Sue Grafton has become one of the most popular female writers, both in the UK and in the US. Born in Kentucky in 1940, she began her career as a TV scriptwriter before Kinsey Millhone and the 'alphabet' series took off. She plans to take Kinsey all the way through the alphabet to Z. Sue lives and writes in Montecito, California, and Louisville, Kentucky.

Discover more at www.SueGrafton.com
and www.facebook.com/SueGrafton

# Sue Grafton

# X

MANTLE

First published 2015 by G. P. Putnam's Sons,
An imprint of Penguin Random House LLC

First published in the UK 2015 by Mantle
an imprint of Pan Macmillan
20 New Wharf Road, London N1 9RR
Associated companies throughout the world
www.panmacmillan.com

ISBN 978-1-4472-6015-8

Visit **www.panmacmillan.com** to read more about all our books
and to buy them. You will also find features, author interviews and
news of any author events, and you can sign up for e-newsletters
so that you're always first to hear about our new releases.

This book is dedicated to my children:

Leslie, Jay, Jamie & Robert.

Caring, hardworking, responsible; my pride and joy always.

# IN THE BEGINNING . . .

Teddy Xanakis would have to steal the painting. What other choice did she have? She believed it was a Turner—a possibility she couldn't confirm unless she shipped it to the Tate in London, where the Turner scholars, Evelyn Joll and Martin Butlin in particular, could make a judgment about its authenticity. Unfortunately, the painting was currently in the basement of the house that was now solely in Ari's name, where it had sat for years, unrecognized and unappreciated. She might have blamed herself for the oversight, but why on earth would anyone expect to find a priceless painting in such homely company?

She and Ari had bought the house when they moved from Chicago to Santa Teresa, California. The estate had been owned by the Carpenters, who passed it down from generation to generation until the last surviving family member died in 1981, having neglected to write a will. The estate attorney had locked the doors and put the house up for sale. Teddy and Ari had bought it fully equipped and fully furnished, right down to the rolls of toilet paper in the linen closet and three sets of sterling flatware in the silver vault. The antiques, including several exquisite Persian carpets, were appraised as part of the purchase price, but in the process a small group of paintings had been over- looked. The attorney had paid the taxes owed, handing the IRS and the State of California the hefty sums to which they were entitled.

Teddy and Ari had made use of a number of the antiques in furnish- ing the mansion's first and second floors. The rest they'd moved into the complex of storage rooms below. The paintings were in a cabinet in an upright rack, each leaning against its neighbor. Teddy had come across them shortly after they moved in. Over the years she'd devel- oped an eye for fine art, but these paintings were drab and uninterest- ing. The subject matter was classical: nymphs, mythological figures, Roman ruins, a seascape, heavy-legged peasant women bringing in the harvest, a still life with a dead duck and rotting fruit, and a floral arrangement in colors she didn't care for.

It was after she and Ari divorced and they'd both signed off on the settlement that she'd realized one of the paintings she'd so carelessly dismissed might be an original by Joseph Mallord William Turner, whose work sold at auction in the millions.

Her rationalization for the contemplated theft was as follows:

1. Ari had no appreciation of art. The collection she'd put to- gether comprised the works of a group known as Les Petits- Maîtres—minor Impressionists like Bartoli, Canet, Jacques Lambert, and Pierre Louis Cazaubon, whose paintings were still affordable because the artists themselves had never achieved the legendary stature of Cézanne, Renoir, Monet, Van Gogh, and their ilk. The collection had already been awarded to her in the settlement, so why not this one small additional painting?
2. If Ari realized the true value of the painting, they'd only get into another wrangle as to which of them was entitled to it.

If they couldn't agree, which seemed inevitable, a judge could force a sale and divide the money equally between them. In this one tiny instance, money didn't interest her. The Turner was a treasure she'd never see again in her lifetime and she was determined to have it.

3. Ari had already screwed her over once, quite literally, by having a dalliance with Stella Morgan, the woman Teddy had once considered her best friend.

Stella's husband, Douglas, was the architect who'd designed the remodel of a condominium Ari and Teddy owned in downtown Santa Teresa. It was while he was overseeing construction that he was stricken with a fatal heart attack. Months passed. After the remodeling work was finished, Ari and Teddy continued to see Stella, who had adjusted to her widowhood as best she could with all that money as compensation.

Then came disaster. That September Teddy spent a weekend in Los Angeles, attending a seminar at the Getty on the Plein Air Painters. On Monday when she arrived home, she hadn't been in the house an hour before an acquaintance rang her up and gave her a blow-by-blow. Teddy's options were limited: fight, flight, play dead, or screw him. She'd slapped Ari with divorce papers within the week.

He got the house, which she couldn't afford to maintain in any event. She got the flat in London. He got a sizable chunk of jewelry, including the necklace he'd given her for their tenth anniversary. She freely confessed she was bitter about that. The stocks and bonds had been sorted out between them. The division was fair and square, which pissed her off no end. There was nothing fair and square about a cheating husband who'd boffed her best friend. In a further cruel twist of fate, in the division of their assets, Teddy had been awarded the very condominium where the architect had breathed his last.

More real estate was the last thing she needed. Her broker priced the condo at a million plus and assured her of a quick sale. After the apartment sat for eighteen months without a nibble, Teddy decided the place would be more attractive if it were properly furnished and decorated. She'd hired a Santa Teresa stager named Annabelle Wright and instructed her to cherry-pick the items in Ari's basement for that purpose. He agreed because the hostilities had gone on long enough and he wanted her out of his hair.

Once the condo was suitably tarted up, Teddy had hired a photographer to do a shoot, and the resulting four-color brochure was circulated among real estate agents in Beverly Hills. A well-known actor had snapped it up—all cash, no contingencies, and a ten-day escrow. The deal was done and all that remained was for the two of them to sign off so Teddy could collect her check.

In the meantime, and this was Teddy's final rationalization:

4. Ari and Stella had gotten married.

Teddy had moved to Bel Air by then, living in the guesthouse of a friend who'd taken pity on her and invited her to stay for an unspecified period of time. It was during the ten-day escrow, while papers were being drawn up, that someone spotted the painting that appeared in the brochure, a seascape shown hanging above the fireplace in the living room. This was a dealer who owned a gallery on Melrose and had an unerring eye for the finer things in life. He'd glanced at the photograph and then brought it closer to his face. A nanosecond later, he picked up the phone and called Teddy, who'd long been a customer of his.

"This looks like a Turner, darling. Could it possibly be genuine?"

"Oh, I doubt it. That's been sitting in the basement for years."

"Well, if I were you, I'd send color photographs to the Tate to see if someone can establish the provenance. Better yet, take the painting yourself and see what they have to say. What harm could it do?"

Heeding his advice, she decided to retrieve the painting and have it examined by the experts. She returned to Santa Teresa, where she signed the final papers on the sale and then drove from the broker's office to the condominium. She'd been told the new owner would be taking possession the following weekend as soon as the place had been emptied, so when she let herself in, she was astonished to see the apartment had already been stripped to the bare walls. No furniture, no art, no Persian carpets, and no accessories. She'd called Ari, who was gleeful. He said he'd known she'd dash in and confiscate any items she took a fancy to, so he'd made a preemptive strike and emptied the place. If she wanted to dispute the move, she could have her attorney contact his.

As she no longer had access to the painting, she approached the photographer and asked to see his proofs. There were several clear shots of the painting, which was really quite lovely now that she had the chance to examine it more closely. It was a seascape with a flat beach and a sky streaked with clouds. In the background, cliffs were visible; probably the Margate Cliffs, a Turner favorite. In the foreground, a boat appeared to have foundered. The boat itself, she learned later, was known as a xebec, a small three-masted ship having an overhanging bow and stern and both square and lateen sails. The tonal quality was delicate, gradations of browns and grays with touches of color here and there. She asked for and was given four prints.

At that point, she realized she'd better buckle down to work. She moved back to town and embarked on a comprehensive self-education. She studied the J.M.W. Turner catalogue raisonné and any other biographical information she could get her hands on. Turner had died in 1851. The bulk of his artistic output he'd left as a bequest to the National Gallery in London. Three hundred and eighteen paintings went to the Tate and National Gallery, and thirty-five oil sketches to the British Museum. The remaining two hundred plus paintings were in private collections in Great Britain and America.

Nine paintings were unaccounted for. The appearance of one such painting, whose whereabouts and size were unknown, had been mentioned in the November 1833 *Magazine of Fine Arts*. Described as "a beautiful little picture," it was hung in the Society of British Artists exhibition that same year. Its owner was one J. Carpenter, about whom nothing else was known except that he had loaned a Hogarth and a Morland to this same exhibition. Teddy's eyes filled with tears and she'd had to honk discreetly into a tissue.

She drove to the Santa Teresa County Architectural Archives and then to the *Santa Teresa Dispatch* to research the family who'd had the painting in its possession for so many years. Jeremy Carpenter IV had emigrated from England to America in 1899, bringing with him a sizable family and a ship's hold filled with household goods. The home he built in Montebello, which had taken five years to complete, was finished in 1904.

Teddy made three trips to the house, thinking she could walk in casually and remove the painting without attracting notice. Unfortunately, Ari had instructed the staff to usher her politely to the door, which is what they did. Of one thing she was certain—she could not let Ari know of her interest in the seascape or her suspicions about its pedigree.

She thought she had plenty of time to devise a plan, but then she learned the newlyweds had leased the house for a year to a couple from New York. Ari and Stella were taking a delayed honeymoon, after which they'd move into the contemporary home that Stella owned. Ari was apparently taking the opportunity to clear out the basement. His intention was to donate the bulk of the items to a local charity for the annual fund-raiser coming up in a month.

She'd have to act and she'd have to do it soon. The task she faced was not entirely unfamiliar. She'd stolen a painting once before, but nothing even close to one of this magnitude.

# 1

Santa Teresa, California, Monday, March 6, 1989. The state at large and the town of Santa Teresa in particular were nearing the midpoint of a drought that had slithered into view in 1986 and wouldn't slither off again until March of 1991, when the "miracle rains" arrived. Not that we dared anticipate relief at the time. From our perspective, the pitiless conditions were upon us with no end in sight. Local reservoirs had shrunk, leaving a wide swath of dried mud as cracked as an alligator's hide.

My professional life was in the same state—always worrisome when you are your sole financial support. Self-employment is a mixed bag. The upside is freedom. Go to work when you like, come home when you like, and wear anything you please. While you still have bills to pay, you can accept a new job or decline. It's all up to you. The downside is uncertainty, the feast-or-famine mentality not everyone can tolerate.

My name is Kinsey Millhone. I'm a private detective by trade, doing business as Millhone Investigations. I'm female, thirty-eight years old, twice divorced, and childless, a status I maintain with rigorous attention to my birth control pills. Despite the shortage of new clients, I had a shitload of money in the bank, so I could afford to sit tight. My savings account had been plumped by an unexpected sum that dropped into my lap some six months before. I'd invested the major chunk of it in mutual funds. The remaining cash I kept in a money market account that I designated "untouchable." Friends, on hearing about my windfall, viewed me as certifiable. "Forget about work. Why not travel and enjoy life?"

I didn't give the question credence. At my age, retirement is out of the question, and even temporary idleness would have driven me insane. True, I could have covered my expenses for months to come with enough in reserve for a lavish trip abroad, except for the following impediments:

1. I'm miserly and cheap.
2. I don't have a passport because I've never needed one. I had traveled to Mexico some years before, but all that was required in crossing the border then was proof of U.S. citizenship.

That aside, anyone who knows me will testify to how ill-suited I am to a life of leisure. When it comes to work, it isn't so much what we do or how much we're paid; it's the satisfaction we take in doing it. In broad terms, my job entails locating witnesses and missing persons, following paper trails through the hall of records, sitting surveillance on insurance scammers, and sometimes tailing the errant spouse. My prime talent is snooping, which sometimes includes a touch of breaking and entering. This is entirely naughty of me and I'm ashamed to confide how much fun it can be, but only if I don't get caught.

This is the truth about me and you might as well know it now. I'm

passionate about all manner of criminals: killers, thieves, and moun-
tebanks, the pursuit of whom I find both engaging and entertaining.
Life's cheaters are everywhere and my mission is to eradicate the lot
of them. I know this speaks volumes about the paucity of my personal
life, but that's my nature in a nutshell.

My quest for law and order began in the first grade when I ventured
into the cloakroom and surprised a classmate snitching a chocolate
bar from my Howdy Doody lunch box. The teacher appeared at that
very moment and caught the child with my candy in hand. I anticipated due process, but the sniveling little shit burst into tears, claiming I'd stolen it from *her*. She received no punishment at all while I
was reprimanded for leaving my seat without raising my hand and
asking to be excused. My teacher turned a deaf ear to my howls of protest. From that singular event, my notion of fair play was set, and, in
sum, it is this: the righteous are struck down while the sticky-fingered
escape. I've labored all my life to see that justice plays out the other
way around.

That particular Monday morning, I was paying my bills, feeling oh-
so virtuous, as why would I not? I'd written and signed all the pertinent
checks and felt only slightly anxious about the drain on my funds. I'd
addressed and sealed the return envelopes. As I licked and placed
stamps, I was humming with satisfaction and looking forward to lunch.
When the phone rang, I lifted the handset and anchored it against my
shoulder, saying, "Millhone Investigations."

"Hi, Kinsey. This is Ruthie. Did I catch you at an okay time?"

"Sure. What's going on?"

"Well, I'm fit to be tied. I swear, about the time I think I'm through
the worst of it, something else comes up. Today I got this official-
looking letter from the IRS. Pete's being audited, of all things. I'm
supposed to call to set up an appointment."

"Can't you tell them he's dead?"

"I could, but that's probably what triggered the audit in the first
place."

Ruthie Wolinsky had been widowed some seven months before, in August of 1988, when her husband was shot to death in what looked like a robbery gone wrong. I'd made Pete Wolinsky's acquaintance ten years prior. Like me, he was a private detective, who'd worked for an agency called Byrd-Shine Investigations. I'd apprenticed with Ben Byrd and Morley Shine when I was racking up the hours I needed for licensing. Pete was a contemporary of theirs. Both of my bosses swore he was once a top-notch detective, but at the point where our paths intersected, he'd fallen on hard times. By then, he was a man so morally bent, I marveled he managed to find work anywhere. While I disliked him, I was then twenty-seven years old and newly employed and didn't feel it was my place to make my thoughts known. Besides which, no one asked and I doubt they'd have listened if I'd volunteered my views.

I'd thought the world of the two seasoned detectives, and I still conducted business in the time-honored ways they'd taught me. Unfortunately, Ben and Morley had quarreled bitterly and the partnership had been dissolved. They went their separate ways, setting up independent agencies. I was already out on my own by then and never heard the details of their falling-out. Whatever the dispute, it had nothing to do with me, so I shrugged it off. Now both were deceased and I assumed the past was dead and buried along with them. As for Ruthie, over the years I'd seen her from time to time, but we didn't become friends until shortly after Pete was killed.

I pondered the historical context while she went on to describe the latest crisis, saying, "Sorry to bother you with this, but let me read you what it says. They're asking for 'Schedule C gross receipts. Year-end papers and reports, including worksheets reconciling books and records for the tax years 1986 and 1987.'" She continued in a singsong voice. "'In addition, please provide any and all business records, files, expenses, and receipts for the period 1975 through 1978.'"

"Are you kidding me? That goes back fifteen years. I thought after seven you could throw that crap out."

"I guess not, at least according to this. Our accountant retired last year, and I'm having a devil of a time getting through to the fellow who took over for him. I was hoping when you and Dietz went through Pete's boxes, you might have come across our old tax returns."

Robert Dietz was the Nevada private investigator whose help I'd enlisted during the period just after Pete was killed. Much more to the story, of course, but I made a point of putting it out of my mind. "I don't think so. I can't swear to it, but the whole point was tracking down his accounts, so anything with a dollar sign attached we shoved in plastic bags, which we handed over to you."

"Too bad," she said. "I've searched those bags twice and there's zilch."

"You want me to try again? It's always possible we missed a box."

"That's just it. I don't have them. All those cartons are gone."

"Where?"

"The dump. A junk dealer taped a flier to my door. He must have been cruising the area, scaring up work. The notice said for fifty bucks in cash, he'd clean out my garage and haul the mess away. I jumped at the chance. I've wanted to park my car under cover for years, but there was never any room. Now I'm looking at an audit and what am I supposed to do? I'm just sick about this."

"I don't know what to suggest. I can double-check, but if we'd come across tax returns, we'd have set them aside. I did keep one box, but those are confidential files from the old Byrd-Shine days. I have no idea how they ended up in Pete's hands."

"Oh, wait a minute. The IRS does list Byrd-Shine in the document request, now you mention it. Hold on."

I heard papers rattling, and then she said, "I can't find the reference now, but it's in here somewhere. You don't need to bother Dietz, but could you check the box you have? I don't need much; I'm guessing a few old bank statements would suffice. If I can hand over *anything*, it would be a show of good faith, which is about all I have to offer."

"I'll inventory the contents as soon as possible."

"No big hurry. I'm driving up to Lompoc this coming weekend to celebrate my birthday with a friend—"

"I didn't know it was your birthday. Happy birthday!"

"Thanks. We're not doing much . . . just hanging out . . . but I haven't seen her since Pete died and I thought it'd be nice to get away."

"Absolutely. When do you get back?"

"Sunday afternoon, which gives you some wiggle room. Even if I called the IRS today, I doubt I'd get in right away. They must have a waiting list a mile long," she said. "Oh. And while you're at it, keep this in mind: Pete had a habit of tucking stray documents between the pages of other files. Sometimes he'd hide money, too, so don't toss out any hundred-dollar bills."

"I remember the wad of cash he buried in the bag of birdseed."

"That was something, wasn't it? He claimed the system was designed to fool the bad guys. He could remember where he'd put all the bits and pieces, but he wouldn't explain his strategy. Anyway, I'm sorry to trouble you with this. I know it's a pain."

"Not a big deal. Fifteen or twenty minutes tops."

"I appreciate that."

"In the meantime, you better talk to a tax expert."

"Ha! I can't afford one."

"Better that than getting hosed."

"Good point. My neighbor's an attorney. I'll ask him who he knows."

We chatted briefly of other matters and then we hung up. Once again, I found myself brooding about Pete Wolinsky, which I was doing more often than I care to admit. In the wake of his death, it became clear how irresponsible he'd been, leaving Ruthie with little more than a mess on her hands. His business files, such as they were, had been relegated to countless dusty and dilapidated cardboard boxes, stacked ten deep and eight high in their two-car garage, filling the interior to capacity. In addition, there were piles of unpaid bills, dunning notices, threats of lawsuits, and no life insurance. Pete had carried a policy that would have netted her a handsome sum, but he'd let the premiums lapse. Even so, she adored him, and who was I to judge?

To be fair about it, I suppose you could call him a good-hearted soul, as long as you included an asterisk referring to the small print below. As a perfect example, Pete had told Ruthie he was taking her on a cruise on the Danube for their fortieth wedding anniversary coming up the following year. He'd intended to surprise her, but he couldn't help revealing the plan in advance. The real surprise came after his death, when she found out he was paying for the trip with money he'd extorted in a blackmail scheme. She asked for the deposit back and used the refund to satisfy some of his creditors, and that was that. In the meantime, she wasn't hurting for income. Ruthie was a private-duty nurse, and her services were much in demand. From the schedule I'd seen taped to her refrigerator door, she worked numerous shifts and could probably name her price regardless of the going rate.

As for the banker's box, I'd put a big black X on the lid and shoved it under the desk in my studio apartment, so the task would have to wait until I got home. I'd been meaning to inspect the contents in any event. If, as I anticipated, the old files were inactive or closed, I'd send them to a shredding company and be done with it.

I'd no more than hung up when the phone rang again. I reached for the handset, saying, "Millhone Investigations."

There was a pause, and a woman said, "Hello?"

I said, "Hello?"

"Oh, sorry. I was expecting a machine. May I speak to Ms. Millhone?"

Her tone was refined, and even through the phone line I could smell money on her breath. "This is she," I said.

"My name is Hallie Bettancourt. Vera Hess suggested I get in touch with you about a personal matter."

"That was nice of her. She had an office next door to mine at California Fidelity Insurance, where I worked once upon a time," I said. "I take it you're a friend of hers?"

"Well, no. We met at a party a few weeks ago. We were having drinks on the patio, and when I mentioned the issue, she thought you might help."

"I'll do what I can. Would you give me your name again? I'm afraid it went right over my head."

I could hear the smile in her voice. "Bettancourt. First name, Hallie. I do that myself. In one ear and out the other."

"Amen," I said. "Why don't you give me a quick summary of the problem?"

She hesitated. "The situation's awkward, and I'd prefer not to discuss it by phone. I think when I explain, you'll understand."

"That's entirely up to you," I said. "We can set up an appointment and you can talk about it then. What's your schedule look like this week?"

She laughed uncomfortably. "That's just it. I'm under a time constraint. I leave town tomorrow morning and won't be until June. If there's any way we could meet tonight, I'd be grateful."

"I can probably manage that. Where and what time?"

"Here at my home at eight o'clock, if that's all right with you. From what I'm told, it's not a big job. To be honest about it, I contacted another agency last week and they turned me down, which was embarrassing. The gentleman I spoke with was nice about it, but he made it clear the work wouldn't warrant the size of their fees. He didn't come right out and say so, but the implication was that they had much bigger fish to fry. I guess I've been gun-shy about reaching out again, which is why I put it off."

"Understood," I said. "We'll talk this evening and see where we stand. If I can't help, I may know someone who can."

"Thank you. You have no idea how relieved I am."

I made a note of the address on Sky View, along with her instructions, and told her I'd be there at 8:00. I was guessing her problem was matrimonial, which turned out to be true, but not quite as I imagined it. Once I hung up, I checked my city map and located the street, which was no bigger than a thread of pale blue surrounded by blank space. I folded the map and stuck it in my shoulder bag.

At 5:00, I locked the office and headed for home, feeling pleased about life. As my appointment wasn't for three hours, I had time for a bite to eat, supping on milk of tomato soup and a gooey grilled cheese sandwich, which I held in a fold of paper towel that neatly soaked up the excess butter. While I ate, I read three chapters of a Donald West-lake paperback. In hindsight, I marvel at how clueless I was about the shit storm to come. What I ask myself even now is whether I should have picked up the truth any faster than I did, which was not nearly fast enough.

# 2

---

Approaching Hallie Bettancourt's property that night, I realized I'd caught glimpses of the house from the freeway on numerous occasions; it was perched on a ridge that ran between the town and the outer reaches of the Los Padres National Forest. By day, sun reflected off the glass exterior, winking like an SOS. At night, the glow was a bright spot, as vivid as Venus against the pale light of surrounding stars. From a distance, it was one of those aeries that seemed impossible to reach, isolated from its neighbors at an elevation sufficient to encourage nosebleeds. The access roads weren't obvious, and without Hallie's instructions, I'm not sure I'd have found my way.

She'd indicated the easiest route was to follow 192 East as far as Winding Canyon Road and then start the ascent. I did as she suggested, taking the narrow two-lane road that snaked up the hill with more switchbacks than straightaways. A mile and a half farther on, I spotted the house number blasted into the surface of a massive sandstone boulder. There was a mailbox nearby, which also touted the address, but the house itself wasn't visible from the road. The driveway angled upward through a thicket of oaks, a precipitous approach that ran on for another quarter of a mile.

When I neared the crest of the hill, the house loomed above me like an apparition. If an alien spacecraft had landed, I imagined it would have had the same nearly menacing presence. Against the shadowy landscape, the stark structure blazed with light, the contemporary style oddly suited to the rugged terrain. The front jutted forward like the prow of a ship and appeared to hang out over the canyon; a sailboat made of glass. Vegetation broke in waves, churning among the concrete pilings, and the wind blew with a high whine.

A parking pad had been hacked out of the stony ground. I pulled in, nosing my Honda up against a stone retaining wall. I got out and locked the car. As I walked, I triggered a series of motion-activated landscape lights that illuminated the path in front of me. I climbed the steep stone steps to the door, careful where I placed my feet lest I topple into the chaparral that stretched out on either side.

From the front porch, as I faced the glass-fronted door, I had an unobstructed view straight through the house to the dark beyond. The Pacific was visible two miles away, where moonlight cast a gray sheen on the water like a thin layer of ice. The ribbon of Highway 101 wound between the shoreline and the town, and a lacework of house lights was draped across the intervening hills. Large patches of darkness attested to the rural character of the area. There were no neighbors close by, and the simplest of daily needs (such as wine and toilet paper) would require a lengthy drive into town.

I rang the bell and saw Hallie appear on the wraparound deck on the far side of the house. She entered the dining room by way of a sliding glass door, a caftan of butter yellow silk billowing around her as she crossed the room. She had a tangled mass of reddish brown hair and a face photographers must have loved. While she wasn't technically beautiful, she was striking. Fine-boned, high forehead. Her complexion was flawless and her narrow nose was prominent, with a bump at the bridge that lent her profile an exotic cast. Her ears were pierced, and a little waterfall of diamonds dangled on either side of her face. The caftan had wide sleeves and intricate embroidery along the cuffs. Only a woman who's genuinely slim can afford a garment so voluminous. Pointed yellow velvet slippers peeked from beneath her hem. I placed her in her midforties.

She opened the door and extended her hand. "Hello, Kinsey. I'm Hallie. Thanks for making the drive. I apologize for the imposition."

"Nice to meet you," I said. "This is quite a place."

She flushed with pleasure, saying, "Isn't it?"

She led the way and I followed as she moved through the house toward the deck. Much of the interior was shrouded in darkness, the furniture covered with tarps in preparation for her departure. When I glanced to my left, I could see that doors leading off the hallway were closed. On the wide stretch of wood flooring, I could see islands of lush-looking Oriental carpeting. Lamps glowed here and there, lighting up decorative vignettes of tasteful objects, artfully arranged.

To our right, a two-story wood-and-glass living room took up one whole end of the house. It, too, was blanketed in shadow, but a spill of light from the dining room reflected clean lines against the generous expanses of exterior glass. Bare white walls formed a gallery for numerous paintings in heavy gold frames. I'm not a connoisseur of art, but they appeared to be museum-quality works: landscapes and still-life images in oil. These were not artists I could identify on sight, but the colors were rich and deep, and my impression was that a lot of money had been spent for the collection.

Over her shoulder, Hallie said, "I hope you won't be cold if we sit outside. I've been enjoying the view. My husband left this morning for the house in Malibu while I close up here."

"Must be nice to split your time that way," I said. Personally, I split mine between my eight-hundred-square-foot apartment and an office half that size.

We went out onto the deck. Exterior lights had been extinguished, and in the lee of the house, the air seemed hushed. I could smell bay laurel, eucalyptus, and night-blooming jasmine. On a narrow terrace below, a bright turquoise infinity pool glowed like a landing strip. An open bottle of Chardonnay sat on a small wooden table flanked by two canvas director's chairs. She'd brought out two stemmed glasses, and I saw that hers was half full. She took the closest chair and I settled in its mate.

She offered wine, which I declined as a way of demonstrating how professional I was. To be honest, with the slightest encouragement (bracing outside temperatures aside) I'd have lingered there for hours, drinking in the view along with anything else she had to offer. We were flanked by two small propane heaters that radiated a fierce but diffused heat that made me want to hold my hands closer, as though to a campfire.

Santa Teresa is almost always chilly after sunset, and once I sat down, I found myself wedging my fingers between my knees. I was wearing blue jeans and boots with a black turtleneck under my good wool tweed blazer, so I was warm enough, but I wondered how she could bear the night air in such flimsy attire, especially with the wind whistling around the edges of the glass. Locks of flyaway hair danced around her face. She removed two hairpins that she held between her teeth while she captured the loose strands and secured them again.

"How long have you owned the house?" I asked.

"I grew up here. This is the old Clipper estate. My father bought it in the early thirties, shortly after he graduated from architectural school. Halston Bettancourt. You may have heard of him."

I made a sound as though of recognition, though I didn't have a clue.

"After he razed the original three-story Georgian-style mansion, he built this, which is how he launched his career. He was always proud of the fact that he was featured in *Architectural Digest* more than any other single architect. He's been gone now for years, and my mother has as well. The place in Malibu belongs to my husband, Geoff. He's a G-E-O-F-F Geoff, not the J-E-F-F kind. We've been married two years."

"What sort of work does he do?"

"He has a law degree, but he doesn't have a job as such. He manages both of our portfolios and looks after our finances."

Fragmented as it was, I had no idea where her commentary was taking us, but I was making mental notes. I couldn't help but wonder how the neighbors felt when her father demolished the old estate and erected this in its place. The house was dramatic, but distinctly short on eighteenth-century charm.

From her remarks, I drew the two obvious inferences: she'd retained her maiden name and she'd held on to the family home. I could imagine her insisting that G-E-O-F-F Geoffrey sign an ironclad prenuptial agreement: separate properties, separate bank accounts, a cheater's clause, and zero spousal support in the event of a split. On the other hand, his fortune might have been more substantial than hers, in which case any stingy financial arrangements might have been his idea.

She crossed her legs and smoothed the yellow silk over one knee, idly pleating the fabric. "I should tell you again how much I appreciate your agreeing to meet like this. Under the circumstances, it's a relief doing business with a woman. No disrespect to men intended, but some things a woman understands intuitively—'from the heart,' you might say."

Now I was thinking about big gambling debts or an affair with a married man. It was also possible her new husband had an unsavory past and she'd just gotten wind of it.

She reached down and picked up a file folder that rested against the side of her chair. She opened the folder, removed a paper clip, and passed the loose pages to me along with a penlight to make reading easier. I was looking at a photocopy of a newspaper article. I checked the date and heading: the *Santa Teresa Dispatch*, June 21, 1979; approximately ten years earlier. The article covered the trial of a kid named Christian Satterfield, a safecracker who'd finally been defeated by a run of cutting-edge vaults and had thrown that career over in favor of robbing banks, which was a much simpler proposition. No maddening array of alarms and exasperating anti-theft devices. Robbing banks entailed pithy notes directed to bank tellers, no weapons, and no mechanical skills. The work was quicker, too.

He'd enjoyed a string of successes, but eventually his luck had run out. He'd been convicted of robbing nineteen banks in the tri-counties area, an impressive number for someone a mere twenty-three years old. The photograph that accompanied the story revealed a clean-cut young man with good facial bones and an open countenance. The three-column coverage on the front page continued for an additional four columns on page four, laying out the reasoning for his choice of banks, his meticulous advance planning, and the carefully worded notes he'd composed. I could picture him licking his pencil point, trying to get the written threats just so, all of the spelling correct and no cross-outs.

I scanned the lines of print, picking up a detail here and there. His successes had netted him close to $134,000 over a period of sixteen months. In his demands, he claimed to be armed, and while he never actually brandished a gun, the tellers were sufficiently intimidated to surrender the cash without an argument. Though this was standard bank policy, three of the young women were so traumatized, they never returned to work.

Hallie waited until I'd finished reading and handed me a folded newspaper with an arrow calling my attention to a notice dated six months before. Satterfield had been released, having served a little over eight years, which I was guessing represented 85 percent of a ten-year bid.

"As you can see, he was released from Lompoc to a halfway house in the San Fernando Valley. Since he was a Santa Teresa resident when he was arrested and tried, I'm told he's most likely been returned to the community by now. I wondered if you could get me his current contact information. I called the county probation department twice and got nowhere."

Her manner of speaking had become more formal, suggesting she was ill at ease. The United States Penitentiary at Lompoc is a federal prison located an hour north of us. The facility opened in 1959 and houses male inmates serving long sentences for sophisticated offenses: white-collar crime, interstate drug deals, tax evasion, and major fraud. As a bank robber, Satterfield must have felt right at home. I wondered about the nature of her interest in him. To me, the two seemed an odd mix.

I said, "He wouldn't have been released to the county. His crime was federal. You'd have to call the U.S. probation department and ask for the name of the agent supervising his parole."

She frowned. "I'm not happy with that idea. I don't know the system and I'd only end up at another dead end. This whole process has been frustrating enough as it is. I leave town early tomorrow. We'll be in Malibu for a few days, and after that we'll be traveling. I'd prefer to have you deal with the situation. As you might well imagine, I have no experience with matters of this sort."

"I'll do what I can, but I make no guarantees," I said. "Parole officers are notoriously tight-lipped."

"All the more reason for you to handle it. I assume your inquiry will be discreet."

"Of course."

"Good," she said. "Once you have his address and phone number, you can send me a note in care of my post office box. My assistant will know where we are and she'll be forwarding mail twice a week."

"May I ask what this is about?"

She paused, her gaze not quite meeting mine. "He's my son."

Intuitively and from the heart, I hadn't seen that one coming and I was taken aback. I said, "Ah."

"I became pregnant and bore a child when I was fifteen years old.

If the choice had been mine, I'd have kept the baby and raised him myself, but my parents were adamant. They felt I was too young and too immature to take on such a burden; a point I could hardly refute. They were convinced he'd be better off in a two-parent home. Given his criminal history, they were obviously mistaken in that regard."

"Does he know who you are?"

Her cheeks tinted slightly. "He does. Some years ago I wrote him a letter in care of the adoption agency. The social worker said she'd keep it in his file. I wanted to make sure he'd have a way to reach me if he were ever interested."

"And did you hear from him?"

"I did. He called shortly after his eighteenth birthday. We met twice, and then I lost track of him. When I saw the brief note about his release from Lompoc, his silence suddenly made sense. That's when I went back and did a follow-up search in the archives at the *Dispatch*."

I glanced at the article. "You first learned he'd been in prison when you saw this?"

"That's correct. I don't ordinarily read the *Dispatch*, but I spotted a copy as I was leaving my dentist's office. When I caught sight of the name, I was so shocked, I had to sit down for a moment and catch my breath. I was also deeply ashamed, as though the fault were mine. I took my time deciding what I wanted to do."

"And that would be what?"

"I'd like to help him if there's anything he needs."

"That's generous."

"It's not about generosity. It's about making amends."

"Does he know how well-off you are?"

Her expression became set. "What difference does that make?"

"You're not worried he might try to take advantage?"

"If he were going to do that, he'd have done so years ago. I've never made a secret of my financial position. I offered him money in the past and he declined."

"What if he's embarrassed about his felony conviction and doesn't want to hear from you?"

"If he decides not to talk to me, then so be it, but I want him to have the opportunity. I feel a sense of responsibility." She picked up the wine bottle to top off her glass and the label caught my eye. I'd seen the same Chardonnay at the liquor store for ninety bucks a pop. While I didn't actually gasp aloud, she must have deciphered my look and held out the bottle. "Perhaps you'll allow me to talk you into it."

"Maybe half a glass."

I watched her pour, taking advantage of the moment to assess her situation. "What about your husband? Where is he in this?"

"Geoffrey knows I had a child and put him up for adoption. All of this happened years before the two of us met. What he doesn't know is that we reconnected, and he certainly doesn't know about Christian's serving a prison term. I intend to tell him, but so far I haven't felt the time was right."

"I can see where it might be an awkward revelation to spring on him after the fact."

"On the other hand, if my son doesn't care to pursue a relationship, why mention it at all? Once you 'fess up, you're stuck. Geoffrey hates deception and he's slow to forgive. There's no point in creating trouble unnecessarily."

"Indeed," I said. Without even meaning to, I was echoing the tone and manner of her speech, and I was hoping the shift wasn't permanent.

"That's why I'm asking you to act as a go-between, using your name and phone number instead of mine. I don't want to risk my husband's intercepting a message before I've told him the whole of it."

"You don't want your name brought into it at all," I said.

"I do not."

"What reason would I give for tracking him down? I've never met Christian Satterfield."

"I'm sure you'll think of some excuse. The point is, I want my privacy protected. I'll insist on that."

I sat there wondering if this was really the way a good marriage worked. I'd been married and divorced twice, so it was difficult to judge. Keeping secrets seemed like a bad idea, but I was hardly qualified to offer the woman marital advice. Aside from that, I've never had children, so the notion of a bank robber for a son was tough to assimilate. His stepdad might take an even dimmer view.

Reluctantly, I said, "I'm not sure a parole officer will give me the information, but I'll do what I can." I studied the black-and-white newspaper photograph and then held up the photocopied pages. "May I keep these? Might be good if I need to identify him on sight."

She reached into the file folder a second time and handed me duplicates. I murmured a thank-you and slid the papers into the outside pocket of my shoulder bag.

"So how do we proceed?" she asked.

"Most new clients sign a boiler-plate contract," I said. "Over the years, I've found it's better to have an agreement in writing, as much for your protection as for mine. That way there's no confusion about what I've been asked to do. In this case, I didn't bring any paperwork. I wanted to make sure I could be of help before I did anything else."

"Sensible," she said. "As I see it, we can do one of two things. You can write up the contract, fill in the particulars, and mail it for my signature, or we can consider this a gentleman's agreement and I can pay you in cash."

There wasn't really much to debate. I'm not equipped to take credit cards, and she must have sensed I wasn't eager to accept a check from a woman who was out of Santa Teresa half the year. She was clearly well-to-do, but if a check was returned for insufficient funds, it would be a pain in the ass to track her down and make it good. The rich are full of surprises. Some hang on to their wealth by stiffing their creditors.

"Does five hundred dollars seem reasonable?" she asked.

"Too much," I said. "We're talking about a few phone calls and then a short written report. Two hundred would more than cover it."

"Unless you fail."

"You're paying for my time, not results. The effort's the same regardless of the outcome."

"Sorry. Of course. I don't expect you to work without compensation. If you'll wait a moment, I'll be right back."

She got up, crossed to the sliding glass door, and went into the house. I took a sip of Chardonnay, feeling for the first time that I could relax. She'd been clear enough about what she wanted, and while acquiring the information wasn't a slam dunk, I had avenues to pursue.

Moments later, she returned with a plain white envelope. She made a point of showing me a portion of the two one-hundred-dollar bills before she slid them fully into the envelope and handed it to me. I put the money in my shoulder bag and pulled out a small spiral-bound notebook. I wrote her a receipt for the cash and tore off the leaf of paper. "I can type up a proper receipt at the office tomorrow."

"Don't worry about it. This is fine." She folded the handwritten receipt and slipped it into the file folder.

"A few things I should ask," I said.

"Feel free."

I went through a list of items I thought needed covering and she seemed happy to oblige, so that by the time we parted company, I had her home address and a mailing address in Malibu, the Malibu home phone, plus her husband's office address and two additional numbers for him at work. Her assistant's name was Amy. Later, I realized I should have asked for Geoffrey's last name, but it hadn't occurred to me.

Once in my car again, I sat in the darkened parking area while the motion-activated path lights went out one by one. Using the Honda's interior light, I jotted notes on a series of index cards that I carry with me as a matter of course. I don't know if she was aware that I was still on the property, but it mattered not. It's always best to capture facts when they're fresh, before assumption and prejudice step in and alter memory.

# X

On the way home, I stopped at the market and stocked up on odds and ends, including paper towels, milk, bread, and peanut butter. Easter decorations and accessories were set up in numerous displays: Easter egg dyeing kits, hollow plastic eggs, foil-covered eggs, big foil-covered chocolate bunnies, marshmallow chickens of a virulent yellow hue, bags of paper shreds resembling grass, wicker and plastic baskets, as well as stuffed animals to be included in the haul.

At that hour, there weren't many shoppers, and since I was the only one in line, I had a nice chat with Suzanne, the middle-aged checkout girl. I paid for my groceries with one of Hallie's hundred-dollar bills, amazed by how little change I was given in return.

I was home by 10:00. I locked up, put away the groceries, grabbed my book, and went upstairs to the loft, where I changed into the over-size T-shirt I sleep in. I brushed my teeth, washed my face, and slid under the covers. Once I found my place, I read until midnight, thinking life was swell.

# 3

In the morning, I did my usual three-mile jog on autopilot. Given the monotony of the weather, there was no chance I'd be gifted with the pleasure of a rainy-day sleep-in. Local homeowners were in such a panic to install low-flow toilets and low-flow showerheads that the retailers couldn't keep up with the demand. A vote on water rationing was in the works. In the meantime, we were voluntarily cutting back on usage.

I'd always made a point of turning off the faucet while I was brushing my teeth. Now even flushing the commode was restricted to only the most serious of business. Everyone (well, almost everyone) in the community pitched in with the conservation effort, primarily because failure to cooperate warranted a stern reproach from the public works department. We were not yet being subjected to neighborhood incursions of the water police, but there were threats to that effect.

I was home by 6:45, including my cooldown and a perfunctory

stretch. After that I showered, shampooing my hair, and donned jeans, a navy blue turtleneck, and my boots. I trotted down the spiral stairs and helped myself to a bowl of Cheerios with 2 percent milk. I had the local television news on in the background, trying to ignore the chirpy weather pundit.

Today it was "Partly sunny."

Yesterday, "Patchy A.M. clouds, then partly to mostly sunny."

Tomorrow, "Partly sunny."

For the weekend, we were promised a "sunny" Saturday and a Sunday marked by "partial sun with areas of A.M. clouds, clearing in the afternoon." For the following week, "mostly clear and sunny with early-morning fog."

I wanted to yell, "Shut up, already!" but I couldn't see the point.

My three-room office is on a side street that occupies one short block in the heart of downtown Santa Teresa in walking distance of the police station, the courthouse, and the public library. I rent the center bungalow of three that resemble the fairy-tale cottages of the Three Little Pigs. I've been in the location now for two years, and while the space isn't slick, at $350 a month, it's affordable.

The outer office serves as a library/reception area. I have a bookcase, an upright cupboard with cubbyholes, and a secondhand armoire that holds my office supplies. There's also room for extra chairs in case more clients flock in. This has never actually happened, but I'm prepared for it nonetheless. The inner office is where I have my desk, my swivel chair, two guest chairs, file cabinets, and assorted office machines.

Halfway down the hall, there's a tiny bathroom that I recently painted a deep chocolate brown on the theory that a tiny room will always look like a tiny room even if you paint it white, so you might as well pick a color you like. At the end of that same short corridor, I have a kitchenette that harbors a sink, a small refrigerator, a microwave, a coffeemaker, a Sparkletts water dispenser, and a door that opens to the outside.

I arrived at 8:00, and while I waited for a fresh pot of coffee to brew, I placed a call to the Santa Teresa County Probation Offices and asked to speak to Priscilla Holloway, a parole agent I'd met while babysitting a female ex-con with a wealthy dad, who'd paid me handsomely to shepherd her about.

When the line was picked up, she said, "Holloway."

"Hi, Priscilla. Kinsey Millhone. I'm hoping you remember me . . ."

"Reba Lafferty's friend."

"Right. You have a minute?"

"Only if you make it quick. I have a client coming in for his monthly ass-kicking, so I gotta get myself in the proper frame of mind. What can I do for you?"

"I need a phone number for the U.S. probation office, Central California district. I'm trying to track down an inmate just coming off a ten-year stint in Lompoc."

"Any agent in particular?"

"No clue. That's what I'm hoping to find out."

"Hang on. I have the number somewhere."

She clunked the receiver on the desk. I could hear her sliding open a drawer and then rustling paper. After a short period, she came back and said, "The parole officer I last dealt with was a guy named Derrick Spanner, but this was three years ago, so who knows if he's still there. This is his direct line in Los Angeles. Area code 2-1-3 . . ."

She gave me the number and I dutifully made a note. I thanked her, but she was gone before the words were even out of my mouth.

I depressed the plunger and then punched in the number. The line rang three times before an answering machine picked up. The outgoing message confirmed that I'd reached Derrick Spanner, so I identified myself by name, pausing to spell it before I said, "I'm calling from Santa Teresa, trying to contact a parolee named Christian Satterfield. I understand he was released from USP Lompoc a few months ago. I'm not sure who's overseeing his parole, but Chris is a former neighbor and he left some personal items in my care. I've since moved and I'd appreciate your giving him my new number. He can call when he has a chance. Thanks so much."

I repeated my name and rattled off my office phone, without pausing to think. The minute the number was out of my mouth, I regretted the choice. If the information was passed along to Satterfield, he wouldn't have the slightest idea who I was, and if he dialed the number I'd given, the first thing he'd hear was me saying "Millhone Investigations." This was not good. For a fellow just out of prison, the notion of an investigation, private or otherwise, would be worrisome. He'd think I was up to something, which I was.

I hung up, thought a minute, and then crossed to my file cabinets, where I opened a drawer and picked my way through the folders until I found the instruction manual for my answering machine. Once I figured out how to change the outgoing message, I recorded one of those generic responses that covers a multitude of sins.

"The party you've reached in the 805 area code is currently unavailable. Please leave your name and number at the sound of the tone and someone will get back to you as soon as possible."

Once that was done, I thought, *Now what?*

Hallie Bettancourt hadn't paid me to sit around waiting for the phone to ring. She hired me to do something else, which was to find her jailbird of a son. Who knew when Derrick Spanner would get around to checking his messages or if he'd actually pass along my name and phone number to Christian Satterfield? Even if Satterfield got the message, I had no confidence he'd call. There had to be another way to get to him.

I opened the bottom desk drawer and pulled out the telephone book—that hoary source of information so easy to overlook. There were twelve listings under "Satterfield" with home addresses that ranged from Santa Teresa proper to Colgate on the north end of town and Montebello to the south. A few were designated with single initials and phone numbers, but no addresses, which was useless for my purposes. I set the matter aside while I went about other business. Tax time was coming up, and I had receipts to sort in preparation for delivery to my accountant.

By the time I reached home that afternoon, it was 5:15 and the light was fading. Now that we were in March, the days were getting longer, but the chill in the air suggested winter wasn't ready to concede to spring. I found a parking place half a block away and hoofed it to my apartment, pausing to pull the mail out of the box before I let myself through the squeaky gate. I angled right, rounded the side of the studio, and moved into the backyard. Henry's lawn was brown, and half his shrubbery had died.

There was a wheelbarrow and spade in the grassy area beyond Henry's flagstone patio, but no sign of him. New to the scene was the recently excavated fifteen-foot half circle that now encompassed two fruit trees at the edge of his dead lawn. He'd mounded the bed with fifty pounds of bark mulch, judging from the empty bags he'd left nearby. I also spotted a hose dangling from his bathroom window, and that stopped me momentarily. What the heck was that about? Probably a water-saving scheme of some sort.

I shrugged to myself and continued to my front door, keys at the ready. As I let myself in, I caught a flash of white out of the corner of my eye. Henry's cat, Ed, shot out of the bushes and across the yard in time to streak into my apartment ahead of me. He'd invented this game himself, timing his run to catch me unawares. Inevitably, I forgot to check his whereabouts before I opened the door and he'd slip through the gap to victory. Sometimes I didn't even see him make his move and only discovered him after the fact, when he announced his win. He was a chatty little thing. Once inside, he usually slowed to a stop so he could sniff the shag carpet in case a mouse had left him a scented love note. Neither Henry nor I had been aware of vermin on the property until Ed came to live with us. Now he made regular patrols and left rodent remains on both our doormats as proof of his superior hunting skills.

Henry had acquired the cat six months earlier, when his brother William carted him from Michigan to California. Their older sister, Nell, who'd be turning one hundred years old on December 31, had adopted the nameless cat as a stray. Soon afterward, she'd tripped over him, taking a nasty spill that left her with a broken hip. William and Rosie had flown from Santa Teresa to Flint to assist with her care. When another brother, Lewis, threatened to have the cat exterminated, William had taken it upon himself to pass the beast along to Henry without permission or prior warning. This was not a good plan. Henry had been vehemently opposed to keeping the cat, until the vet informed him that Ed was a Japanese Bobtail, a rare and ancient breed known for their intelligence, their talkativeness, and their affinity for human companionship. Henry had promptly named him Ed and now the two were inseparable—except for those occasions when the cat came to visit me.

Henry and I had agreed that Ed would be strictly an indoor cat. The street we lived on wasn't subject to speeding cars, but there was sufficient traffic to be hazardous. There was also the issue of the occasional dog running loose, and while we felt Ed could defend himself, he was too precious to risk. Ed, of course, had other ideas, and we'd no sooner confine him to Henry's house than he'd find a way out. We were still trying to determine how he managed. It was embarrassing that he outwitted us so easily.

I dropped my shoulder bag on a kitchen stool, tossed the mail on my desk, and turned on a lamp in my living room. There were no messages on my answering machine. Ed had leaped up on the counter, where he was now reclining, watching me with interest, his devotion largely inspired by the fact that I plied him with treats. I stepped into the kitchen and took out his bag of crunchy party mix. I opened the package and tilted a selection into my palm. He chose a few kibbles shaped like chickens, leaving the fish and mice for another occasion.

I put his treats away and then picked him up and carried him under one arm as I pushed the thumb lock of the patio door to the open position, went out, and pulled the door shut behind me. Ed's purring was an audible rumble in the vicinity of my ribs as I crossed the patio. I knocked on Henry's door. I heard a muffled command, which I assumed was encouragement to let myself in. I peered through the glass and spotted him lying on the floor, stretched out on his back. I could see shorts, long bare feet, and a portion of his sweatshirt, while his head and shoulders were positioned halfway into the cabinet under the kitchen sink.

I opened the door and stuck my head in. "Is everything okay?"

"Plumbing issue." He exhibited a wrench, which he waved in my direction before he went back to work. He'd placed a five-gallon plastic bucket on the floor to one side, along with an assortment of cleansers, liquid dishwashing soap, window spray, sponges, and rusty S.O.S pads he usually kept out of sight.

I set Ed down on all fours and closed the door behind me. "You have a leak?"

"I have a *plan*," he said. He put the wrench down and inched his way carefully from under the counter, holding a J-shaped ninety-degree fitting made of PVC. "Sink trap."

"I can see that."

He struggled to his feet, shaking his head at his own creakiness. Henry is eighty-nine years old and in phenomenal shape for a man his age (or any other age, now that I think of it). He's tall and lean, with thick snow white hair and eyes the color of bluebells. He held up the trap and tilted it, emptying the contents into the plastic bucket. "Water creates a seal that prevents sewer gas from passing from the pipes back into the room."

"I thought the trap was to catch stuff in case you dropped a pricy diamond ring down the drain."

"It does that as well." He moved the bucket into position under the sink, which I could see now was filled with soapy water. "Watch this."

He pulled the plug and the sink full of water drained noisily into the bucket below. "What you're looking at is Step One in my new water conservation system. I can dump this bucket full of gray water in the toilet to make it flush. I can also use wastewater to irrigate my lawn."

"Which is why you have a hose hanging out the bathroom window, yes?"

"You got it. I'll keep the tub stoppered while I shower and then siphon the water out the window into my shrubs. Think of all the city water I can save. I probably waste a gallon every time I run the tap, waiting for the water to get hot. Last week, I ordered a book on gray water use, and we'll see what more we can do."

"Sounds good. Is that a new flower bed?"

He looked at me blankly.

"I saw the empty mulch bags."

"Oh! No, no. The mulch bed is there for purification purposes. You can't store gray water for more than twenty-four hours because of the bacteria content, so any runoff has to pass through healthy topsoil."

"News to me."

"And to me as well. My big shock was the water bill, which jumped sky-high. I called the water department and the woman checked the meter readings, which she swore were accurate. She says landscape irrigation is the prime culprit. Household use is minimal by comparison. The more lawn I can eliminate, the better off I'll be. For the moment, the water department is asking us to voluntarily reduce our usage by twenty percent. I'm hoping to get ahead of the game."

"Well, I'm being careful."

"I know that and I appreciate your efforts. We still have to tighten our belts. If the city restricts us further, I want to be prepared."

"You can count on me."

He clapped his hands together once. "Let me change clothes and we can have supper up at Rosie's. With all this going on, I haven't had a chance to shop today, let alone cook," he said. "Almost forgot to tell you. We have new neighbors."

"Since when?"

"January first, from what I hear. Shallenbargers, on the driveway side. Joseph and Edna."

"Good news. I knew the house was on the market, but I didn't know it sold. I'm sure the Adelsons are thrilled," I said. "What's the story? Are they young, old?"

"No one eighty-five and under is old. They're retired. I just met them this morning. She and Joseph were in the backyard, planting flowers on their little doggie's grave."

"What happened to him?"

"Her. Old age. She died shortly after they arrived. I guess they'd been expecting it because they seemed to be bearing up okay. Joseph's in a wheelchair, so he doesn't get around so well. His walker's a bit of a struggle, too, when he's crossing the grass."

"At least they're quiet. I had no idea anyone was living there."

"She says now they're settled, they plan to spruce up the place, which it could sorely use. Their backyard used to look worse than mine. It's already looking better than it did."

He retreated down the hall on his way to his room, calling over his shoulder, "Help yourself to wine. I'll be right there."

"I can wait," I said.

# 4

We ambled the half block to Rosie's through the gathering dark. Streetlights had come on, forming shapeless yellow patches on the sidewalk. Once there, Henry opened the door and ushered me in ahead of him. The tavern's atmosphere was subdued, much as it had been before the place was taken over by the local sports enthusiasts whose various league trophies still lined the shelf Rosie had had installed above the bar. The 1988 football season had been capped by Super Bowl XXIII on Sunday, January 22, when the 49ers defeated the Bengals by a score of 20–16. For reasons unknown, this had triggered an exodus. One week the sports rowdies were in evidence; the next, they were gone. In one of those inexplicable migrations of restaurant patrons, they'd abandoned Rosie's as mysteriously as they had appeared. Almost at once, police department personnel drifted in to fill the ecological niche.

Until recently, the favored hangout among cops had been the Caliente Café, or CC's, as it was known. Then on New Year's Day, a kitchen fire had broken out, and by the time the fire engines arrived a scant seven minutes later, the entire back side of the restaurant was engulfed in flames and the better part of the structure was reduced to charcoal briquettes. There was some suggestion the devastating fire wasn't entirely accidental, but whatever the facts, the doors and windows had been boarded over and there was no talk of reopening.

Rosie's was off the beaten path and less than a mile away, which made it the natural successor for those dispossessed of their watering hole. Rosie's wasn't a popular spot. The décor, if one could call it such, was too tacky to attract a sophisticated crowd, and the ambience too staid to appeal to the young. Now police officers and civilian employees stopped in after work and plainclothes detectives from the criminal investigations division had begun to frequent the place, attracted by its anonymity. The cheap prices also exerted an appeal. Absent were the chief of police, assistant chiefs, and others in upper management, which was just as well.

In hopes of engendering loyalty, Rosie had purchased a popcorn machine. Napkin-lined baskets of freshly popped corn were now stationed down the length of the bar with shakers of Parmesan cheese and garlic salt. The smell of hot oil and burnt kernels formed a pungent counterpoint to the scent of Hungarian spices that saturated the air.

It was early yet and neighborhood regulars would soon trickle in, augmented by off-duty police as the evening wore on. For the time being, the television screen was blank and all of the overhead lights were on, illuminating the dispirited collection of mix-and-match furnishings Rosie had assembled from garage sales over the years. The secondhand chairs had wood or chrome frames with padded vinyl plastic seats, and the Formica-topped tables were only made level through the tricky use of shims. The wooden booths that lined the right-hand wall were darkly varnished, with surfaces perpetually sticky to the touch.

William was behind the bar, polishing stemware. Rosie was perched on a bar stool, consulting a collection of cookbooks that were open in front of her. There was only one other customer, and he sat four stools away from her, his back turned while he read the newspaper and sipped a glass of beer.

As Henry and I took our seats, I glanced over and realized the lone man at the bar was Cheney Phillips, who worked in the homicide unit at the Santa Teresa Police Department. Cheney was roughly my age, with a dark mop of unruly curls as soft as a poodle's coat. Brown-eyed, clean-shaven. Two years before, we'd had what I suppose could be called a "romance," though I feel compelled to put the term in quotes. While the initial sparks had never taken hold, I didn't think either of us had ruled out the possibility. Now even the most casual encounter sometimes triggered intimate images that made my cheeks color with embarrassment.

I pushed away from the table, saying to Henry, "I'll be right back."

"You want white wine, yes?" he asked.

"I do. Thanks."

As usual, Cheney was nattily dressed: gray slacks, navy blazer, under which he wore a white dress shirt with an expensive-looking silk tie in shades of gray.

I crossed to the bar and tapped him on the shoulder. "This is a pleasant surprise. I don't usually see you here at this hour. What's up?"

He smiled. "I just finished my annual physical, for which I received a multitude of gold stars. I thought that warranted a beer."

"Congratulations. Good health deserves celebration."

He lifted his glass. "To yours."

Cheney Phillips came from money. His father owned a number of private financial institutions in the area, while his mother sold high-end real estate. Both were perplexed when he forswore the banking business in favor of the police academy. Once onboard at the STPD, he'd worked his way up from traffic to his current position as a homicide detective, where the pay was adequate but no cause for rejoicing. Still, Cheney managed to live well, which should have come as no surprise. Wealth begets wealth. Some years before, his uncle had died and left him an inheritance that he'd used to purchase a rambling two-story Victorian home next door to my friend Vera, whose house was its mirror twin.

Rosie caught sight of me and her gaze flicked to Henry, alone at his table. She closed her cookbooks, stood, and reached for an apron she tied around her waist. Idly, I watched her move around behind the bar and pour a Black Jack over ice for him. William passed her a sparkling wineglass and she filled it with Chardonnay and placed it on the bar in front of me. The wine would be second-rate, but the service was superb. She delivered Henry's whiskey, while Cheney pulled out the stool next to him and patted it. "Have a seat. How've you been?"

"Good."

As I settled next to him, I caught a whiff of his aftershave, and the familiar associations set off a warning bell. I shifted into business mode.

"You're actually just the man I was looking for," I said. "You remember the name Christian Satterfield? Convicted of nineteen counts of bank robbery, according to the *Dispatch*."

"Know him well," he said. "His last two jobs, he targeted the Bank of X. Phillips."

"Your father's bank?"

He pointed at me to confirm. "The dummy hit the same branch twice. First time, he walked off with thirteen grand. Second time, my cousin Lucy Carson was at the teller's window as a trainee, which was bad news for him. He couldn't find the note he'd written, so he told her he had a gun and threatened to shoot her in the face if she didn't empty her drawer and fork over the cash. He handed her a canvas tote, so she did as requested and then pressed the button for the silent alarm."

"Good for her. Serves him right. The paper said a couple of tellers were so stressed out, they quit."

"Not her. Just the opposite. She testified at his trial, but downplayed the shooting threat. She said he was a gentleman, soft-spoken and polite. She said she only went for the alarm because she could see he was hurting and wanted to be caught. Once he went to prison, they carried on a feverish correspondence, pouring out their hearts. Her more than him. He's the kind of guy women think they can rehabilitate."

"She have any luck?"

"Nah. She was twenty-two years old and fickle as they come. Last I heard, she'd taken up with a biker accused of killing his ex. Nothing like a bad boy in need of emotional support. What's your interest?"

"I've been asked to get a contact number for him now that he's out on parole. This is for his bio-mom, who's got money to burn. She'd like to smooth his transition, should the need arise."

"Nice."

"I thought so myself. I left a message with one of the federal parole officers, but I don't want to sit around hoping he'll call back. I figure when the kid was arrested, he must have listed a local address, so I thought I'd start there."

"I can help you with that. Back then, he was living with his mom over on Dave Levine. I'll have someone in Records pull up the address. I'll call tomorrow and give you what we have."

"I'd appreciate it. Can I buy you another beer?"

"Thanks, but I better pace myself. I'm having dinner with a friend."

"Catch you later then," I said as I slipped off the stool.

I returned to Henry's table and took a seat.

"What was that about?" he asked.

"Work."

"Everything with you is work."

"No, it's *not*."

Rosie reappeared and gave us each a setup: a paper napkin wrapped tightly around a knife, fork, and spoon. She usually presented us with a mimeographed menu, which was strictly window dressing, as she told us what she was serving us and brooked no argument. She tucked her hands under her apron and rocked on her feet. "Tonight is big treat."

"Do tell," Henry said. "We can hardly wait."

"Calf brain. Is very fresh. How I prepare is rinse and place in large bowl into what's trickling cold water from tap. I'm peeling off filament is like membrane covering. Then I'm soaking in vinegar water one and haff hours, all the time cutting away white bits . . ."

Henry closed his eyes. "I may be coming down with something."

I said, "Me too."

Rosie smiled. "Just teasing. You should see the look on you two faces. Wait and I'm surprising you."

And surprise us she did. What she brought to the table were plates on which she'd created a visual composition of grilled kielbasa, puffy fresh herb omelets oozing pale cheese, and two salads with a light vinaigrette. To one side, she placed a basket of dinner rolls Henry'd made the day before. For dessert, she served us baked plums wrapped in a flaky pastry with a cap of softly whipped cream.

We finished dinner and Henry took care of the check while I shrugged myself into my jacket. We'd just stepped into the chilly night air when Anna Dace appeared, coming toward us through the newly minted dark. The two of us were related, though I'd be hard-pressed to define the family connection, which stretched back a generation to my grandmother, Rebecca Dace. My father was *Anna's* father's favorite uncle, making us (perhaps) second cousins. I might also be her aunt. She had her hair pulled up in a careless knot she'd secured with a clip. She wore a navy blue peacoat over jeans, and military-style boots. I may have neglected to mention that she's shamelessly pretty— not a trait I consider relevant, though men seem to disagree.

She brightened when she caught sight of Henry and clutched him by the arm. "Hey, guess what? I took your advice and put my money in mutual funds. I allocated the investment over the four types you talked about."

I stared at her. *Allocated?* Shit. Since when did she use words of more than one syllable?

She and her two siblings had come into money at the same time I did, though the source was different. I'd expected all three of them to burn through the funds in a heartbeat. Being the mean-spirited creature I am, I experienced a pang of disappointment that she was exhibiting good sense.

Henry said, "Not the whole of it, I hope."

"No way. I set twenty grand aside in a separate account, so I'd have access to it. Not that I'd touch it," she added in haste.

"I'm giving you an A-plus," he said.

"I invested in mutual funds. How come I didn't get an A-plus?" I interjected. Neither paid the slightest attention.

When Henry realized Anna was on her way in to Rosie's, he pushed the door open again and held it, allowing her to pass in front of him. As he did so, I looked up and saw a truncated slice of the interior, a vertical slat that included a narrow view across the tables to the bar where Cheney sat. In that split second, I saw him turn and catch sight of Anna. His face creased in a smile as he got up. The door closed, but the image seemed to hang in the air.

Cheney's throwaway line hadn't really registered until then. *Dinner with a friend?* Since when was Anna Dace a *friend?*

# 5

The next morning, the office phone was already ringing as I turned the key in the lock and pushed open the door. The phone continued to ring as I crossed the outer office in giant steps and flung my bag on my desk. I was poised to snatch up the handset when my outgoing message kicked in. "The party you've dialed in the 805 area code is currently unavailable . . ."

My first thought was that this might be Christian Satterfield's parole officer, or perhaps the parolee himself. I was just about to answer when I heard Cheney's voice. I stayed my hand, which hovered in midair as he tossed off a hasty greeting and then read aloud the phone number and the address on Dave Levine Street that Christian Satterfield had used at the time of his arrest. I picked up a pen and made a note of the information as Cheney neared the end of his recital. After he signed off, I played the message again, making certain I'd heard the numbers correctly.

I opened my bottom desk drawer and hauled out the phone book again. I flipped over to the S's and ran a finger down the column. There were no Satterfields living on Dave Levine, but I found a match for the phone number under the name Victor Satterfield on Trace Avenue, which was not a street I knew. I removed the Santa Teresa street map from my shoulder bag and opened it to the full. I spread it across my desk and checked the street index. I found Trace at the axis of G on the horizontal and 31 on the vertical. The street was a block and a half long and butted right up against Highway 101. If I was correct in my recollection of the house numbers on Dave Levine, this address was no more than five blocks away from the one Satterfield had claimed ten years earlier.

I picked up the phone and dialed. I probably should have cooked up a ruse in advance, but sometimes action without planning makes just as much sense. And sometimes not. The phone rang three times, and then someone picked up. "Hello?" Female, gravelly voiced, and blunt.

I pictured a habitual smoker over the age of fifty. She'd uttered only one word and somehow managed to sound rude. "May I speak to Chris?"

"Who?"

"Christian?"

There was dead silence for a beat. "Honey, you're not going to have any luck with that one," she said.

And then she hung up.

I replaced the handset in the cradle, wondering what she meant. I wasn't going to have any luck with that one, meaning asking for someone named Chris or Christian? Or I wasn't going to have any luck with the man himself? Were women calling the house all day long and bombing out right and left? All I'd wanted to know was whether the number would net me one parolee. Calling again probably wasn't going to prove any more informative. I needed to settle the issue, and Hallie wasn't paying me enough to extend the task any longer than was absolutely necessary.

I picked up the folder in which I'd tucked the copy of the newspaper clipping that included Satterfield's photograph. I slid the file into the outer pocket of my shoulder bag, locked the office, and trotted out to my car. I'd recently sold my 1970 Mustang, a Grabber Blue Boss 429 that was much too conspicuous for the work I do. I'm supposed to blend in to the background, which was much easier with my current boring vehicle, a Honda so nondescript that I sometimes failed to spot it in a public parking lot. The only element common to the two cars is the overnight bag I stash in the trunk in case of an emergency. My definition of an emergency is being without a toothbrush, toothpaste, and fresh underpants. I slid under the wheel and turned the key in the ignition. I missed the resounding throatiness of the Mustang's oversize engine as it rumbled to life. It always sounded like a Chris-Craft powerboat to me.

I drove to the end of the block and turned right on Santa Teresa Street, continuing six blocks north before I cut over to Dave Levine. I took a left and followed the one-way street south toward the ocean. I spotted Trace Avenue, passed it, and then found a parking place a block away. I locked the car and walked back.

The house at 401 Trace turned out to be a small one-story frame structure on the corner of Trace and Dave Levine. A wide apron of dead grass formed an L on two sides of the property, and a plain wrought-iron fence marked the perimeter. The house itself sat on a slab of poured concrete made level by a low wall of cinder block with a planting bed along the upper edge. The shrubs, like the lawn, were so brown, they looked singed.

The windows were sliding aluminum-framed panels, tightly closed and rendered blank by lined drapes. Up close, I knew the aluminum would be pitted. The porch was small. To the right of the front door, there was an upholstered chair covered in floral cotton, blue and green blossoms on a ground of red. To the left of the door there was a houseplant, probably fake. I crossed the street at an angle, waiting until I was out of range to pause and look back. No sign of the inhabitants.

The rear of the house suggested more space than I'd imagined. I was guessing three small bedrooms, one bathroom, living room, kitchen, and utility porch.

The neighborhood seemed quiet, made up almost entirely of single-family homes that had probably been built in the 1940s. A few of the cars parked at the curb were new; maybe two out of fifteen. The rest were three to five years old and in good shape. Most were American-made. This was not an area where banged-up vehicles were parked three-deep in the driveways. The houses were well-maintained and most of the lawns were tidy, given that dead grass is so much easier to control.

I returned to my car and drove around the block, this time parking on a side street to the north and perpendicular to Trace. For a while, I sat there and thought about life. I needed a vantage point from which I could keep an eye on the house. With luck, Christian Satterfield would arrive or depart, thus allowing me to confirm his whereabouts. Here's the problem with stationary surveillance, otherwise known as a stakeout: Most people arrive at a destination, park the car, and get out. Almost no one with a lawful purpose sits in a vehicle staring through the windshield at a building across the street. Sit in a car for any length of time and you look suspicious, which means somebody's going to call the cops and then your cover will be blown. The trick is to think of a legitimate reason to be loitering—a proposition more slippery than one would imagine. In the past, I'd feigned car trouble, which is only effective as long as some Good Samaritan doesn't approach and offer assistance. I'd also faked a traffic survey, which I managed to extend for two days until I spotted my prey. Here, there was no point in pretending to count cars, because mine was the only moving vehicle I'd been aware of since I arrived.

I locked the car and proceeded on foot. As I approached the corner, I spotted two small businesses: a convenience store on one side and a bar and grill called Lou's on the corner opposite. The mailman, with his rolling cart, was just ahead of me on the far side of the street. Despite the chilly weather, he wore blue shorts, a matching blue shirt with a USPS patch on one sleeve, and what looked like a pith helmet. The mailboxes were stationed along the sidewalk, so instead of having to approach each house on foot, all he had to do was open the box and insert the relevant bundle of bills, magazines, and junk mail for any given address.

I kept pace with him and watched when he turned the corner, moving toward the cul-de-sac where the highway cut through. I thought I might catch up with him and quiz him about the occupants of 401, but I worried the inquiry would get back to them. My mailperson is a friendly gal with whom I chat from time to time. If someone came skulking around with questions about me, she'd not only stonewall the stranger, she'd tattle the first chance she had. If I wanted to know the names of the persons receiving mail at 401 Trace, all I had to do was look. I glanced at the house. No one peered out from behind the drapes and no one emerged to collect the mail, so I took the liberty of lowering the flap. I removed the mail and sorted through the collection as though I had every right to do so.

Geraldine Satterfield was the addressee on a number of bills, Southern California Edison, AT&T, and Nordstrom among them. None of the envelopes was rimmed in red, so I assumed her accounts were current. A Pauline Fawbush had received her copy of *People* magazine, but that was the extent of the mail in her name. Impossible to know if it had been Geraldine or Pauline who'd answered the phone. The catalogs were for Occupant or Current Resident. Nothing for Christian, but he'd only been a free man for a short while, assuming he was there at all. I didn't picture him on anybody's mailing list. I closed the box and moved on.

On the far side of the street, I spotted two houses with For Rent signs in the yards. One sign in small print said DO NOT DISTURB TENANTS, which suggested someone was still in residence. The house two doors to the right looked more promising. There were cardboard boxes piled up on the curb along with four bulging black plastic bags. There were also assorted discards: a chair with a spring poking up through the seat and a swing-arm lamp with a missing locking nut and springs. This fairly cried out for further investigation. I lifted my gaze and did a casual survey. No dogs barked. I didn't pick up any cooking smells or the whine of a leaf blower being operated nearby.

I traversed the street at an angle and walked up the short driveway, circling the house to the scruffy yard in the rear. I climbed two steps to the back porch and peered in through the glass-paned window in the kitchen door. The place was a mess. These people were never going to get their cleaning deposit back. The four-burner stove was spattered with grease. The counters were littered with open containers that ants were raiding in a feverish display of industry. In the center of the room, there was a garbage can filled to the brim. Even through the glass, the rotting foodstuffs smelled like they'd been sitting for a week.

I tried the knob and the kitchen door swung open with the sort of creak reserved for horror movies. Technically speaking, this wasn't breaking and entering since I hadn't broken anything. I made a few "yoo-hoo" noises just to satisfy myself that I was the only one on the premises. I'd seen this same floor plan in countless California cottages. Kitchen, living room, dining area, and two bedrooms with a bathroom between. I moved down the hall to the living room and looked out the front window toward the house at 401, which was hard to my right. I couldn't see much. I unlocked the dead bolt on the front door and stuck my head out. The front porch was small, surrounded on three sides by a half wall, bisected by a short flight of steps. White latticework trellises extended from the top of the low porch wall to the roofline. The vines that had originally climbed up the trellises were long since dead, and the brown leaves created a cozy retreat. The angle of the view was sharp, but it did encompass Geraldine Satterfield's front door and part of the driveway to the left.

I closed the front door, which I left unlocked as I continued my walk-about. In the bathroom, I tried the taps and was delighted to find running water. I opened the toilet lid and discovered the little present left by the former tenant. I pushed the lever and was rewarded with a vigorous flushing. Despite the absence of toilet paper, a working commode is always an asset to a hard-boiled private eye.

I left by way of the back door and went out to the street. I strolled to the corner, where I turned right and returned to my car. I opened the trunk and hauled out a folding camp stool suitable for golf or tennis matches if I were the sort who attended sporting events. I opened the driver's-side door, leaned across the seat, and flipped open the glove compartment. I removed my binoculars, locked the car, and then checked the parking signs to make sure the Honda wouldn't be towed away while I was on the job.

Before I returned to the empty house, I went into the convenience store and picked up a turkey sandwich sealed in cellophane. The sell-by date wasn't coming up for another two days, so I figured I was safe. I opened the glass-fronted refrigerated case and chose a bottle of lemon-flavored iced tea. I added a two-pack of one-ply toilet paper and paid for the items at the cash register in front.

I entered the empty house a second time by way of the back door, tested the toilet, which was still in good working order, then went out onto the front porch and assembled my temporary campsite. I opened the folding canvas stool and positioned it close to the trellis, set my bag of supper items to one side, and then trained my binoculars on the house at 401. I cursed myself when I realized I'd neglected to bring anything to read, which was probably just as well. This left me with no choice but to sit and stare through the X's of the trellis until I spotted my subject or gave up my quest for the day. As time passed, to amuse myself, I divided the total hours on the job into the two hundred dollars I'd been paid. In calculating my hourly rate, I couldn't help but notice a steep decline as time went on.

This is what I saw: a woman I took to be Pauline Fawbush fetched the mail from the box and then settled on the porch in the floral upholstered chair and read her *People* magazine. Pauline appeared to be in her late seventies, and I was guessing she was Geraldine's mother and

Christian's grandmother. She was occupied for forty-five minutes, after which she returned to the house and came out moments later with
her manicure kit. Oh, boy. I watched her paint her fingernails with a
shade of polish called Love's Flame, the label clearly visible through
my binoculars.

At 5:00, a glossy black limousine appeared from my right, turned
the corner onto Trace, and pulled into the Satterfield driveway. The
driver was a middle-aged woman in a black pantsuit with a white
dress shirt and a black bow tie. The rim on the license plate read PRES-
TIGE TRANSPORTATION SERVICES INC. From that, I surmised she was a driver
for a limousine company, a guess I later verified through other sources.

She went into the house. I spotted her moments later in the kitchen,
which was on the Dave Levine side of the street at the rear. Pauline
joined her, and the two occupied themselves with preparing the evening meal. As they chopped at waist level, I couldn't identify any of
the foodstuffs. I was about to pass out from boredom. Not that carrots
would have been exciting. I ate my sandwich, which was better than I
had any reason to expect. My neck hurt, I was cold, my butt was sore,
and I was cranky. My right leg had fallen asleep. My hourly rate continued to drop precipitously. Ninety-two cents an hour isn't even close
to minimum wage. I saw the porch light go on.

It was fully dark when I saw a fellow approach from the right on
foot. He went into the house. In the murky light, I'd only caught a flash
of him, but I recognized Christian Satterfield from his photograph. I
waited another thirty minutes before I packed up my gear and de-
camped.

I drove to the office and let myself in. I hauled out my portable
Smith Corona and placed it on my desk. I removed the top of the
hinged case and set it to one side. Then I pulled out a few sheets of
letterhead stationery along with a few pieces of blank paper that I
used to compose a rough draft of my report, laying out the information
in that faux-neutral language that infuses a professional summary of a
job when it's done. The report was short, but covered the information

my client had requested: Christian's current address, a home phone, and visual confirmation that he was in Santa Teresa and had entered the premises on at least this one occasion. My guess was that he'd gone back to living with his mom, but I might have been wrong about that.

I reread the report, editing a line here and there. Then I rolled a sheet of stationery into the typewriter and made a proper job of it. I ran off two copies of the report on my new secondhand copy machine, signed the original, and folded it in thirds. The two copies I placed in the file folder I'd created for that purpose. I cranked a number 10 envelope into the machine and typed Hallie Bettancourt's name and the post office box she'd provided. I affixed a stamp, snapped the lid onto the Smith Corona, and tucked it under the desk. Then I grabbed my shoulder bag and the report, turned out the lights, and locked up.

On my way home, I stopped by the post office, where I pulled up at the curb and tossed the envelope into the collection box.

# 6

The rest of the week went by, the days filled with the sort of do-nothing business not worth mentioning. I should have savored the mindless passage of time, but how was I to know? Monday, March 13, I went into the office as usual and diddled around until noon, taking care of clerical matters. I was halfway out the door on my way to lunch when the telephone rang. I hesitated, tempted to let the machine record the caller so I could be on my way. Instead, I reversed direction and dutifully picked up.

"Millhone Investigations."

Ruthie laughed. "I love that. 'Millhone Investigations.' So businesslike. This is Ruthie. I was afraid you'd left for lunch."

"I was just on my way out. How was your trip north?"

"Good. Actually, it was great. I enjoyed myself," she said. "I was wondering if you'd had a chance to check the contents of that box."

*Box?*

I said, "Shit! I forgot. I'm sorry. Honestly, I blanked on it."

"Well, I hate to nag, but I called the IRS agent this morning and he was Johnny-on-the-spot. My appointment's tomorrow afternoon at one."

"That was quick," I said. "Which IRS office, local or Los Angeles?"

"He's coming to the house. I thought I'd have to make the trip downtown, but he says it's just as easy for him to stop by."

"Accommodating of him."

Somewhat sheepishly, she said, "I confess I was sucking up to him. I'm playing the 'poor widder woman' with a lot of 'woe is me' thrown in. I can't believe he fell for it."

"You gotta work with what you have."

"I'll say. Tell you the truth, he frightened me with all his talk of interest and penalties."

"How much does Pete *owe*?"

"That's what the agent is trying to determine. He says failing to pay taxes is one thing. Failing to *file* is a federal offense. It's not like he wants to get me in hot water; just the opposite. If I come up with any documentation at all, he thinks he can get the issue resolved in my favor."

"What issue? Is he talking about personal or professional?"

"Professional, but not the 1988 returns. He dropped that idea. I told him Pete had one client this entire past year, so he shifted gears. Now he's focused on Byrd-Shine."

"That's ridiculous. Pete wasn't a partner in the agency. He wasn't even a full-time employee. It was all contract work. Who bothers to hang on to old 1099s?"

"I'm just repeating what he said. I don't want to argue with the man when I'm trying to pass myself off as a conscientious citizen. Pete swore he had access to all the old records, but they weren't close at hand."

"When did he talk to Pete?"

"A year ago, I guess. He says Pete assured him he had the paperwork in storage, but it was a hassle to get to and that's why he was dragging his feet."

"It does sound like him."

"Doesn't it? He never did anything he could put off."

I said, "Here's what seems weird: as broke as he was, why would he shell out money for a storage unit?"

"Hadn't thought of that. You think he lied?"

"Not my point. I'm saying if he'd rented a self-storage unit, you'd have heard about it by now unless he paid a year in advance. Otherwise, the renewal would have come up, don't you think?"

"True. I guess he might have stuck the paperwork in the attic. I mean, we don't really have an attic, but we have the equivalent."

"Which is what?"

"Junk room might be the kindest way to describe it. Most of it's mine from when my mother died and we had to clean out her house. Always possible Pete shoved a box or two in there. It would be easy to overlook."

"Sounds like it's worth a try."

"I've been meaning to do it anyway. I could use the space. Enough about my mess. I better let you get to lunch."

"Don't worry about it. I'll do a quick search and get back to you within the hour. Will you be there?"

"I've got errands to run, but it shouldn't take me long. I'm not crazy about the idea of your using work time for this. Why don't you drop the box at my place and I can tackle the job? Play my cards right and I can probably talk the IRS guy into lending a hand. I could swear he was moments away from volunteering."

"Well, aren't you the charmer? He's really falling all over himself. So what's this guy's name? If I get audited, I'll be sure to ask for him."

"George Dayton, like the city in Ohio. You sure you won't change your mind about bringing the box to me?"

"No, no. I'll take care of it. I should have done it a week ago."

"Well, I thank you. Let me know what you find."

. . .

I decided I might as well grab lunch at home, thus combining feed-time with the task I'd forgotten. As I rounded the corner of the studio, I spotted Henry standing to one side of the yard in a white T-shirt, shorts, and flip-flops. He has the long, lean lines of a distance runner, though I've never seen him engaged in formal exercise. He's a man in constant motion, who keeps his intellect sharp by way of crossword puzzles and other tests of memory and imagination. The genetic code for all of the Pitts kids has tapped them for long lives. His brothers William and Lewis share Henry's lean build. Charlie and Nell, now ninety-seven and ninety-nine years old, respectively, are constructed along sturdier lines, but enjoy the same extended longevity. Charlie's hearing has dimmed, but the lot of them are smart, energetic, and mentally acute.

I crossed to Henry's side and looked down, noting he'd dug a twelve-inch-deep hole in the lawn, into which he'd inserted a measuring stick. The cat sat nearby, staring attentively into the hole, hoping something small and furry would appear.

Henry picked up his watering can, filled the hole with water, and took a quick look at his watch.

"What's this about?" I asked.

"I'm measuring soil perk. This dirt has heavy clay content, and I need to find out how fast the water drains."

I studied the water in the hole. "Not very."

"I'm afraid not." He glanced at me with a wry smile. "I made a discovery today. You know how Ed's been getting out?"

"No clue."

"Dryer vent. The tubing came loose and I spotted the hole when I was crawling through the bushes checking water lines."

"You close it up?"

"I did. He'll probably find another way out, but for now he's house-bound."

Apparently, Henry hadn't noticed the cat at his feet, and I made no mention of him.

On a side table next to one of his Adirondack chairs, I spotted an oversize paper edition of *Grissom's Gray Water Guide*.

"I see you got your book."

"Came in Friday's mail. I've been reading up on the difference between separate flow and collection plumbing."

"What's that about?"

"Reuse efficiency, among other things. I've set up separate flows, but now I'm not sure that's the best choice. Grissom's talking about maintenance and troubleshooting, which hadn't occurred to me. This fellow's not a fan of the slapdash."

"Sounds like you need a plumber."

"Might," he said. "My house and yard are small, so I was hoping to minimize the cost, but there's no point in building a system that doesn't do the job."

"Wouldn't hurt to ask an expert."

"I'll give someone a call," he said. He continued to stare at the water in the hole, which was, so far, stationary. He shook his head, disheartened.

"Yoo-hoo, Henry. Excuse me . . ."

Both of us turned to see a small round face rising like a moon above the wood-plank fence that separated Henry's driveway from the house next door. Henry lifted a hand in greeting.

"Edna. Good to see you. This is Kinsey."

"How do," she said. "I heard voices and wondered if there was a problem."

Her face was framed by a thin braid she wore wound around her head. Her teeth, even at a distance, looked like a replacement set. She had thin shoulders and thin arms that she rested on the fence support. Her dress was black with tiny white dots and a wide white collar edged with lace. Under her collar, a red grosgrain ribbon was tied in a perky bow. I was surprised she was tall enough to peer over the fence.

"She's standing on a box," Henry said, half under his breath. And to her, "I'm explaining my water conservation plans."

"I hope you'll share the information," she said. "Our water bill's been going up. I wish someone had told us how expensive it is living here. It's been a shock."

"Where were you before?" I asked.

"Perdido. My husband worked for the city. He took early retirement because of an injury. He receives his social security and disability checks, of course, but his pension doesn't go as far as we thought, and now we're feeling the pinch. Are you Henry's daughter?"

"His tenant. When he built his new garage, he converted the old one into a rental unit."

She blinked. "Well, that's a wonderful idea. Our garage is sitting empty. Joseph isn't allowed to drive, and I'm much too nervous on the road these days. With gas prices so high, it made sense to sell our car. A tenant would be a nice way to add to our income."

"I doubt you can get the necessary permits," Henry said. "Zoning laws have changed, especially with drought conditions getting worse. The city's tough on new construction."

"I don't know what we're to do," she said. "If an item's not on sale, I have to take it off the list. I never thought I'd see the day when I'd be clipping coupons."

"I do that as well," he said. "I make a game of it, seeing how much I can save from week to week."

"Sometimes I serve chili with chopped onions over corn bread as our main meal of the day. Fine as far as it goes, but eighty-nine cents for a can of chili beans is too much," she said. "So-called 'land of plenty,' and here you have little kids and old folks going hungry. It's not right."

"If you need to go to the market, I'll be happy to give you a lift the next time I go," Henry said, riding right over her complaints.

Her small face creased with a tremulous smile. "That would be wonderful. I have one of those wire carts, but it's too far with my bad ankle."

"You put a list together. I'll be making a trip in the next couple of days."

She turned to look at the house as though in response to a sound. "Joseph's calling," she said. "I best go see what he needs. Nice meeting you, Miss."

"You too," I said.

She disappeared, and moments later we could see her struggle as she climbed her back porch stairs, clinging to the rail.

"Bit of a sad sack," I remarked.

Belatedly, he frowned. "Aren't you home early?"

"I promised Ruthie I'd look for Pete's financial information. She's got an IRS audit tomorrow and any relevant documents would be a blessing. I doubt I'll find 'em, but I said I'd try. There are some old Byrd-Shine files I need to sort through anyway."

"You need help?"

"Nah. It's one box. I should have done it days ago, but I forgot."

He glanced back at the hole. "Water's still sitting there."

"Bummer," I said. "Anyway, I told Ruthie I'd get back to her within the hour. Will I see you later at Rosie's?"

"I'm attending an adult education water conservation workshop at seven, but I'll stop by afterward."

I headed for my front door. I glanced back, noting that Ed the cat had taken himself inside and now sat on Henry's high bathroom windowsill, his mouth moving mutely in what I took to be a plaintive cry to be let out.

"You just stay where you are. I'm not letting you out," Henry said.

# 7

I sat down at my desk and dragged the banker's box out of the knee-hole space. The lid was askew because the files were jutting up above the rim. It looked like someone had jammed the lid into place, trying to force a fit. Half the file tabs were bent and mangled in consequence. I lifted the box, using the handhold on either end, and set it on my desk.

This was the same cardboard carton in which I'd found Pete's tape deck wedged some months before. I'd since moved the recorder to my bottom drawer. The old Sony was oversize and had the look of an antique compared to those currently in use. On the cassette he'd left in the machine, I'd found the illegally recorded phone conversation he'd used in the blackmail scheme that eventually got him killed. It really was a wonder he'd lived as long as he did.

I emptied the box, hauling out file after file: bulging accordion-style folders, correspondence, case notes, and written reports. Byrd-Shine had a document-retention policy of five years, so most were long out of date. The major portion would be duplicates of reports sent to the various attorneys for whom Ben and Morley had worked. My plan was to assess the contents, set aside anything sensitive, and deliver the remainder to a shredding company. I wasn't sure what would qualify as "sensitive," but occasionally lawsuits drag on for years, and it was always possible a case might still be active, though no longer under the purview of the now-defunct agency.

Pete must have cherry-picked these client files, perhaps hoping to generate business after the agency was dissolved. Given his questionable code of conduct, he would have felt no compunction about reaping the benefits of Ben and Morley's split. The fifteen files I counted seemed randomly assembled. Pete probably had a game plan, but so far I hadn't discerned the underlying strategy.

Among the cases, the only one I remembered was a lawsuit in which an attorney named Arnold Ruffner had hired Byrd-Shine to do a background check on a woman named Taryn Sizemore, who was suing his client for intentional infliction of emotional distress. The defendant, Ned Lowe, was accused of stalking, harassment, and threats. His attorney paid Byrd-Shine a big whack of money to find evidence that would undermine the plaintiff's credibility. Morley Shine had handled the matter.

At the time, I was still in training, so I wasn't involved. Eventually, the suit was dropped, so Morley must have delivered the goods.

Remembering Ruthie's caution about Pete's penchant for hiding cash, I turned each file upside down and riffled the pages. I wasn't even halfway through the process when a piece of folded graph paper fell out. I opened it and found myself looking at handwritten columns of numbers, eight across and twelve down, the numbers grouped in subsets of four.

| 1216 | 0804 | 1903 | 0611 | 2525 | 1811 | 1205 | 1903 |
| 2407 | 0425 | 0825 | 1509 | 1118 | 1222 | 1100 | 0000 |

| 1903 | 2509 | 0403 | 0403 | 1314 | 0304 | 2500 | 0000 |
| 2407 | 0425 | 0825 | 1509 | 1118 | 1222 | 1100 | 0000 |
| 1016 | 0619 | 1908 | 1217 | 0910 | 1908 | 2500 | 0000 |
| 1003 | 0413 | 0813 | 0922 | 1100 | 0000 | 0000 | 0000 |
| 0511 | 0406 | 2512 | 0820 | 0326 | 0904 | 0300 | 0000 |
| 1211 | 2505 | 1105 | 0304 | 0312 | 1122 | 1100 | 0000 |
| 1207 | 1211 | 2505 | 0319 | 1409 | 0413 | 0000 | 0000 |
| 1603 | 2513 | 0304 | 1209 | 2525 | 2300 | 0000 | 0000 |
| 1711 | 2503 | 0526 | 1122 | 0600 | 0000 | 0000 | 0000 |
| 0507 | 2212 | 0925 | 1120 | 0000 | 0000 | 0000 | 0000 |

I checked the other side of the paper, which was blank. There were no torn edges, so it didn't appear the page had been removed from a financial ledger. No dollar signs, no commas, and no decimal points. Many numbers were repeated. Eight of the twelve lines ended in sets of zeroes, which might have been place holders used to round out the grid. I couldn't imagine what it was, but I assumed the data was significant, or why would he have hidden it? Knowing how devious he was, I didn't want to underestimate his thinking process—but I also didn't want to overestimate his smarts. I put the paper in the outer compartment of my shoulder bag and went back to the job at hand.

I thought the case names I came across would trigger memories, but it was the sight of Ben Byrd's precise penmanship that called up images of the past. He'd used a fountain pen and a particular brand of ink, so his field notes were easily distinguished from the scribbles Morley had made with assorted ballpoint pens. All the final reports were neatly typed. The originals had gone to the clients' attorneys and the carbons were filed in descending date order, the most recent on top. Ben had insisted on storing the rough draft notes with the finished versions, making sure both were retained. I could remember a couple of occasions when critical information hadn't made it into the typed report, and it was Ben's policy that had saved the agency embarrassment.

He and Morley had been a study in contrasts. Ben was a statesman and a gentleman, tall, elegant, and dignified, while Morley was the rumpled, overweight jack-of-all-trades who generally flew by the seat of his pants. Morley relied on intuitive leaps, where Ben operated by the methodical accretion of detail. Morley was quick off the mark and insights came to him intact. At the outset, he couldn't always justify his position, but nine times out of ten he was right. Ben might come to the same conclusion, but his was a carefully rendered composition, where Morley's was a quick sketch.

In one expandable file folder, I found a stack of annotated index cards, wrapped with a rubber band that broke the minute I lifted the packet from the depths; Ben Byrd's bold blue cursive again. He was the one who'd taught me the art of the interview without the use of a notebook or tape recorder. Didn't matter to him if he was dealing with a client or a culprit, an adversary or a confidential informant. His policy was to listen with his whole being, mind open, judgment held in reserve. He absorbed tone and body language, trusting his memory as the conversation went on. After each exchange, he converted facts and impressions into written form as soon as possible, using index cards to record the bits and pieces regardless of how unimportant they might have seemed in the moment. He was also an advocate of shuffling and reshuffling his makeshift deck of cards, convinced that even a random rearrangement would sometimes suggest a startling new view. Until that moment, I wasn't even aware how thoroughly I'd absorbed the lesson. I'd forgotten his habit of dating his index cards and decided it might be a smart idea to adopt the practice myself. I could see the virtue of keeping track of the order in which information was acquired along with the content itself.

After that brief detour, I worked quickly, doing a spot check here and there, still hopeful I might find pertinent financial statements. That Pete might slip personal business papers in among agency documents made no particular sense, but I didn't want to rule out the possibility. The folders themselves were shopworn, tabs ragged and bent, a consequence of the box's being too shallow for the contents. Since banker's boxes are designed to accommodate standard-size files, I was perplexed by the poor fit.

I studied the bottom of the empty box, noting that the cardboard "floor" was uneven along the edge. I'd constructed many identical cartons, which arrived in flat packages for assembling in place. There were always tricky diagrams labeled Flap A and Flap B with arrows pointing this way and that. I thought of it as an IQ test for office employees whose job was to pack up documents for long-term storage. The puzzler was that the final flap should have fit seamlessly, and here it did not. I retrieved a letter opener from my pencil drawer and wedged it into the gap, using it as leverage. I cringed at the harsh shriek of cardboard on cardboard, but did succeed in popping out the makeshift rectangle that had been cut to fit.

Under it was a ten-by-fifteen padded mailing pouch, addressed to a Father Xavier, St. Elizabeth's Parish in Burning Oaks, California, a small town a hundred and twenty-five miles northeast of Santa Teresa. The return address was 461 Glenrock Road, also in Burning Oaks. The package was postmarked March 27, 1961, roughly twenty-eight years before. I removed the mailer and studied it, front and back. Originally, the padded envelope had been taped and stapled shut, but someone had already opened it, so I felt at liberty to take a peek myself.

Inside, there were a number of items that I removed one by one. The first was a red-bead rosary; the second a small Bible with a red leatherette cover embossed with LENORE REDFERN, CONFIRMED TO CHRIST, APRIL 13, 1952. The name was written again on the frontispiece in a girlish cursive. Knowing little about the Catholic Church, I imagined young girls were baptized or confirmed at age twelve or so. I wasn't sure if baptism and confirmation were synonymous or different religious rituals, but I thought the taking of a First Communion figured in there somewhere.

I reached into the mailer again and removed a crude handmade card on red construction paper. The simple lettering said *Happy Mother's Day!* In the center, there was a child's diminutive handprint outlined in white tempura paint with the name *April* printed under it, doubtless under the guiding hand of an adult. At the bottom of the mailer was an unsealed envelope that contained a child's birthday card. On the front was a teddy bear holding a balloon with a button affixed. The button read: NOW I AM 4! Inside, the handwritten message read: *I love you with all my heart! XOXOXOX Mommie*

Four one-dollar bills had been enclosed; one for every year of the child's life.

I returned to the Bible, where I found a black-and-white snapshot tucked into the New Testament. The young girl pictured wore a white dress, a headband with a short white veil attached, white socks edged with lace, and black patent leather Mary Janes. She was posed on the front steps of a church. Dark hair, dark eyes, and a smile that revealed endearingly crooked teeth. In the current context, I thought I was safe assuming this was Lenore Redfern.

Tucked in the back cover of the Bible, almost as an afterthought, I found a wedding announcement, dated March 13, 1988, clipped from the *Santa Teresa Dispatch*.

### LOWE-STAEHLINGS

April Elizabeth Lowe and Dr. William Brian Staehlings were united in marriage on February 20, 1988, at the United Methodist Church in Santa Teresa, California. April, the daughter of Ned and Celeste Lowe of Cottonwood, is a 1981 graduate of Pomona College and more recently the Santa Teresa Business College. She's currently employed as a legal secretary for the law firm of Eaton and McCarty. Mr. Staehlings is the son of Dr. Robert Staehlings and the late Julianna Staehlings of Boulder, Colorado. A graduate of the University of California, Santa Teresa, and Loma Linda University

School of Dentistry, Dr. Staehlings opened a private practice, specializing in orthodontics, with an office on State Street in Santa Teresa. The newlyweds honeymooned in Hawaii and are now "at home" in Colgate.

April, not yet four years old when the items were mailed to Father Xavier, had done all right in the world. She'd managed to educate herself, find gainful employment, and fall in love. I read the wedding announcement again and stopped three sentences into it at the mention of the bride's father. Ned Lowe was the defendant in the lawsuit I'd just come across. I was assuming Ned Lowe was April's father and Lenore Redfern was her mother. Ned was now married to a woman named Celeste, so if Ned and Lenore were April's parents, they'd either divorced or Lenore had died and he'd moved on. Pete must have spied the announcement in the paper and added it to the old file, creating an addendum to the now-dead legal dispute.

The remaining item was a four-by-six-inch red leather frame that contained a studio portrait of a mother posed with a little girl sitting on her lap. The mother-daughter relationship was reinforced by the fact that the two wore matching red plaid tops. The little girl's wispy blond curls were shoulder-length and her face was lighted by a smile that showed small perfect teeth. She held an Easter basket in her lap that contained a big blue bunny, dyed Easter eggs (one pink, one blue, one green), and assorted foil-wrapped chocolates nested in bright green paper grass. Lenore and April? I put the two photographs side by side. Lenore at her confirmation and Lenore with her child.

The grown-up Lenore bore only a passing resemblance to her younger self. Her hair was now blond and worn in a style vaguely suggestive of vintage movie star glamor. She must have been in her late teens or early twenties; her pale complexion was so smooth and clear, it might have been carved from alabaster. Her expression was withdrawn, anger turned inward, as though motherhood had somehow robbed her of animation. The contrast between mother and daughter was troubling. The camera had caught the child close to bouncing, happy and secure and utterly unaware of her mother's demeanor.

I returned the items to the pouch and then returned the pouch to the bottom of the box and wedged the cardboard panel in on top. I assumed Pete had created the hidey-hole, though I couldn't be sure. I shoved the batch of files into the box in no particular order. I wondered how these keepsakes had ended up in his hands so many years after the fact, especially when they'd been mailed to a Catholic priest. Pete, of course, was a mercenary at heart and may have intended to deliver the memorabilia to the newly wed April and accept a reward if she should press one on him in gratitude. The notion was crass, but in perfect keeping with his character.

I placed the banker's box near the front door. In the morning, I'd take it to the office and lock the mailing pouch in my floor safe. I couldn't imagine who'd want it, but if Pete thought it worth concealing, then I'd do the same. At that point, for lack of a better plan, I put a call through to Ruthie. The number rang repeatedly, and then her answering machine picked up. I listened to the outgoing message, and after the beep, I said, "Hey, babe. No tax returns and no financial records. Sorry 'bout that. I'll be trotting up to Rosie's in a bit, so if you feel like joining me, I'll buy you a drink and we can catch up."

# 8

As I'd forgotten to eat lunch, I prepared a nutritious dinner at home: a peanut butter and pickle sandwich on a multigrain bread so textured, I could count the seeds, nuts, hulls, and bits of straw baked into the loaf. I rounded out the fiber content with a handful of Fritos while I sipped a Diet Pepsi. At eight, I grabbed the banker's box and rested it on my hip while I locked the studio door behind me. As I passed my car, I unlocked the trunk and hefted the box into the space, locking the car again before I continued the half block to Rosie's.

William was at his usual post behind the bar, looking chipper in a three-piece navy suit with a pale blue dress shirt; no tie. He'd donned a white apron and he was polishing wineglasses with the special microfiber cloth he favored for eradicating water spots. When he saw me, he lifted a hand in greeting. He placed a glass on the bar, filled it with white wine from one of Rosie's oversize screw-top jugs, and then winked to let me know the glass was meant for me. I crossed to the bar and settled on a stool. "How are you doing, William?"

"Good. How are you?"

"Good. Thanks for this," I said as I lifted the wineglass.

"My treat," he said, and then lowered his voice. "Rosie suggested no tie tonight. If you think it's disrespectful to the other patrons, just say the word."

"William, you're the only one in here who ever wears a tie, so it might be a relief."

"I appreciate that."

He glanced to his left, where one of the day-drinkers had bellied up and was now signaling for his usual. William poured two fingers of Old Crow and walked it down the bar.

I turned on my stool. Anna Dace was seated at a table at the rear in the company of two girlfriends, one dark, one fair. Given the chill March evening, all three seemed too scantily dressed: tank tops, mini-skirts, and high heels. They had their heads together, and Anna seemed to be reading the palm of the blonde, who appeared to be the younger of the two girls. I watched her trace a line along the blonde's thumb, speaking earnestly. Nothing so fascinating as being the focus of someone else's rapt attention.

Monday nights are quiet in most neighborhood watering holes, but the recent influx of police personnel opened the door to chance encounters with officers I didn't usually have occasion to run into. A case in point being Jonah Robb, who sat in a booth by himself. I eased off my perch and crossed the room. "You up for company?"

"Of course. Have a seat. It's good to see you," he said.

I slid into the booth across from him. He looked gloomy, but he was otherwise aging well; trim, graying at the temples. He was what's referred to as Black Irish, which is to say black-haired and blue-eyed, an irresistible combination from my perspective.

I'd first met him when he was working missing persons and I was looking for one. For years, he'd been married to a girl he'd met in seventh grade when they both were thirteen years old. He thought marriage was for life, but Camilla's commitment was on-again, off-again. She left him at intervals, taking their two daughters with her, leaving Jonah with a year's worth of frozen dinners she'd done up herself. Jonah was hopelessly smitten with her, and the worse she treated him, the more hooked he seemed to be. At one point she left with the two girls and came home pregnant by someone else. Jonah took her back without a murmur of complaint. That little boy, Banner, was coming up on three years old by my count.

Rosie appeared from the kitchen and made a brief stop at the bar before she headed in our direction. Now that police department personnel were gracing the tavern, she'd begun to make eye contact with new patrons, whereas before she generally looked to me or to someone familiar to translate requests from strangers. She delivered a fresh glass of Michelob on tap for Jonah and a basket of freshly popped corn for the table. I sprinkled Parmesan cheese over the surface and began to munch.

"What's happened to you? You look great," I said.

"That's a backhanded compliment."

"I didn't mean it that way. You look fabulous."

"What makes you say that?" he asked. "I'm not fishing for compliments. I'm really curious."

I studied him. "Good haircut. You've lost weight. You look rested. Also, depressed, but that's not always unattractive in a guy."

"Camilla's back."

"Good news."

"She's perimenopausal."

I paused with a handful of popcorn halfway to my mouth. "Which is what?"

"Hot flashes and night sweats. Irregular menses. Loss of libido. Vaginal dryness. Urinary tract infections."

"Shit, Jonah. I'm trying to eat."

"You asked."

"I thought you'd talk about mood swings."

"Yeah, well, those too. She says she's home for good. No more fooling around."

"Then why so glum?"

"I just got used to her being gone. The girls have been living with me for the past year, and we do great. Camilla parked Banner with us when she took off. That was last September as a matter of fact. Kid's in preschool; bright, verbal, well-adjusted. She comes back and now he's wetting the bed and socking classmates in the mouth. I get calls from his school twice a week. Camilla wants us in counseling and she thinks he should be on medication."

I decided to steer off that subject. The pair had been in counseling off and on for years at Camilla's insistence and look where it had gotten them. "How old are the girls now?"

"Courtney's seventeen. Ashley's fifteen."

"Are you serious?"

"Sure. That's them over there."

Astonished, I turned and stared. These were the two young women in consultation with Anna Dace. All three of them were gorgeous, which I'm sure wasn't true of me at that age. "I don't believe it."

"Trust me."

"Hey, no offense intended, but I remember snaggled teeth, tangled hair, weak chins, and bodies shaped like sausages. What happened?"

"All it took was countless beauty products and seven thousand dollars in braces."

"Not Dr. Staehlings, by any chance?"

"Dr. White," he said.

"Well, they look fantastic," I said. "They must be happy to have Camilla home."

"Ha! They hate it. She's all over them. No phone calls after six P.M. No boys coming to the house. Curfew's at nine."

"Doesn't sound bad to me. So what's your parental game plan?"

"I don't need a game plan. I treat 'em like adults. All it takes is common sense. She doesn't have a clue what they're about."

I checked my watch and made a face. "Wow. Eight forty-five. With a nine o'clock curfew, shouldn't they be heading home?"

"This is my night out with them. She's got Banner."

I said, "Fun. Just like being divorced. Which of you pays child support?"

"Don't make jokes."

"Sorry. I didn't mean to be flippant," I said. "So what happens now?"

"I expect we'll work it out. Change is tough." The glum expression was back after the few brief moments of animation.

"Jonah, how long has this been going on? Five years? Ten? As long as you buy into the program, why would anything change?"

"You're missing the point. My parents were divorced. I wouldn't wish that on any kid."

I didn't think I'd missed the point at all, but there was no arguing with the man. I glanced at the door just as Henry came in. "Henry's here. I'll catch you later. Good luck."

"Good seeing you," he said.

"You too."

I eased out of the booth, relieved at the excuse. There's nothing as aggravating as watching someone else make a hash of life. Jonah had all the cards and he refused to play the hand. What was Camilla's hold on him? I hadn't seen her for years, and then only at a distance. The woman had to be a bombshell. Why had he put up with her? He was good-hearted, handsome, steady, responsible, even-tempered. I'd dallied with the man myself on a couple of the occasions when Camilla had gone off to "find herself." It hadn't taken me long to figure out that Jonah was never going to set himself free. He knew better, but unhappiness was apparently preferable to taking risks.

I crossed to Henry's table, taking my wineglass with me. "How was class?" I asked as I sat down.

He made a face; tongue out, eyes crossed. "I left early. It's not that gray water's boring, but the subject does have its limits. How are things with you?"

"Nothing much to report."

"There's your friend Ruthie."

I followed his gaze and spotted Ruthie coming in the door. I waved and she wound her way among the empty tables. Ruthie was in her mid-sixties, tall and thin, with a lean face, a high forehead, and gray-brown hair she wore in a braid down her back. Her jeans, sweatshirt, and running shoes seemed incongruous on someone who seemed innately elegant.

When she reached us, I said, "Good. You got my message."

She looked at me blankly. "What message?"

"The one I left an hour ago."

"I just stopped by the house and there wasn't anything on my machine. What was the message?"

"That I'd be here and if you were up for it, I'd buy you a drink. Isn't that why you came?"

Henry stood and pulled out a chair for her.

She said thanks and sat down. "I came looking for you. I thought you were always here. When I drove past your place and saw the lights were out, I made a beeline."

"Why were you looking for me?"

"Being alone in that house has been giving me the creeps." She turned in her chair, looking around with interest. "Has this place changed hands? I remember beefy guys in baseball uniforms, spilling beer and smoking cigarettes. The quiet is lovely."

"The sports enthusiasts have moved on and now we have off-duty cops, which is better from my perspective."

Henry said, "Can I buy you a drink?"

"Vodka martini. Three olives. Thanks for asking."

"What about you, Kinsey?"

"I'm fine for now."

"I'll be right back," he said. Ruthie watched him cross to the bar.

"How old is he?"

"Eighty-nine."

She studied him. "He's cute. Really, he doesn't seem old to me. Does he seem old to you?"

"Knock it off, Ruthie. I got dibs on him."

We chatted about nothing in particular, and it wasn't until Henry returned carrying her martini and a Black Jack for himself that she brought up the subject of the box.

"So how'd it go?" she asked.

"The search was a bust, which was also part of the message you missed."

"You didn't find anything?"

"Nope."

"Too bad. I was hoping you'd provide me with ammunition."

Henry sat down and carefully placed Ruthie's martini in front of her. "Ammunition for what?"

"Hang on," she said. She held up an index finger, and I watched her lift the icy vodka to her lips and take a sip. She made that sound that only a vodka martini seems to inspire among connoisseurs. "That is *so* fine."

I answered on her behalf while she savored the alcohol. "She has an appointment with the IRS tomorrow, trying to sidestep an audit. She was hoping I could provide documentation, but no such luck."

"Oh well," she said. "What are they going to do, put me in jail?"

I said, "Actually, I found something else. It probably won't help, but it's interesting."

I leaned to my right and plucked the piece of graph paper from the outside pocket in my shoulder bag. I unfolded the page and put it on the table in front of her, then pointed to the grid of numbers. "You have any idea what this is?"

I watched her eyes take in the numbers on the page. "Looks like gibberish, but it's Pete's handwriting. No doubt about that," she said.

"He loved graph paper and he was a big fan of those technical pens. He kept dozens on hand."

Henry leaned forward with interest. "Code."

I turned to look at him. "You sure about that?"

"Of course. It's alphanumeric and not terribly sophisticated. If I'm correct, he assigned a number to each letter of the alphabet and then grouped the letters in fours to make it trickier to crack."

"How'd you come up with that?" Ruthie asked.

"I play word games. Cryptograms, anagrams, word scrambles. You see 'em in the paper every day. Haven't you ever done one?"

"Not me. Pete loved that stuff. Most days I feel dumb enough as it is, which is why I don't do crossword puzzles." She pointed at the page. "So translate. I'd love to hear this."

"I can't off the top of my head. I'd have to work with it. Let me take a look." He picked up the paper and let his eye run down the columns from left to right. "This is actually a cipher as opposed to a code. In a true code, each word is replaced by a specific word, which means you have to have a big awkward code book to accompany your secret messages. No respectable spy does that in this day and age."

"Plain English please. I'm not following," Ruthie said.

"It's not difficult. In a cipher, each letter is replaced by a different letter or symbol. This looks like a simple number substitution. If he'd stuck to ordinary English, we could start breaking it down by looking for single letters, which are almost always 'I' or 'A.'"

"What else?" Ruthie asked, chin on her palm.

Really, I could have done without her moony-eyed look at him.

Henry tapped the paper. "A two-letter word usually has one vowel and one consonant: 'of,' 'to,' 'in,' 'it,' and so forth. Or you might start with short words: 'was,' 'the,' 'for,' and 'and.' 'E' is the most commonly used letter in the English language, followed by 'T,' 'A,' and then 'O.'"

I said, "I figured the zeroes were placeholders."

"That would be my guess; rounding out the grid," he said. "A block of numbers has an elegant look, as opposed to ragtag lines of different lengths."

"Wonder why he went to so much trouble?" I said.

"He must have worried someone would read his notes," he said. "Where did you find this?"

"He'd slipped it between the pages of a document, a lawsuit dating back to the old Byrd-Shine days."

"You think the two are related?" Henry asked.

"No clue," I said. "Ruthie warned me about his habit of hiding papers, so I was turning files upside down, riffling pages when it fell out. If he hid this, the information must have been sensitive."

I took a few minutes to describe the compartment at the bottom of the box and then detailed what I'd found in the padded mailing pouch: the Mother's Day card, the two photographs, the birthday card, the rosary, and the Bible embossed with Lenore Redfern's name.

"A regular treasure trove," Henry remarked. "Wonder how it ended up in Pete's possession."

"No telling. The pouch was mailed to a Father Xavier at St. Elizabeth's Parish in Burning Oaks, California. This was in March of 1961."

Ruthie said, "I remember Pete's driving to Burning Oaks, but that must have been sometime in March of last year. He never said a word about a Catholic priest."

"I also came across a wedding announcement he'd clipped from the *Dispatch*. This was the marriage of a young woman named April Lowe and a dentist named William Staehlings."

"What's the relevance?" Henry asked.

"April's the daughter of the defendant in that same lawsuit, a man named Ned Lowe."

"Must have rung a bell," he said.

"Which would explain why he saved the announcement, but not why he made the trip to Burning Oaks," Ruth replied.

# X

Henry pondered the point. "Might be part of an investigation. From what Kinsey's told me, he was once a fine detective."

I couldn't remember ever voicing such a claim, but I kept my mouth shut on the off chance he was simply being kind.

Ruthie smiled. "He *was* a good detective. Ben used to say Pete had 'a nose for iniquity.' In his heyday, at any rate," she amended.

"I remember that," I said. One of Ben's rare compliments where Pete Wolinsky was concerned.

"So perhaps he was persuaded to take a case," Henry said.

Ruth made a face. "I doubt it. He only had one paying client the whole of last year."

"Might have been pro bono work," Henry said.

*Good, sweet Henry,* I thought. *Working so hard to make Pete look like a better guy than he was.*

"I appreciate your defense of him, but let's be honest. We are what we are," she said.

"He could have had a crisis of conscience," Henry said. "Just because he made one mistake doesn't mean every choice he made was wrong. People change. Sometimes we have reason to stop and take stock."

Ruth regarded him with interest. "Actually, you might have a point. You knew he had Marfan syndrome."

"Kinsey mentioned it."

"One of the complications is an enlarged thoracic aorta. A ruptured aneurysm's fatal in minutes, so Pete had an annual echocardiogram to monitor his condition. After his physical in February, his doctor told me he'd urged Pete to have surgery to make the repair. Pete never said a word to me and, knowing him, he blocked the idea entirely. What he didn't want to deal with he put out of his mind and never thought about again."

Henry cleared his throat. "You're saying if the shooting hadn't killed him, he might be dead anyway."

Ruthie shrugged. "More or less. The point is Pete told the doctor he'd already lived more years than he had any reason to expect. On one hand, he was a fatalist—what will be, will be. On the other hand, why risk surgery?"

"I don't understand how this relates," I said.

Henry turned to me. "She's saying I might be right. He knew all that stood between him and death was a roll of the dice. If he discovered something significant, he might have translated the information into code as a way of hiding it."

Ruthie closed her eyes. "You're a nice man," she said. "And don't I wish that it were true."

# 9

In the morning, I arrived at work at 8:00 on the dot, toting the banker's box I'd retrieved from the trunk of my car. I sidestepped the pile of mail that had been shoved through the slot from the afternoon before and proceeded into my inner office. I dropped the banker's box and my shoulder bag on the desk and walked down the hall to the kitchenette, where I put on a pot of coffee. While the coffee brewed, I picked up the mail and sorted through the accumulation of bills and junk. Most of it, I tossed. Once the coffee was done, I returned to the kitchenette and poured myself a mug.

I set down the mug and took the lid off the box. I piled the files on my desk, removed the false cardboard "floor," and took out the mailing pouch. I crossed to the near corner, pulled back a flap of carpeting, and opened my floor safe. I had to bend one end of the mailing pouch in order to make it fit, but it seemed like a better idea than leaving it where it was. I locked the safe, put the carpet back in place, and pressed it flat with my foot. I repacked the files and set the box on the floor near my office door.

I'd just settled at my desk when I heard the door in the outer office open and close. "I'm in here," I called.

The man who appeared in the doorway looked familiar. Offhand, I couldn't place him, but I pegged him as a cop of the plainclothes variety. Late thirties, nice-looking, with a long, narrow face and hazel eyes.

"Detective Nash," he said, introducing himself. He opened his coat to reveal his badge, but I confess I didn't peer closely enough to commit the number to memory. This was because his badge was attached to his belt in close proximity to his fly, and I didn't want to seem too interested. "Sorry to barge in unannounced," he went on.

"Not a problem," I said. I stood and we shook hands across the desk. "Have we met before? You look familiar."

He handed me a business card that identified him as Sergeant Detective Spencer Nash, of the investigative division of the Santa Teresa Police Department. "Actually we have. Mind if I sit?"

"Sorry. Of course. Be my guest."

Detective Nash took one of my two visitors' chairs and gave the place a cursory assessment while I did the same with him. He wore dark slacks and a blue dress shirt with a tie, but no sport coat. "You used to be over on State Street. The nine hundred block."

"That was six years ago. I was working for California Fidelity Insurance in exchange for office space. Did our paths cross back then?"

"Once, in passing. There was a homicide in the parking lot. I was a beat officer and first at the scene."

I felt a small flash of recollection and an image of him popped up. I pointed. "A claims adjuster was shot to death. I'd just driven up from San Diego and stopped by the office to drop off some files. You were manning the crime scene tape when I asked for Lieutenant Dolan. I remember you had a little divot right here in your front tooth."

Dimples appeared as he ran his index finger across his front teeth. "I had it fixed the next week. I can't believe you remember."

"A quirk of mine," I said. "How'd you chip it?"

"Bit down on a piece of floral wire. My wife was making a wreath with pine cones and one of those Styrofoam rings. You wouldn't think a little nick would be so conspicuous, but I felt like a redneck every time I opened my mouth."

"That's what you get for being helpful," I remarked. "Bet your mom told you not to use your teeth for stuff like that."

"Yes, she did."

I glanced at his card. "You've moved up in the world."

"I work property crimes these days."

I half expected him to take out a pen and notebook, getting down to the business at hand, but he was apparently content to take his time. Meanwhile, I reviewed my behavior, doing a quick scan of present and past sins. While I'm occasionally guilty of violating municipal codes, I hadn't done anything *lately*. "Was there a burglary in the neighborhood?"

"I'm here about something else."

"Not something I did, I hope."

"Indirectly."

I thought, *Shit, now what?*

He took his time, probably deciding how much he wanted to share. "A marked bill was passed in this area a week ago."

I watched him, waiting for the rest of it.

"We believe it came from you."

"Me? I don't think so," I said.

"Do you remember using cash for a transaction on the sixth?"

"No. You want to give me a hint?"

"I could, but I'd prefer not to color your recollection."

"What's to color? I don't remember anything of the sort."

"Take your time."

81

I was getting annoyed. "What kind of bill? Five, ten, a twenty?"

He jerked his thumb upward.

"A hundred? I don't carry hundreds. They're useless. Too hard to change."

I was about to go on when an "uh-oh" popped to mind. I leaned forward and squinted. "Are you talking about the hundred-dollar bill I used to pay for *groceries* last week?"

He pointed at me, like he was calling on me in class. "Can you tell me where you were?"

"At the grocery store obviously; the Alpha Beta market on Old Coast Road in Montebello." I was only adding the details to show I had nothing to hide. My righteous tone sounded bogus, but that might have had more to do with the look he was giving me.

"We're wondering how that particular bill ended up in your hands."

"I was hired to do a job and I was paid in cash," I said. "That bill was *phony?*"

"Not quite. Six months ago, the Alpha Beta chain initiated use of a device that counts, sorts, and bands currency. It's also programmed to spot counterfeits and capture serial numbers. The machine tagged the bill as marked, and the store manager tracked it to the cashier who took it in trade. She doesn't usually work that shift, so she remembered the transaction."

"Suzanne," I said, supplying her name.

"What kind of job did you do?"

"None of your business."

"Hired by whom?" he asked, not the least bit perturbed.

I hesitated. "I'm not sure I should tell you my client's name. Give me a minute to think about it."

"I can do that. When were you hired?"

"That same night. So you're telling me that bill was marked?"

"Not literally marked. We recorded serial numbers on a stack of cash that changed hands two years ago in the course of a felony."

"What felony?"

"I'll get to that in a bit. I have a few questions first, if you don't object."

"I might object. I don't know yet. Why don't you ask and I'll tell you what I can?"

He opened his notebook, flipping to a blank page, and clicked the tip of a ballpoint pen into place. "Let's go back to your client's name."

I went through a hasty internal debate. If I'd been working for an attorney in a civil or criminal matter, the question of confidentiality would have been clear-cut. In my dealings with Hallie Bettancourt, there were no legal issues at stake. The information I'd been hired to find seemed uncomplicated on the face of it. If Hallie paid me with tainted cash, the act might or might not have been intentional. Therefore what? My recollection of the ethical niceties was as follows: *No privilege exists between the investigator and a third party, nor does it exist in communications outside the scope of the reason for legal representation.*

So how did that apply to the current circumstance? Was I at liberty to blab her business to this nice plainclothes police detective? Ordinarily, I'm protective of clients, but in this case, I thought a police inquiry took precedence.

"Hallie Bettancourt," I said. I paused to spell her name for him and watched him make a note of it before I went on. "Now it's my turn to ask. We'll trade off. You ask me and then I'll ask you."

"Fair enough. Go ahead."

"You said 'felony.' So what was the crime?" I watched him deciding how forthcoming he should be, the same debate he'd gone through moments before.

Finally, he said, "Nineteen eighty-seven, a painting was stolen from a wealthy Montebello resident. His collection was uninsured and the painting in question was valued at one-point-two million."

"Yikes."

"That was my reaction. He was in a white-hot sweat to get the painting back and decided to offer a reward. We opposed the plan, but you can only push people so far, and he ended up winning the argument. He posted the reward, and shortly afterward, someone contacted him, claiming to know the painting's whereabouts."

"Which 'someone' would be happy to confide as soon as the arrangements were made," I said. "How much was the reward?"

"Fifteen grand. The caller was a 'she' in this case," he said. "The woman insisted on the reward being bumped from fifteen to twenty-five grand; five thousand of it in hundred-dollar bills and the rest in smaller denominations."

"More like ransom."

"Exactly. My turn now, isn't it?"

I conceded the point with a careless wave of my hand.

He checked his notes. "Aside from that Monday, how many times did you meet with your client?"

"First and only time. She lives up on Sky View in Montebello, off Winding Canyon Road. The old Clipper estate, in case you're about to ask." I gave him the house number and watched him make a note. "I can't believe I missed this whole ransom thing."

"It was only in the paper briefly. A reporter got wind of it and ran with the story before we could shut her down. We wanted to keep a lid on it, figuring if word got out we'd have a rash of copycats," he said. He checked his notes again. "Can you give me Ms. Bettancourt's phone number?"

"I didn't get a local number. There wasn't any need. When she called the office, I was here and I picked up the phone. After we met, I didn't have occasion to call her. She was leaving town the next morning, so she gave me a couple of numbers in Malibu. She and her husband have a second home down there. He has an office in Malibu as well."

As he was about to ask anyway, I reached into my bag and pulled out my index cards, sorting through until I found the relevant numbers, which I recited while he made notes.

"And she hired you to do what?"

"Nuh-uh. My turn. What happened to the reward? Did the woman collect?"

"Unfortunately, yes. We advised the victim not to pay, but he was adamant. The best we could do was talk him into letting us record the serial numbers on the bills. Long story short, he paid, the painting came back, and that was the end of it until that bill showed up," he said. "What did she hire you to do?"

Another quick debate, but I couldn't see how the job I'd been hired to do was in any way connected to the painting-for-ransom scheme. "She wanted contact information for a kid she put up for adoption thirty-two years ago. The story's more complicated, but essentially that's it."

"Whose idea was the cash?"

I thought back to the conversation. "Hers, though I'd have suggested it if she hadn't brought it up herself. She said she'd be out of town until June. Under the circumstances, I would have been leery about taking a check. Please note I just allowed you an extra question."

"You're sure the bill came from her and not someone else?"

"Positive. I stopped at the market on the way home. I don't usually carry hundreds. The money was in an envelope I put in my shoulder bag, and I spent it within the hour. While we're on the subject, I've already done the job and put my report in the mail, if it's relevant. You think this same woman stole the painting?"

"Possible," he said. He squinted at me in delayed disbelief. "You did a job for a hundred bucks?"

"Oh, sorry. She offered five, but that was too much, given what I'd been asked to do. I suggested two, and that's what she ended up paying me."

"Still sounds like a bargain."

"It does, doesn't it?" I hesitated and then said, "Crap. I guess you might as well have the other hundred. You'll ask for it anyway."

I reached into my shoulder bag and removed the envelope from the outer pocket, holding it by one corner. "My prints are on this, but so are hers. Run 'em and you might get a hit in case she turns out to be a criminal mastermind."

He smiled. "I'll mention that to the techs. Chances are she came by the cash the same way you did, but maybe we can track it back to the source."

"Meanwhile, what? I'm out the money?"

"I'm afraid so. The supermarket lost out, too, if you want to get right down to it. The bill you passed, they turned over to us without recompense. At least you got groceries out of the deal."

"I hope they don't take it out of Suzanne's pay," I said.

"Depends on store policy. I'm guessing not."

I thought about his story. "You said this was two years ago. I wonder why the money's showing up now?"

"No idea."

"But clearly someone's been sitting on it, right?"

"Theoretically, yes. Some of it could have been circulated in other parts of the country. We have no way of knowing that."

"Bad paper's a bitch," I said. "You need anything else?"

"Nope. What about you? Any questions?"

"I'd like a receipt for that bill, which I'm assuming will be booked in as evidence."

"Oh, right."

I watched while he fashioned a receipt, writing down the date and serial number before he passed it across the desk to me. "I hope your client makes good on the loss," he said.

"Hey, me too, but I wouldn't count on it."

"Probably smart. In the meantime, this is a sensitive operation, so steer clear if you would." He stirred and stood up.

I stood at the same time.

He said, "We appreciate your cooperation. Sorry to be the bearer of bad news."

"Not your fault. If I hear from her again, I'll be happy to let you know."

# X

He pointed to the phone number on his business card. "That's my private line. You need me, leave a message and I'll get back to you. I'm currently on loan to an FBI/ATF task force. Technically, the PD's not involved, and they want to keep it that way. You call the department looking for me, they're going to play dumb."

"Got it," I said. We shook hands again, as though closing a deal. "Thanks for the backstory. You didn't have to put me in the loop on this."

"We'd be grateful for any help."

The minute I heard the door close behind him, I opened Hallie's file again and tried her home phone in Malibu.

After three rings, I got a message saying the number was not in service. Odd. I tried her husband's two office numbers with the same result. I could feel the mental punctuation form above my head: a question mark and an exclamation point.

# 10

I leaned back in my swivel chair and put my feet on the desk while I did a quick assessment. Hallie didn't strike me as a high-end art thief, but what did I know? She'd told me her husband didn't have a job, so maybe this was his way of generating income—stealing art and trading it back to the rightful owner in exchange for a "reward." Detective Nash had suggested I leave the matter to law enforcement, but he hadn't *forbidden* me to do anything. Not that a clever course of action occurred to me. For now, the situation was irksome, but not pressing. True, I'd done the work and shipped off my report. Also true, groceries aside, I was no longer in possession of the cash I'd been paid. Added to that annoyance was the fact that the phone numbers she'd given me were duds. On the plus side, I knew where she lived, so she'd have a tough time dodging me once she returned in June. Worst-case scenario, I'd wait until then, explain the difficulty, and ask to be reimbursed. If she'd been the inadvertent recipient of marked bills, she'd be as irritated as I was to hear the cash was now evidence in a criminal case. Even if she felt no obligation to make good, I was only out a hundred bucks. I wanted what I was due, but with a shitload of money in the bank, I wasn't desperate.

I should have relegated the issue to the back of my brain, but alas, I could not. I picked up the handset and rang Vera at home. Three rings. Four. I was gratified when she finally picked up, though she did seem winded.

"Hey, Vera. This is Kinsey. Did I catch you on the run?"

"What makes you ask? The fact that I'm huffing and puffing and gasping for breath?"

"Pretty much," I said. "If this is a bad time, I can try you later."

"This is fine. To what do I owe this rare contact?"

"I'll overlook the snotty remark," I said. "I need to contact Hallie Bettancourt, but the numbers she gave me in Malibu turned out to be no good."

There was a moment of silence. "I don't know anyone named Hallie."

"Sure you do. You met her at a party and gave her my name."

"Nope. Don't think so. When was this?"

"A couple of weeks ago. I don't know the date."

"I haven't been to a party in two years."

"Okay, maybe not a party, but a social gathering of some sort. You had a conversation with a woman who needed the services of a private investigator."

"No."

"Don't be so quick! I haven't finished yet. She was trying to locate the kid she gave up at birth and you thought I could help. Which I did."

"I have no idea what you're talking about."

"I did a job for a woman named Hallie Bettancourt, who said she met you in passing—"

"You've said that already and I'm still not following. I'm pregnant with twins. Enormous. We're talking the size of a whale. Seven months. Actually, it's closer to eight. I don't drink. I don't go out, and the only people I talk to are under thirty-six inches tall. Except Neil, of course. I hope I don't sound bitter or cross."

"A tiny bit cross," I said. "Not to argue the point, but I only took the job because she mentioned you by name. Otherwise, I might have turned her down." I was fibbing of course. I'd been delighted to be gainfully employed.

"*What's* her name again?"

"Bettancourt. First name Hallie. Her husband is Geoffrey, last name unknown. This is one of those modern marriages where everybody hangs on to what's his or hers. They live on the old Clipper estate. Half the year, at any rate. The rest of the time, they're in Malibu or traveling the world. Tough life."

"Uh, Kinsey? The Clipper estate's empty and has been for years. No one's lived in that house since the old lady died back in 1963."

"Bullshit. I met Hallie up there a week ago."

"No, you didn't."

"Yes, I did."

"No."

"Yes, Vera." Slowly, as though to a half-wit, I said, "Here's how it went, and I will swear to this. She called and set up a meeting to discuss a personal matter. On your say-so, please note. I drove up to the house. We had wine on the deck looking out over the city while she told me a long sad tale about the baby she gave up for adoption thirty-two years ago."

"Did you find him?"

"Yes, I did. He's a safecracker-turned-bank-robber just out of prison, and I've already sent her the information she asked for."

"She set you up. She must have talked a good game."

"I don't see how she could have been bullshitting. She told me all kinds of things about the house."

"For instance, what?"

90

"For instance, her father's the famous architect who tore down the original Georgian mansion and built the contemporary structure that's up there now."

"Her *father?*"

"Halston Bettancourt. At least I think that's his name."

"Wrong again. *Her* name was Ingrid Merchant. She was a San Francisco architect who was all the rage in the 1930s."

"I don't *think* so," I said. I did hear the note of uncertainty that had crept into my voice. "Are you sure about that?"

With exaggerated patience, she said, "I know I'm hormonal. I know my IQ's dropped a good twenty points, but I'm still the reigning queen of local real estate. That's what I do for jollies when I'm not giving birth."

"I remember that. You scour the Sunday papers and go to all the open houses. Your knowledge is encyclopedic."

"That's right, which is how I know about the Clipper estate. It's a relic. A white elephant. It's been on the market so long, it's a joke. The foundation's cracked and the wooden joists are riddled with termites. The only thing holding it together is the selling agent's high hopes. Hallie Bettancourt set you up."

"How many children do you have now?"

"Including the soon-to-be-born twins? Five."

"What happened to Peter and Meg?"

"Those are my first two. They still live with us. Not to accuse you of neglect, but you missed Abigail entirely, and you're just about to miss Travis and Scott."

"Maybe I'll stop by sometime," I said weakly.

She didn't actually hang up on me. There was some kind of ruckus in the background, and I heard her say, "Oh, shit!" Then the line went dead.

I stared at the phone. This was bad. Worse than I'd thought. Had Hallie lied to me about *everything?* It was clear she'd played fast and loose, but what was the point? She'd conned me into doing the legwork in her efforts to locate an ex-con named Christian Satterfield, who might not be related to her at all. He was for real, a convicted bank robber out on parole. I'd seen the article about his crime spree and I'd seen the man himself (at least as far as I could tell in the dark and at a distance). I'd provided Hallie with contact information, neatly keeping her name out of it as requested, but the story about giving a child up for adoption now seemed questionable. I wasn't even sure the name Hallie Bettancourt was real. Probably not, now that I thought about it.

There had to be a way to track her down. How could she appear and disappear without leaving a trace?

I picked up my leather bag by the strap and slung it over my shoulder, fishing in one of the outer pockets for my keys. I locked the office and trotted out to my car. I took the back road through town, skirting the city limits as I hit the 192 and headed east toward the Clipper estate. Now the route looked different, nearly disorienting with its surfeit of visual information. At night, many houses disappeared, fading into the surrounding darkness under the cover of trees. During the daylight hours, the trajectory of the east-west mountain range was brought into high relief.

Sunlight warmed the chaparral and the dry conditions intensified the volatile oils in the dense, low-growing vegetation. The still air was heavy with the woody smell of eucalyptus, black sage, and California lilac. Manzanitas and canyon live oaks, while drought tolerant, are also highly flammable—nature's bottle rockets. Given current conditions, with the slightest miscalculation in human judgment, the landscape could ignite, turning into an ocean of fire that would take everything in its path.

I turned left onto Winding Canyon Road, following a series of switchbacks that angled ever upward. Houses were fewer here and farther between. There were no intervening side roads. An occasional driveway led off to some unseen habitat, but I saw no other motorists. I spotted the big sandstone boulder with the house number blasted into it and I turned in as I had the week before. When I reached the parking area below the house, I shut down my engine and got out. I stood for a moment, turning by degrees until I'd taken in the whole of the property, which Vera claimed had been on the market for years. Of course there was no For Sale sign. Montebello residents frown on anything so crass. I suspect in any economic decline, countless homes are listed on the quiet, with no suggestion to the outside world that owners are scrambling around trying to scare up quick cash.

I lifted my gaze to the house that towered over me. The expanses of exterior glass looked blank and lifeless. Before, believing someone was in residence, I'd seen signs of life, projecting the appropriate appearances. Now, if what Vera had told me was correct, I was seeing the structure as it really was: deserted and suffering neglect.

Scanning the foundation, I didn't spot any cracks, but maybe they'd been puttied over and painted to match the rest of the poured concrete footing. I could certainly see where the termites were at work. A moldering cord of firewood had been stacked up against the house on the uphill side where it was cozied up next to an exposed beam. Some of the quartered logs looked fresh, and I was guessing that if a tree went down, the gardener assigned to maintain the property dutifully split and stacked the wood. Aside from that, there were no other indications that anyone had tended to the place in recent months. I climbed the rugged stone stairs, careful where I stepped.

When I reached the front door, I cupped my hands to the glass and peered in. The place was empty. No paintings, no furniture, no tarps, no glowing lamps. The floors were plain wood with no sign of the Oriental carpets I'd seen. I realized my perceptions on the prior occasion were colored by my expectations. Now the white walls were bare and looked slightly dingy. I tried the knob and found it locked.

I followed the deck as it skirted the house in a wide arc. On the far side, looking out over the city, the view seemed flat—two-dimensional instead of the diorama I'd admired by night. On the terrace below, the infinity pool was hidden under a tattered automated cover. There were no deck chairs, no side table, no heaters, no remnant of fine Chardonnay. Dead leaves were scattered across the surface of the deck, caught here and there where the wind had blown them up against the railing. I glanced down. There between the beveled planks of the decking, I saw a line of dull silver. I squatted and peered, then used my thumbnail to loosen and lift the object. I held it up with a long, slow smile. "First mistake," I said aloud.

This was the paper clip Hallie had used to secure the copies of the newspaper articles she'd given me.

I did a full exterior search, checking two trash cans, which were empty. I'd hoped to find the Chardonnay bottle, but maybe she'd taken it back to the liquor store, hoping for the deposit. Pick away as I might with the sprung paper clip, I couldn't jimmy any of the locks, so I had to be content with peering into assorted windows as I circled the house. If the house had been on the market for years, there must be some provision for local agents to get into the place to show prospective buyers.

I looked around with interest. Where would I put a lockbox if I were in charge? Not on the front or back doors. That would have been the same as an invitation for someone to break and enter, which is against the law. I went down the outside stairs to ground level and went around the house again—tough work on a hillside that steep. I'd just about reached my original point of departure when I found an old-fashioned lockbox attached to a hose bib and secured by a combination lock. I checked the lockbox, surprised the device wasn't electronically controlled. Maybe no one had thought to replace it with one more sophisticated. In my perimeter search, I hadn't come across evidence of an alarm system. If the place had been empty since the sixties, it was possible proper security had never been installed.

The lock was small and looked about as effective as the ones on rolling suitcases. There were four rotating wheels, numbered zero through nine. Even with my rudimentary math skills, I was looking at ten times ten times ten times ten, or ten thousand possibilities. I

# X

tapped an index finger against my lips, trying to determine how much time that would take. More than I could spare. I trudged a few steps up the hill to the woodpile, grabbed a handsome chunk of freshly split oak, returned to the lockbox, and hauled back in my best batter-up mode. I swung and whacked the lock so hard, it flew off into the brush, and then I picked up the key.

# 11

My tour of the interior was largely unproductive. Hallie Bettancourt had left nothing behind. Somehow she'd managed to furnish the place and then eliminate any trace of physical evidence. Except for the paper clip, of course, which was so ubiquitous as to be insignificant. The house had that odd smell that seems to emerge when human occupants have moved on. I wandered down the hall and peered into the powder room. I tried the wall switch. The power was on. I turned the faucet and discovered the water had been shut off. I moved on to the kitchen. While the residence was designed along sleek, contemporary lines, the bathroom and kitchen fixtures were fifty years old and looked every bit of it. What was top-of-the-line when the house was built was by now sadly outdated.

The walls had recently been painted white, but in the spots where two coats had failed to cover, I could see the original pea green hue. The counters and splashboards were tiled in white, three-by-six rectangles laid horizontally. Subway-style tiling is all the rage again, but here the look was curiously dated. Appliances had been removed, and the refrigerator- and stove-size gaps made the room seem stark and unfriendly. A breakfast nook at one end of the room sported a built-in table with a bench on either side. The padded seats were upholstered in a fabric I remembered from one of the trailers we'd lived in when I was growing up. The pattern bore a black background with violins, clarinets, and jaunty musical notes in lemon, lime, and tangerine. I couldn't imagine why the seat fabric hadn't been freshened, but maybe the vintage look was thought to contribute a note of authenticity. I slid into the bench seat and pretended I was a family member waiting for the maid to bring me my breakfast of cream of wheat, zwieback, canned orange juice, and Ovaltine.

In the center of the table, there was a stack of fliers detailing the number of bedrooms (six), the number of bathrooms (seven), and the pedigree of the house, which was on the National Register of Historic Places. I studied the particulars. According to the hype, the architect was indeed Ingrid Merchant, whose landmark work was coveted among home buyers in Montebello. A line in small print at the bottom read PRICE AVAILABLE UPON REQUEST, meaning a sum so astronomical, the agent didn't dare write it down. Someone had provided the floor plan, showing rooms that were surprisingly small and poorly laid out for a structure that appeared so grandiose from the outside.

The listing was held by Montebello Luxury Properties. The agent was Nancy Harkness. A two-by-four color photograph of her showed a woman in her fifties with streaked blond hair worn in a shoulder-length bob immobilized by spray. I folded the flier and put it in my bag. I was already leaning toward not buying the place, but I wanted to be fair. With a property on the market as long as this one had been, there was probably some wiggle room in the asking price.

It had been clever of Hallie to whisk me through the dining room to the deck beyond, with its cozy propane heaters and its stunning views. I was so dazzled by the expensive wine and her exotic yellow caftan, it hadn't occurred to me to look closer. Lucky for her. If I'd asked to use the ladies' room, she'd have been forced to refuse. In the seven bathrooms I'd seen, there wasn't even one roll of toilet paper.

As there seemed to be nothing left to discover, I let myself out the front door and locked it behind me. I scrambled partway down the hill and shuffled through the underbrush until I found the combination lock. I returned the key to the lockbox and left the lock dangling ineffectually in the busted hasp. I was guessing the entire search (including breaking and entering) had taken less than thirty minutes. Since I was already in the Montebello area, I wound my way down the mountain and drove into the lower village.

Montebello Luxury Properties was tucked into a quaint cottage with an undulating thatched roof, mullioned windows, and a Dutch door painted red. There was a modest strip of parking to one side, and I snagged the only available space. I locked my car and went in, activating an old-fashioned shopkeeper's bell on a spring. I knew I wasn't projecting the image of someone wealthy enough to be house hunting in Montebello, unless I was pegged as one of the eccentric rich dressed like a bag lady.

The interior had been renovated and enlarged to a sprawling warren of offices, the entrance to which was guarded by a receptionist whose nameplate identified her as Kim Bass, Receptionist. Like I might have mistaken her for the company president. She was chatting on the phone, taking notes on a spiral-bound stenographer's pad. When I reached her desk, her gaze rested on me briefly, then returned to her notebook, where she was busy scribbling information. She raised a finger, indicating she was aware of me.

She said, "What time is the Cal-Air on the twenty-fourth?" She listened for a moment, saying, "Um-hum, uh-huh. And the Pan Am is at ten P.M.? What's that number again?" She made a note. "Anything earlier out of ST? No, that's fine. I was just asking on the off chance."

I watched her write: *Cal-Air 2287 dep STA 5:45p, arr LAX 6:52p.*

*Pan Am 154 dep LAX 10:00p, arr LHR 8:25am.* The entire page was covered by fragments; phone numbers without identifiers, names without references indicated. She knew what she meant while she was taking notes and she assumed she'd remember what she was talking about, but when she came across the same page in four days, she'd be clueless. At the same time, she wouldn't have the nerve to throw out her scribbles in case the notes turned out to be critical.

I finally got tired of being ignored and ambled over to the wall-mounted photographs of the current agents. The women outnumbered the men, and most were closer to fifty years old than thirty. All of the names were easy to pronounce. Catherine Phillips was the #1 Sales Associate for Montebello Luxury Properties, selling over $23 million for each of the past three years. Several exclamation points were affixed to the news!!! If the office took a 6 percent cut and Ms. Phillips collected even half of that amount (minus expenses), she was doing better than most. In her photograph, she appeared to be in her mid- to late sixties and quite attractive.

I sat down in one of the comfy upholstered visitors' chairs. Kim was still deep in her phone conversation. While I was cooling my heels, I cast about for a cover story to present as soon as she was free. I'd intended to slide in with a ruse that would allow me to pump the listing agent for information about the Clipper estate. Specifically, I was curious how someone might have commandeered the property as Hallie had. There was bound to be a system in place, but I wasn't sure how it worked. Agents from other companies had to be in possession of the combination that would open the lockbox that held the house key. Otherwise, Nancy Harkness would have to be present for every showing, a nuisance if nothing else.

I let my gaze drift back to Ms. Bass, who was now asking about United and Delta. I placed her in her forties—dark-eyed, with red hair worn in a style that suggested a wind machine at work. She wore a tank top, and her arms were so beautifully muscled, I envied her.

Her tan was uniformly dark except for a mottled streak along her left forearm, where she'd misapplied her Tan-in-a-Can. (When I try such products, my skin takes on an orange tinge and smells faintly spoiled.)

To hurry her along, I got up and crossed to her desk. She made eye contact, apparently surprised to find me still waiting. She circled a set of numbers, murmured a few remarks, and hung up. She cocked her head in a deft move that shifted her torrent of hair. "May I help you?"

I don't know how she managed it, but her tone implied I was the last person on earth she'd be willing to accommodate.

"I'm here to see Nancy Harkness."

No hesitation whatever. "She's gone for the day."

I glanced at the wall clock. "It's ten fifteen."

"She has buyers in from out of town. Is there anything else?"

"Actually, there is. I need information about the Clipper estate. She's the listing agent, isn't she?"

Kim widened her eyes and worked to suppress a smile. "Are you in the market for a house?"

"I'm in the market for information about the Clipper estate." I had no sense of humor whatever and I thought I'd better make that clear.

"If you leave a number, I can have her call you later in the week. She's tied up with clients for the next three days."

I thought rapidly to the mug shots of other agents in the office and remembered only one. "What about Catherine Phillips? Is she here?"

Kim Bass, Receptionist, didn't look favorably upon this request. "I doubt she'd have time to see you. *What's* this in reference to?" She asked this as though I'd told her once and she'd forgotten what I said.

"Business."

"And you are?"

I took out a card and placed it on the desk in front of her. She picked up the card and read it, then focused on me fully, a response I'm often subject to from those who've had little or no experience with private investigators.

"You're a private *detective*?" she asked.

"I am."

She waited for me to elaborate, and when I said nothing, she picked up the handset and pressed two numbers. Her expression suggested a smackdown was forthcoming from someone higher up in the chain of command. For this, she could hardly wait.

"Good morning, Ms. Phillips. I have someone here who'd like to see you. No, ma'am, she doesn't have an appointment." There was a pause; Ms. Phillips was apparently asking for additional information.

Kim shot me a look, and her gaze returned to the card I'd given her. "Kinsley Millhoney," she said, pronouncing "Millhone" as though the second syllable rhymed with "baloney" instead of "bone."

I leaned forward. "Millhone. Accent on the first syllable." No point in tackling the "Kinsley" issue.

Kim corrected herself, saying, "*Mill*hone." As she listened, her manner underwent a subtle shift. "Well, yes, ma'am. I'll let her know. I can do that," she said. She hung up. "She'll be right out. May I offer you coffee or bottled water?"

"I'm fine," I said. I was as surprised as she was that Catherine Phillips intended to emerge from her office to greet me personally. No wonder she was first in her class.

In a remarkably short period of time, she appeared from the corridor, holding out her hand. "So nice to meet you," she said warmly. "I'm delighted you stopped by. Come on back to my office where we can chat."

We shook hands and I worked to make my grip as firm and forthright as hers.

I wanted to send Kim Bass a smug look, but I restrained myself. Ms. Phillips ushered me into the corridor and then moved ahead so she could show me the way.

She was elegantly dressed in an understated way: black wool gabardine suit with a tailored jacket and knee-length skirt, white silk shell, medium heels with sheer black hose. She was trim and her hair was unabashedly gray, blunt cut, with a sheen to it. She reminded me of my Aunt Susannah, with whom I'd been smitten on sight. In moments like this, the desire for a mother fills me with something akin to pain. Mine died when I was five, and I carry a vision of her like an exemplar against which all women are tested. Ordinarily, Rosie is as close to a mother as I get. Granted, she's opinionated, bossy, and overbearing, but at least she *cares*. This woman was my ideal: warm, lovely, gracious, encompassing. My inner self mewed like a kitten while my outer self sailed on.

"I hope Kim offered you coffee."

"She did. Thanks."

"You couldn't have come at a better time. My ten o'clock canceled and I was at loose ends."

I said, "Ah."

This was worrisome. She was being so *nice*. She must have mistaken me for someone else, and what was I to say? I'd asked for her on a whim, and now I couldn't think of one earthly reason I'd be quizzing her about the Clipper estate. Any hope of a convincing fib went straight out of my head. I pride myself on lying well, but I was drawing a blank. I wondered if I'd be forced to fall back on the truth—a risky proposition at best.

Entering her office, this is what I learned: when you gross 6 percent of $23 million annually, you can decorate your personal space any way you want. Hers was understated elegance, like the public area in a high-class hotel, only with a number of personal touches thrown in. There were fresh flowers on her desk, and I could see angled silver picture frames that probably showcased family members: husband, children, a goofy, lovable dog rescued from the pound.

She offered me a seat on a couch upholstered in dove gray. The cushions must have been filled with down because I sank with a sigh of air. She sat in a matching chair, just close enough to suggest intimacy without invading my personal space. The coffee table between us was glass and chrome, but most of the other furnishings were antique. "Janie's talked about you so often, I can't believe our paths have never crossed," she said.

Oh dear. I don't know anyone named Janie, and I was just about to pipe up and confess when I realized what she'd actually said was "Cheney." I felt my head tilt metaphorically, and then the penny dropped. My mouth didn't actually flop open, but I was momentarily without speech. This was Cheney Phillips's *mother*. I remembered then that while his father was X. Phillips of the Bank of X. Phillips, his mother sold high-end real estate. All I could think to say was, "I need help."

"Well, I'll do what I can," she said without missing a beat.

I described the situation as succinctly as possible, starting with the phone call from Hallie Bettancourt and moving on to our meeting. I repeated the lengthy tale of woe she'd laid on me, and then detailed Detective Nash's subsequent revelation about the marked hundred-dollar bills. I capped the recitation with my confusion when Vera assured me the Clipper estate had been empty for years.

I could see her curiosity mount as mine had, point by point, including the fact that the phone numbers Hallie had given me were nonoperant. When I finally paused, she took a moment to reflect.

"She went to a great deal of trouble to pull the wool over your eyes," she said.

"And it worked like a charm. Honestly, she didn't have to persuade me of anything. She offered me the bait and I took it. I thought her relationship with Geoffrey was odd—assuming she *has* a husband by that name—but I didn't doubt for a minute she'd given birth to a son out of wedlock and put the child up for adoption. It didn't even occur to me to question the fact that she hoped to make contact with him while keeping her husband in the dark. I quizzed her on a point or two, but I didn't really dig into the story. When she cautioned me to be discreet, it all made perfect sense."

"I suppose in your line of work, clients are keen on discretion."

"Always," I said. "What I don't understand is how she got into the house. She had to be in cahoots with someone in real estate, didn't she? I mean, I can't think how else she could manage it."

"Could she have broken in?"

"No evidence of it that I saw. At the same time, I'm assuming anyone with the right combination could open the lockbox on the property."

"True. All that's required for access is to dial it in. Our system's ancient. Some companies are moving to a new device that utilizes an electronic 'key' and keeps a running log of which agents have come and gone, but that's a year or two in the future for us, which is no help to you now."

"In the meantime, what's the procedure?" I asked. "I mean, suppose someone has a client who wants to see the house? Then what?"

"The agent checks the MLS . . . the Multiple Listing Service," she amended when she saw my look. "Standard instructions are 'LB/cf,' which means 'Lockbox, call first,' or 'LB/apt,' meaning an appointment is required. In the case of the Clipper estate, all the agents know the house is empty, so no one bothers with either one."

"So you're saying anyone and everyone has access."

"As long as they've been given the combination."

"In other words, you couldn't just stand there punching in numbers randomly, hoping to hit it right."

"I suppose you could if you were lucky," she said. "Come to think of it, how did you get in?"

I made a face. "I hauled off and smacked the lock with a chunk of wood, knocking it to kingdom come. I'll be happy to pay to have the lock replaced."

"Don't worry about it. I'll have Nancy take care of it. She was given the listing because she's worked here for all of two months and she's low man on the totem pole. She'll be thrilled with the mission. We can stop by her office and I'll introduce you on the way out."

"She's not here."

"Of course she is."

"Really? I thought she was gone. Kim said she had clients in from out of town and she was off showing property."

"I don't know where she got that. Nancy's right around the corner."

I didn't press the point. As much as I'd have loved to get Kim in hot water, I wanted to stay on track. "Here's the other thing," I said. "The night I was up there, the place was fully furnished. Lots of Oriental carpets and paintings on the walls. She had deck chairs and outdoor heaters. Where did all that come from?"

"It's called staging; common practice in real estate. If a house goes on the market unfurnished, the feeling is that most buyers who tour an empty house lack the imagination to see the possibilities. A stager will show an appealing living room arrangement and set up the dining table and chairs, complete with table linens, flatware, and a centerpiece. Sometimes a buyer even asks to have the furniture included in the purchase price."

"Isn't that expensive?"

"Quite."

"So if Hallie hired a stager to furnish the house short-term, who paid for it?"

"She would have, I guess, though the cost would have been prohibitive. I believe you said this was for one night, yes?"

"More or less. I met her at the house last Monday and there was stuff everywhere. Now it's empty," I said. "Why prohibitive?"

"A stager has to maintain a large inventory of furniture because they're often handling eight or ten big houses at the same time. Part of their overhead is the warehouse space for items not in use. That gets factored in to the client's overall cost. There's also the expense of moving furniture into a house and then out again at the end of a contract. In this case, that's a lot of time and effort."

"I wonder if any of the neighbors saw the moving van?"

"In that area? Doubtful. On the other hand, all she had to do was create the *illusion* of furnished rooms. How much of the house did you actually see?"

"Not much, now that you mention it. The furniture in the living and dining rooms were largely covered in tarps. I guess there could have been old cardboard boxes under them."

"Sleight of hand," she said.

"I can't believe I fell for it."

"You're fortunate in one respect. Under ordinary circumstances, you wouldn't have caught on to the trick at all. You'd have tracked down the information, sent off your report, and that would have been the end of it. If that police detective hadn't come into your office with the story about the marked bills, you'd still be in the dark."

"You think there's any point trying to find the stager?"

"Probably not. We all know one or two, but there's no formal list. Hallie either paid handsomely or the stager was doing her a personal favor. It's also possible she didn't need outside help at all. She might have brought in all the items from home."

I said a bad word, but Catherine Phillips never flinched. This is probably what comes of having a grown son who works for the police department.

Soon afterward, I rounded out our chat with a few incidental questions and then excused myself. I didn't see any point in talking to Nancy Harkness. Catherine Phillips had been more than generous with her time, and my curiosity was tapped out. "Hallie Bettancourt" had taken me for a ride for reasons that eluded me. I'd have to give the situation some serious thought before I decided what to do next. In light of the hundred-dollar bill I'd forfeited, I was already in the hole, and I couldn't see what there was to be gained by pushing the point.

When I passed the front desk on my way out, Kim Bass, Receptionist, was nowhere to be seen. This was fortunate, as I was so irritated with the way she'd treated me, I might have bitten her on the arm. I'd been a biter as a kid and I can still remember the feel of flesh between my teeth. It's like biting a rubber bathing cap, in case you're curious.

# 12

When I arrived back at the office, Henry was sitting on my front step with a handful of papers. Ever the gentleman, he rose to his feet as I approached. "I've been playing with Pete's number grid," he said.

"You broke the code?"

"Not yet, but I have an idea. If I take a look at your Smith Corona, I can tell you if I'm right."

"Sure thing," I said.

I unlocked the door and he followed me in. I continued on into my inner office, talking over my shoulder. "I thought I gave you a key. Why didn't you let yourself in?"

"I might have if you hadn't shown up when you did. Otherwise it would have seemed cheeky."

"God forbid," I remarked.

I put down my shoulder bag, pushed aside my swivel chair, and hauled my typewriter from the knee space under my desk. I placed

it on top, removed the lid, and then turned the machine so it was facing him.

He sat down in one of my two visitors' chairs and placed his papers
on the desk to his left. The top sheet was the graph paper where Pete
had recorded his grid of numbers. Henry reached for one of my letter-
size yellow legal pads and jotted a column of numbers along the left
margin, one through twenty-six. I could see his eyes trace a line back
and forth between the keyboard and the grid. I walked around the
desk so I could look over his shoulder.

He was clearly pleased with himself. "Good man! I knew he was
doing something of the sort. Pull up a chair and take a look."

I scooted the second chair closer and sat down.

Henry said, "Remember I said this was probably a number-letter
substitution code? I figured chances were good he used a format of
some kind, a matrix or template that would govern the assignment of a
particular number to a given letter. He could have done this any number of ways. He might have written the alphabet, A B C D and so forth,
and then used 1 for A, 2 for B, 3 for C, down the line. Pete constructed
his cipher along other lines, which is what I've been trying to pin
down."

"Swapping one number per letter would make it twenty-six altogether, yes?"

"Right."

"What about that number? The 1909," I said, pointing to a four-
number group.

Henry said, "I suspect that's the number 19 followed by the number
9. I'm theorizing Pete put a zero in front of any letter between 1 and 9.
So 03 is something and 04 is the next in the sequence, whatever the
sequence is."

"I guess you have to start somewhere."

"It's basically trial and error, though if you do these often enough
you get a feel for what's going on. The obvious system where 1 is A, 2
is B, and so forth didn't work, which didn't surprise me in the least.

Pete was too wily for something so simplistic. So I said to myself, what's next? As kids, we used a system called Rot 1—Rotate 1— which means that B becomes A, C becomes B, and so forth. I experimented with that and a few other well-known systems and got nowhere. And then I wondered if this could be a keyboard pattern, which is why I needed your Smith Corona."

He looked up with a sly smile, tapping the paper with his pen. "This is a QWERTY code, starting with the top row of letters on a typewriter. Read left to right and keep on going. Q is 1, W is 2, E is 3, or 03 the way he writes it. R is 4 or 04. You'll see I'm completing that first row of letters and then starting again left to right, moving down all three rows. The last row is Z X C V B N. Do you see what I'm doing here? M is the last letter, which in this format makes it the twenty-sixth."

"Just tell me what it says."

Henry rolled his eyes. "So impatient. Give me a minute and I'll write it out for you."

"You want some coffee?"

"Only if you're making some," he said, distracted. He was already busy writing down the letters he matched with the numbers on the grid.

I left him where he was and went down the hall to the kitchenette, where I picked up the coffeepot and filled it with water. I poured the water into the reservoir and then opened a packet of coffee, the grounds neatly sealed in a filter that I tucked into the basket. I flipped the switch and stood there until I could hear the gurgling begin.

Moments later, I placed both mugs of coffee on my desk and resumed my seat. Henry was still translating, so I waited for him to finish. "This is a list of names," he said. "Six of them. I'll start with the first. You see the numbers 1216, then 0804 and so forth. The 12 is the letter S, followed by 16, which is the letter H. Here, 08 is the letter I, followed by 04, which is the letter R. I won't go through every single grouping. Trust me when I tell you the first name is Shirley Ann Kastle.

The line under her name reads 'Burning Oaks, California,' with the state abbreviated."

"Never heard of her."

"Next is the number series starting with 1903 2509 and on down the line. This line spells the name Lenore Redfern, also from Burning Oaks, California, which is the line under the name. I believe hers was the name written in the Bible you found."

"April's mother," I said. "It looks like she wanted April to have her Bible and the other items. I'm not sure why she mailed them to the priest, unless he was supposed to hold them and pass them on in due course. According to April's wedding announcement, Ned's now married to a woman named Celeste. Go on. I didn't mean to slow you down."

"The third name is Phyllis Joplin, Perdido, California, again the state abbreviated. Are you familiar with the name?"

"Nope."

"Under her name, if you'll look at my cheat sheet, you'll see that 05 is T, the number 11 is A, 04 is R, 06 is Y . . ."

I checked the next number in the sequence. "And 25 is N, and the name is Taryn," I said. I knew exactly who this was. "Surname is Sizemore."

"That's right. He's written 'Santa Teresa, California' on the line beneath, so she must be local. You know her?"

"She was the plaintiff in the lawsuit I mentioned earlier."

"Much of this seems to hark back to that lawsuit," he said.

"Could be coincidental."

"Possible. Fifth name on the list is Susan Telford, who apparently lives in Henderson, Nevada. Ring a bell?"

"Nada."

Henry said, "Speaking Spanish now. Very nice."

I pointed to the next sequence of numbers. "Who's that?"

"Last name is Janet Macy in Tucson, Arizona."

"Which doesn't ring any bells." I thought about the names for a moment. "I can't imagine what the relationship is among these women."

"It might help if you talked to someone in Burning Oaks. Father Xavier would be the obvious choice."

"I'm not planning to do anything unless I figure out what Pete had in mind."

"I'm not sure how you'll arrive at that. I gather he didn't confide in Ruthie, at least where this business is concerned," he said. "Is that a copy machine?"

"It is."

Henry picked up the single sheet of graph paper and the yellow pad, crossed to the machine, and pushed the power button. While he waited for the machine to warm up, he neatly tore off the top two sheets of lined yellow paper, and when the Ready light went on, he opened the cover, placed the first sheet facedown on the glass plate, and lowered the cover again. He pushed Print and we stared, transfixed, as a line of light moved down the page and a copy emerged from the innards of the machine. I didn't have a clue how the process worked. He then copied the second sheet, and last he made a copy of the grid of numbers.

When he finished, he handed me the originals and folded the copies, putting them in the pockets of his shorts. Indicating the first sheet he'd given me, he said, "That's the key, written down the left-hand margin; the QWERTY letters with a number value next to each. You come across any other eight-place grids, you should be able to translate. I'm not sure what you'll do with the names, but I'll leave you to ponder the possibilities."

"I'll do that, and thanks."

"I enjoyed watching Pete's mind at work," he said. "Nearly forgot to mention I had a plumber out this morning to take a look at the irrigation issue. He was full of good advice. He kept saying 'reduce before reuse.'"

"You already knew that," I said. "Nothing practical?"

"You want to hear his recommendation? Tear out the lawn. Get rid of all the grass. 'It's dead anyway' was what he said. He recommended Astroturf. Can you imagine it?"

"Well, it would be green all year round."

"I told him I'd think about it and get back to him. Then I put a call through to someone else. At any rate, I'll see you back at the house."

Once he left, I sat and chewed on the significance of what I'd learned. Henry had provided the key to the list without supplying the point. Pete's purpose wasn't obvious, but the six women must have had something in common. The fact that he'd encrypted the names suggested he thought the list worth protecting, but I had no idea why. Who did he imagine might come across information so sensitive that he couldn't leave it in plain English?

I picked up the handset and punched in Ruthie's phone number. The machine picked up and I dutifully left a message at the sound of the beep. "Hi, Ruthie. Sorry I missed you. This is Kinsey with another update. Henry's broken the code and I'll tell you what it says when you have a minute. Meanwhile, the files are here at the office. I'll search again if you think there's any point. Fat chance in my view, but you're the boss. Hope your appointment went well. Give me a call as soon as you get home. I'm panting to hear."

I stacked the sheets, folded them, and put them in my bag. More from curiosity than anything else, I pulled out the telephone book and checked the white pages for residential listings in hopes of spotting Taryn Sizemore. In the ten years since the lawsuit, she might have married, died, or left town, in which case there'd be no sign of her. Under the S's, I found ten Sizemores, none of whom were T. or Taryn. I shifted my search to the business section of the white pages and found her: Sizemore, Taryn, PhD. No clue as to the field she was in. College professor, educational consultant. She might be an audiologist or a speech therapist. The address was in downtown Santa Teresa with a phone number. I pulled out my index cards, made a note, and then replaced the rubber band and returned the cards to my bag.

I was still torn. What in heaven's name was Pete Wolinsky up to? Probably nothing good. If he was extorting money from the women on the list, then lucky them. He was dead and they wouldn't have to pay another cent. If he was operating from other motives, then what? It would behoove me to chat with Taryn Sizemore in hopes she had some idea what was going on. I was in information-gathering mode and I'd make a decision when I had a few more facts in hand.

In the meantime, when it came to "Hallie Bettancourt," I was concerned that in passing along Christian Satterfield's contact information, I might have put him in harm's way. At the very least, I felt I should alert him that he'd been the subject of the inquiry. I locked the office and hoofed it to the *Santa Teresa Dispatch*, which was six blocks away. I needed the air, and the exercise allowed me to free up my brain. I thought I was correct in estimating Hallie's social status. She looked like big bucks and she'd carried herself with a classy air that was impossible to fake. How did she know about Christian Satterfield and what did she want from him? Unless she hoped to supplement her income by robbing banks, I couldn't imagine how locating a parolee would serve her.

When I reached the *Dispatch* building, I went into the lobby and took the stairs to the second floor. The newspaper archives were housed in an area dense with file cabinets, the drawers packed with news clippings dating back to the 1800s. The librarian was a woman named Marjorie Hixon, who was in her eighties. Tall and refined, gray-green eyes, high cheekbones, gray hair streaked with white. I'd dealt with her on many occasions and I'd always found her cooperative and down-to-earth.

"How're you doing, Marjorie? It's been a while," I said.

"This place is a madhouse and has been for months. Last July, we moved from paper to a newfangled electronic system: words, pictures, and graphics, including maps. Don't ask me how it's done. I have no idea. I'm still partial to an old-fashioned card catalog, but that's beside the point. We used to have drones typing headlines on envelopes as they stuffed stories into them. The files were even cross-indexed, which I thought was fancy enough. Now an extraordinarily patient soul named John Pope ensures new stuff is transcribed from paper into an electronic format. All way over my head."

"Hey, mine too. I don't even own a computer."

"I have an old Mac my son-in-law passed along when he bought his new one, but I can't make heads or tails of it. He says it's user-friendly, but I've got news for him. Time was, I could have mastered the darn thing in a day or two, but now there's no way. Might be time to retire. I'll be eighty-eight August nineteenth, and my best years may well be behind me."

"I'm sure that's not true. You know more than anyone else around here."

"Well, I thank you for the vote of confidence, but I'm not too sure. This is a young man's game. Reporters and editors these days are all kids in their fifties. Too much ambition and energy for my taste. They cuss, they wear jeans to work, and most can't spell without help, but they dearly love their jobs, which is more than I can say."

"But what would you do if you retired? You'd go nuts."

"That's a worry, now you mention it. I'm not one for needlework, and you can only read so many books before your eyesight fails. Someone suggested volunteer work, but that's out of the question. I'm accustomed to being paid, and the idea of giving away my time and my skills is an affront. Braver women than I fought decades for equal compensation in the workplace, so why would I undo their accomplishments? Anyway, I doubt you came here to hear me complain. What can I do for you?"

I wrote the name Christian Satterfield on a slip of paper and pushed it across the counter. "I'd like to see the file on this guy. I have two clippings, but I'm hoping there's more."

X

She read the name. "Let me see what I can find."

Within minutes I was seated at a desk along the side wall with the envelope in front of me. There wasn't much in it beyond the articles Hallie had passed on to me. The only other item of note was a brief mention of an academic scholarship he'd been awarded on graduating from Santa Teresa High School in 1975. He'd been accepted at UCLA, where he hoped to major in economics. The guy was smart and, if his photograph was representative, good-looking as well. How had he ended up in prison? I'd had classmates—dull-witted, dope-smoking losers—who'd ended up better off than he had.

I returned the folder to Marjorie. "I have a question. I believe someone came in making a similar request for information about this guy. This would have been a woman in her forties. Tall, thin, masses of red-brown hair, a beaky nose—the sort of face you'd see in a snooty magazine ad."

"I'd remember someone of that description. Of course, I was out on vacation over Christmas, and she could have come in then," she said. "I can ask around, if you like. Someone might remember her. We don't get much business up here these days. One day soon newspapers will be a thing of the past."

"That can't be true. You think? I mean, people want to know what's going on in the world. A television broadcast is never going to take the place of hard news."

"All I know is there was a time when a newspaper was the heartbeat of the city. Now, not so much. It's like the lifeblood is draining out."

"Well, that's depressing."

"Try looking at it from where I stand," she said.

# 13

I walked back to the office and retrieved my car. I had time for one more stop before I headed home. I checked my index cards to verify Taryn Sizemore's address. I cruised up State and turned right onto a side street, approaching a bar and grill called Sneaky Pete's, which had closed and reopened under a new name some years before. Despite the new moniker, it was still referred to as Sneaky Pete's. What loomed large in my mind's eye was the vision of the specialty of the house: a sandwich made with spicy salami and melted pepper jack cheese, topped with a fried egg, the whole of it served on a Kaiser roll that dripped with butter as you ate. I would have pursued that fantasy, but I spotted Taryn Sizemore's office address directly across the street. I had to make a hasty turn at the next corner and swing back around. It was well after five by then, and many of the area businesses were closed for the day, which made street parking a breeze.

I locked my car and entered the renovated Victorian structure, which apparently now housed an entire complex of psychologists' offices. From this, I cleverly deduced that Taryn's PhD must be in marriage and family therapy, counseling, or social work. She'd probably had years of professional training in how to feign interest in what others had to say. This might work to my advantage until she realized I wasn't in the market for a shrink.

Hers was suite 100 on the ground floor. I went in and found myself in a small, comfortably furnished waiting room complete with an apartment-size, chintz-covered love seat and two small easy chairs. The color scheme was a soothing blend of blues and greens, probably designed to calm clients whose emotional tendencies ran to upset and agitation. There were no windows and only one other door, which I assumed opened into her office proper.

To the right of the door was a glowing red light. I took this to mean she was currently occupied. It was dead quiet. I checked my watch, hoping I hadn't missed the boat altogether. It was 5:25. It was my understanding that therapists operated on a fifty-minute hour, but I had no idea when the hour began. I sat down, noting that she subscribed to six women's magazines, all current. I picked up a copy of *House & Garden* and turned to an article about easy Easter-themed entertaining for eight, then realized I don't know eight people, let alone eight who'd suffer my cooking even if I invited them.

After fifteen minutes passed, I got up and tiptoed to the door, listening for sounds from within. No comforting murmur of conversation, no shrieks or sobs. I sat down again. Having arrived without an appointment, I didn't feel I had the right to bang on the door and complain. It was always possible she'd left for the day, but surely she'd have locked the front door. At ten minutes of six, the light switched abruptly from red to green. No one emerged. There must be a separate outside exit so a loony-tunes patient was never subjected to the indignity of crossing paths with another nut job.

At six, the door to her office opened and a young woman appeared at a brisk pace. She stopped dead when she caught sight of me. "Oh, sorry! I didn't know anybody was out here." She turned and glanced at the room behind her in dismay. "Do you have an appointment?"

"I don't. I stopped by on the off chance I might catch you before you left for the day. Are you Ms. Sizemore?"

She held out her hand. "Taryn, yes."

"Should I have said 'Doctor' Sizemore?"

"Taryn's fine. Even with a PhD, I don't call myself 'doctor' anything. It seems pretentious."

"Kinsey Millhone," I said as the two of us shook hands. "Do you have a few minutes?"

I watched her make a quick decision. "I have to be somewhere at seven, but I can give you until six thirty if that helps."

"That would be great."

"Come on in."

She turned on her heel and I followed her into her office, waiting while she closed the door behind us.

She was tall and lean, towering over me in black high-heeled boots. She wore a short white knit top over jeans that were belted low on her hips. A strip of bare midriff flashed when she moved. Her pant legs were long enough to break across her instep, which made her slim legs look even longer. I took in the rest of the picture as she crossed to the telephone and activated the message machine. Dark eyes, shoulder-length brown hair arranged in a messy tumble. Big hoop earrings, red lipstick.

I did a visual survey of my surroundings. This room had the same homey feel as the reception area. Instead of a desk, she had a refectory table, bare except for a low vase filled with drooping pink and yellow roses that had opened to the full. I could see a leather-bound appointment book, a tidy row of ballpoint pens, and color-coded file folders in an upright rack. Bookshelves lined the walls on two sides, with two windows dead ahead and an exterior door that opened onto the side of the building. One arm of the walkway probably circled to the street and the other to a parking area in the rear. If she had file cabinets, I saw no sign of them.

She offered me a choice of a couch, a sleek chair of leather and chrome, or one of two chairs upholstered in a blue-and-green floral print. I chose one of the two matching chairs, and she elected to settle on the couch with the coffee table between us. I wondered if my selection was psychologically significant, but decided not to fret about the point. Her nails were clipped short and without polish. No wedding ring and no other jewelry except a loose, bracelet-style watch that she adjusted with her free hand. I saw her flick a practiced glance at the watch face, noting the time. She seemed open, waiting for me to set the subject and tone of the conversation.

I hadn't thought about how to summarize the story, so I was forced to jump right in. Really, I should mend my careless ways. This was the third time I'd been caught without a story prepared in advance. *Oh, what the hell,* I thought. "I'm a private detective looking for information. The story's complicated, and if I stop to spell it out, it's only going to slow us down. I thought I'd lay out the situation and you can tell me if you need anything clarified before you reply. Assuming you're willing to answer questions."

"Fire away," she said.

"Does the name Pete Wolinsky mean anything to you?"

"Sure. I knew Pete. Not well, but when I heard he was shot to death, I didn't know what to think. Is that why you're here?"

"Not exactly. The police arrested the perpetrator, but the case hasn't been set for trial. What interests me is peripheral. Was he a patient of yours?"

"I prefer calling them 'clients,' but no."

"Good. That's great. I'd hate asking you to violate a confidence."

"No danger there," she said with a polite smile.

"Can you tell me how you knew him?"

"Call it 'old business' for simplicity's sake. Our paths crossed years ago, and then he showed up again last spring."

Chances were good the "old business" she was referring to was the lawsuit she'd filed against Ned Lowe. I nearly mentioned him, but I decided to wait, curious to see if she'd volunteer the name.

"So Pete initiated contact?" I asked.

"Yep. We got together twice, with maybe three or four weeks between meetings. When I didn't hear from him again, I didn't think anything about it. When I found out he'd been killed, I was taken aback."

"That was a tough one," I said, my tone noncommittal.

"What's the nature of your interest?"

"His widow's a friend of mine. Pete left Ruth with a pile of debt and his affairs in disarray. She's got an IRS audit coming up, so we've been going through his effects, looking for financial records. Yesterday I found a mailing pouch concealed under a false bottom in a banker's box. The mailer was addressed to a priest in Burning Oaks, postmarked 1961. There was also a list hidden in the pages of a document in the same box. Your name was on it."

"What kind of list?"

"Six women's names, which he'd encrypted for reasons unknown. My landlord identified the cipher and provided me the key."

"I didn't know Pete was into cloak-and-dagger stuff."

"I guess he was; in this regard, if nothing else."

She studied me. "Now you're trying to determine if there's a link between the names."

"Exactly."

"Can you give me the other five?"

"Sure."

I opened my shoulder bag and took out my index cards. I removed the rubber band and sorted through the first few until I found the notes

I'd made. "There's a Susan Telford in Henderson, Nevada, and a woman named Janet Macy in Tucson, Arizona."

She shook her head to both.

"Shirley Ann Kastle from Burning Oaks?"

"I know who she is, but the reference is secondhand. I never met her myself. And the fourth?"

"Lenore Redfern, also from Burning Oaks. There's also a Phyllis Joplin from Perdido."

"This is about Ned Lowe, isn't it?"

"It's possible. I'm not sure."

"Back up a step. You said Pete's widow is a friend. Were you and Pete also friends?"

"Sorry. I should have filled you in. We worked for the same detective agency many years ago. I was just starting out and needed six thousand hours for licensing purposes. Pete was pals with Ben Byrd and Morley Shine, the guys who ran the firm. To be honest, I know about the lawsuit you filed against Ned Lowe in that same time period."

"How long did you work there?"

"From 1975 to 1978, when I left to open an office of my own."

"I thought Pete was a partner in the agency."

"Is that what he told you?"

"Not directly, but that was the impression he gave."

"Well, it's not true. He didn't even work there full-time. He did occasional contract work." I was doing a poor job of concealing my dislike, which might have been a mistake. If she was crazy about Pete, I didn't want to put her off.

Her response was mild. "You say that like it's a bad thing."

"I don't like his distorting the facts. Ben and Morley kept him at arm's length."

"And why was that?"

I considered my reply. No reason to offend on the off chance she thought he was a model citizen. "I don't see the point in going into it," I said.

"If you're asking about Pete, your history with him is relevant, don't you think?"

I entertained a small debate. If I wanted information from her, I was going to have to prime the pump. The problem was I'd have to be circumspect, which is not my strong suit. I chose my words carefully. "Pete had trouble distinguishing right from wrong. He was usually hard up for cash and willing to cut corners when it came right down to it."

"Really," she said, bemused. "He didn't strike me as morally compromised, which is what you're suggesting."

"Let's put it this way: what got him killed was extorting money from someone with something to hide. Maybe he was different in his dealings with you."

"Possible."

"You know, I appreciate your professional reticence, but so far this is like pulling teeth. Can we loosen up a bit?" I asked. "I'm trying to decide how much time and effort to expend, so a tiny bit of information would be a boon."

"Ask anything you like. I'll tell you what I can."

"I'd appreciate it. Let's start with Lenore Redfern. Am I correct in thinking Ned was married to her?"

"Years ago, yes. According to the story I heard, Lennie suffered postpartum psychosis after their little girl was born. When the child was three, Lennie killed herself, and now he's married to someone else."

"Celeste. I ran across her name in a wedding announcement Pete clipped from the local paper."

"You're talking about April's marriage," Taryn said. "I saw the notice myself and remember thinking her life must be turning out okay after all."

"Given her mother's suicide?"

122

"Yes."

"What do you know about Shirley Ann Kastle? I'm assuming she's connected to Ned in some way. As nearly as I remember, she wasn't named as a party to the lawsuit."

"She wasn't. Shirley Ann was peripheral."

"Meaning what in this context?"

"Meaning I don't want to go into it quite yet. I'm not saying I won't, but I have concerns to satisfy first. How much do you know about the lawsuit?"

"Ned's attorney hired Byrd-Shine while I was there. You sued for intentional infliction of emotional distress, and they were asked to do a deep background check."

"On me, yes. I'm painfully aware."

"I thought you dropped the suit."

"We reached a settlement."

"Really. According to the talk around Byrd-Shine, you had him nailed. They were sweating bullets. Why did you back off?"

"Because I panicked. When Ned's attorney—I notice I'm blanking on the name . . ."

"Arnold Ruffner."

"Of course. How could I forget? When Ruffner took my deposition, he tore me apart. He had information that would have been devastating if we'd gone to trial."

"Like what?"

She closed her mouth and shook her head once before she went on. "Sorry to do this to you, but I've said enough for now. That was a difficult time, and I really don't want to go into it."

"When I mentioned Lenore's name and then Shirley Ann's, you jumped right to Ned. Why was that?"

"He grew up in Burning Oaks."

"He was born there?"

"Don't think so. I know that's where he went to high school. Phyllis Joplin was his second wife."

"Well, that's a help. I take it you weren't the one who gave Pete the list?"

"He must have put that together on his own."

"Do you know why?"

"I can make a reasonable guess, but I'd prefer not to spell it out. I hope you won't push."

"Of course not. I appreciate what you've told me so far, and I want you to feel okay about sharing more. I hate the word 'sharing,' by the way."

"Oh, me too," she said, and we both smiled. She shifted positions slightly. "Is there a connection between the list and the mailer you mentioned?"

"Don't know yet. Intuition says yes, but that remains to be seen. Meanwhile, it strikes me the two of us do much the same job. We study people's lives, determine what went wrong, and try to make it right. That lawsuit was ten years ago. What harm could it do if you talked about it now?"

"That whole subject still makes me squirm because I blew it. It's embarrassing to admit this, but I made every mistake imaginable. Starting with my attorney."

"What was wrong with him?"

"He was *kind*."

"Oh, boy."

"Really," she said. "I was an emotional mess, and he seemed so *sympathetic*. The minute things got rough, he gave up."

"So how much was the settlement?"

"I signed a confidentiality agreement, which I'd be violating if I revealed the terms. It was an ugly business. I've had to put it behind me and move on with life. I will say the settlement allowed me to finish my degree with enough left over to set up the office I'm in."

"Doesn't sound like such a bad deal."

"It wasn't. More importantly, I made my peace with it. End of story. Until Pete showed up."

"To do what?"

She thought about that briefly. "Look, I'm not unwilling to help, but I have to protect myself. If you'll give me your phone number, I'll get back to you when I've decided what to do."

"Works for me," I said. I pulled out a business card and handed it to her. "I hope you'll see your way clear."

# 14

I left my car parked on the street and crossed to Sneaky Pete's. The meeting with Taryn Sizemore had been promising, but she'd have to decide how far she could trust me before we could continue our conversation. I didn't object to her wrestling with her conscience as long as she ponied up in the end. In the meantime, I wasn't going to pass up the consolation of a hot, gooey spiced salami sandwich.

The place was sparsely populated, a mere sprinkling of patrons. The jukebox was dark and the television set turned off. I'd hoped to run into Con Dolan, but there was no sign of him. The bartender was reading the paper, which he'd laid flat on the bar in front of him. I ordered a sandwich and a Diet Pepsi. He conveyed the food order to the kitchen and then popped the top on the Pepsi can and passed it across the bar to me along with a glass of ice. I carried both to a two-top near the front window. I took out a pen and my index cards and took notes on everything I could remember from the conversation with Ms. Sizemore. I took out the sheet of graph paper on which Pete had meticulously encoded the list of names. I put Henry's breakdown beside the original and studied the number-to-letter translation. Taryn had identified two names on the list: Lenore Redfern, Ned's first wife, and Phyllis Joplin, his second. She was apparently acquainted with the name Shirley Ann Kastle, though she hadn't trusted me sufficiently to fill me in. When the sandwich arrived, I set my pen aside and ate with full attention to the gustatory joys at hand.

I was home by 7:15. Henry's kitchen was dark, and I assumed he was up at Rosie's. I let myself in and checked for messages, but there was no winking red light. Ruthie's appointment with the IRS had been scheduled for 1:00, and I was hoping she'd call to fill me in. I'd done what I could to help, and while she wasn't *obligated* to report, it would have been nice. On impulse, I leaned across the desk, picked up the handset, and punched in her number. She picked up after three rings.

"Hey, Ruthie. It's Kinsey. How'd it go today?"

"How did what go?"

"Your appointment. I left a message earlier."

"I didn't have any messages."

"Are you *sure* your machine's not on the blink? I called to ask how it went with the IRS."

"Oh. He never showed."

"You can't be serious! After the horseshit he put you through?"

Abruptly, Ruthie said, "Is there a chance you could get over here? Something's come up."

"I can do that. Are you okay? You sound odd."

"Someone's been in my house. The police just left, and I don't want to be here by myself."

"Shit. Why didn't you say so? Absolutely. I'll be right there."

．．．

I didn't break any speed laws, but I'll admit I slid through two stop signs and a yellow light that turned red while I was still under it. Ruthie's house was only ten blocks away, so it didn't take me long to get there. When I pulled up in front, there were so many lights on, the place looked like it was on fire. In rooms downstairs and up, every lamp and overhead fixture was ablaze. I could see Ruthie standing at the front window, peering from behind the sheers. When she spotted my car, she disappeared from sight. I didn't even have to knock because the door opened before I reached it. She grabbed my hand and pulled me inside as though I might be pursued by demons. Her face was pale and her hands were icy.

"What's going on?"

"I don't know. Maybe nothing, but I'm freaked out." She twisted the key in the dead bolt on the front door and moved through the hall to the kitchen. I followed, looking over my shoulder in the same furtive manner she displayed.

She pointed to a seat at the kitchen table where she'd set an open bottle of wine and two glasses, one half full and a second one empty. I settled in the chair while she poured wine for me as though I'd need to fortify myself. She pushed the glass in my direction, picked hers up and drained it.

"What happened?"

She sat down and then she got up again and began to pace. "When I got home from work, the back door was standing open. I will swear to you someone was in here. Not right then, but earlier. I turned around and went straight next door and called the police. Two officers showed up six minutes later."

"Sounds like they took you seriously."

"They did. Very much so. They were great. The older one—I think his name was Carew—could tell I was scared to death. I told him it was *possible* I didn't close the door all the way when I left for work, but

I know I did. I always push until I hear the latch catch, and then I try the knob to make sure it's locked. Anyway, the other one—a gal named Herkowitz—did a complete walk-through, checked all the doors and windows, looked in closets, looked under the beds, checked for tool marks. There was nothing. House was empty, and as far as I can tell nothing's missing."

"Well, that's good news. You think it was kids?"

"Doing what? I don't keep cash or drugs on the premises."

"Addicts will break in anywhere. If neighbors know you're a nurse, someone might assume you keep narcotics on hand."

"Doubtful. The medicine cabinets in both bathrooms were untouched. No drawers pulled out and dumped. No evidence that anyone tore through in search of valuables. My camera, TV set, and jewelry are all accounted for. Not that I have much."

"Maybe someone was trying doors at random and found yours unlocked."

"The police said the same thing. I can't rule it out, but it doesn't feel right. They wrote up an incident report and suggested I get someone in to change the locks. I called a locksmith with a twenty-four-hour emergency service, but I haven't heard back."

"Who else has a house key?"

"My next-door neighbor's the only one with a spare. I have one for his house as well for occasions when one or the other of us is out of town," she said. "Is it possible someone picked the lock?"

"Of course it's *possible*, though picking locks requires more skill and practice than you'd think. You'd still have to wonder why anyone would bother."

She finished her wine and then refilled her glass. Her hands were shaking so badly, she had to use both to steady the bottle while she poured. She carried the glass with her while she crossed the room and then came back to the table.

I took a few sips of my own wine, hoping to quell the anxiety I was feeling in response to hers. "Why don't you give me the details?"

"Forget it. I'll just get all riled up again."

"Come on. You'll feel better. It'll be cathartic. What time did you get home?"

"I don't know. Six thirty or so. I worked noon to six, covering for another private-duty nurse who had to be somewhere. I put the car in the garage and came in the back way like always. It wasn't 'til I was halfway up the back porch stairs that I realized the door was standing open. And I'm not talking 'ajar' open. This was wide open. If my neighbor hadn't been home, I don't know what I would have done. I would not have stepped that first foot inside for any reason. Not on your life. The whole place was cold. Still is. I don't know how long the house was open. A long time."

I said, "Sit down. You're fine. Take a deep breath. You're doing great."

She sank into a chair and I covered her hands with mine.

"Look," I said, "we'll have the locksmith come in, and once he's done, you can spend the night at my place. If you stay here, you won't sleep a wink."

"I won't sleep anyway. I feel like I'm hopped up on something . . ."

"Adrenaline."

"Worse. Feels like my veins are full of Freon." She put her hands between her knees and then leaned forward and put her arms around her waist, hugging herself.

"Are you feeling faint?"

She pressed two fingers to her lips and shook her head. "Might throw up. I shouldn't guzzle wine on an empty stomach."

"You have any cheese and crackers? You should eat."

"Great idea."

She got up and opened the refrigerator, rummaged in the meat drawer, and then seemed to lose track of what she was looking for. I moved over to the kitchen counter and opened one cabinet after another until I unearthed a box of Ritz crackers that I placed on the table.

I took her place at the refrigerator and found a block of cheddar while she took a cue from my action and pulled a slicer out of the utensil drawer. I took the slicer and began carving off chunks, which I mounted on crackers and passed to her in rapid succession. I couldn't help but make one for myself while I was at it. I was still chewing, holding a hand in front of my mouth lest I spray her with crumbs, as I said, "At Rosie's the other night, you mentioned the house giving you the creeps."

"I know. I remember."

She took over the cheese-and-cracker duties and fed herself two more, which seemed to calm her to some extent. "Something else. I had another friend complain about my not returning calls, and it bothered me. When you said you left that first message, I shrugged it off, thinking you dialed wrong or there'd been a power outage, something like that. But then I couldn't figure out how your message *and* hers could just evaporate. So then I held down the Play button and brought up old messages. I had sixteen, which I played and deleted as fast as I could because most I'd heard but neglected to erase. Then yours popped up, and two from her were on there as well. I had to ask myself what the hell was going on, and the only answer I could think of was someone was in here and listened to them first. Once you play a message, the message light no longer blinks."

"Which means you'd have no idea the message was ever there."

"That's what I concluded."

"You think someone was in here before the incident today?"

"I do. On more than one occasion." She dropped her gaze and shook her head. "Once it occurred to me, I realized I've had the same feeling for the past couple of weeks. Like something was off."

"Give me an example."

"Little things. Nothing obvious. I'd put mail on the counter and come back later to find it not quite where it was. I'd see books leaning at odd angles in the bookcase, which is a bugaboo of mine. Or a light would be on when I distinctly remembered turning it off. I do that automatically because it's what my mother taught me. Leave a room, turn the light off. I kept dismissing and discounting my perceptions."

"This is bringing up the hair on the back of my neck."

"Well, it's scaring the shit out of me, too."

Suddenly, the phone rang and we both jumped.

Ruthie crossed to the counter, and when she picked up, it was quickly apparent she was talking to the locksmith who'd returned her call. I disconnected my attention while she went through the exercise of explaining what had happened and what she needed done. He was available, and the two agreed to his arrival within the hour. Once she hung up, she sat down again, and I could tell she was feeling better now that help was on the way.

"Why would someone do that?" I asked.

"What, move things around? To spook me, I guess. It wasn't with an eye to ripping me off. There was ample opportunity for that. This was something else. 'Sly' is the only way I can describe it."

"Had to be a guy. I can't picture a woman pulling the same stunt."

"A woman would certainly be capable, but I agree. You know what's weird? Anybody who could slip in like that could slip out again without leaving a trace. This was deliberate. It wasn't until today I felt the reality sink in. Even then, if you'd told me it was my imagination, I'd have taken your word for it."

"No alarm system?"

"Well, no. When Pete was alive, we didn't need one. After he died, I could've had one installed, but I'm not used to thinking that way. The neighborhood is quiet and it's always felt safe. It's not like we have vandals or burglars. I've checked all the windows and doors, and there's nothing out of line. Locks, window latches, everything's closed up tight, so how's this fellow getting in?"

"We'll come over in the morning and do a proper search. I'd rather tackle it by day so we can see what we're doing."

"I'm not making this up, am I? Really, this is making me feel crazy."

"Don't worry about being crazy. I just met a good shrink and I can probably get you a discount."

It took her three seconds to realize I was joking, and even then I knew the attempt at humor was lame.

The locksmith arrived and rekeyed the front and back doors, along with a little-used side door. While Ruthie threw a change of clothes and toiletries in an overnight bag, I gave Henry a call to tell him Ruthie would be spending the night and asking if she could leave her car in his driveway. I knew I'd manage to find parking, but I didn't want her driving around in the dark in an unfamiliar neighborhood. Of course Henry agreed. I didn't stop to explain what was going on, and he didn't press. There'd be plenty of time for that when I knew what we were dealing with.

When the locksmith was finished, she wrote him a check and then walked him to the front door. After that, the two of us made the rounds, assuring ourselves that the windows and doors were secure. I followed Ruthie upstairs and walked with her from room to room, watching as she turned out the lights one by one. I was dimly aware that something was bothering me, but the immediacy of the moment required my undivided attention. The notion was like someone knocking at a distant door. Twice, I paused and turned my head as though I might identify the source.

I walked with her to the garage at the rear of the property and waited while she backed her car into the alleyway. I closed the garage door after her and circled the house to the front, where my Honda was parked. Meanwhile, she'd driven along the alley and pulled around to the front, where she eased her car in behind mine. We proceeded in a slow two-car motorcade. I kept an eye on her in my rearview mirror, noting how anxiously she scanned the darkened streets. At Henry's, I left my car with the engine running while she parked in his drive. I let her into the studio and then went back out to scout for a parking place of my own.

Once that was taken care of, it didn't take long to get Ruthie settled.

I keep the sofa bed made up with fresh sheets, so all I had to do was add two pillows and a quilt. At 10:00, we said our good nights and I climbed the spiral staircase and got ready for bed. It was comforting to have someone else on the premises. I was reminded of the nights Dietz had camped out on the same sofa bed. Waking in the wee hours, if I peeked down from the loft, I'd see him reading or watching television with the sound turned so low, I could have sworn it was off.

I slid under the covers and I was just about to turn out my bedside lamp when I identified the idea my subconscious had been trying to bring to my attention. I got out of bed and crossed to the railing where the loft overlooks the living room below. I could see Ruthie propped up in the sofa bed, a book open in her lap.

"I didn't have a chance to tell you. Henry broke the code on the number cipher Pete created. Turned out to be a list of women's names. Six of them."

She looked up. "You want to come down or talk to me over the rail?"

I padded down the stairs barefoot, my oversize T-shirt skimming the tops of my knees.

She moved her feet so I could perch on the bottom of her fold-out bed. I could feel the bed frame through the mattress and wondered how she could bear it. I'd never had a complaint, but the supports felt like the metal struts on a sewer grate.

Ruthie set her book aside. "So six women's names. Was mine one of them?"

"Nope. So far, I don't think this has anything to do with you."

"You know who they are?"

"The first two are Shirley Ann Kastle and Lenore Redfern, both from Burning Oaks. The third is Phyllis Joplin, who's either from Perdido or currently living there. The fourth is a psychologist named Taryn Sizemore. I talked to her. Number five is a woman named Susan Telford in Henderson, Nevada. The last name is Janet Macy in Tucson, Arizona. Four are definitely connected to Ned Lowe, and I suspect the other two are as well."

"Ned Lowe's the guy whose daughter got married? What's that about?"

"I'm not sure. I had a chat with Taryn this afternoon. She's the one who pointed out the link."

"Name's familiar, but refresh my memory."

"Oh, sorry. She's the gal who sued Ned Lowe back in 1978."

"Right. I remember now."

"Lenore Redfern was Ned's first wife. Phyllis Joplin was his second. Taryn said she knew about Shirley Ann Kastle, but that's as far as she'd go. I haven't identified the other two, and Taryn didn't recognize the names. I'm curious why Pete put together the list of names and why he encrypted them."

"Don't look at me. He never said a word about any of this," she said. "You have a theory?"

"I do, but you won't like it."

"Why is that relevant?"

"I don't want to get your dander up. I'm just playing with ideas."

"Fine. Duly noted. Now get on with it."

"I think Pete was collecting hush money."

"Oh, for heaven's sake. Blackmail?"

"I knew you wouldn't like it."

"Of course not. So who's he blackmailing now? And don't say Ned Lowe."

"I won't say Ned Lowe, but that's what I'm thinking."

"Bullshit."

"Don't be so defensive. Suppose it *was* Ned Lowe and Pete was pressuring him. Pete's killed and at first the guy thinks he's safe and everything's good. Then he gets worried Pete had something that would prove incriminating if it ever came to light."

"But why Ned Lowe in particular? As far as I know, Pete never even met the man."

"You can't be sure of that, and neither can I. Pete kept a lot of information to himself. The point is, he was working for Byrd-Shine

when the lawsuit was filed. It was their job to find dirt on Taryn Sizemore, which apparently they did. Pete might have learned something
just as damning about Ned Lowe. The list is a roster of women, and I
believe all of them are tied to Ned Lowe in some way. Girlfriends,
wives—romantic interests would be my guess. What I don't know is
why the list constitutes a threat."

"Pure speculation."

"Of course it is. On the other hand, if Pete blackmailed one victim,
why not two?"

"Why are you always so quick to put him in the wrong?"

"I'm not. I'm just trying to construct an explanation for all the bits
and pieces."

"Sorry to disappoint you, but I'm not buying it."

"You don't have to be so *cranky*."

"I'm not cranky!"

"Good. Fine. May I continue then?"

"Have at it."

"Taryn Sizemore sued Ned Lowe for stalking and threats. Intentional infliction of emotional harm, to use the proper legal term. Maybe
Pete found out more about Lowe than he should have."

"You said the lawsuit was dead."

"It is, but what if Lowe turned out to be vulnerable in some other
way? What if Pete had evidence that was damaging?"

"Like *what*?" she said, exasperated.

"I don't know. Maybe Lowe doesn't know, either. My point is Pete
had *something* on the guy."

"Can you hear yourself? Do you see how unfair you're being? In
your view, if something bad went down, Pete must have been at the
heart of it, hoping to make a buck."

"I'm not accusing him of anything."

"Yes, you are! You're suggesting he had the goods on Ned Lowe and
was extorting money to keep quiet."

# X

"That's not exactly unprecedented in Pete's repertoire of bad behavior."

She held a hand up. "Enough. I'm tired. I've had a hard day. We can talk about this tomorrow. Right now I'm turning off the light."

Which is what she did.

I sat for a moment, nonplussed, and then padded back up the spiral stairs, got into bed, and turned out my own light. I knew she was angry, but I felt curiously unaffected. So she was pissed off? Big deal. I still thought the idea had merit. She must have thought so too, or why get so bent out of shape?

# 15

---

In the morning, I slipped out of the studio before Ruthie was up and got in my three-mile run. By the time I returned, bringing in the morning paper, the sofa bed was made and she was in the shower. I put on a pot of coffee and set out the milk, a box of Cheerios, two bowls, and two spoons. I turned on the television set with the sound muted. When she emerged from the bathroom, showered and dressed, we ate our cereal while we passed sections of the paper back and forth. I noticed she'd repacked her overnight bag, which was now resting by the front door.

"You sure you don't want to stay one more night?"

"Don't think so. I'll sleep better in my own bed."

"I can relate to that," I said.

Pete's name was never mentioned, and neither of us made reference to our little chat the night before. This is not a bad strategy. The practice of baring all, analyzing every nuance embedded in a quarrel, is a surefire way to keep an argument alive. Better to establish a temporary peace and revisit the conflict later. Often, by then, both parties have decided the issue isn't worth the relationship.

As we were preparing to leave for Ruthie's, Henry appeared on my doorstep. He was still in the dark about this latest development, so I gave him a quick rundown on the intruder and the changing of the locks. "We're on our way over to her house now to see if we can figure out how the guy got in."

Henry was shaking his head. "Terrible."

"All's good with you?" I asked.

"Actually I have to go out shortly, and I was going to ask you to move your vehicle so I can get my marketing done."

She held up her car keys. "I'm on it, champ."

He turned to me. "I wonder if I might have a word with you? It won't take two shakes."

Ruthie picked up her overnight bag. "I'll go on over in my car, and you can follow in yours when it suits."

"You're okay going in the house on your own?"

She waved away the idea. "If I get nervous, I'll wait for you on the back porch."

Once she pulled out, Henry held up a handwritten list. "This may not work if you're going to be at Ruthie's for any length of time. I told Edna I'd take her to the market, but Joseph's not feeling well and since she only needs a few items, I said I'd do her shopping along with mine. The problem is I have a plumber coming this morning between ten and noon and I'm not sure how long I'll be gone. I was wondering if you could be here when the guy arrives. If I'm not back, you can show him around. I've already told him what I need, but you may have to answer questions about hose bibs or sprinkler heads."

"Sure. I'll make a point of being back by nine forty-five and I'll hang out until you get home."

. . .

Ruthie had pulled her car into her garage while I parked mine along the rear property line. I retrieved a flashlight from the glove compartment, locked the car, and followed the back walk to the porch, doing a cursory visual survey in the unrelenting morning light. The house probably dated back to the early 1900s; a story and a half of wood frame, bereft of the usual gingerbread trim that might have lent it some character. The structure was serviceable, incorporating all of the relevant elements, minus style, personality, and appeal. I tapped at the door and she let me in.

Aside from my brief visit the night before, I hadn't been in the house in months, and I was struck by its shabbiness. Pete hadn't been blessed with handyman talents, so if something needed repairing, either Ruthie took care of it or it was left in its funky state. Pete had also been averse to hiring outside help because his pride prevented his admitting that even the simplest job was beyond his poor skills. To spare him, Ruthie had learned to make do. Drawer handles were missing. In the kitchen window, cracked wood putty had pulled away from the glass and short sections were gone. The vinyl tile flooring in the kitchen had buckled in places, as though water had seeped in and loosened the underlying mastic. Now that Ruthie was alone, what difference did it make? Pete's clutter was gone, so the house was tidier. She'd also removed the stained and threadbare area rugs in the downstairs hall and waxed the pale hardwood floors to a high shine.

She'd removed a drawer and placed it on the counter, where she'd unloaded the contents. She'd been sorting the miscellany and tossing the discards in a wastebasket. She'd bought drawer dividers to organize the salvageable items.

"I'll put some coffee on," she said. "Don't mind the mess. I decided to tackle some of Pete's crapola."

"A good idea," I said. "Mind if I go ahead and look around?"

"Please."

I dropped my shoulder bag on a chair and shoved my flashlight in my back pocket while I made a circuit of the first floor, checking window latches, locks, and door hardware. Ruthie had made the same search the night before and she'd sworn the house was secure, which did seem to be the case.

I climbed the stairs to the second floor, peering out of windows as I moved through a small guest bedroom with an adjoining bathroom, a hallway, and a second bedroom currently used for storage. This must be the junk room. Ruth had relegated miscellaneous furniture, hanging clothes, and seasonal items to the ten-by-twelve-foot space. There were also short stacks of assorted cardboard boxes with scarcely room to walk in between. The wallpaper was pink and blue, with tiny floral bouquets tied with ribbons, which suggested this might have been a nursery once upon a time. Now it was essentially a closet jammed wall to wall with articles better suited to a charity donation box. We'd both faulted Pete for being disorganized when, in truth, this wasn't much of an improvement. Looking out the window, I couldn't see any trees growing close enough to allow an intruder to shinny up and enter a second-story window.

I returned to the first floor. The smell of fresh coffee was strong in the downstairs hall, but I didn't want to interrupt the search for a coffee break. The front door was solid wood, not one of the flimsy hollow-core doors so popular in residential construction these days. The back door was also solid wood, with mullions in the upper third separating four small panes of glass. The side door was fashioned along similar lines, with solid wood below and the top half made up of six equal-size six-by-eight-inch panes of glass. The knob was sturdy and the lock was a double-keyed dead bolt. In the interests of fire safety, the key had been left in the lock on the inside should a hasty exit be required.

I unlocked the door and went outside. No tool marks to suggest that someone had forced the lock. A dense twenty-foot hedge along the walk separated Ruth's house from her neighbor's. I turned to my right and toured the exterior, looking for signs of a breach. Like many California homes of this era, there was a crawl space below the house, but no basement. A scrim of trellising had been affixed to the framing to shield the space from urban wildlife, but sections had been chewed away. A tuft of coarse hair was caught in the splintered wood where a beast had squeezed through the gap.

I took out my flashlight and got down on my hands and knees, peering into the space under the house. I allowed the beam of my flashlight to illuminate the area, which stretched its length and width. The "floor" was rubble and exposed dirt with cinder block footers at irregular intervals. Metal brackets secured plumbing to the floor joists, and a large furnace duct, wrapped in shiny insulation, shot across at an angle and disappeared into a large hole cut into a concrete wall.

Electrical wires sagged into view, and between the joists pink and gray insulating material hung in tatters. The far corners were in deep shadow, but my flashlight caught the two bright eyes of a creature that scuttled out of sight. There were no vents, and the underside of the subflooring was dusted with a white substance that could only be mold. I saw no evidence of trapdoors connecting the crawl space to the rooms above, so there was no way an intruder could enter the house from below. Absent were scuff marks to suggest that someone had belly-crawled across the surface, which resembled nothing so much as the bleak landscape on a distant planet man had once visited and found wanting.

I got up and dusted myself off, then continued circling the house. At the back of my mind, I was still testing my belief that Pete was up to something. Why put together six names and then convert the list to code unless he was worried it would fall into the wrong hands? Why would a list like that mean anything to anyone except Ned Lowe? Ruth could protest all she liked, but it didn't add up any other way; at least as far as I could see.

When I arrived at the side door again, I noted what looked like a thin line of a lighter color along the mullion nearest the door. I leaned close, picking up the scent of oil-based paint. I drew back a step. The original dark blue trim had been covered with a shade that wasn't quite a match. I ran a finger across the surface and found it faintly tacky to the touch. I went inside and checked the same panes of glass. Adjacent mullions and trim were the original dark blue. Only the pane nearest the door handle had been touched up. Outside again, I dug a fingernail into the paint and found the window putty as soft as cheese.

I peered through the glass at an angle. The key in the dead bolt sat within easy reach. I pictured the intruder using a knife blade to chip away the ancient putty that secured the glass. Once the pane was lifted out, it would be easy to reach through the opening and extract the key from the lock. Any hardware store could duplicate that key. Many of the same hardware stores sold dark blue exterior paint. All the intruder would have to do is return the original key to the lock, replace the pane, and putty it into place. After that, he'd apply a line of fresh paint, and for all intents and purposes, the glass would appear as it had been.

I wondered if he'd anticipated the arrival of the locksmith and the rekeying of the lock. Having left the door standing open, he must have assumed she'd have the locks changed. No big deal to him. All he had to do was wait. The next time she left the house, he could employ the same technique to supply himself with a new key while she'd go on thinking she was safe. I noticed I was neatly tiptoeing past the name *Ned Lowe*. Ruthie's bristling aside, I still harbored the strong belief that Pete had been operating in the usual shakedown mode with Lowe as his target.

I closed the door, turned the key, and removed it from the lock.

"What are you doing?"

I jumped and said, "Shit!"

Ruthie was standing behind me. "Sorry. You were gone so long, I came looking for you. What's the matter with the door?"

"This is how he got in," I said. I gave her a quick summary, watching as her expression shifted from disbelief to dismay.

"How do I know he didn't get in again last night after the locks were changed? He might already have a copy of that key."

"Better have the locksmith out again, and let's hope he offers you a discount. You should have an alarm system installed."

"I guess I'll have to, but I'm pissed off just thinking about how much it will cost."

"No point in getting mad when you don't have a choice."

"Right, and I'm angry about that, too," she said.

"You have a company in mind?"

"My neighbor used an outfit called Security Operating Systems. He had an alarm installed last year and he's a big fan."

"Security Operating Systems. S.O.S. Very clever," I said. I placed the key in the palm of her hand. "In the meantime, you might want to install a chain where he can't get to it."

"How did he know he could break in to begin with? What if I'd been home?"

"Come with me," I said.

I ushered her into the kitchen with me where I pointed at the refrigerator door, which was papered with odds and ends. Under assorted magnets shaped like vegetables, there was a photograph of Pete, a dental appointment reminder card, two fliers, and a calendar on which she'd noted her work hours. "Look at this. You have your schedule posted where anyone can see it. The first time he broke in, he was taking a big risk. After that, he knew what shifts you worked, so he could come and go as he pleased."

Ruth put a hand on my arm. "I really have to pee. If I stand here one more minute I will wet my pants."

"Go and pee," I said.

She left the room. I could feel my own mental processes at work, ideas tumbling over one another as though escaping from a cage. I turned back to the refrigerator door. Dead center was the junk hauler's flier, headline hand-drawn in mock-three-dimensional letters, fashioned after the messages left under bridges by a tagging crew. I pushed aside the magnets and freed the flier, which read:

No Taste for Waste? Want Junk Displaced?
Fifty Bucks in Cash Eradicates Your Trash
Call (805) 555-2999
Leave your name, address, and a list of the items you want re-moved. One-time offer, so don't delay!
Cash only. No checks. No credit cards.
We accept carpet, scrap metal, discarded furniture, lumber, tires, appliances, leaf & garden waste, mattresses, and anything else you want to get rid of.
We'll be in your neighborhood on Monday, October 24.

The ad was catchy and the guy made it easy to take him up on his offer. Fifty bucks was cheap, especially since it had to cover the fees at the local dump. Robert Dietz and I had spent the better part of two days searching the very boxes the junk hauler had carted off. I remembered loading some of them into Henry's station wagon, moving them from Pete's office to my studio, where Dietz and I sat cross-legged on the floor, going through them item by item. I was guessing we'd barely finished the search when the junk hauler began canvassing the neighborhood in his search for work.

Ruth returned, saying, "Sorry about that."

"This is the flier the junk man left?"

She nodded. "I kept it in case my neighbor needed him. I swear he cleans his garage every other month."

"Didn't the timing strike you as odd?"

"Are you kidding? It was perfect. I don't know what I'd have done with all that crap if he hadn't come along when he did."

"So two days after Dietz and I searched the boxes, someone just happened to stick this in your screen door."

"Yes."

"You read the flier and did what in response?"

"Just what it said. I left a message telling him I had a garage full of stuff I needed to get rid of. I knew he'd be in the neighborhood the twenty-fourth, so all I had to do was give him my address. I had to be at work, so I put the fifty bucks in an envelope and taped it to the back door. I came home, he'd emptied the garage, and everything looked great."

"So you never actually laid eyes on him and you never got his name?"

"I needed the garage cleaned. I wasn't looking for a friend. What's the matter with you?"

"I'm not a fan of coincidences. I know they happen in life, but you've been plagued with happy accidents and it seems off to me. You mind if I try the number?"

She seemed skeptical, but she gestured her assent.

I carried the flier as I crossed to the phone. I picked up the handset and punched in the number. The line rang twice, and then a three-tone signal sounded at an earsplitting pitch. I held out the handset so mine wasn't the only hearing under assault. An automated operator in a singsong voice said, "I'm sorry, but the number you've dialed is no longer in service." She went on to tell us what we could do about it, which was precious little.

"The number's been disconnected. Why should I care?"

"Put the incident in context. This unseen guy carts Pete's boxes away. Four months later you receive a letter from the IRS."

"What's one have to do with the other? I'm not getting it."

"We're talking about three men you never met. The junk dealer, the IRS agent, and the guy who broke in. Doesn't that bother you?"

"No."

"Well, it should. I mean, think about it. The junk dealer walks off with Pete's business records. Then the IRS agent comes along and expects you to find documents that date back fifteen years. And now you've got some thug going through everything you own."

"I agree it's creepy."

"Not my point. What if they're the same man?"

"Like they're in cahoots?"

"I'm saying one man instead of three. And not just any man. We're back to Ned Lowe."

Her expression was pained and included a rolling of the eyes.

"Don't roll your eyes at me. Just listen. Two days after Dietz and I finish searching Pete's boxes, this anonymous junk man leaves a note in your door and you jump at the chance to have the same boxes carted off. End of problem as far as you're concerned. Meanwhile, the guy is now in possession of all Pete's files. He goes through everything at his leisure, trying to find what he's looking for."

"How do you know he's looking for anything? He took a bunch of crap to the dump."

"You don't know that. All you know is he's taken it off your hands. I'm asking you to consider that the arrival of this flier was more than serendipitous. What if Lowe was looking for something in those cartons? No luck, so he comes back around posing as George Dayton from the IRS. The letter specifically asked about Byrd-Shine, insisting on documents and records from 1978. That seemed nutty on the face of it, and I said so at the time."

"You told me there weren't any Byrd-Shine records, so I turned around and told the IRS guy the same thing."

"But suppose he didn't believe you. 'Dayton' told you he talked to Pete last spring and Pete swore he had paperwork in storage, which may or may not have been true. Pete might have been bullshitting, or maybe he was too lazy to actually hunt up the files in question. Whatever the case, 'Dayton' assumes you're holding out on him. As a last resort, he breaks in and has a go at it himself."

"George Dayton's a real guy. Honestly. I didn't create him out of whole cloth. I talked to him myself."

"But you never met him, and I bet you never saw any IRS identification. You don't even know what that would look like. What's he got, a badge? A business card? You received a notice on IRS letterhead with an address and phone number, but that could have been faked. The day the two of you are finally supposed to meet, he's a no-show."

"That's true," she said reluctantly. "On the other hand, I don't have anything of value. They can search all they like. One man or three. Who cares?"

"I don't think it's about you at all. I think it's about Pete."

"Crap. Now you're back to the theory he was shaking someone down."

"If you're so sure Dayton's on the up-and-up, call the local IRS office and ask for him."

"Here we go with the calls again."

"I was right about the first one."

"Okay, I'll call, but what am I supposed to say?"

"You don't have to say anything. Just ask for him. I want to know if he's legitimate. All you have is his word he works for the IRS. We assume people are telling the truth, so most of us wouldn't dream of calling to verify employment, but what if he's lying through his teeth?"

"Why would he do that?"

"How do I know? If he's a real IRS agent, then at least you find out for sure, and if he's not, you'll learn that as well."

"What if he's there?"

"Then ask why he missed his appointment with you. I can't believe I'm having to spell it all out. Use your imagination."

"What if they ask who's calling? Am I supposed to give my real name?"

"Of course. You can use a fake name if it makes you feel any better. Don't you know how to lie?"

"I can't believe you'd ask. I don't lie to people."

"Well, no wonder you're so ill at ease. Lying's a skill. You can't just open your mouth and expect a convincing lie to flop out. It takes practice."

Ruth laughed.

"I'm serious," I said.

"Oh. Sorry. Let me scare up his letter and I'll call."

"Not that number. It might be rigged to an answering machine. Here."

I moved a potted African violet that was sitting on the telephone book. I paged through the listings in the front: city offices, Santa Teresa County offices, California State offices, United States government offices. I ran a finger past Agriculture, Air Force, Army, and Coast Guard, whizzing right along until I reached Internal Revenue. There I had my choice of Taxpayer Assistance Center, Need a Tax Form, Checking on a Refund, and ten variations on a theme. All were 800 numbers except the last, which was designated the Local Area Office. I circled the number and turned the book so Ruth could see it. I picked up the handset and held it out to her.

She took it and punched in the number, tilting the phone so I could hear both sides of the conversation. The line rang four times.

A woman picked up, saying, "Internal Revenue. This is Christine Matthews. How may I help you?"

Ruthie said, "Hiiiii. Could I speak to George Dayton?"

"Who?"

"Dayton, like the city in Ohio. First name, George."

"You have the wrong number. This is the Internal Revenue Service."

"I know. I looked you up in the phone book. I called on purpose."

"There isn't anyone named Dayton working here."

"Are you sure? George told me he was an agent with the IRS. That's why I called this number."

"He told you he worked here?"

"He did. I guess he might work in Perdido or another office in the area. Do you have a directory?"

"Ma'am, I hope you won't take offense, but I've worked for the IRS thirty-two years, and there's no George Dayton. Never was for that matter."

149

"Oh. Sorry. Thanks."

I depressed the plunger and returned the handset to the cradle. Despite the fact that Ruthie and I locked eyes, I knew she wasn't ready to yield.

"I still don't see what this has to do with Ned Lowe," she said.

"Trust me, it does. I don't know how yet, but there's no point in beating the subject to death. You're not convinced and I don't have proof."

"Even if the names do connect to Ned Lowe, that doesn't mean Pete was extorting money from him."

"I'm through trying to talk you into it. If I find supporting evidence, I'll let you know."

"Kinsey, I know you mean well and I'm sure you believe every word you've said, but I was married to the man for close to forty years. I don't believe he was greedy and avaricious. That's just not the man I knew."

"All I'm trying to do is make sense of what's going on," I said. After an awkward beat, I changed the subject. "At least we figured out how the guy was getting in."

"I'll call S.O.S. today. I should have done it months ago."

# 16

There was already a plumber's truck in Henry's driveway when I pulled up in front at 9:35. The garage doors were open and Henry and the fellow were standing in the backyard. Henry gestured as he explained the situation and the plumber nodded in response, asking the occasional question. He was a man in his seventies and rail-thin, wearing khaki overalls and thick-soled brown brogans caked with mud. His cap was brown with MCCLASKEY PLUMBING machine-stitched in red just above the bill.

When I joined them, Henry introduced us and the plumber raised his cap half an inch. "Nice to make your acquaintance."

We shook hands briefly. His palm was damp and threw off a scent of moist earth and cast-iron pipes. He had a lined face and mild brown eyes. His cap forced tufts of gray hair to protrude above his ears, and when he'd doffed it, I saw that his forehead was still dead white where it was shaded by the bill.

"Mr. McClaskey was just telling me about the sources of salt in a gray water system," Henry said, returning to the subject at hand.

The plumber used his fingers to tick off the sources of salt, reciting in a tone that suggested constant repetition of the self-same points. "We're talking about sweaty bathers, cleaning products, water softeners, and pi— Excuse me, ma'am, urine. Your water softener can add high levels of sodium chloride that adversely affect the soil. I'm quoting from an expert in the field, who happens to be a local fella name of Art Ludwig. The way he puts it, 'Urine is where the majority of the body's salt ends up.' Finds its way into your gray water reuse system via toilets, bed pans, and people peeing in the shower."

I saw a pained look cross Henry's face. "Kinsey and I would never dream of peeing in the shower."

"I understand and I applaud your restraint. Good news on urine is it's full of plant nutrients; nitrogen, in the main, but also potassium and phosphate."

Henry looked at his watch. "Sorry to cut this short, but I have an errand to run, so I'll leave you to poke around. Kinsey will be in her studio if you should need her. We can chat when I get back. I'll be interested in your recommendations."

"Happy to oblige. I'll do an in-depth analysis and tell you what I think." McClaskey doffed his cap again.

Henry went into the garage. I heard the station wagon door snap shut smartly and the engine hum to life. Shortly afterward, he backed down the drive, swung into the street, and drove off. I looked over to see Edna crossing the grass toward the fence that separated their backyard from Henry's driveway.

Half a second later, she rose into view, having climbed to her position on the box. Oversize dentures aside, her features were delicate: button nose, Kewpie doll lips. Broken veins on her cheeks looked like two sweeps of rouge. Her wardrobe had a girlish cast; today she had ruffles down the front of her blouse with its Peter Pan collar and puffed sleeves.

"Good morning, Edna. How are you?"

"Doing well. How is Henry's project coming along? I saw the plumber's truck pull in while I was sweeping the porch."

"The plumber's making up a list, so we'll see what he suggests."

I could see what type of neighbor she'd be. Every noise would have to be investigated, every visitor would generate a quiz, any small change would be grounds for scrutiny and debate. If the telephone rang, if a package arrived, Edna would be right there, making sure she knew exactly what was going on. Henry would find no fault with her. He was a softie where women were concerned—including me, of course, so I could hardly complain.

"Where's Henry off to?"

"The market, but I expect him back before long. I believe he's picking up a few items for you."

"He offered and I couldn't bring myself to refuse. Joseph's having a bad day and I didn't think I should leave him alone. In Perdido, we had a neighbor who'd step in on occasion, and what a godsend that was. Sadly, we don't know many people in this area and I can't think who I'd ask."

I can recognize a hint when I hear one, but I knew better than to pipe up. She'd introduced the subject hoping I'd step into the breach. This is not a good idea. Agree to such an arrangement once and you're on call from that time forth. I envisioned an endless succession of good deeds stretching out to the horizon if I didn't sidestep the trap. "Why don't you call the Visiting Nurse Association?"

She dropped her gaze. "Well, honey, he doesn't require skilled nursing care. I'm talking about someone spending a few minutes with him when I have to be somewhere else. He's no trouble."

She closed her mouth and waited for my next idea, which was sure to bring us back around to my being tapped for the honor.

"I don't know what to suggest. That's a tough one," I said. I lobbed the ball back to her side of the court. "Was there anything else?"

Grudgingly, she held up a baking tin. "I wanted to return Henry's pan. He brought us fresh cinnamon rolls this morning."

"I can give it to him if you like."

"Well, I wouldn't want to inconvenience you."

"It's not a problem. I'll be happy to take care of it."

I approached the fence and took the pan. It was one of those flimsy disposable tins, still sticky from the glaze he used to top his cinnamon buns. The sides of the pan were bent, and I suspected he'd toss it in the trash, but that was his to decide. My Aunt Gin, overbearing though she was, taught me that in returning a dish, it was polite to have it properly washed and packed with a homemade delicacy as a thank-you. This was a cultural nicety unknown to Edna.

I gave a little wave and headed for the studio, eager to avoid further conversation. She sank from sight, her head bobbing into view again as she crossed the grass to her back steps. She looked pouty from the back.

While I waited for Henry, I put the tin in the sink, filled it with hot, soapy water, and left it to soak. I tidied the studio, making a point of scrubbing the downstairs bathroom. I took Ruth's damp bath towel, tossed it in the dryer with a small sheet of fabric softener, and ran a quick cycle so it would emerge dry and smelling sweet. If she changed her mind and decided to stay another night, at least she'd feel welcome. I put away the bowls, spoons, and coffee cups we'd used that morning and then washed out the baking tin, which was thoroughly deformed by my efforts to get it clean.

When I heard Henry's car pull in, I went out to the garage and helped him carry in his grocery bags. By then, the plumber was standing by with a list in hand and an expectant look on his face.

"You want me to take Edna's groceries over so the two of you can talk?"

"I'd appreciate it," he said as he passed me a loaded plastic bag. "I packed her items separately along with her receipt."

"Be right back."

# X

I scurried around to the front of the studio and passed through the squeaky gate. I took a short left and traversed the Shallenbargers' walk to the front door. Their lawn wasn't large, but the grass seemed to be in good shape. I couldn't remember seeing their sprinklers on, so they must have been watering when the sun went down as we'd all been advised. I rang the bell, and while I waited, I made an idle check of the grocery receipt—$25.66—before I returned it to the bag.

When half a minute went by without a response, I knocked.

Shortly afterward, Edna opened the door and peered out at me. "Yes?"

I held up the bag. "The items you asked for. Receipt's in the bag."

"Thank you," she said as she took it. "Tell Henry how much I appreciate his kindness. He's considerate of others."

"How's Joseph feeling?"

For a fraction of a second, her look was blank, and then she caught herself. "Better. I fixed him a bowl of soup and now he's having a rest."

"Good to hear." I expected mention of reimbursement, but it didn't seem to occur to her. When she moved to close the front door, I caught it by the edge.

"You want to pay him in cash or write a check?"

She dropped her gaze. I wondered what I'd have seen if she'd continued to make eye contact. She smiled with her lips together, creating a dimple in each cheek. The effect was curious. Malice surfaced and then disappeared.

"You didn't tell me how much it was," she murmured, as though the fault were mine.

"Receipt's in there if you want to take a look."

"Of course. If you'll wait, I'll find my pocketbook."

She took the bag and retreated, leaving the door ajar. I could hear her steps receding on the hardwood floor. When she returned minutes later, she handed me a twenty-dollar bill and a five. No change and no receipt, which meant I couldn't call her on the fact that she'd shorted Henry by sixty-six cents.

. . .

On my way back to the studio, I saw McClaskey and Henry seated at his kitchen table with their heads bent together. I was fuming about Edna's mistreatment of Henry, but if I brought it to his attention, he'd wave the matter aside. Sixty-six cents was minor. He'd never make a fuss about something so insignificant, and he'd never believe she'd acted out of spite that was actually directed at me. He was good-natured and generous. As is true of many such souls, he assumed others operated out of the same good will that motivated him.

I could feel the office beckon. Lately, I've noticed an impulse to retreat to a place where I feel competent. Though I was reluctant to admit it, in addition to being annoyed with Edna, I was irritated with Ruth. I had a hypothesis that made perfect sense, and she wasn't buying it. It was obvious someone was sniffing around the edges of her life. Of course, I had no proof it was Ned Lowe. I'd debunked "George Dayton's" phony claim, but neither of us knew who he really was or why he'd gone to such lengths. Beyond that, I had no support for my suspicions about the junk man. It meant little that his phone was not in service. His business might be seasonal, and undercapitalized at that. He was a citizen with a big truck and a willingness to dirty his hands.

This is the downside of intuition: when it feels so exactly right, other people's skepticism is infuriating. Once again, I was reminded I hadn't been hired to do anything and I wasn't getting paid. I thought I was being "helpful," which is usually a mistake. If I wanted to prove my point, I'd have to tackle the list and fill in the blanks. I had the name Susan Telford in Henderson, Nevada. I also had Janet Macy in Tucson and Phyllis Joplin, Ned's second wife. I might start with her. Perdido was twenty-five miles south. I'd pick up a phone number for her from directory assistance as soon as I had a minute.

I parked in the short drive that ran between my bungalow and the one on my right. I let myself in and picked up the mail strewn on the floor just inside the door. The air smelled unpleasant. There was the strong overlay of scorched coffee, and I chided myself for forgetting to turn off the machine the day before. I caught a whiff of another odor suggestive of plumbing issues. Meanwhile, the message light was blinking on my answering machine. I tossed the mail on the desk, leaned over, and pressed Play.

"Hi, Kinsey. This is Taryn Sizemore. Sorry I missed you, but I was hoping to stop by your office this morning. It finally dawned on me there's no reason in the world I shouldn't talk to you about Ned. Apologies for the paranoia, but I'm afraid the man has that effect. If you're tied up, let me know. Otherwise, I'll be there as soon as I'm finished with my ten o'clock appointment. My number in case you don't have it is . . ."

I was busy jotting down the number, so it took me a moment to register my surroundings. I set the pen aside, and when I looked up, I uttered a yelp of dismay. Every item on my desk—including papers and pens, my blotter, my calendar, and the telephone—was off by two degrees. File drawers were open half an inch. The window blinds had been raised and secured at an incline. This doesn't sound like a big deal, but believe me, it is. As was also true of Ruthie, I like things squared up. Being tidy is essential to my peace of mind. In the chaotic world of crime and criminals, maintaining order is my way of asserting control.

I made a three-hundred-and-sixty-degree turn.

My entire office looked like a playful, slightly destructive breeze had rippled through, lifting items and setting them down askew. None of the angles matched. My copy machine was canted to the right. My two visitors' chairs faced opposite directions, but only by three inches. Even my desk had been offset, leaving shallow indentations where the legs had formerly rested on the carpeting.

I went to the door and took in the sight of the outer office. Textbooks were tilted this way and that. My crummy travel posters had been removed from the wall and then retaped off the true. I walked down the short corridor to the bathroom, where the disarray continued. The small venetian blind hung from the box bracket on the right-hand side of the window frame. The entire roll of toilet paper had been unraveled and lay on the floor in a loose mound. The lid to the toilet tank was cockeyed, the seat was up, and a bar of hand soap floated on the surface of the water in the bowl.

I moved on, a whisper of dread roiling in my gut.

In the kitchenette, the back door stood open and all of the cabinet doors yawned, though the contents hadn't been displaced. As it turned out, I hadn't left the coffee machine on at all. Someone had filled the apparatus with an inch of water and then run a brewing cycle. The result was a layer of heat-laminated sludge in the bottom of the glass carafe that must have sat on the burner for hours. I flipped the button to the Off position. I'd probably have to toss the carafe, as there was no way I'd ever scrub it clean. The roll of paper toweling had been removed from the holder and now rested in the sink, where the hot water faucet had been turned on to a trickle. I turned the water off, wondering how much my water bill would jump in consequence.

I removed the plastic wastebasket from under the sink, intending to toss in the sodden roll of paper towels. As usual, I'd lined the waste bin with a plastic bag to simplify trash removal. A small gray mouse leaped ineffectually up the sides of the bag, frantic to escape, but unable to achieve sufficient purchase. This was made all the more problematic by the fact that the same man who'd gone to such lengths to touch everything I owned had also defecated in the bin.

# 17

I took the wastebasket out the back door, laid it on its side, and watched as the mouse skittered off and disappeared into a patch of grass behind the bungalow. Gingerly, I removed the plastic bag and deposited both the bag and its unsavory contents in the rolling garbage bin. I returned to the kitchenette and locked the door, using the hem of my T-shirt to preserve any latent prints the intruder had probably been too smart to leave behind. I went into my inner office and sat down.

This was the long and short of it, at least in my analysis: The mouse was free, so good news on that score. If I notified the police—a decision I hadn't arrived at yet—it would not be because I expected anyone to be charged with breaking and entering, vandalism, or malicious mischief. Shitting on a mouse is not expressly forbidden under California law. A nice officer would arrive in response to my 9-1-1 call and he'd write up an incident report, much as the nice officers had done when Ruthie made a similar call. No APB would result. A forensic specialist would not perform a DNA analysis on the turd left in the wastebasket, nor would the turd data be entered into the National Crime Information Center database for comparison to criminal turds nationwide. Whether I called the cops or not, I'd have to have my locks changed and an alarm system installed. I had no doubt my intruder and Ruthie's were the same man. Prove it, I could not, which meant I had no recourse. I was royally pissed off.

I heard the door open in the outer office.

"Kinsey?" The voice was Taryn Sizemore's.

"Just the person I was hoping to see."

She appeared in the doorway and then stood transfixed as she took in the sight. "Oh, wow. Poor you. Ned Lowe's been here."

"Thanks. I'd be interested in your reasons for saying so."

She wore a starched white cotton shirt with the collar turned up, belted over tight jeans. Big bracelets, big earrings, high-heeled boots with buckles up the sides. I could still see the roller shapes in her shoulder-length curls. I'd look ridiculous in that outfit. She looked great. I envied her black leather shoulder bag, which was bigger than mine and appeared to have more compartments.

She dropped her bag on the floor. "It's his style: hostile and aggressive. Wherever he is now, he knows what he's done to you and he's happy with himself. You'll never walk in here again without bracing yourself on the off chance he's been in while you were gone."

"What a shitheel."

"This is just for openers. There's probably more where this came from."

"Oh joy."

She chose one of the two visitors' chairs and took a seat, pausing to align the chairs so they were parallel. Her eyes strayed to the window blinds. "You mind?"

"Have at it. Eventually, I'll tidy up, but I thought I'd sit here and appreciate the care and planning that went into this."

She crossed to the window and adjusted the blinds, corrected the blinds on the other window, closed the file drawers, and then sat down again. "You must be his type, the same way I was."

"That makes three of us, including Pete's widow, Ruth."

"He paid her a visit, too?"

"She found her door standing open when she came home from work. Scared the hell out of her. I can't figure out how he knew about me. It looks like he's been getting into her place to listen to phone messages and diddle around with her things, but that doesn't explain how he came up with my name and address."

"It's probably something obvious, but you'll worry about it for days, which is all part of his plan. Aren't you going to ask why I'm here?"

"Who cares? I'm glad to have company while I'm freaking out."

"I should let you decompress."

"I don't want to decompress. I want to call the police."

She slid her watch around on her wrist so she could check the time. "Call 'em later. Took me eight minutes to walk over here. We'll assume another eight on the return. I have a client coming in on her lunch hour, so I need to get back in time to intercept her."

"I hope you're here to help."

"I am," she said. "Feels odd, though. I'm not used to being on this side of the confessional."

"What made you change your mind?"

"I'm tired of having Ned rule my life. You want to know about my relationship with him, I'm happy to oblige."

"Ready when you are."

"Fine. Let's start with the lawsuit and why I settled instead of fighting the good fight. I had a nervous breakdown when I was eighteen. The doctors decided on a diagnosis of clinical hysterical personality, derived from the Perley-Guze checklist: fifty-five symptoms, any twenty-five of which had to be present in at least nine of ten predetermined symptom groups. Can you believe this shit? I was having extended panic attacks that presented as psychotic breaks. I was in the hospital for two weeks and I came out on a cocktail of prescription medications. Once they got the mix right, I was fine. Chat therapy, of course, but that was more to benefit the psychiatric staff, composed of—guess what? All guys."

"And that's what Byrd-Shine came up with when they did the deep background on you?"

"Oh yes. They turned up the name of the hospital, admission and release dates, my doctors' names, and all the drugs I was on."

"How hard did they have to dig? You must have had friends willing to supply all the nitty-gritty details."

"That was my assumption. None of my friends were sworn to secrecy, but I assumed I could trust their discretion. What a disappointment."

"So what was the big deal? You spend two weeks in the hospital and then you're fine. Where could Ned's attorney go with that?"

"Character assassination. He'd paint me as a basket case— unstable, vindictive, and paranoid. I was suing Ned for emotional harm. All Ruffner had to do was to point out how nuts I was and Ned became the victim of my delusional state."

"Didn't you have proof he harassed and threatened you?"

"I had phone records, but no witnesses. I didn't realize how carefully he set me up."

"Meaning what?"

"I had all the notes he left on my car and my front porch and my mailbox and anyplace else he could think of that might unnerve me. You wanna know what the notes said? Things like 'I love you.' 'Please forgive me.' 'You mean the world to me.' 'I wish you'd let me get close.' I could see how it would look to a jury. I'd have been burned at the stake."

"How'd you get involved with him in the first place?"

"We worked for the same company. I was marketing. He was outside sales."

"Wasn't that a no-no?"

"Yes and no. Generally, it was frowned on, but the policy wasn't spelled out in any great detail. As long as we didn't let the relationship impact our work, everybody looked the other way."

"How long did you date him?"

"A year and a half. The first six months were great, then things started to get weird. Ned's a photography buff, so he wanted to take pictures of me, which doesn't sound bad on the face of it, but believe me, there was some kind of pathology at work. He insisted I wear this special outfit, along with a wig and makeup. I could see what he was up to: turning me into someone else. I'm just not sure who. He also had sliiightly kinky taste when it came to sex."

"Oh please, no details," I said in haste. "Had to be about control, don't you think?"

"Absolutely. And that was just the beginning. He became obsessed with what I did and who I saw and whether I talked to friends about him, which I didn't. I didn't dare. He checked phone bills and read my mail. If I mentioned someone else at work—male or female—he was all over it. 'What did you talk about?' 'How much time did you spend?' 'If everything was so innocent, why wasn't I included?' On and on it went.

"He's the master of escalation. Any protest I made, any step I took to protect myself, he upped the ante. At one point I got a temporary restraining order, and you know what he did? He called the police and claimed I'd thrown a pipe wrench that hit him in the head. He was bloody and he had a knot the size of my fist, but he did it to himself."

"The police actually showed up?"

"Of course. I was arrested and put in *handcuffs*. I spent eight hours in jail until I got someone to post bail. After that, at the slightest provocation, he'd threaten me with the cops."

"And you were still working with him?"

"Uh, no. What happened was I went to my boss and told him what was going on. I got fired. Ned got promoted."

"Can we talk about the settlement? I don't mean to put you in an awkward position."

She dismissed that. "Not a problem. Honestly. I've thought about it and I can't see that I'd be in jeopardy even if you broadcast details, which I don't think you'd do. At the time, Ned scared the shit out of me, but I see now he was more frightened of me than I was of him. The settlement was seventy-five."

"Thousand?" I asked in disbelief.

She nodded.

I said, "Oh, man. That's not good. If you'd told me five grand, I'd have said it was a token payment, Ned trying to get you out of his hair. Seventy-five thousand sounds like a payoff motivated by guilt. He must have thought you had him by the short hairs, or why cough up that much?"

"Not my attorney's response. He told me it was a good deal. More than I'd have gotten from a jury even if they'd sided with me, which he didn't think they would. He urged me to take it."

"I'll bet he did. He wanted to make sure you could pay his bill, which must have been substantial."

"He took fifteen thousand off the top."

"How does Pete fit into this? You said he showed up a year ago."

"He came to apologize."

The four words were not what I'd expected. "Apologize? For what?"

"You won't believe it."

"Try me."

"Okay, so here it is: Pete told me Morley Shine got drunk one night and admitted he'd broken into my psychiatrist's office. That's how he got the information. He photocopied my file and turned everything over to Ned's attorney. Of course it was illegal, immoral, and unethical, but what good did that do me? Pete had felt guilty about it for years and he wanted to set the record straight."

"Too little too late, wasn't it?"

"Not at all. In a weird way, it helped. I felt vindicated. In some sense of the word Ned 'won,' but only by playing dirty."

"Would have been nice if Pete had spoken up back then."

"Oh, he did. That's the point. He went to Ben Byrd and told him what Morley had done. Ben confronted Morley and they had a knock-down, drag-out fight. After that, I gather Ben never spoke to Morley again."

I closed my eyes and lowered my head. "That's why the partnership broke up."

"Basically, yes. Morley blamed Pete for blowing the whistle on him, and I guess Ben blamed him, too, even though Morley was the guilty party. In the end, Pete was left out in the cold. Any work he did after-ward was strictly catch-as-catch-can."

I sat, pondering what I already knew in light of this new informa-tion. "So what's the list of women's names about?"

"You know Pete was an insomniac. He roamed the streets at night."

"Right. He was doing that when I knew him way back when."

"He had a protective streak. He knew Ned was treacherous and he took to hovering over the women who'd come in range of him. Me, Ned's daughter, his wife, Celeste."

"His daughter's name and his wife's weren't on the list."

"Maybe he intended to add them. He told me he'd spoken to both."

"What about Shirley Ann Kastle? Who is she?"

"Ned's high school sweetheart. That's as much as I know about her."

"I figured all of you were victims of a blackmail scheme."

"No, no. You're wrong about that. Pete was a purist."

"A *purist*? You gotta be kidding me! The guy was a crook."

"Not so," she said. "I saw him as someone so passionate about jus-tice, he was destined to fail."

I made a sour face. "You met with him, what, twice? I knew him for the better part of ten years."

"Hold on and just listen to me. I have clients you'd swear up and down were total, unmitigated slobs, but they're actually the opposite—so hell-bent on 'clean and tidy,' they can't even start. Rather than fail, they give up. Their standards are so high, they're overwhelmed before they start. To them, it's better not even tackling the job."

"That's a stretch."

"Talk to Ruth. She understood him better than you did."

"No doubt."

"You want my opinion?"

"Are you speaking as a person or as a shrink?"

"I'm always speaking as a shrink."

"Then I don't want to hear it."

She smiled. "I'll give it to you anyway. No charge to the recipient."

I raised a hand. "I'm serious. I don't want to hear it."

Taryn went on as though I'd never opened my mouth. "This is as much about you as it is about him. You're entangled with the man. I don't know how or why, but I can see it as clear as day."

"I'm not 'entangled.' Bullshit. Where'd you get that? I didn't like him. I disapproved of the choices he made. That's hardly 'entanglement.'"

"You felt no compassion for his Marfan syndrome?"

"Oh, come on. We all have a cross to bear. His life was tough, but his problems were self-generated. The Marfan was the least of them. Most were the result of his basic dishonesty, which is something you can't fix."

"He didn't need fixing. He needed to get back to who he was before he lost track of himself."

"Too late for that now."

"No, it's not. That's what you're here for, to tie up loose ends."

"Wait. Excuse me. This is about him. It has nothing to do with me."

She seemed to be enjoying herself, her manner animated. "You said it yourself. We 'do much the same job. We study people's lives, determine what went wrong, and try to make it right.'"

I laughed. "You're quoting me back to myself? That's a low blow. I was referring to the two of us. You and me. Not Pete and me."

"He left work undone. Whatever his plan was, I'm sure you'll figure it out."

"*I'll* figure it out? I don't think so. Since when is this my problem?"

"Since the day he died," she said.

I shook my head, smirking, as though her comment warranted no legitimate response. Then I noted my body language. I'd crossed my arms over my chest, which I thought she might misinterpret as stubborn and defensive. I uncrossed my arms and then couldn't think what to do with them. I leaned forward and put my elbows on the desk. "No offense, Ms. Sizemore, but you are full of shit."

She reached for her bag and rose to her feet. "We'll come back to this. Right now I have a client coming and I have to run."

# 18

"Who asked you?" I called after her. The rejoinder was not only weak, but she'd already left by the time I delivered it.

I turned and peered out the window, catching sight of her as she retreated down my walk. She waved over her shoulder, confident she was having the final word. Well, wasn't I cranky and out of sorts? I thought therapists were supposed to keep their opinions to themselves. I wasn't even a client and there she was challenging my view of Pete's character when I'd known the man for *years*. I was the one who'd witnessed his moral failings. The idea that I was going to come along in the wake of his death and tidy up his unfinished business struck me as ludicrous. What especially annoyed me was the fact that I'd already been planning to unearth the remaining women on the list and see what they could tell me. In Taryn Sizemore's analysis, that was tantamount to taking on Pete's investigation, which was certainly not the case. I had work of my own to do. Sort of.

# X

I had intended to file a police report about the break-in, but what was the point? I could picture writing out my complaint about an intruder unraveling a roll of toilet paper. This would not be compelling to officers whose sworn duty was to battle crime in our fair city. I might have legitimate grounds, but in the larger scheme of things, this was chickenshit. I did a circuit of the inner and outer offices, testing locks and righting the remaining disorder Ned had created. Took all of three minutes. I had no proof it was him in any event, so scratch that idea.

I returned to my office proper, and I'd no more than crossed the threshold when I stopped in my tracks.

Where was the banker's box with the X on the lid?

I stared at the floor as though I'd already registered the empty spot. The box should have been sitting near the door where I'd left it, but there was no sign of it. I knew I'd brought the box to work with me. I'd removed the padded mailer from its hiding place, crammed the pouch into my floor safe, and set the box aside. I'd meant to go through the contents a second time, but now it was gone. I felt a sharp pang of regret, grasping at alternative explanations. I hadn't left it at home, had I? I remembered toting it to the car and then bringing it into the office.

Feeling anxious, I pulled back the carpet, ran the combination to the safe, and opened it. The manila mailing pouch was still there. I pulled it out, opened it, and eyed the contents. Everything was accounted for. I returned the pouch, then closed and locked the safe. I made another circuit of the bungalow, knowing I wouldn't find what I was looking for. I sat down at my desk and stared out the window, trying to come up with an explanation other than the certain knowledge that someone had stolen it. "Someone" being Ned Lowe.

I knew my current obsession was an emotional state called "psychological assessment"—an endless revisiting of events in hopes the outcome would change. I stopped myself. It was done. The box was gone. If I'd failed to find something critical, it was too late. Really, *had* I left the box in the trunk of my car? I didn't think so.

*Time to get practical,* I thought. Instead of fretting about what I didn't have, maybe it was time to go back to what I had. I pulled out the list of names. Of the six, the last two women were still unaccounted for. I picked up the handset, dialed directory assistance in Tucson, Arizona, and asked for listings for last name, Macy. There were twenty-one of them. I didn't think the operator would have the patience to read all of them out to me one by one, so I asked for the first ten with the accompanying numbers, which I jotted on an index card: Andrew, Christine, Douglas, E. (probably Emily or Ellen), Everett P. . . . On and on it went.

I thanked her profusely and depressed the plunger, determined to launch into the first batch before I lost heart. I wasn't quite sure of my approach. I could, of course, simply call and ask for Janet by name, hoping for the best, but I felt I should also be prepared to explain the reason I was asking for her. I could feel myself waffle. Making cold calls is time-consuming and tedious, and the longer I put it off, the more tempting it would be to avoid the chore altogether.

I checked the ten numbers and dialed the first. Six minutes later, I'd left messages on four answering machines, two numbers were disconnects, two parties hadn't answered, and one didn't know a Janet Macy. The effort had been pointless, but at least it hadn't taken long. As I dialed the last number, I made up my mind that this was it for the day.

When a woman picked up, I said, "I'm sorry to bother you, but I'm calling from Santa Teresa, California, trying to track down a Janet Macy. Is this the correct number for her?"

"Not anymore," she said. She sounded elderly, tired, and perturbed.

"Ah. But this was her number at one time?"

"Yes, it was."

"Do you have her new number?"

"There's no new number as far as I know. Janet left some time ago, and I haven't heard from her. I can't say it surprises me. She was never good about things like that. Are you a friend?"

"Actually, I'm not. A mutual acquaintance is hoping to locate her, and I offered to help." This explanation made no particular sense, and if the woman pressed me, I'd be at a loss to elaborate. "Are you her mother?"

"I am. Her dad passed a year ago."

"I'm sorry to hear that."

"Took him long enough."

"That must have been difficult," I said.

She said, "Well."

I was afraid she'd launch into his medical history, so I moved right along. "Do you remember when you last spoke to Janet?"

"Let me think about that now. It must have been three years ago this spring. She wanted to pursue a modeling career in New York City. I was against the whole idea. I told her she was too young and inexperienced, but she was bullheaded and wouldn't listen. She picked that up from her dad, if you want to know the truth. A very unattractive character trait."

"How old was she?"

"That's just it. She was not quite sixteen and she couldn't very well leave without my permission. She had no money, for one thing, and she didn't drive. She was still in high school. She was never a good student anyway, so it's no big loss there."

"If she was broke and didn't drive, how did she intend to get to New York?"

"Greyhound bus, I imagine. She might have had enough for a one-way ticket. It's possible she hitchhiked, which she knew I was opposed to."

"Did she know anybody in the city?"

"She did. She met this photographer who thought she had promise. He worked for a big modeling agency and he was helping her put together a portfolio. I didn't think anything would come of it and I didn't appreciate her taking off without a word."

"As young as she was, did you report her as missing?"

"Of course I did. Regardless of her opinion, I'm still her mother. I went down to the police station and talked to someone. He took the information, but didn't seem that interested."

"Was there any follow-up?"

"Not that I'm aware. I filed a report, but nothing's come of it. The police officer was nice about it. He said it was probably nothing to worry about and I should be sure to let him know if I heard from her, which I have not. What did you want with her?"

"Just making sure she's okay, I guess."

"No way to know how she is unless she calls me one of these days. I look for her picture in the fashion magazines, but I haven't seen her yet. I always told her hard work was required if you wanted to be a success. I guess she's finding that out."

"I suppose she is," I said. "Well, I thank you for your time. I appreciate your courtesy."

"You're entirely welcome."

I made a note beside the number. I drew a line under her name. For some reason Pete had thought she was of interest, but I didn't see a link.

The phone rang. I picked up the handset, saying, "Millhone Investigations."

"Kinsey? Spencer Nash. I've got a plane to catch, but I thought I'd give you an update on your pal Satterfield. You have a sec?"

"Absolutely. What now?"

"I got word last night he was huddled with a gal in a bar off Dave Levine Street. Place called Lou's. The two had their heads together and the talk was intense. No description of the woman, but it could have been your Hallie Bettancourt. Timing's right if she found him on the basis of information you provided her."

"Nice. I'd about given up on her."

"Well, don't give up yet, because there's more. For the past twenty minutes, Satterfield's been sitting in a limousine idling outside the

Santa Teresa Shores Hotel. You know the area where the shuttle to LAX picks up?"

"Sure."

"Well, the next run leaves at three twenty this afternoon. If she's the one he's waiting for, you've got time enough to get down here. Long shot, but I'm giving you the heads-up. You want to check it out, she's yours."

"Why are you suddenly so interested?"

"I mentioned your encounter with her to a pal in vice. Hallie he doesn't care about, but he thinks Satterfield is promising. He likes the idea of grooming him as a confidential informant."

"In what context?"

"Money laundering's my guess. At Lompoc, he was tight with guys who run a gambling syndicate on the outside."

"I won't be stepping on toes?"

"Get results and I'll take care of any flack you generate."

"Where are you calling from?"

"Lobby at the Shores, which is where I sign off. I'd pursue this myself, but I'm out of here."

"How long?"

"Two days max. I'll call when I get back. Meantime, you interested?"

"I'm on it."

"Great." He clicked off.

I grabbed my shoulder bag, locked the office, scooted out to the Honda, and slid under the wheel. As I backed out of the drive, I glanced at the dashboard and realized I'd committed the two cardinal sins in the catechism of a private eye:

1. Never allow your car to get low on gas. I was looking at a third of a tank at best. Now I was in a hurry and had no time to top it off.
2. Never pass up a chance to pee.

I traveled surface streets. The Shores was on Cabana Boulevard across the street from the turnaround point on my usual morning jog. The location must have seemed perfect to tourists who flocked to our city in June and July, not realizing we'd be socked in by a marine layer that blocked the sun and chilled the summer air. The hotel itself had seen better days. Age and the sea damp had taken their toll, though the facility still played host to small conventions.

I hadn't had a chance to tell Nash that Christian's mother, Geraldine, worked for Prestige Transportation Services Inc. I had no doubt she was at the wheel of the limousine, decked out in her stern black suit, white shirt, and black bow tie. I couldn't imagine why she'd ferried him to a bus stop unless it was a habit left over from his grade school days when his morning dawdling required her to load him in the car and drive him to prevent his being late.

I turned left at Cabana and followed the boulevard as it paralleled the beach. The entrance to the Shores was on a small street that ran behind the hotel. An adjacent parking lot allowed guests the use of valet services. A few hundred yards to the left, a passenger pickup area was designated for the airport shuttle that made the round-trip to Los Angeles eight times a day.

Across the street, the limousine was idling at a length of curb painted red, despite numerous posted signs that forbade parking, stopping, and loitering. One of the Shores' minivans was parked directly behind the limousine in a spot designated for passenger loading and unloading. I pulled the Honda to the curb behind the minivan, which allowed me a modicum of cover while I kept the stretch in view. Rear and side windows were heavily tinted, creating the impression that someone famous was currently on board. On the street, people would turn and stare, wondering who it was. I saw the front driver's-side window descend. The driver reached out to adjust the side-view mirror. In the convex oval, I saw a portion of Geraldine's face reflected before she withdrew her arm and closed the window.

I considered scurrying into the hotel lobby in search of the ladies' room, but worried the limousine would take off while I was gone. Instead, I unearthed my index cards and recorded the content of Detective Nash's phone call and the bits of information I'd gleaned. I wondered who at the STPD hoped to cultivate Christian as a source. Cheney had worked vice once upon a time, but he was now assigned to homicide. Next time I saw him, I'd quiz him on the subject.

I tapped my pen against my lower lip. If Christian was taking the Airbus to LAX, why hadn't his mother simply dropped him off and reported for work? Maybe her intent was to drive him the hundred-plus miles, in which case, why was she still sitting there with the engine running? I checked my rearview mirror.

On the street behind me, as though on cue, a beige VW Bug appeared, slowed, and turned right into the hotel drive. The Shores had provided a portico to shelter guests from the sort of inclement weather we hadn't seen for years. I noted the woman at the wheel, returned my attention to my notes, and then did a double take.

I could have sworn I'd caught sight of Kim Bass, the receptionist at Montebello Luxury Properties. I leaned forward, hoping to bring her into focus as she got out of the car. Most of what I saw were the masses of hair and her bare, deeply tanned arms. She opened the rear car door and reached into the back seat for her luggage. The abundance of red hair, white silk blouse, short black skirt, trim hips. Her calves looked muscular above her very high black patent leather heels. Kim Bass in the flesh. She hauled out her overnight case and then turned to the parking valet, who handed her a ticket. She proceeded to the outside desk, heels clicking audibly on the pavement. She chatted with a fellow in uniform who was apparently in charge of the valet services. Much nodding and gesturing, with questions and answers that seemed to satisfy both. He handed her a receipt. She slid the stub into her purse, picked up her overnight bag, and crossed the street, moving in my direction.

Geraldine was already out of the limousine. I leaned down and busied myself with the floor mat, averting my face on the off chance Kim would turn to look. By the time I peered over the dashboard, Geraldine had opened the rear passenger-side door. Kim Bass handed her the overnight case and slipped into the backseat. I watched Geraldine pass the overnight case into the vehicle after her. She closed the car door and returned to the driver's seat.

I turned the ignition key and waited briefly until the stretch limousine pulled into the street and took a slow and stately right-hand turn. The stoplight changed from red to green and the limousine turned left. I had time enough to ease into the street and turn left on Cabana before the light turned red again. There was sufficient traffic on Cabana that my Honda wasn't conspicuous. Not that anyone would notice it in any event. I allowed a two-car margin, keeping a close watch on the limousine ahead. I concentrated on careful driving while my brain buzzed with this latest revelation. Christian Satterfield and Kim Bass? What was that about? If I'd expected to see him with anyone, it was his faux bio-mom: professional liar Hallie Bettancourt. Detective Nash had said just enough to allow me hope of running into her again.

What was Kim Bass doing in the car with him? As an employee of Montebello Luxury Properties, she'd certainly know the combination to the lockbox at the Clipper estate. She had to be the confederate who'd given Hallie access the night I met with her. I wondered what Kim thought when I appeared at the office, asking for the agent who represented the estate. Must have put her in a white-hot sweat. No wonder she'd abandoned her desk by the time I left.

Ahead of me, the limousine sailed on, passing the Santa Teresa Bird Refuge on our left. I saw the brake lights flash briefly as the vehicle approached the southbound freeway on-ramp and slowed in preparation for merging.

Shit.

While I'd flirted with the notion that Christian's mom was driving him to the Los Angeles International Airport, I'd hoped I was wrong. I took another anxious peek at my gas gauge. I was probably okay for the drive, but the bladder issue was more pressing, so to speak. The limo cruised south at a leisurely pace. Most commercial drivers are scrupulous about traffic laws, and Geraldine was no exception. That's because a ticket for a moving violation could result in her getting her ass fired.

We passed the off-ramps for Cottonwood, Perdido, Olvidado, and points beyond. I devoted thirty-two seconds to the idea of abandoning the pursuit, but I knew better. I pictured myself presenting Detective Nash with some startling revelation about where the pair was headed and what they were up to. Ego puffery will get you into trouble every time, but what else was I to do? It was 1:15. There were few cars on the road at this hour and the day was clear. No accidents. No construction delays. I reserved the right to cut out, turn around, and drive home. In the meantime, I kept my eyes pinned to the rear end of the stretch—close enough, but not too close.

From the outskirts of Santa Teresa to the San Fernando Valley, travel time was approximately sixty minutes. When the southbound 405 loomed into view, Geraldine eased into the right-hand lane and I followed suit. This route was still consistent with a trip to LAX, which suggested another set of problems. What if the pair boarded a domestic flight to who-knows-where? I was capable of impulse travel, but it ran contrary to my conservative nature. Determining where they were headed would be tricky enough. The purchase of same-day plane tickets would cost an arm and a leg, even assuming there were seats available. It would also be an extremely risky move if I had to slow-walk, single-file, onto an airplane where seated passengers had nothing better to do than watch those still traipsing down the aisle. While Christian didn't know me by sight, Kim Bass did. If their flight was international, I had no hope of pursuing them.

I considered surrendering to the Zen of "living in the moment," but

I knew my bladder would be right there living in the moment with me and clamoring for relief. To distract myself, I thought about all the cusswords I knew and arranged them in alphabetical order.

Once we merged onto the southbound 405, traffic picked up. The freeway climbed the hill that crosses a stretch of the Santa Monica Mountains. To my relief, as we neared Sunset Boulevard, the limousine eased into the right lane again and exited. I was by now six cars back, but I could see the long black stretch slide through the green light and turn left onto Sunset. I got caught at the same light, and by the time I made the turn, the limo was nowhere in sight.

Sunset Boulevard, eastbound, rolls out in a series of blind curves, each concealing the fast-moving vehicles ahead. I had to take it on faith that the limousine would remain steady on its course. If Geraldine turned off on one of the intervening side streets, I could easily miss the maneuver altogether.

I sped up, keeping an eye out for the Beverly Hills Police. It was helpful that everyone else on Sunset was barreling along at the same merry clip. Within a mile, I caught sight of the limousine again. I closed the gap and stayed within a four-car range from that point on. Mansions and gated homes materialized on either side of Sunset. At the intersection of Sunset and Beverly Glen, Geraldine turned right. I tagged along as far as Wilshire Boulevard and turned left in concert with the limousine, still keeping a few cars back. We proceeded east and remained on Wilshire when it crossed Santa Monica Boulevard. The limousine passed the Rodeo-Wilshire Hotel, slowed, and turned right at the next corner.

I slowed and waited briefly before I eased forward and turned right as well. Ahead, I spotted the limousine doing a wide turn into a steel-and-glass-covered entrance that ran the width of the hotel. At the mouth of this avenue was a sign:

> *This is a private motor plaza*
> *intended for guests of the Rodeo-Wilshire Hotel.*

*Use is restricted and enforced by municipal code.*
*No public access.*

I pulled forward just far enough to see what was going on. A bell-man in gray livery stepped forward, opened the rear door of the limousine, and offered Kim a hand as she emerged. Christian followed, carrying her overnight bag and a Dopp kit that I assumed contained his personal toiletries. The two disappeared into the lobby through the hotel's revolving glass doors. The bellman shut the door to the limousine, and I watched as it pulled away and exited onto the street at the far end of the passage. *Farewell, Geraldine.* I wondered if she'd be coming back for them. Like a good mom, she'd dropped off the kids for a sleepover date.

I thought it best to park and proceed on foot until I'd settled on a course of action. I found an available meter and parallel-parked my way into a spot. Four quarters, two dimes, and a nickel netted me twenty minutes. I double-timed it back to the hotel, passed the motor plaza, and proceeded to Wilshire Boulevard, where I hung a left and entered the hotel lobby through the main street entrance.

Natural light flooded through tall arched windows overlooking Wilshire on the east side and the motor plaza to the west. Classical music was audible at an almost subliminal level, as though a symphony orchestra was toiling away nearby. At the level of the third floor, I could see a dimly lighted loggia that circled the lobby.

Dead ahead, Kim Bass and Christian Satterfield waited in a short line at the registration desk. So far, neither seemed to sense they were being observed, but I didn't want to push my luck. To my left, directly across from the hotel bar, I spotted a glass-enclosed gift shop that offered newspapers, magazines, books, and a smattering of health and beauty products. I went in, grateful for protective cover.

I picked up a paperback mystery and read the blurbs on the back while I watched through the window. The two approached the desk clerk in his navy blazer and pearl gray vest, signature attire for hotel employees not in livery. Kim was accustomed to interfacing with wealthy real estate clients, so she looked right at home, comfortable with the deference accorded guests in five-star hotels. There was a brief exchange and the desk clerk tapped on his keyboard and then checked his computer screen. He must have found her reservation because the two conferred. She handed over a credit card as the two continued to chat. The young man's manner was polite, polished, and attentive. I watched Christian flick the occasional uneasy glance at his surroundings.

The lobby was elegantly furnished with antique chairs and love seats upholstered in pale green silk and arranged in conversational groupings. An indoor forest of potted palms and ficus trees dotted the vast space, effectively breaking the whole of it into smaller areas. The floral arrangements were oversize and dramatic, exotic blooms mixed with gilded branches in grand proportions.

While Christian bore no visible prison tattoos, he looked scruffy, unshaven, and out of place. His dark, shoulder-length hair had separated into strands, some of which he'd tucked behind his ears. His gray sweatshirt was pulled out of shape, his jeans bagged, and his deck shoes, which he wore with white crew socks, looked like something a bum might pick out of a garbage can. Surely he hadn't robbed banks in such a state of dishevelment. In the black-and-white photograph taken in the courtroom while he was on the witness stand, he'd had an air of easy confidence. Now that was gone. Then again, USP Lompoc wasn't known for its emphasis on charm and social etiquette. Whatever he'd learned there—and I was guessing it was plenty— tasteful dressing wasn't part of the curriculum. He must have been unnerved by the power structure in play. Here class and courtesy dominated and aggression represented no coin at all.

In the gift shop, I moved to the counter and studied a display of candy bars and high-priced fatty snacks. I chose a granola bar and paid for it along with the paperback, barely netting change from my twenty-dollar bill. Meanwhile, at the registration desk, the desk clerk summoned a bellman and handed him a key card. The bellman in turn gestured for Kim and Christian to accompany him. The trio proceeded to a short corridor on the left where I could see a bank of elevators. The trio paused near the last of these, waiting for the doors to open. There was some incidental chitchat, the bellman probably asking if they'd stayed at the Rodeo-Wilshire on prior occasions. I left the shop and crossed the lobby to a spot from which I had a better view.

The second elevator was stationary on the twenty-third floor. As I watched, the number dropped to twenty-two, then twenty-one, while the first elevator moved from the eighth floor to the ninth. The numbers above the third elevator dropped from three to two to one in rapid succession, and then the doors opened. The threesome stepped in, and as soon as the doors closed again, I moved closer. I kept an eye on elevator three as the numbers climbed to the fourteenth floor and hung there. I pictured their exiting, though the stop might have been for another hotel guest. No way to know if the two had separate rooms on the fourteenth floor or if they were sharing. I'd have to find out because the answer to that question seemed loaded with significance. Until a scant two hours before, I'd had no idea the two were even acquainted. Now I was not only curious about their relationship, but puzzled about their connection to Hallie Bettancourt.

I spotted the ladies' room in one corner of the lobby and took the blessed opportunity to avail myself of the facilities. On my return, I headed for the registration desk, noting that the same desk agent who'd assisted Kim and Christian was now free to assist me. His name, according to the tag he wore, was Todd Putman. Up close, he was fresh-faced and had perfect white teeth—always a plus in my book. I asked if a room was available, sheepishly confessing I had no reservation. I half expected an expression of fake regret, followed by a smug announcement that I was shit out of luck. Instead, young Putman couldn't have been more accommodating. I requested a low floor, which I was given, no explanation required. My credit card was swiped and approved without incident. Once I had my key card in hand, he asked if I needed help with my luggage. I thanked him, but said I could handle it myself. I glanced down at the desk, where a series of business cards had been arranged on one of a line of small acrylic easels. On the first of these, I saw the name Bernard Trask, Guest Services Manager. I plucked one from the stack. "May I keep this?"

"Of course. If you need assistance, please feel free to contact Mr. Trask or anyone here at the desk. We'll be happy to be of help."

"Thanks."

I exited the hotel through the Wilshire Boulevard entrance, scurried around the corner, and retrieved my car. The meter was expired and I'd narrowly missed the meter maid, who was five cars behind me with her chalk-laden tire marker. I shifted my perpetually packed overnight bag from the trunk, where I keep it, and moved it to the passenger seat, drove around the block, passed the entrance to the hotel, took the next right-hand turn, and pulled into the motor plaza.

The same bellman in livery who'd assisted Kim stepped forward and opened my car door. "Checking in?"

"I'm registered," I said, holding up my key card, neatly tucked in the little folder with the hotel logo. Todd Putman had written my room number across the front. I grabbed my overnight bag and got out of the car.

The bellman handed me a parking receipt, which I slipped in my shoulder bag. I went into the lobby.

By now I was familiar with the expanses of polished marble flooring and the massive framed mirrors that reflected endless smoky images of those crossing the palace-size Oriental carpeting. I drank in the scent in the air, which was light and flowery. Unwilling to risk an elevator encounter with Kim or Christian, I found the stairwell and climbed the intervening flights to the eighth floor.

# 19

I emerged from the stairwell and did a quick walk-about on the eighth floor. In the transverse corridor where the elevators were located, there was a seating area. In the center was a fruitwood credenza crowned by a large mirror with an upholstered chair on either side. A house phone sat on the credenza along with two potted plants and a row of magazines.

I found room 812 and let myself in. The space was handsomely proportioned and beautifully decorated. The color scheme was neutral—tones of charcoal, beige, and pale gray with textured and small-print fabrics in repetitions of the same shades and hues. King-size bed, desk, large-screen television set, and two comfy reading chairs with a table between. Good lighting, of course. This was a far cry from my usual accommodations, which might best be described as the sort of place where protective footwear is advisable when crossing the room.

My windows overlooked the swimming pool two floors down. The chaise longues were unoccupied. I could see a bar and grill at one end, but it was shuttered.

The directory of hotel services was sitting on the desk. I leafed through, noting that a hotel guest could order up just about anything, including massages, valet services, and babysitters. The indoor pool, the workout facility, and the spa were located on six. I went into the bathroom, which was done up in pale gray marble with thick white towels and an assortment of Acqua di Parma amenities. These people thought of everything. I could learn to live like this.

I pocketed my key card, left my room, and did a full tour of the eighth floor, noting the location of the ice and vending machines. I spotted a door marked STAFF ONLY that I couldn't resist. Slipping through, I found myself in a short hallway that housed two freight elevators, a row of cleaning trolleys, and a room service cart waiting to be returned to the kitchen. A secondary door opened into a linen room, where clean sheets, towels, and an array of pillows were shelved in neat rows, along with bins of mini shampoos, conditioners, body lotions, and soaps. This area was strictly no-frills: bare concrete floors and walls painted the chipped, utilitarian gray of a prison set.

I moved back into the corridor, which was U-shaped with a stairwell at either end. The three guest elevators were in a transverse corridor midway between. I counted twenty-four rooms, some doubtless larger than others, a guess I later confirmed by consulting the fire map I found on the back of the closet door in my room. There was an X indicating my location with an arrow directing me to the stairs. I was warned not to use the elevators in case of fire, so I swore solemnly I would not. I went up to the ninth floor to assure myself that the layouts were identical and then checked the seventh floor as well.

When I returned to 812, I sat down at the desk, dialed an outside line, and left a message for Henry, summing up my unexpected journey to Beverly Hills. I told him I had no idea how long I'd be gone, but that I'd call him when I got home. After I hung up, I opened the desk drawer and found a leather binder that contained hotel stationery of two kinds: sheets of five-by-eight notepaper bearing the hotel logo, and five-by-four note cards, also neatly embossed with the hotel name and logo. There were six matching envelopes.

Toting my key card, I went out into the hall and sat down in one of the two chairs that flanked the credenza. On the off chance a call could be traced to my room, I picked up the house phone and asked the operator to connect me with Christian Satterfield.

When he picked up, I said, "Good afternoon, Mr. Satterfield, and welcome to the Rodeo-Wilshire Hotel." I used my most cultured tone, smiling as I spoke, which I felt would lend warmth and sincerity to what was otherwise bullshit.

"*Who's* this?"

Unruffled, I said, "This is Ms. Calloway in Guest Services. I'm sorry to disturb you, but it would appear that when you checked in, Mr. Putman neglected to enter your credit data in our computer system."

"My room's paid for."

"Wonderful. Lovely. Do you have a card on file?"

"Someone else is paying. I just told you that."

"Oh, I see now. You're traveling with Ms. Bass."

"Why is that any of your business?"

"I wonder if I might ask you to confirm your room number on the fourteenth floor. I show 1424."

"You show wrong."

"Well, I'm not sure what's happened here. According to our records, we have you in 1424."

I waited, hoping he'd correct me. For six seconds, we breathed in each other's ears.

Then Christian Satterfield depressed the plunger, disconnecting us. So much for that plan.

I didn't dare roam the hotel for fear of running into the pair, so I did the next best thing, which was to post the Privacy Please sign on the outside of my door and nap for an hour. When I rose, refreshed, I brushed my teeth and took a shower. This necessitated my donning the only clean pair of underwear I'd brought. I took a few moments to wash out my step-ins, using the hotel shampoo. I rolled them in a towel to squeeze out excess moisture and hung them on the faucet in the bathtub. I can just about promise you Philip Marlowe was never as dainty as I.

At six, I pulled out a hotel note card and matching envelope from the desk drawer and slid both into the outside compartment of my shoulder bag. I added my key card, closed the door behind me, and took the stairs down to the lobby. I was operating on the premise that Christian and Kim would descend to the elegantly appointed bar to have drinks at cocktail hour. I sure as hell would. I returned to the gift shop and bought a magazine to use as a prop. Through the glass, I surveyed the foot traffic in the area outside the shop. No sign of them.

I crossed the lobby to the bar, which was open but dark inside except for a tasteful sconce or two and the lighted rows of liquor bottles behind the bar. No hostess, eight small tables, and a stretch of six leather booths along each side wall. I chose the first booth on the left and slid into the seat, keeping my back to the door. A line of mullioned windows that ran the length of the room afforded me a truncated view of the lobby. Not a perfect vantage point, but it would have to do. A waiter materialized and I asked for a glass of Chardonnay. He handed me a bifold drink menu in which six were listed. I chose the Cakebread, which seemed to meet with his approval, as well it should have at the price listed.

Five minutes later he returned, bearing the wine bottle and an empty glass on a tray. He placed the glass on the table. He held the bottle so I could read the label and then poured half an inch for my approval. I tasted it, nodded, and he filled my glass with a flourish. He set down a bowl of cashews along with the bar tab, which he'd tucked in a leather folio with the hotel logo on the front. As he turned to go, I caught sight of Hallie Bettancourt in the doorway.

I rested my hand lightly against the right side of my face. She took no notice of me. She paused, apparently searching for sight of Kim and Christian. I opened my magazine and leafed through the first twenty pages, which were all glossy advertisements for items I couldn't afford. Out of the corner of my eye, I watched Hallie cross to the bar. She removed her jacket and placed it over the back of a tall swivel stool and then took her seat. Her back was turned, which allowed me to breathe. I kept my focus on the magazine in front of me, knowing if I looked at her fully, she'd sense my gaze and turn to look at me.

The bartender approached and she ordered a drink. Within four minutes, Kim and Christian appeared in the doorway, pausing as she had. When they spotted her, they crossed to the bar and took a stool on either side of her. Kim was wedged into the same tight black skirt, but she'd swapped her white blouse for a silver tunic, over which she wore a long black jacket. Christian looked exactly as he had earlier, except that he'd removed his white crew socks and now wore his deck shoes without.

I was not crazy about this scenario. I didn't dare leave for fear of calling attention to myself. Hiding in plain sight is a nerve-racking game. I sat where I was and willed myself invisible. Casually, I sipped my wine and made a leisurely meal of the salted cashews. I went ahead and signed the bar bill in case I'd need to depart in haste. I added a five-dollar tip to the eighteen-dollar glass of wine, which I charged to my room. The nuts were free as far as I could tell. Under ordinary circumstances, given my cheap nature and limited experience of the finer things in life, I'd have sat and fretted about all the money I was coughing up. On this occasion, I was focused on blending into my surroundings. In point of fact, I had money in the bank, so why sweat it?

Over the next forty-five minutes, time crept by. Pretending to do something when you're doing nothing is an art form in itself. Finally, I saw movement. Hallie gestured for the bill and the bartender slid the leather folio in her direction. She did a quick tabulation, added a tip, and then scribbled her name across the bottom of the check. When she got up, Christian helped her into her jacket. I reached to my left, searching in the depths of my shoulder bag for an important item that required all of my concentration. The three moved past me and ambled out of the bar. I leaned forward and strained, peering out the window to my left as the trio reached the doors that opened onto Wilshire Boulevard. Christian stood back and allowed the two women to walk out ahead of him before he followed.

I waited a beat and eased out of the booth. The bartender was at the far end of the bar, and the waiter was taking an order from a couple across the room. I let my gaze return to the leather folio, still resting on the bar near Hallie's now-empty stool. I could even see the white paper cash register receipt extending from the fold. I picked up my bill in its leather folio and slid out of the booth. I carried it with me, keeping my mind blank, as I moved to the bar. When I reached Hallie's seat, I placed my bill on the bar and picked up hers.

I opened it and let my gaze skim the receipt from top to bottom, where she'd neatly printed her name, Theodora Xanakis. In the line below, she'd scrawled her signature, shortening the Theodora to Teddy. According to the cash register tally, she'd charged two martinis, a cosmopolitan, one glass of champagne (shit, $24 for that?), and two Miller Lites to her room, which was 1825. The total was $134, including a tip in the same amount I'd left. Seemed stingy to me, but then I had a flash of insecurity wondering if I'd overpaid.

I closed the folio and placed it on the bar beside mine, then strolled into the lobby. Glancing upward, I found myself looking at the third-floor loggia, still in shadow. I crossed to the registration desk.

Todd Putman, my favorite hotel desk clerk, was still on duty, and he smiled at my approach. To my astonishment, he remembered me by name. "Good evening, Ms. Millhone. I hope you're enjoying your stay."

"I am, thanks." I leaned my elbows on the counter and lowered my voice. "I have a favor to ask."

"Certainly. How may I help?"

"I just found out my friend Kim Bass is staying here and I'd like to surprise her with a bottle of champagne. I'm worried if I order it through room service, my name will appear on the bill."

"I can handle that for you. I take it you'd like to charge it to your room?"

"I would. I'd also appreciate having it delivered in the next hour so she'll find it waiting when she gets back from dinner. Is that something you can arrange?"

"Absolutely. No problem at all. Do you have a label in mind?"

"Actually, I don't. What would you suggest?"

He reached under the counter and presented me with the same wine list I'd seen in the bar, only his was opened to sparkling wines and champagnes by the bottle. I sincerely hoped my eyes didn't bulge, cartoonlike, when I saw the prices. The least expensive "label" was $175.

He was saying, "The Veuve Clicquot is popular, though my personal preference would be the Taittinger."

"Wonderful. Let's do that," I said. "You promise she won't find out the gift is from me?"

"You have my word. We'll take care of it right away."

"One more question." I pointed upward to the loggia balcony. "What am I looking at up there?"

"The mezzanine, which has conference and banquet rooms. To reach the mezzanine, use one of the guest elevators. You'll see the M before the numbered floors pick up."

"Thanks."

He was already on the phone as I moved away from the desk.

Having seen Kim and Christian depart the hotel in Teddy Xanakis's company, I had no qualms about taking the elevator to the fourteenth floor.

Once in the corridor on fourteen, I paused at the credenza and selected a magazine called *Beverly Hills Exclusive* from those on display. I tucked it under one arm and then did another quick walk-about to verify that the freight elevators on this floor were located where I'd seen them on floors seven, eight, and nine. Sure enough, the Staff Only door opened onto an identical utility area. I closed the door and wandered back to a point in the corridor where I could see anyone who might pass. I leaned against the wall and leafed through my magazine.

Another hotel guest, a gentleman, walked by and flicked a look at me. "Maid's in my room," I remarked.

He nodded and smiled briefly. Maybe the same thing had happened to him.

Ten minutes later, the Staff Only door opened and a room service waiter rolled a cart into the corridor. There was a crisp white cloth over the top and the bottle of Taittinger was nestled in a silver ice bucket, beaded with condensation. Also included were two champagne glasses, a nosegay of yellow roses in a crystal vase, and a cut-glass bowl of fresh strawberries with a side of whipped cream. Nice touch, that, and I would surely be charged accordingly. The waiter checked his order pad and proceeded to a room halfway down the hall. I remained where I was, but kept an eye on him.

He knocked. No answer. He knocked a second time, and after a brief wait, he used his pass key to open the door. He reached down for the door stop that he used to keep the door ajar as he pushed the cart inside.

I took a seat in one of the two comfy chairs provided on either side of the credenza. From my shoulder bag, I removed a pen and the hotel note card, scribbled "With our compliments" on the inside, and dashed off an illegible signature. I slipped the card into the matching envelope along with the business card for the guest services manager I'd collected from the registration desk.

Two minutes later, the room service waiter crossed my field of vision, this time without his cart. I waited until I heard the Staff Only door open and close. Then I tiptoed to the main corridor and looked both ways. No one. I turned left and scampered the short distance to the room he'd just left, which turned out to be 1418. I slid the note under the door.

# X

That done, I had another piece of business to take care of. I went down to the lobby and out to the motor plaza. I fished out my valet parking ticket and passed it to the valet car parker, along with a five-dollar bill. When my car swept into view, I got in and headed for Wilshire Boulevard. Seven blocks later, I found a gas station and filled my tank. I drove back to the hotel motor plaza, where I left my car for the night. My clean underwear was still damp, so I set up the ironing board and iron and sizzled them dry.

# 20

As I had time on my hands, I amused myself by perusing the room service menu, which boasted no food item with a price of less than fifteen bucks. Well, coffee was ten, but that wasn't saying much. I finally scarfed down the granola bar I'd bought earlier, chiding myself once again for my nutritional failings. At 9:00, armed with my paperback and my key card, I sallied forth. I took the elevator down to the mezzanine, where I got off and had a look around. The corridors were dimly lit, and I seemed to have the entire floor to myself. I peered over the balcony railing at the lobby below. While I couldn't see the motor plaza entrance, the doors that opened onto Wilshire Boulevard were easily in view.

Behind me, chairs were arranged in twos and threes outside the empty meeting rooms. I dragged one closer to the railing and sat down. I read my mystery novel, glancing up often for fear I'd miss Teddy, Kim, and Christian passing through the lobby. At 10:45, they returned, not drunk by any stretch, but relaxed and laughing. They paused just inside the revolving doors and there seemed to be a discussion of whether to share a nightcap. I was praying they would not. It was irksome enough that I'd had to hang around waiting as long as I had. Finally, they disappeared from sight, moving toward the lobby elevators.

I scooted over to the elevators on the mezzanine, keeping a close eye on the call pattern. I saw elevator two descend from the fifth floor to the lobby and then watched it go up again, passing the eighth, ninth, and tenth floors and stopping finally on fourteen. I pictured Kim and Christian getting off. When the elevator continued, the numbers climbed as high as eighteen, where it paused again: Teddy Xanakis heading for 1825.

I found the stairwell and climbed to the eighth floor. I sat in my room for an hour and a half. At midnight, I left my book behind, slid my key card into my jeans pocket, and ventured into the hall again. I took the stairs from eight up to fourteen, where I opened the stairwell door and peered into the corridor. That portion of the hallway was empty, but I heard two women chatting from a point around the corner and I withdrew.

I climbed from the fourteenth floor to the eighteenth, where I found the corridor empty. All seemed to be quiet. I walked as far as the corner and ventured a peek. Teddy's room was somewhere along the right-hand side past the transverse corridor where the elevators were located. Beyond that point was the utility hall where I'd seen the freight elevators. To reach her room, I was going to have to brave the journey with no detours, no cover, and no way to disguise my purpose.

I made my mind a blank and began to walk. The wall-to-wall carpeting muffled my footsteps. When I reached Teddy's room, I paused. On the knob, along with the Privacy Please sign, was a breakfast order card. I tilted my head against the door, listening. No sound. Then again, the hotel was sturdily constructed and the walls well-insulated. I looked at the bottom of the door, but there was no way to determine if the lights were on in her room. I lifted the breakfast menu from the knob and read her order. She'd circled French press coffee, fresh-squeezed orange juice, and the fresh fruit plate. Included was her last name, her room number, and the time she wanted breakfast delivered, which was between 8:00 and 8:15. I looped the order form back onto the doorknob.

I went to the fourteenth floor, where I stuck my head into the corridor and listened again. When I determined I was alone, I proceeded to 1418, where I was happy to see Kim Bass had placed her breakfast order on her doorknob, ready to be picked up. Like Teddy, she'd requested room service between 8:00 and 8:15. Diet Pepsi and pancakes.

I still had no idea if she and Christian were sharing a room. If so, she didn't intend to feed him. The Pepsi and pancakes could have been his, but he seemed more like a bacon-and-eggs kind of guy. I took a step back and let my gaze travel the entire corridor, eyeballing the doorknobs. I walked as far as the corner and peered at the rooms on the short arm of the hall. No other breakfast orders.

As I reversed my steps and headed for the stairwell, a desk clerk emerged from the elevator with a sheaf of papers in hand. He turned into the corridor and proceeded down the hall just ahead of me. At certain designated rooms, he stooped and slid a paper under the door; 1418 was one. Had to be the final bill, which suggested Kim would be checking out. I followed him around the corner and watched him slip a copy under two other doors as well. He turned and walked back along the corridor, this time facing me. I smiled politely and murmured "Good evening" as I continued to the stairwell.

As I passed room 1402, I spotted a plastic shoe bag that had been hung on the knob in anticipation of the complimentary shoe shine. The name handwritten across the bottom in marker was Satterfield. I opened the bag and verified the presence of the battered pair of deck shoes he'd been wearing earlier. I was tempted to steal them just for the mischief of it, but decided to behave myself.

I trotted down the stairs to the eighth floor. Safely ensconced in my room, I called the front desk and said I'd be checking out in the morning and I'd appreciate having my bill sent up. Within twenty minutes, it came shooting under the door to me.

In anticipation of the trio's departure, I got up at 7:00, threw my few belongings into my overnight bag, and called downstairs asking to have the Honda brought around. Bag in hand, I took the stairs down and paid my bill. Then I waited just outside in the glass-covered motor plaza until the parking valet pulled up in my car. I tucked my overnight bag in the trunk and handed him a ten-dollar bill to keep it parked close by until I needed it.

As is true of most surveillance work, I spent more time avoiding discovery than I did acquiring information. In point of fact, none of my skulking about was productive until close to 10:00 A.M. I was, by then, sitting in the darkened hotel bar. A discreet signpost near the entranceway indicated that the hours were noon to midnight. I had slipped in, attracting no notice whatever, and settled in a booth with the lobby elevators in full view.

Teddy Xanakis appeared first, decked out in a two-piece red wool suit and a pair of red heels. She was trailed by a small rolling bag that accompanied her like an obedient dog while she approached the front desk and took care of her bill. When Kim and Christian joined her, I could see that Kim wore her black skirt for the second day in a row, this time with a matching black sleeveless top and a wide frothy silver scarf. She was clearly one of those women who knows how to travel with two or three separates she could mix and match, creating countless outfits. Even from a distance, I could see that each coordinating piece could be folded to hankie size and shoved in an overnight case without wrinkling. Christian's ensemble, on the other hand, must be smelling ripe by now.

They entrusted their luggage to the bellman and proceeded to the revolving doors that opened onto Wilshire Boulevard. The three disappeared, leaving me blinking rapidly. I'd pictured them driving to Santa Teresa together, so I was expecting Teddy to have her car brought around. It took me to a count of thirty before I realized they weren't going to reappear. Either her car was being delivered to the front or they were setting off on foot. I slid out of the booth and followed, keeping my pace unhurried so as not to call attention to myself.

I pushed through the revolving glass doors and reached the walk in front of the hotel in time to see them cross Wilshire Boulevard and continue down Rodeo Drive. I walked to the corner, where I was forced to wait for the light to change. Ahead of me, the three didn't seem to be in any hurry, and Teddy's red suit made her easy to track even from a block behind.

I kept to the opposite side of the street and picked up my pace. Street parking was at a premium and there was a surprising amount of traffic, which afforded me a modicum of cover. Most of the buildings were two stories high, constructed shoulder to shoulder on both sides of the street. The walks were lined with tall palm trees. Islands of pink and red geraniums were planted at every corner. The businesses were a blend of pricy designer boutiques, where shoes, handbags, and clothing were tastefully displayed. I saw the occasional beauty salon, an art gallery, and two jewelry stores.

The trio paused and peered into the window of a shop called Pour Les Hommes, which I knew from my high school French class meant "For the Men." So often, foreign-language courses come in handy. Now I wished I'd taken more than the one. I watched them go into the shop and then I checked my immediate surroundings. The store directly behind me was a gourmet food emporium, with a parfumerie on one side and a lingerie shop on the other. I couldn't imagine loitering inconspicuously in any one of the three. There was a bench near the curb and I took a seat. Someone had left a newspaper, so I picked it up and read the front page while I kept an eye on the men's shop across the way. Forty-five minutes passed before the trio emerged. Teddy now toted two oversize shopping bags, with Kim and Christian bringing up the rear with one shopping bag apiece. They walked half a block and went into a place called Epiphany. From where I sat, I wasn't even sure what kind of establishment it was.

I was not unmindful of the possibility that this expedition might turn out to be a wild-goose chase. I'd launched my surveillance on the basis of a phone call, Detective Nash expressing his belief that something was afoot. He'd been under no obligation to keep me in the loop, so I'd leaped at the idea, intrigued by his suggestion that Satterfield had met with a woman who might be Hallie Bettancourt. That this turned out to be Kim Bass instead made the matter all the more interesting.

Surveillance work is a commitment. You're in it for the duration, no ifs, ands, or buts. Half the time there's no payoff at all, but that's not the point. This was information-gathering at its most basic, which is to say, boring beyond belief. By 12:30, I was getting restless. I folded the newspaper and tucked it under my arm and crossed the street, approaching Epiphany at an angle. Once in range, I could see that under the name of the shop, in teeny tiny letters were the words STYLISTS TO THE STARS, REVISE, REFRESH, REFINE. This was some sort of beauty spa. Teddy and Kim must have been having their hair and nails done while I sat cooling my heels, reading the same depressing front section of the *Los Angeles Times*.

I was almost at the entrance when I caught a splash of red. Teddy exited the store, pausing to hold the door for Kim. This allowed me time to pivot to my right and head toward Wilshire Boulevard. If the two women were returning to the hotel, they'd be walking a path identical to mine. I didn't dare turn around to confirm. At the next store I passed, I pushed open the door and went in.

Once inside, I slowed to a stop, shielded by a window display of faceless bone-white mannequins in black leather pants and halters studded with silver nail heads. They stood in various aloof postures that conveyed boredom and superiority, as well they should have, as they were decked out in thousands of dollars' worth of Italian designer garments.

Outside, Teddy and Kim sauntered by with Christian tagging behind. As he passed, he stole a look at himself in the glass. I was tucked inside, a good ten feet away, and his attention was focused on his reflection in the plate glass window. He stared at himself while I took in the sight of him as well. He still wore jeans, but this pair was beautifully cut. Instead of the stretched-out gray sweatshirt he'd worn on arrival, he now wore a tan poplin sport coat over a casual pin-striped dress shirt with the collar open. The cut of the sport coat was flattering, nipped in at the waist and perfect across his shoulders.

Teddy had apparently become aware that Christian had hung back. She appeared beside him and tucked her hand through the crook of his arm in a gesture that was both possessive and companionable. The two moved out of visual range while I was still reacting to the indelible image of the parolee transformed. Not only was he clean-shaven, but his hair had been cut and styled. Gone were the dark clumps he'd sported before. Now the strands appeared silken, laced with blond strands that hinted that he'd just returned from a Caribbean cruise, an illusion further enhanced by his visible tan. More remarkable to my way of thinking was the shift in his bearing. Instead of looking ill at ease and out of place, he carried himself like a man who was just figuring out how good-looking he was.

# 21

I arrived in Santa Teresa at 3:15 Thursday afternoon and found a rare parking spot within steps of my studio apartment. Parking in the neighborhood had become a major pain in the ass. Henry, in shorts and a T-shirt, was at the curb on his hands and knees with his butt in the air. Beside him was the rectangle of concrete that formed the cap for the recessed city water meter. He'd used a screwdriver to lift the cover, which he'd set to one side. He picked up his flashlight and directed the beam at the face of the meter. He recorded the numbers on a scratch pad and then settled the cover into place. He stood and dusted off his bare knees. "This was McClaskey's suggestion, and I thought the idea was sound. He told me to check the last few water bills for the billing date to determine when the meter reader comes by from month to month. Turns out it's the twenty-sixth, so now I know my end date. By keeping track of the running numbers, I can monitor my usage."

"How often do you have to take a reading?"

"Twice a day. When I water the shrubs by hand, I can check before and after to see how many HCFs it takes."

"I love how casually you toss the terms around. What's an HCF?"

"Hundred cubic feet. A cubic foot is seven hundred and forty gallons. Since I have two residential structures on the property, once rationing takes effect, I'd be allowed more than someone with a single-family dwelling, like Joseph and Edna next door. They'd probably be allocated four HCFs where I get five."

"So five times seven hundred and forty gallons is . . ."

"Three thousand seven hundred gallons."

"Really? We use thirty-seven hundred gallons of water a month? Doing what?"

"That's the question, isn't it? The low-flow toilets use one-point-six gallons. My dishwasher's an older model, so it uses six gallons per cycle. The newer ones use half that amount. Instead of running the dishwasher, McClaskey recommends switching to paper plates and plastic utensils and doing the rest by hand. You might adopt the same plan. Think of all the water you'd save."

"I don't have a dishwasher."

"Oh. That's true, now you mention it. Why didn't I give you one?"

"I wasn't interested."

"What about your washing machine?"

"I only run full loads, and that's once every two weeks. People complain because I wear the same outfit six days in a row."

"Very sensible of you."

"Thanks. What's your average water use?" I asked, and then interrupted my own chain of thought. "I can't believe we're seriously discussing this."

"It's high time. Average usage is next on my list. I'll sit down and compare water bills for the past four months with the same four months last year."

"Well, I admire your spirit, but don't you think your obsession is premature? So far, there's no water rationing in effect."

"I think of this as the fact-finding phase. Once I have my spread-sheet in place, I'll move on to implementation."

"I've never known you to be so *zealous.*"

"This drought's serious business. Anyway, enough on the subject. How was your trip to Beverly Hills?"

"Expensive. I haven't added it all up yet because I don't want to know." I did a brief recap of events, which sounded even more point-less in the telling than it had at the time.

"Theodora Xanakis? I know the name, but I can't remember the context."

"Doesn't ring a bell with me. Maybe Detective Nash will know. Not Hallie Bettancourt, that's for sure."

I went on to tell him about my office intruder, the missing box, and the arrival of Taryn Sizemore with all the information she'd laid on me. By the time I'd rounded out the story, the two of us had ambled into Henry's kitchen, and next thing I knew, I had a glass of wine in hand and he was busy fixing supper while he sipped his Black Jack over ice.

I was home by 8:30 and went to bed shortly afterward.


Let's skip the talk about my morning jog, which felt the same as it al-ways did. Good for me, but b-o-r-i-n-g. I showered, ate breakfast, and went into the office, where I spent the morning on the phone, first making an appointment with an S.O.S. technician to come out and talk about installing an alarm system, then talking to the guy who owns the bungalows to ask for his approval. He balked until I said I'd pay for it myself. I pointed out that if I should move, the system would stay in place, providing improved security for anyone who occupied the office after me. He was on board the minute he realized he wouldn't have to pony up a dime.

The S.O.S. technician arrived at one o'clock to give me an estimate. Cullen, last name unspecified, was young and earnest and seemed to take his job seriously. He devoted fifteen minutes to "reviewing the site," though I'm sure he could have designed the whole system in the time it took him to scratch his chin, measure, make notes, and ponder the possibilities. My office is modest and I knew the wiring wasn't complicated. He filled out the paperwork and gave me a bid for putting contact wires on all the windows and doors, installing two alarm panels, and the monthly monitoring. To his estimate, I added another smoke detector, a motion detector, a glass-break detector, a radon detector, a carbon monoxide detector, and a couple of passive infrared beams for good measure. I noticed he didn't argue about the redundancies and add-ons, which made me wonder if he was salaried or working on straight commission.

We scheduled the installation for the following Tuesday at noon, and he made a point of mentioning the fact that payment in full was due on completion. There was something obnoxious about his saying so, as though I might be the type who'd hold out on him. I made a mental note to pop by the bank and move sufficient funds into my checking account to cover the expense. Now that I was accustomed to spending money, there didn't seem to be an end in sight. This is how lottery winners end up broke. He did say he knew a locksmith who could rekey my door locks at the same time.

Late in the afternoon, I called Ruthie. "Drinks and dinner at Rosie's tonight?"

"What time?"

"How about six o'clock?"

"Sounds good. What's the occasion?"

"There isn't one. I heard a story I'd like confirmed."

"Hope it's juicy."

"We'll see about that," I said.


At five, I locked the office and I was on my way out to the car when I turned around and went back. I let myself in, set my shoulder bag on the desk, and peeled back a corner of the wall-to-wall carpet. I opened my floor safe and pulled out the mailing pouch, locked the safe again, then headed for home.

I drove through town, taking State all the way down to Cabana Boulevard, where I turned right. It was one of those perfect Santa Teresa days I sometimes take for granted. The temperature was in the mid-sixties with clear skies, sunshine, and a light breeze. Nearing Bay, I got caught at the traffic light, and when I glanced to my right, I spotted Edna and Joseph toddling in my direction, he in his wheelchair, she pushing from behind. He had a basket affixed to the front of his chair and he was using it to tote a number of bulging plastic bags. I was momentarily annoyed that Edna intended to impose on Henry to ferry her back and forth on her weekly shopping trips when Joseph was more capable than he let on.

I kept an idle eye on them as I waited for the light to change. Edna and Joseph were apparently unaware of my observation. I watched her slow and then stop as they reached the motel trash bins set out at the curb. Joseph pulled himself upright, and while she lifted the lid, he removed one plastic bag from his basket and tossed it in. He resumed his seat. She pushed his wheelchair as far as the next bin, where the two of them did it again. The entire transaction took fewer than five seconds, so smoothly accomplished I thought I must be seeing things. Could they possibly be tossing their garbage in other people's bins?

The light changed and I turned right onto Bay and then left on Albanil. Trash bins up and down the block had been moved to the curb, including the two Henry used. There was no bin in front of the Shallenbargers' house, and now that I thought about it, I couldn't remember seeing a bin out on the curb since the Adelsons had moved. I was still shaking my head when I pulled into Henry's driveway and parked. Should I mention it to him? He'd as good as adopted them and I knew he'd be reluctant—if not wholly unwilling—to hear petty complaints about the pair.

Their actions bugged me nonetheless. Parceling trash into other people's bins, while questionable, doesn't constitute a crime. If Edna and Joseph chose to sidestep a bill from the waste management company, it was no skin off my nose. I put their cost-cutting measure in the same category as snitching discount coupons from someone else's mailbox. I wouldn't have done it myself, but as violations go, it wasn't that big a deal.

I should have reminded myself that people willing to cheat a little bit are generally dishonest throughout.

Once home, I turned on the lights and scanned the living room for a place to hide the mailer. I had no reason to believe Ned Lowe knew where I lived, but he'd managed to find my office, so why not my home address? I stood in the middle of the room and let my gaze move from surface to surface. All the possibilities seemed obvious. I considered locking the package in the trunk of my car, but all he'd have to do then was bash out a window, reach in, and open a door, which would give him access to the lever that opened the trunk.

I made a detour into Henry's garage, where I placed the mailer on the shelf where he stores empty paint cans before he drops them off at the nearest hazardous waste collection point.

When I walked into Rosie's, I headed for an empty four-top, where I placed my shoulder bag, claiming occupancy on the off chance a flock of hard-partying patrons suddenly rushed the place. William was tending bar in a white dress shirt, red bow tie, black dress pants, and a jaunty pair of red suspenders.

"Well, look at you," I said. "I don't think I've ever seen you decked out in such finery."

"No point in getting complacent at my age. I've worn the same three-piece suit for close to fifty years. Not that it's anything to be embarrassed about. The quality's excellent and the tailor swore it would wear like iron, but a change now and then is good. The bow tie I knotted myself. I don't believe in clip-ons, do you?"

"Definitely not."

He reached under the counter and came up with a corksrew and a bottle of Chardonnay sealed with an actual cork. "I bought this for you. I know those screw-top wines make your lips purse. May I pour you a glass?"

"I would love it. Thanks so much."

"I'll bring it to the table. Are you on your own?"

"Ruthie's coming in and we'll have supper in a bit. Is Rosie cooking anything we should be warned about in advance?"

His expression showed skepticism. "Carp fillets with sauerkraut, which is actually better than it sounds. She's making quark, but that won't be ready for another day." He held up a hand to forestall my question. "Curdled whole milk with the whey drained away."

"Yum."

By the time Ruthie appeared, he'd brought a generous pour of Chardonnay for me and an icy vodka martini for her.

She took a sip and I watched a shiver run down her spine. "I can't believe you don't drink these," she said.

"No, thanks. Any sign of your intruder?"

"He's out of luck. I had the locks changed again and my alarm system went in today. I feel better having all those buttons to push." She propped her chin on her fist. "So what's the story you want confirmed? I hate when you say things like that without filling me in."

I gave her a synopsis of Taryn Sizemore's tale about Morley Shine breaking into her psychiatrist's office and stealing enough personal data to blow her lawsuit out of the water. I didn't go into detail about the facts themselves, just the manner in which Morley acquired them. "Is the story true?"

Ruthie held up a hand. "Gospel. Morley confessed to Pete one night when he was in his cups. He considered it a coup, and Pete said he was positively gleeful about it, chortling on at length. He compared the break-in to Watergate, only without the political fallout. Ha. Ha. Ha. What a card our Morley was."

"Did Ruffner know what Morley did?"

"He made a point of not probing too deeply. He was happy to have the leverage and didn't much care how it fell into his hands. Pete was horrified, of course, though he didn't let Morley know how upset he was. I urged him to tell Ben, but Pete was unsure and he agonized for weeks."

"What was the debate?"

"He knew he was skating on thin ice. Ben and Morley had been partners for fifteen years and fast friends for years before that. Pete was low man on the totem pole and hardly a pal to either one. He was well-trained—Ben made sure of that—but he didn't have the social skills to pick up jobs on his own. They'd parcel out the odd assignments, but he was there on sufferance, especially where Ben was concerned. Pete and Morley got along okay, until this came up."

"So in the end, he decided to tell Ben."

"For better or for worse. You know what a stickler Ben was for the rules. What Morley did was a criminal offense, which put Ben in jeopardy and the agency at risk. But what bothered Pete as much as anything was the effect on the woman who filed the suit. Ned's attorney presented her as a gold digger out for as much as she could get. His problem was he didn't have anything to use against her in court. Then Morley provided Ruffner with all the ammunition he needed. Meanwhile, Pete came to believe Ned Lowe was dangerous and Byrd-Shine, in essence, had given him carte blanche."

"Why didn't you tell me about this?"

"I just did."

"Before now. Why haven't you ever said anything?"

"You worked for the agency. I assumed you knew. I'm surprised Ben didn't take you into his confidence."

"Not a word. It must have come close to the end of my tenure with them. I'm guessing Ben was too appalled to admit Morley's breach. By the time the agency broke up, I was out in an office of my own. There weren't any rumors around town about why they broke up."

"Weird, since that's all Pete and I talked about. He ended up the bad guy, and that bewildered him. He hadn't *done* anything, you know? Morley broke the law and Pete took the blame. I'm sure if you and I had known each other back then, we'd have chewed the subject to death."

"Wonder why Pete never mentioned it to me."

She studied me. "He was under the impression you had no use for him."

"Well, that's not true," I said. "I'll admit I disagreed with some of what he did."

"Oh, come off it. You didn't 'disagree.' You disapproved."

"Okay, fine. Maybe I did, but I never let on. What he did was his business. I kept my personal views to myself."

"No, you *didn't*. Pete knew exactly what you thought of him."

"He did?"

"Kinsey, the man wasn't an idiot. You're not that good at covering."

"But he was always so nice to me."

"Because he *liked* you. He thought the world of you, the same way Ben did."

I put my elbows on the table and put my hands over my eyes, saying, "This is not good. I truly had no idea my opinion of him was so obvious."

"Too late to worry about it now," she said.

I shook my head, saying, "Shit."

# 22

I thought about Pete as I walked the half block home. Sometimes I turn to Henry for counsel and advice, but not in this case. I'd erred, and it was up to me to make amends. I'd misjudged Pete Wolinsky; not entirely, but in certain essentials. Even then, if you'd asked me what sort of man he was, I'd have said he was a crook, someone who chose self-interest over honesty and never hesitated to coax a few bucks from a deal if he could manage it. I did take note that even as I was exonerating him, I continued to condemn him in equal measure, proof positive that our prejudices are nearly impossible to scotch.

The best I could manage for the moment was to concede he could be guilty of bad deeds and still retain a basic goodness at the core. Pete had done what he thought was right, which was to tell Ben Byrd that Morley was corrupt. The Byrd-Shine agency was dissolved, and while Ben never spoke to Morley again, he'd damned Pete in the bargain. I'd damned him as well, thinking myself clever for not revealing my true opinion. All the time Pete knew what I thought of him and yet he'd borne my disdain without complaint. Ruthie, too, had been aware of my scorn, and while she'd challenged my views, she'd continued to offer me her friendship. I was going to have to do something, wasn't I? As Taryn Sizemore predicted, I now felt compelled to pick up where Pete left off and finish the job for him.

And what was that job? Pete was in possession of the mailing pouch, which he'd gone to some lengths to conceal. As nearly as I could tell, the contents were intended for Lenore's daughter, and I was curious why he hadn't handed them over to her. I was hesitant to complete delivery until I understood what was going on. Twenty-eight years had passed, and April would want to know what the delay was about. What was I supposed to tell her when I had no clue? I'd have to drive to Burning Oaks and unearth the story before I did anything else.

I'd just made an impromptu trip to Beverly Hills and the last thing I wanted to do was hit the road again, but if Pete had driven to Burning Oaks, I'd have to do the same. While I continued to whine internally, I was outwardly preparing for the inevitable. I hauled out my map of California, spread it on my kitchen counter, and decided on a route. This was a two-hour drive at best on winding back roads, which were my only choice. I'd take the 101 south as far as the 150 and then head east. Where the 150 met Highway 33, I'd drive north and east on an irregular path that would deposit me in Burning Oaks.

I retrieved my overnight case from the car and replenished my supply of sundries. This time I packed a change of clothes, including three pairs of underpants and the oversize T-shirt I wear as a "negligee." I added two paperback novels and a hundred-watt lightbulb. I was prepared for anything. Before I went to bed, I reclaimed the mailing pouch from its hiding place in Henry's garage.

I still carried the grid Pete had constructed with its alphanumerical code. The paper was in my shoulder bag along with Henry's translation, which had netted me the list of six women's names. Taryn Sizemore I knew. In addition to Lenore Redfern's name, there was also

Shirley Ann Kastle's, she being his former high school sweetheart. Both were from Burning Oaks. The three remaining names would have to wait. Phyllis Joplin I knew about, which left Susan Telford and Janet Macy. I'd tend to them when I got back.

In the morning, I slipped a note under Henry's door before I hopped in my car. It was by then 7:45 and I'd been through my usual exercise, shower, and breakfast routine. On the way out of town, I filled the tank with gas and then headed south, overnight bag on the passenger seat. I didn't expect to be gone long enough to utilize the change of clothes, but I didn't want to be caught short.

During the early portion of the drive, I was traversing the Los Padres National Forest, which covers 175 million acres, spread out over 220 miles south to north. The road I was on climbed from sea level to an altitude of 7,000 feet. To speak of the national "forest" doesn't nearly convey the reality of the land, which is mountainous and barren, with no trees at all in this portion of the interior.

On either side of the road, I could see wrinkled stretches of uninhabitable hills where the chaparral formed a low, shaggy carpet of dry brown. Spring might be whispering along the contours, but without water there was very little green. Pockets of wildflowers appeared here and there, but the dominant color palette was a muted gray, dull pewter, and dusty beige.

The descent from the summit carried me into the westernmost reaches of the central valley. The big draw in the area was its recreational waterway, which had all but disappeared with the onset of the drought. All I saw were the wooden docks that extended onto an apron of cracked mud. Where the waters had receded, the metal dome of a partially submerged car sat like an island, baking in the sun. Beyond, in the empty channel that had once carried a tributary, there was only more mud and long sloping banks of rock, exposed now after years of being hidden. Wide flat fields, bordered by distant mountains, awaited spring planting. The drought had tapped out all the natural springs, and the man-made irrigation systems were silent. I missed the reassuring *fft-fft-fft* of water cannons firing tracers out over newly sown fields.

I barreled along a straightaway where a series of signs boasted of asparagus, peppers, sunflowers, and almonds for sale. All of the farm stands were closed except one. The small wooden structure was set up on the right side of the road, a hinged panel lowered to form a shelf piled high with asparagus spears bundled with fat red rubber bands.

A middle-aged woman sat in a metal folding chair. Beside her, on the dusty berm, an old man stood holding a hand-lettered sign. As I passed, he turned his face and followed me with his gaze. I missed the message, but I could see that his arms trembled from his efforts to hold the sign aloft. Just off the road, a thirty-foot-tall telephone pole had three signs attached, one at the top, one in the middle, and another close to the ground. I put on the brakes, slowed, and pulled to a stop. I put the car in reverse and backed up until I was twenty-five feet away. I parked and got out. I told myself I was interested in buying fresh asparagus for Henry, but in truth I was struck by the old man himself.

I spoke to the woman, saying, "How much is the asparagus?"

"Dollar a bunch."

My eyes strayed to the old man, who appeared to be in his late eighties. His weathered face was darkened by years of exposure to the relentless valley sun. His pants were too long, bunched across his shoes and tattered at the hem where they had perpetually dragged along the ground. His plaid flannel shirt had faded to a pale graph of gray lines, and where his sleeves were rolled up, his forearms were tanned.

The message on the sign was rendered in a formal lettering he'd probably learned in elementary school. He'd been educated in an era when children were taught the value of good penmanship, good manners, a respect for their elders, and a love of country. The sign read:

*Behold, the waters shall subside and the*
*land shall falter and collapse in its wake.*

I was guessing he was the one who'd posted the signs mounted on the telephone pole because the materials were the same: poster board and black ink. Each sign was approximately eighteen inches long and eight inches tall, large enough to be legible to drivers in passing cars as long as they weren't clipping along as fast as I had been. Now that I was standing in range, I had to tilt my face and use a hand to shade my eyes in order to see the sign near the top, which read "1925." Midway down, a sign read "1955," and close to the bottom, "1977."

I gestured, saying, "What is this?"

The woman sitting at the card table responded on his behalf. "Land subsided twenty-eight feet. Sign at the top shows where it was in 1925. Bottom shows where it sank to by 1977. Monitoring system's down, so it's been twelve years since anybody measured."

I was assuming she was his daughter, as they shared similar facial contours and the same electric blue eyes.

The old man watched me with interest. I shifted my gaze to him.

"Are you saying the land has literally sunk twenty-eight feet?"

"Land don't hardly rise unless an earthquake buckles her in two. My pappy and my pappy's pappy farmed this valley from 1862 onward. My grandpappy was thirteen years old when he first put his hand to a plow. Youngest boy of ten. They worked the land through the terrible drought of 1880 and come out good enough from what I hear tell. In those days the land was a paradise on earth, and it looked like the bounty wouldn't never end.

"Then the government came along and proposed moving water from up yonder to down here and then on. They called it the State Water Project. More like Steal Water, you want my opinion. Good for growers. Good for flood control. A help to everybody is what they said. They built the Delta-Mendota Canal up north, the Friant-Kern Canal, and the California Aqueduct. Regulate and irrigate. Water flows. Water goes. The drought's come around again and the water's gone."

"Daddy, that's enough. This lady don't want to hear you yammer on about the end of the world."

"Actually, I'd like to hear what he has to say."

"The groundwater was once plentiful. Runoff from snowpack in the high Sierras. Rain and more rain and the rivers were full up. One hundred and fifty years back, water was diverted at People's Weir on the Kings River. The Kern River was diverted as well. Drought came around again and the water was cut back again as well, so the farmers around here refurbished the old pumping plants and drilled new wells. Nobody thought about the consequences. But the shallow aquifer declined and the deep aquifer declined. Land sinks when there's nothing under her to hold her up. Twenty-eight feet's a fact."

His daughter said, "Compaction's what it's called, but all adds up to the same thing."

I handed her two one-dollar bills and she put two bundles of asparagus in a brown paper bag.

"Where you from?" she asked.

"Santa Teresa."

"Where you headed?"

"Burning Oaks."

"I was there once. Didn't much care for it. Maybe we'll see you on your way home."

"Always possible."

Thirty minutes later, I hit the outskirts of Burning Oaks, where a sign indicated a population of 6,623. After the total, someone had added "give or take" in small print. The region was once known for its petroleum and natural-gas reserves and even now produced a continuous supply of crude oil. The local job economy had also enjoyed a boost from the Burning Oaks Correctional Institute, a privately operated low-security prison. The town itself was bigger than I'd imagined, covering fifteen square miles.

I drove the twenty-block width and the eighteen-block length in a grid pattern, taking in the whole of it. There was one Catholic church, St. Elizabeth's, constructed in the style of an old California mission, which is to say, a number of rambling one-story stucco buildings connected under a zigzagging red tile roof. All of the other churches were outposts of off-brand religions. Apparently, the good citizens of Burning Oaks did not hold with the Baptists, the Methodists, or the Presbyterians.

The residential streets were five lanes wide, as generous as the commercial avenues that bisected the downtown. The homeowners seemed to favor raw board fences, picket fences, and tidy alleyways where trash cans had been set out waiting for the pickup. In addition to three mobile home parks, there were one-story frame and stucco houses of modest proportions. Neighborhoods were punctuated by tall palms, feathery pepper trees, paddle cactus, and telephone poles that listed to one side or the other, straining the overhead wires.

I stopped at the first service station I saw and picked up a local map, where points of interest had been flagged with small representative drawings. There was a library, a movie theater, and four elementary schools, a junior high school, a high school, and a community college. In addition to numerous supermarkets, I spotted a hospital, two hardware stores, a feed store, a boot museum, a dry goods emporium, coffee shops, drugstores, a retail tire business, three beauty shops, a fabric store, and a store selling Western attire. I couldn't think why anyone would choose to live here. On the other hand, I couldn't think why not. The town was clean and well-kept with more sky overhead than scenic wonders at ground level.

I was assuming that when Pete arrived in Burning Oaks the previous spring, he did so without the benefit of the mailing pouch. I couldn't imagine how he might have acquired it unless he'd met with Father Xavier, who had delivered the items into his hands. Because of Pete's preliminary work, I'd been provided with two critical points of reference: the name and address of the priest and the return address of the sender in the upper left-hand corner of the mailer.

I circled back to the library and pulled into an empty slot in the fifteen-space parking lot. I locked the car and went in, mailing pouch tucked under my arm. The one-story structure was of an uncertain architectural style that probably dated to the years just after World War II, when the country was recovering from steel shortages and throwing together new construction with whatever materials happened to be at hand.

I went into an interior made cozy with oversize paper tulips cut out of construction paper and mounted under a row of clerestory windows, like the flowers were yearning for the light. The space smelled of that brand of white library paste so many of us loved to eat in elementary school. Assorted preschoolers sat cross-legged on the floor while a young woman read aloud from a book about a bear who could roller-skate. To these tykes, the world was full of novelties and a skating bear was only one of many. Older adults, retired by the look of them, claimed the comfortable chairs along the far wall. Not surprisingly, much of the rest of the space was taken up by row after row of book-shelves, filled to capacity.

I approached the main desk, where a librarian was sorting and loading books onto a rolling cart for a return to the shelves. According to her name tag, she was Sandy Klemper, head librarian. She appeared to be fresh out of graduate school; a blonde in her early twenties, wearing a mint green sweater over a white blouse with a green-and-gray tweed skirt.

She looked up with a quick smile. "May I help you?"

"I'm hoping you have copies of the Haines and Poke Directories going back thirty years. I'm researching someone who lived here in the late fifties, early sixties."

"We have directories starting in 1910. Genealogy?"

"Not quite. Something similar."

"Telephone books should help," she said. "We have newspapers on microfiche, and you might take a look at voter registration records, which are available at city hall."

"Thanks. I'll keep that in mind. This is my first run at the project, so we'll see what kind of luck I have."

She showed me to the reference section, where an entire wall of shelves was devoted to city directories, old phone books, and historical accounts of the settling of the area. "Let me know if I can be of any further assistance," she said, and left me to my work.

I found both the Haines and the Polk from the years that interested me—1959, 1960, and 1961—along with the telephone books for those same years. I also picked up the current year's editions of the Haines and Polk so that I could trace information forward. I was hoping to find someone who'd been acquainted with Ned and Lenore during the period before her death. For sleuthing purposes, gossip is like freshly minted coin. If I could find someone at a given address who'd been in residence in 1961, I might strike it rich.

I sat down at an empty table and spread my books across the surface. I started with the 1961 Haines and worked my way through the alphabetical street listings until I reached Glenrock Road. Then I followed the house numbers from 101 as far as the 400s. The occupants at 461 were Elmer and Clara Doyle. Elmer owned a carpet-cleaning business. Clara was a homemaker. I flipped over to the 1961 Polk Directory and found the Doyles listed by last name, with the same address and a telephone number, which I made note of. I turned back to the Haines and jotted down the names of the neighbors on either side of the Doyles, Troy and Ruth Salem at 459 and John and Tivoli Lafayette at 465. I tried those same names in the current telephone book and found Clara Doyle, a widow, listed, still at 461. There was no sign of the Salems or the Lafayettes.

Out of curiosity, I returned to the shelves and pulled the Haines and the Polk for 1952, the year Lenore Redfern was "confirmed to Christ." There were four Redfern families. The listing that sparked my interest was for Lew and Marcella at 475 Glenrock, a few doors away from the Doyles.

I had no idea how or why the Doyles, husband or wife, had sent the mailing pouch to Father Xavier, but I was hoping Clara could enlighten me. In the 1961 Polk, under the last name Lowe, I found Ned and Lenore Lowe at 1507 Third Street. From April's wedding announcement, I knew that Ned and his current wife, Celeste, lived in Cottonwood, six miles to the south of Santa Teresa. The 1961 Haines confirmed Ned Lowe's name and indicated he worked in sales and his wife, Lenore, was a homemaker. I wrote down the names of nearby neighbors: the Wilsons, the Chandlers, and the Schultzes. Taryn Sizemore had told me Ned attended Burning Oaks High School, which might be another source of information.

My final search was for the last name Kastle, in hopes of tracking down Shirley Ann's parents. The only Kastles I found were Norma and Boyd on Trend. I went through the current Polk and the Haines, along with the current telephone book, and came up empty-handed. Oh, well. It was probably unrealistic to expect to score in every single category. I returned the volumes to the shelves, sent the librarian a friendly wave, and went out to my car.

# 23

Clara Doyle lived in a boxy one-story white frame house with a pitched roof and a row of windows that glassed in the original porch. From the street, it was hard to imagine an interior large enough to accommodate much more than a living room, an eat-in kitchen, one bedroom, and a bathroom. Enclosing the porch had probably added a much-needed hundred and fifty square feet of space. There were two very tall palm trees in the yard, each growing from the center of a circle of white rocks. Green fronds formed feather dusters at the top, while shaggy brown fronds hung down along the trunk almost to the ground. In Santa Teresa, Norway rats will shelter in the crevices if city mainte-nance crews let too much time pass between trims.

There was no doorbell in evidence. Through the glass in the upper half of the door, I could see a woman sitting at a table in the front room, working on a jigsaw puzzle. I tapped on the glass, hoping I wouldn't startle her. When she caught sight of me, she pushed her chair back and got up. She was tall and stout, with a round face, thin white hair, and glasses with oversize red plastic frames that made her eyes look enormous. She wore a pink cotton floral-print housedress with a pinafore-style apron over it. She opened the door without hesitation, saying, "Yes?"

I couldn't believe she was so trusting. How did she know I wouldn't burst in, smite her about the head and shoulders, and take all her cash? "Are you Clara Doyle?"

"I am, and who might you be?" She had a sturdy set of yellowing teeth, darkly discolored at the gum line, but otherwise looking like the set she was born with.

I handed her a business card. "Kinsey Millhone. I drove up from Santa Teresa this morning hoping you might give me information about Lenore Redfern. Her family lived down the street at 475—"

"I know where the Redferns lived, but they've been gone for years," she said. She slid my card into her apron pocket. "Why have you come to my door?"

"Because of this." I held up the mailing pouch, the face of it turned toward her, as though I meant to read her a story, pointing to the pictures as I went along. "Do you recognize it?"

"Of course. Why do you have it when it was mailed to someone else?"

"A colleague drove up from Santa Teresa a year ago. I believe he met with Father Xavier."

"You're referring to Mr. Wolinsky, the private detective."

"You met Pete?"

"He came to me with questions about Lennie and her husband, Ned. I advised him to talk to our parish priest."

"How did he know you were acquainted with Lenore?"

"He had the Redferns' old address and started knocking on doors. All of the neighbors from the old days have died or moved on except me. He said our conversation was confidential, so I'm not entirely clear why he told you."

"He didn't. I came across the mailer among his personal effects." I could see her fix on the word "effects."

"He passed?"

"In August."

"Well, I'm sorry to hear of it. He was a very nice man."

"I'm trying to find out what brought him to Burning Oaks in the first place. Did he say anything about that?"

"I'm still not clear what this has to do with you."

"Sorry. I should have explained myself. Pete's widow is a good friend. She asked me to help settle his business affairs. I was hoping to deliver this to April, but I wanted to make sure I was doing the right thing. I came to you first because yours was the return address."

She thought about that briefly. "You'd best come in."

She held open the door and I stepped into the glassed-in front room. She closed the door behind me and returned to the jigsaw puzzle.

The tabletop was a large sheet of plywood, probably forty-eight inches on a side, resting on two sawhorses. Chairs had been placed around the partially completed puzzle so that several people could work at the same time. The light pouring in through the front windows brought the haphazard arrangement of puzzle pieces into sharp relief. She was apparently a purist, because there was no sign of the box top with the finished picture in view. The portion she'd pieced together was in tones of black and white. When I saw the subject matter, I leaned forward and looked more carefully.

The figures were small; a cartoonlike assortment of medieval peasants in a landscape rendered in minute detail. There were weapons everywhere—spears and crossbows and swords. Also, lizards and strange birds. Naked men and women were being variously whipped and beaten, pecked, and cut in half with a giant knife. All of the edge pieces were in place and she'd completed certain areas along the left-hand side, including a naked fellow, impaled on a stick, being roasted over an open fire.

"I hope you don't mind if I work while we talk. My great-grandchildren will be here after school and I promised I'd get this started. Their patience is limited."

"May I?" I asked.

"Of course."

I pulled out a chair and sat down, putting the mailing pouch on the floor at my feet. I was transfixed by the horrors in the jigsaw puzzle. "What *is* this?"

"I'm teaching them about the Seven Deadly Sins. The two older ones are too busy to visit, so I'm having to focus on the little ones. Kindergarten through third. I started with an explanation of Gluttony and Sloth. They had no idea what I was talking about and couldn't have cared less even when I explained. Then I found these puzzles, and now they can't wait to help."

"What am I looking at?"

"Pieter Bruegel the Elder did a series of engravings with the Seven Deadly Sins as his subject. This one is Anger. You can talk about Greed or Pride being wrong, but it doesn't mean much to children. Eternal damnation's an abstract, so what do they care? On the other hand, they know about tantrums and school yard fights, with all the scratching, biting, and kicking that accompanies them. They also have a keen understanding of punishment. This is a hell they can see with their own eyes. You'd be surprised how much fun we have."

She was searching for a particular piece, so I held my tongue. "Where are you, you little dickens?" she murmured to herself.

I stole a quick look at my surroundings, which included the living room and a portion of the kitchen. The furniture was the sort I've seen at Goodwill donation centers: serviceable and well-used. No antiques and no pieces that would even qualify as "collectible," except for the oven, which was a four-burner O'Keefe and Merritt with a center griddle, a fold-down shelf, drop-in salt and pepper shakers, and a clock that displayed the correct time. Henry would have given an arm and a leg for it.

Idly, she said, "I'm sorry to hear about Mr. Wolinsky. Was he ill?"

"He was killed in a robbery attempt," I said, without going into any detail. "He went to some lengths to hide the mailer, so he must have been worried about its falling into the wrong hands. Do you have any idea why Father Xavier gave it to him?"

"Mr. Wolinsky told me April was living in Santa Teresa. I'd imagine he told Father Xavier the same thing. He saw her wedding announcement in the paper and that's what set him thinking." She picked up a puzzle piece and pressed it into place. "Gotcha. Hah! I haven't laid eyes on that package in years. I expect Father Xavier asked him to deliver it."

"How well did you know Lenore?"

"Her family attended St. Elizabeth's the same as we did. I sat for Lenore when she was just a tiny little thing. I called her Lennie, but I might have been the only one who did. Once she married Ned, I looked after April if she was having a bad time of it. I raised six babies of my own and I know how rough it can be."

"May I ask why she used your return address instead of her own?"

"She worried the package might be sent back. She didn't want Ned to know she'd sent the keepsakes to Father Xavier."

"Why?"

"He wasn't a Catholic. I'm sure she didn't trust him to pass along the Bible and the rosary. Sometimes he got in a rage and destroyed things."

"Was that often?"

"More so as time went on. He had no patience with her. She was subject to low days. Migraine headaches, no energy, poor appetite. She had a nervous disposition and it was clear she needed help. By then, my children were grown and I missed having little ones underfoot. Ned was often on the road, so it fell to her to take care of everything. When he was home, she had to be Johnny-on-the-spot. He'd snap his fingers and she was supposed to hop to."

"You think she was suffering postpartum depression?"

"'Baby blues' they called it back then, though that was a personal matter and not something anybody talked about. Lennie would sink into black moods. These days, you read about women killing their own kids, but I don't believe she ever thought about hurting April. Ned claimed she threatened to, but I never believed a word of it. He'd be all down in the mouth, talking about how worried he was, asking my advice, but it was all done for effect."

I studied her, wondering how much she might be willing to confide. I picked up a puzzle piece shaped like a one-armed ghost and tried to find a home for it. "Was there a question about how she died? I was told she killed herself."

"She was a Catholic. Devout. Suicide's a mortal sin. If she'd killed herself, she'd be condemning her own soul to Hell."

"So you don't believe she'd do such a thing."

"No, I do not."

"What if she were in unbearable emotional pain?"

"She had Father Xavier and she had her faith. She also had me."

I tried placing the piece near the left-hand edge and I was startled when it popped into place. "What time of year was it?"

"Spring, which is another reason suicide made no sense. Her favorite holiday was Easter, which fell on April second that year. She passed on Good Friday, two days before. That week, we dyed Easter eggs together and hid them on the church grounds for the children's Easter egg hunt. We were set to bake cookies and we'd been looking at recipes. She wanted to do bunny shapes with pink and blue icing. Ned hated anything to do with the holiday, but she ignored him and did as she pleased for once."

"How did she die?"

"Valium. An overdose."

"How much Valium do you have to take before you overdose?"

"Ned said she mixed it with vodka."

"Valium is a prescription drug. Why would a doctor write her a script, given the state she was in?"

"A goodly number of housewives took Valium in those days. They referred to it as Vitamin V. If you complained about anything, Valium was the cure. Her family doctor actually suggested it."

"Did she leave a note?"

Clara shook her head.

"Doesn't her sending those items to Father Xavier suggest suicide was on her mind?"

"It might have been on her mind, but I don't believe she would have done such a thing. She was frightened."

"Of what?"

"Ned, obviously."

"It may seem obvious now, but it must not have seemed obvious back then or the police would have investigated her death as a homicide."

"That's not necessarily the case. He was clever. The chief of police was a friend of his. Ned cultivated friendships with many of the officers and he was generous with his donations to their foundation. He laid the groundwork, confiding in everyone how distressed he was about her mental illness."

"Personal relationships aren't relevant. I don't care how clever or charming Ned was in those days. The pathologist's opinion would have been based on autopsy results, not schmoozing with him."

"I'm not saying he did anything, so I should refrain from comment. To do otherwise is unchristian."

"Don't hesitate on my account. I don't even go to church."

"For shame," she said mildly, still surveying the loose pieces for another fit.

"Was she unhappy?"

"Of course. Divorce was impossible for the same reason suicide was. Marriage is a sacrament. Lennie's mother was furious she'd gotten pregnant to begin with and scandalized when she talked about leaving him."

"Really? She told her mother she was leaving him?"

"She hinted at it. There'd never been a divorce in the family, and Marcella said Lenore was not going to be the first."

"Did Ned know she talked about leaving him?"

"If he did, Marcella's the one who told him. She was crazy about Ned. He played up to her. He was downright flirtatious, for lack of a better word. I could see what he was doing, but Marcella would brook no criticism, and it wasn't my place to interfere."

"Just a stab in the dark here, but didn't Lenore get pregnant because of the Church's stance on birth control?"

"She got pregnant because she was naive and inexperienced. Ned told her it wasn't that easy. I'm sure he'd have said anything to get what he wanted from her. By the time I set her straight, it was too late."

"What about Ned? Was he unhappy in the marriage as well?"

"If so, I'm the last person he would have told."

"Do you believe he killed her?"

"You asked me that once."

"I'm just wondering if he had reason to get rid of her."

"I don't know why a man like that does anything. I said the same thing to Mr. Wolinsky. All I'm offering is my opinion."

"Fair enough. Let's put it another way. Did *other* people believe he killed her?"

"I don't know what other people believed. I heard talk, which I won't repeat because it's not my place."

"Are Lenore's parents still alive?"

"Oh my stars, no. Marcella died of cancer in 1976; her husband a year later of a heart attack."

"So there's no family left?"

"Two sisters, but they both married and moved away. This was some time after she died. The family was devastated. I don't know where either girl ended up. Father Xavier might know."

I thought about the two photographs I'd found. "I came across a snapshot of Lenore the day she was confirmed. She must have been twelve or thirteen."

"Eleven and a half. I was there that day. She was a lovely child and a lovely young woman."

"Why did she dye her hair?"

"Who?"

"Lenore. In the photograph of her with April, I was struck by how unhappy she looked. She'd dyed her hair a bleached blond that made her look hard. I wondered if the change was a sign of her illness."

Clara looked at me in confusion. "Lennie never dyed her hair. She was always a brunette."

"Not in the photograph I found."

"I don't think so. There must be some mistake."

I reached down and removed the photograph of Lenore and April in the red leather frame and passed it across the table to her.

She barely glanced at it. "That's not Lennie."

"Who is it then?"

"Ned and his mother, Frankie," she said. "That photograph was taken two days before she left."

I took another look. "You're telling me that's a boy? I assumed the child was April."

"She was the spitting image of Ned at the same age, but that's not her. It's him."

"Doesn't that look like a little girl to you?"

"Of course. Even though the boy was almost four, Frankie refused to have his hair cut. It wasn't until she left that his daddy took him to a barbershop and had it all shaved off. Poor little boy cried like his heart would break."

I took one more look, still only half convinced, and then returned the photograph to the pouch. "Is there anyone still around who was with the police department back then? Because I'd love to talk to someone who actually remembers Lenore's death."

"I know a gentleman who worked for the coroner's office. Stanley

# X

Munce is retired now, and I'm not sure how helpful he'd be. He's off visiting his daughter, but I can ask when he gets home. I don't believe there was much of an investigation."

"Did Pete intend to talk to anyone other than you and Lenore's priest?"

"Father Xavier's the only one I know about."

"I'd like to talk to him myself. It was my primary reason for driving up."

"He'll be at the rectory. Do you know where that is?"

"I passed it earlier when I was touring the town," I said. "Would it be all right with you if I mentioned our conversation?"

"You don't need my permission. I keep no secrets from him. He still hears my confession every week, though I must say my sins are so boring, he falls asleep half the time."

"You have my card," I said. "If you think of anything else, would you give me a call? You're welcome to make it collect."

"No need of that. I'll tell Mr. Munce about your questions and we'll see if he remembers her."

# 24

The rectory at St. Elizabeth's was a short ten-minute drive. Given the fact that I have little or no experience with the Catholic Church, I wasn't sure what kind of reception to expect. I got out of the car with the mailing pouch in hand, which I thought of by now as my calling card. I had my choice of the church proper, the administration building, and the religious education building, which also included St. Elizabeth's Parish School, serving prekindergarten through eighth grade.

I went first to the sanctuary, where the outside door stood open. I passed into the dimly lighted foyer and found that the double doors leading into the church were closed. I paused long enough to pick up a copy of the program for that week. The Pastor and Pastor Emeritus were listed, along with Father Xavier, Retired, and Father Rutherford Justice, Weekend Associate. Masses were said daily at 7:45 A.M., with two on Saturday and two on Sunday. Baptisms were the first and second Sundays of the month, and weddings could only be scheduled if the bride and groom were already registered, contributing, and active members of St. Elizabeth's Parish for at least one year before requesting a marriage date. Clearly, no hasty marital shenanigans would be tolerated.

I shifted the mailing pouch to my left hand and slid the four-page newsletter into my shoulder bag. I returned to the parking lot, where I saw a sign pointing to a small building I thought might house the nuts-and-bolts business of running a parish church. I felt like an interloper, which of course I was, unclear on the underlying etiquette of secular matters in a sanctified setting.

I reached a door that said OFFICE and peered through the glass window. There was no one in evidence. I tried the knob and found the door unlocked. I opened it and stuck my head in.

"Hello?"

No response. I hesitated and then stepped inside. The interior was quite ordinary. Aside from a smattering of religious art and artifacts, the office was simply office-like: two desks, office chairs, file cabinets, bookcases.

I heard approaching footsteps and a woman appeared from a short corridor to my right. She was in her midseventies, with iron gray hair worn in a halo of tiny frizzy curls. The look reminded me of the ads for Toni Home Permanents back when I was a little girl. In those days, a beauty salon permanent cost fifteen dollars, while a Toni Home Permanent kit cost two dollars, sulfur-scented waving lotion and curlers included. The savings alone was thrilling, especially when you considered that a refill was only a dollar more, which further reduced the cost. My Aunt Gin's friends were smitten with the prospect of beautification at home. Aunt Gin sniffed at the very idea. In her mind, spending even one dollar on beauty products was a waste. As it turned out, she was the only one among her friends who had the patience to follow directions, so our trailer was the source of an entire army of frizzy-haired women smelling of spoiled eggs.

I said, "I'm looking for Father Xavier."

"Well, you've come to the right place. I'm Lucille Berrigan, the parish secretary. Is he expecting you?" She wore a navy blue rayon pantsuit and crepe-soled shoes.

I handed her a business card, which she didn't bother to read. "I don't actually have an appointment, but I'm hoping he can spare a few minutes of his time."

"You'll have to be quick about it. He's out in the garden with his sun hat and trowel and looks to be settling in for a snooze."

"Would it be better if I returned another time? I hate to interrupt."

"Now is fine unless this is something I might help you with . . ." She glanced at the card. ". . . Ms. Millhone."

"I have questions about Lenore Redfern."

"Then he's definitely the one to consult. He was close to the family. Wonderful people. If you're interested in matters of chronology, we have handwritten records of every marriage, baptism, confirmation, funeral, and sick call going all the way back to the turn of the century."

"You do?"

"Yes, ma'am. Looking after our families is one of the roles we fill."

"I'll keep that in mind. If you can show me where he is, I'll let you get back to work."

"Of course."

She motioned me to the window and pointed to an old gentleman in jeans and a black shirt with a clerical collar. He'd settled on a weathered wooden bench with his legs outstretched and a wide-brimmed canvas hat tilted down over his face. She gestured for me to follow, and I trotted after her to a side door that opened onto a hard-packed dirt-and-gravel path. The garden itself was enclosed by a round-shouldered adobe wall that looked like it had been there for a century.

I stood for a moment, reluctant to disturb his nap. She made an impatient shooing motion, urging me to move on. She gestured in roughly the same manner as my Aunt Gin when I was five and waiting in line to see Santa Claus. On that occasion, I'd burst into tears and refused to talk to him at all. What upset me was that his lips were too wet and he had a wen beside his nose that looked like a kernel of burnt popcorn.

"Father Xavier?"

His bony hands were loosely clasped across his waist, and I could see his lips puff outward with every breath. He had to be in his late eighties; well into the shrinking part of life. He was thin, so narrow through the shoulders and hips that he probably had to buy his pants in the boys' department.

I cleared my throat. "Father Xavier?"

"Listening."

"Sorry to bother you, but I have some questions about Lenore Redfern and the package she sent you. I was hoping you could tell me about the circumstances."

I thought he was formulating a response, but then his lips made a tiny sound as they parted with the next breath.

I waited a beat. "Just in your own words would be fine."

No response.

I sat down beside him on the bench and checked my watch. It was just after the noon hour—12:17 to be exact. I surveyed the area, thinking how heartily Henry would have approved of the garden. The sun was hot. The earth surrounding us was largely hard-packed dirt. No grass at all. The plants were roughly divided between cacti and succulents. No sprinklers, no soaker hoses. I did see a birdbath, but it was empty. A chickadee, undismayed, enjoyed an extravagant dust shower and flew away. The air smelled like rosemary. I could do with a snooze myself.

I glanced at the office window, where Ms. Berrigan was acting out an elaborate pantomime of waking the priest, urging me to shake his arm. I couldn't do it. I put a hand behind my ear as though I'd failed to comprehend. She turned and looked behind her, which I took to mean the phone was ringing or someone else had appeared in the office, requiring help.

I checked my watch again and saw that one whole minute had flown by. I took a quick look at Father Xavier, whose dark eyes were open. His face was pleated with wrinkles. His pupils were almost engulfed by the pouches above and below his eyes. He sat up, looked at me briefly, and then saw the mailing pouch.

"What's that doing here? Mr. Wolinsky said he'd see that April received the contents as her mother intended. He promised he'd deliver it."

"Pete was a friend of mine. He died in August."

Father Xavier crossed himself and kissed the cross that hung around his neck on a chain. "My apologies if I was abrupt. I didn't expect to see that package again."

"I found it among Pete's effects. I intend to pass the items along to April, but I wanted to understand the situation first. I drove from Santa Teresa this morning, hoping you'd explain."

"Of course. It was good of you to make the trip, and I'll tell you what I can."

"It's my understanding Pete paid you a visit a year ago. Why did he want to see you?"

"I believe he was interested in background information."

"On Lenore?"

"No, no. It was Ned he was inquiring about. Something to do with a lawsuit. He'd come to believe Ned had serious psychological problems that might have showed up early in his life. He asked about Ned's childhood. His family of origin."

"Do you remember what you told him?"

"It wasn't much. I wasn't acquainted with his family. Ned wasn't a Catholic. This is a small town, but it's not that small."

"You knew Lenore?"

"Oh, yes. From baptism to her First Communion and right up until her death."

"I'm assuming she sent you these items because she wanted April to have her confirmation Bible and her rosary."

"As keepsakes, yes," he said. "You knew Lenore took her own life."

"That's what I was told. I had a conversation with Clara Doyle and we talked about that. I noticed Lenore included a card for April's fourth birthday."

"I believe that's correct."

"Do you think she bought the card because she knew she wouldn't be around when the time came?"

"So it would seem. She sent me the package to hold on to until such time as April was confirmed. After Lenore died, Ned took the child and left Burning Oaks. I had no idea where they went, but I kept the mailer in the expectation I'd hear from him. I intended to place it in April's hands myself once she was of an age to appreciate the meaning. To tell you the truth, I forgot all about it until Mr. Wolinsky showed up. He told me April was married and living in Santa Teresa. Ms. Berrigan was the one who reminded me the mailer was in storage, so I gave it to him to deliver. You'll have to forgive me if I sounded cross when you first arrived. I thought Mr. Wolinsky failed to make good on his promise to me."

"No need to apologize. I understand completely."

"I appreciate your patience."

"Clara told me Lenore died just before Easter. This was postmarked March 27. Did you realize the extreme emotional state she was in?"

"We were all aware of her distress. I spoke with her parents on a number of occasions. Naturally, they were worried about her and hoped I might intervene. I did what I could, but Lenore was very fragile by then, almost beyond reasoning."

"So you weren't shocked or surprised when she overdosed."

"I was saddened. I took it as a failure on my part."

"Did she tell you what she intended to do?"

"She told her husband and he came to me. She was a very troubled young woman. Since Ned wasn't Catholic, they'd wed in a civil ceremony at the courthouse. He believed Lenore was upset in part because

233

she knew they weren't married in the eyes of the Church. He assured me he was willing to take instruction and convert if it would ease her suffering."

I felt an inappropriate laugh bubble up and coughed to cover it. I said, "Really? He thought the basis for her depression was his failure to convert to the Catholic faith?"

"I believe it was more a matter of his desire to do what he could for her."

"That speaks well of him, assuming he was sincere."

"I'm certain he was. I've no doubt of it. We had a lengthy chat, after which I counseled Lenore to allow him the opportunity to demonstrate his good intentions."

"Did she seem open to the idea?"

"She was upset."

"And why was that?"

"She said I'd taken his side. She said I was all she had left and now he'd poisoned the well. She felt he'd turned me against her, which wasn't true." He blinked and his nose reddened. "I assured her it wasn't the case. I wanted her to give him the benefit of the doubt."

"Because you felt he was acting in good faith?"

"He gave me every reason to believe he'd follow through. I encouraged him to come to Mass with her. I also suggested he join the group class we offer on the Rite of Christian Initiation for Adults so that he could learn Church history, as well as our beliefs and values. He needed a sponsor, of course, and I explained that if all went well, once the end of the liturgical cycle neared, he would be deemed 'an elect.' At that point, he'd prepare for the Rite of Election, the Call to Continuing Conversion, and the Easter Vigil."

"He hadn't yet taken instruction, so you're talking about his conversion Easter of the following year?"

"I am."

"Sounds like a lengthy process."

"And rightly so. There are many steps along the way."

"Am I correct in assuming he was eventually baptized a Catholic?"

"Unfortunately, he was not. Lenore's death was a devastating blow. I'd hoped his faith would shore him up, but I could see he was faltering. We spoke many times and I thought he was coming around, but then he took little April and left town without a word. I've heard nothing from him since."

I hesitated, unsure how hard to push. "There are people who believe he killed her. Were you aware of that?"

"If Clara Doyle said as much, she's to be censured."

"No, no. She refused to comment. This was an inference I drew, but not from anything she told me. I suspect Pete was tracking the idea, or why else would he drive all this way?"

"There are always those willing to believe the worst. It's unfortunate."

"Did you ever hear rumors to that effect? That Ned might have done it?"

"None that I gave any credence to."

"What about the police? Did they investigate?"

"I'm certain they did. I don't know the particulars, but they must have been satisfied she acted of her own free will."

"Clara tells me Lenore had two sisters. Do you have any idea where they are at this point?"

He shook his head. It seemed to me his attitude had chilled.

"You mentioned Pete's asking about Ned's family of origin. What happened to his mother? Clara told me she left."

"I believe he was four when Frankie walked out."

"Is there someone who might confirm that?"

Father Xavier shook his head. "I can't think of a soul."

"Were Norma and Boyd Kastle your parishioners?"

He brightened. "Oh yes. I knew them well. She was a lovely woman. Even in her final illness, she was just as gracious as she could be."

# 25

I found a drive-through fast food restaurant and ate in my car. Cheese-burger, limp fries, a Diet Pepsi, and a piece of gum that I chewed as a substitute for brushing my teeth. After this elegant repast, I sat and made notes, filling up three dozen index cards that ended up smelling of onions as well. So far, I had no access to the past except for other people's recollections, which are often telling, but not always to be trusted. Memory is subject to a filtering process that we don't always recognize and can't always control. We remember what we can bear and we block what we cannot. I wondered if there was anything to be learned from the local police, who would at least have access to the investigator's report from the time of Lenore's death.

I was pleasantly surprised by how easy it was to gain access to the Burning Oaks chief of police. It helped, I'm sure, that Burning Oaks is a small town with a low crime rate, most of which is property-related as opposed to crimes against persons. In addition to DUIs, driving without a valid license or proof of insurance was the number-one cause of traffic arrests. I was also guessing the public relations aspect of the department was a point of pride. This was the kind of law enforcement that made little kids want to grow up to be cops.

Seventeen minutes after I arrived at the police department and asked to see the chief, I was sitting across the desk from her. In the interim, I read a free color brochure, complete with photographs that covered the department history and its current makeup, which consisted of one police chief, an administrative assistant, one lieutenant, three sergeants, and eight patrol officers. In addition, there were three school resource officers, five dispatchers, two community service officers, an animal control officer, and a code enforcement officer.

Chief Ivy Duncan was in her late forties, dark-haired and dark-eyed. She was attired in the usual black short-sleeved uniform with her chief of police badge, her Burning Oaks Police Department patch, a pin that said CHIEF on each side of her collar, her name tag, two pens in her shirt pocket, and the tools of her trade attached to her belt, which creaked every time she moved. I'd been a sworn officer for a two-year period early in my career, and I can assure you the getup looked better on her than it ever did on me.

I'd given her one of my business cards, which she studied while I stood across the desk from her. From her expression, I couldn't tell whether she felt antagonistic or kindly disposed toward private investigators.

She tossed the card on the desk and leaned back in her chair. "Welcome to Burning Oaks. What can I do for you?"

I sat down without invitation and put my shoulder bag on the floor by my feet. Psychologically speaking, I didn't want to tower over her. I wanted us eye to eye like we were equals. Her more than me.

"I'm wondering how I could obtain a copy of the autopsy report on a woman who died here in 1961. Her maiden name was Redfern, first name Lenore. She married a man named Ned Lowe. She died of a drug overdose from what I'm told."

"If you're talking about an autopsy close to thirty years ago, that file would be in storage. Burning Oaks is a small town. We rely on contract pathologists, most of them located up in Bakersfield. No offense, but asking one of my staff to track that down would be a pain, and what's the point?"

"What about the investigator's report?"

"I doubt they'd make that available, but even assuming you laid hands on it, paperwork like that would be useless. In those days, officers weren't as well-trained. Case notes were sketchy and sometimes incoherent. Some of the spelling errors are downright comical. Generally speaking, no agency's going to open their files to scrutiny by someone outside law enforcement. We could get our butts sued. People are entitled to privacy, even dead ones. Especially dead ones."

"Is there anybody here who might actually remember the case?"

"I'll be happy to ask around, but it doesn't sound like it would have generated much buzz. What's the husband's name again?"

"Ned Lowe."

"And he's still here in town?"

"He left four months after his wife's death."

"They have kids?"

"One. A little girl who was three at the time. She's married now and living in Santa Teresa."

"You have a copy of the death certificate?"

"I don't."

"Write to Sacramento. Maybe you'll discover something pertinent."

"Thanks. I should have thought of it myself."


I returned to my car and made notes, although I noticed I was feeling sheepish. Chief Duncan had been polite, but she'd made it clear we weren't going to sit around discussing old news. She didn't know the case and wouldn't speculate. If I'd thought about it, I'd have known how little encouragement I'd get. I rubber-banded the cards and returned them to my bag.

I checked the map for Burning Oaks High School and headed in that direction. I wondered if Pete Wolinsky had had better luck than I was having. For the first time in my life, I wished he were in the car with me. We could have compared notes or bounced around ideas about how to get what we were after. For all the corner-cutting he did, he was a wily old bastard and doubtless had a million clever tricks up his sleeve.

I parked on the street down the block from the high school and walked to the entrance, passing the football stadium, which was empty. There was a curious lack of activity, but it wasn't until I reached the double doors and pushed that I realized the building was locked and dark. I stared, perplexed. Shit, this was Saturday. I backed up and scrutinized the facade, but there were no signs of life. Well, now what?

I returned to my car and circled back to the public library. I parked and went in. The prekindergartners were gone and the comfy chairs were filled with a different set of patrons. Most of the tables were now empty. Saturday afternoons were meant for movies, the local mall, and the park. I wasn't sure what else small-town kids did these days.

I caught sight of Sandy Klemper showing a high-school-age student how to thread microfilm through a machine. She glanced up and smiled, raising a finger to let me know she'd seen me. I waited at the desk.

"Back again," I said.

"I see that. Are you having any luck?"

"I was until I realized it was Saturday and the school's locked up tight. You have copies of the yearbook?"

"The *Clarion*? We do," she said. "Are you looking for classmates?"

I shook my head. "These kids were all ten years ahead of me."

"What year did you graduate?"

"Nineteen sixty-seven, but not from here. I went to Santa Teresa High. The yearbooks I'm interested in are 1955 through '57."

Her expression shifted. "Why the sudden interest in Burning Oaks High School? I had a man in here a few months ago looking at the same years."

"Pete Wolinsky. That was actually a year ago. He was a friend of mine."

"I wasn't sure what to make of him. He was nice; a bit weird-looking, but we ended up chatting for a long time. Did you know he was a detective?"

"I did. We trained together at the same agency."

"Wow. Guess you could have quizzed him and saved yourself a trip."

"I would have if I'd had the chance. He died. I've been asked to follow up on a case of his."

"I'm sorry. I didn't mean to be flippant."

"No way you could have known."

"Still, I shouldn't have commented on his appearance. That was uncalled for."

"He wouldn't have taken offense," I said. "You want to point me in the right direction? I can find the yearbooks on my own."

"No need. I'll round them up for you."

"Thanks."

I took a seat.

When she reappeared, the yearbooks she carried included 1954 and 1958 in addition to the three I'd asked for.

"Thanks. This is great."

"Let me know if you need anything else."

I started with the 1954 *Clarion*, looking for Lenore Redfern, who was nowhere to be found. There was no index to the photographs and references to individual students. I suppose with a sizable student body that would be too much to expect. I leafed through page by page, finding nothing until I finally realized '54 was before her time. I found one photograph of her in the 1955 *Clarion*, her sophomore year, and one picture of her in the 1956 *Clarion*, her junior year, ages fifteen and sixteen, respectively. Amazing how quickly I felt myself transported. I'd been out of high school for roughly twenty years and even the idea of it was making my stomach hurt.

I knew my impression of Lenore was colored by what I knew of her history, truncated as it was, but certain characteristics seemed evident. She wasn't smiling in either photo, which left her looking pale and insecure. Even in a one-inch-by-one-inch format, her posture was poor. She was too thin and her hairstyle was a miserable combination of bangs cut too short, a spit curl on either side of her forehead, and the remaining hair held back with bobby pins. She wore a white blouse with a small triangular scarf knotted at the collar. Same blouse, two different scarves. The photographs, of course, were in black and white, but even so, she looked pinched. It troubled me knowing the young Lenore had no idea she'd never reach the age of twenty-two.

Ned Lowe was better represented, but not by much. To my surprise, I realized he owed his entire photographic presence to Shirley Ann Kastle, who seemed to be everywhere. She was one among six junior varsity cheerleaders. In the 1954 *Clarion*, her junior year, she posed in her saddle oxfords, white crew socks, and her flippy little skirt, holding pompoms aloft. I spotted her photograph among members of the glee club, the pep club, the home economics club, and the drama club. Nothing that required brains or academic excellence, but she was pretty. I hate to admit how much that matters when you're sixteen years old.

That same year, she was one of six princesses at the junior prom, where she and Ned Lowe posed with Matt Mueller and Debbie Johnston, the homecoming king and queen. Ned had given Shirley Ann a wrist corsage. Shirley Ann also appeared in the high school production of *Our Town*, playing the part of Emily Webb, the play's main character, if my memory was correct. This was the Friday night cast. Having a Saturday night cast as well allowed twice the number of students to participate. I noticed that in the Friday night cast, the part of Joe Stoddard, the undertaker, was played by Ned Lowe. There were three staged-looking photographs from the production itself, and Shirley Ann appeared in two. The only picture of Ned was in the group shot of the Friday night cast, second row on the left. I leaned close, but couldn't determine much about him except that his hair was cut very short on the sides and arranged in a pompadour on top. I found a better picture of him among the juniors: a postage stamp–size black-and-white image. He was handsome in a pouty sort of way.

I wondered what I would have thought of him if I'd gone to high school with him myself. Mentally, I stepped back and studied the class officers, the representatives to Boys State, the merit scholarship winners, and the members of student council, comparing Ned's image to those of his classmates. He struck me as technically attractive, but marginal. I was guessing he met Shirley Ann Kastle as a result of their casting in the school play. I couldn't imagine why she'd taken up with the likes of him.

I checked the pictures of graduating seniors in the 1955 *Clarion* and there he was again. By then, his smile was practiced. He'd learned that setting his teeth in a certain way created the impression of a smile without his having to experience anything worth smiling about. Beside his picture in the brief few lines accorded each student, he listed his activities as glee club and pep club. Shit, everybody was in the pep club. Under Hobby, he listed "photography." Ambition: "to be rich and successful." Memory: "junior prom." Song: "You'll Never Walk Alone." Pet Peeve: "stuck-up girls."

There was no sign of Shirley Ann among graduating seniors. Had *she* died? Surely not.

I flipped back to Lenore Redfern's photograph that same year, knowing she was a junior the year Ned graduated. What must she have thought when the semi-attractive Ned suddenly turned his phony smile on her? I turned to the 1956 *Clarion*, but there was no sign of her photograph among the graduating seniors.

I sat for a long time thinking about the three: Ned Lowe, Shirley Ann Kastle, and Lenore Redfern. I remembered the intensity of high school, all those hormones, like spotlights, casting events in high relief. Everything felt like forever. Love, betrayal, impossible crushes, breakups, jealousies, and yearnings. How had poor little Lenore ended up in Ned Lowe's sights? What was the story? More important, how was I going to find out?

I did make one unexpected discovery that so startled me, I yelped aloud, thus drawing the stares of two people at an adjoining table. As I leafed through pages devoted to school activities, I spotted Ned's photograph among members of the German club, which wasn't interesting in and of itself. What caught my attention was an enlarged photo of the president of the organization—a fellow whose name was George Dayton.

Suddenly I understood where the fake IRS agent had come up with his alias. I'd been almost certain Ned Lowe was behind Ruth's trumped-up audit request. It didn't help with my current query, but at least a wee piece of the puzzle had fallen into place. I couldn't wait to tell Ruth, who'd scoffed at my suspicions.

I closed the yearbooks and stacked them, gathered my shoulder bag and my notes, and repaired to the main desk, where the librarian was perched on a stool.

"How'd you do?"

"Not bad," I said.

"If you don't mind my asking, are you investigating someone in particular?"

"A guy named Ned Lowe. His wife committed suicide in 1961, and there's a question about what went on. I thought background information would help. Would any of the teachers from the midfifties still be around?"

"I doubt it. I mean, not that I know, but we can certainly find out. Let me check with Mrs. Showalter. She retired just last year, which is when I came on. She might know one or two faculty members, and if she doesn't, I'm sure she can suggest someone who does."

# 26

I was introduced to the former history teacher/football coach by phone. Drew Davenport, who'd agreed to take my call, had been on the faculty at Burning Oaks High during the relevant years. He had no recollection of Ned or Lenore. He sparked to my mention of Shirley Ann Kastle, but had nothing new to add. He referred me to a guy named Wally Bledsoe, who owned a local insurance agency and supposedly knew everything about everyone.

Bledsoe worked Saturdays and invited me to stop by his office in greater downtown Burning Oaks. Like Drew Davenport, he drew a blank when it came to the three, but said his wife had graduated from Burning Oaks High School in 1958. Not perfect, but I'd take what I could get. When I chatted with her by phone, she told me she'd *hated* high school and had happily repressed all her memories thereof. As it happened, however, she sang in the church choir with a woman whose sister was a 1957 graduate. By the time I found myself standing on

Marsha Heddon's front porch, ringing the bell, I was appreciative of the virtues of small-town life.

She'd apparently been awaiting my arrival because she opened the front door before the sound of the chimes faded. By my ten-digit accounting system, she was close to fifty, but looked twenty years younger. Her youthful appearance was the function of her being wonderfully round, with flushed cheeks, bright blue eyes, and plump lips. Her wrap-front dress framed extravagant curves that she seemed happy to possess.

When I introduced myself, she interrupted with a wave of her hand. "Deborah told me all about it. A reunion coming up and you're looking for the lost."

"Not quite. I'm hoping for information on three kids who were at Burning Oaks with you."

"Oh. Well, I can probably do that, too. Come on in."

I followed her past the living room and through the kitchen to a glassed-in back porch that had been attractively furnished with a white wicker love seat and matching armchairs upholstered in a sunny yellow fabric.

"This is the Florida room," she said as we sat down. "My hobby's interior decorating."

"Must come in handy. You did this yourself?"

"Well, I didn't upholster the furniture, but I did everything else. This used to be a mudroom, full of junk. You couldn't even walk through without bumping into something. Now we're out here all the time."

"It's cozy. I like the yellow."

"Thank you." She paused to fan herself, flapping one hand. "Don't mind me. I'm overheating. Whew! Now, tell me who you're looking for."

I gave her the three names. "You remember them?"

"Not Lenore so much, but the other two of course. Who didn't know Shirley Ann? She was a goddess. Two years ahead of me from elementary school on up."

"What about Ned?"

"I'm not sure anybody knew him well. He was one of those guys you see on the street and you can't remember his name to save your soul. There's only so much room at the top of the heap. The rest of us are fill dirt."

I laughed because I knew exactly what she was talking about. "I hope none of my high school classmates are saying that about me. Bet they are, now that I think about it. I didn't even date."

"The thing about Ned? He had no impact. He wasn't popular. He wasn't funny. He wasn't a class officer, didn't play in the marching band. Not an athlete, didn't win science awards. No talent or skill that I recall. Just a gray guy taking up space."

"According to the yearbook, he was in *Our Town*."

"But he didn't have a big part. That's my point. When the script says 'crowd murmurs,' you have to have somebody there to mill around onstage. It's kind of like dog food. You can only have so much real meat and the rest is by-products."

"Got it," I said.

"You want a cup of coffee or anything? I don't know what's wrong with me for not asking in the first place."

"No, no. I'm fine. Go on."

"*Our Town* was where it started. Shirley Ann was cast as the female lead. No big surprise. She was good at everything and just as nice as she could be. Completely down-to-earth. She was going steady with this guy named Bobby Freed. There were two Bobby Freeds in our class. Spelled differently—the other one was F-R-I-E-D—but they sounded the same, so there was Big Bobby and Little Bobby. She dated Big Bobby. He was on the tennis team, captain of the swim team, class president. You know the type. He was a hunk. Stuck on himself, but who wouldn't be?"

I kept my mouth shut and let her run on. My job here was to supply the occasional prompt and otherwise keep out of the way.

"Anyway, Big Bobby got mad because she was spending so much time in rehearsals and I don't know what. It was just one of those things. Big fight and he broke up with her. I'd see her in the hall sobbing her heart out with a cluster of girls around her patting her and being sweet. Suddenly Ned's in the thick of it with his arm around her shoulder, making sure she's okay. I remember thinking, 'Where did he come from?' Nothing wrong with him, except he was a dud and she was a star. It was just so wrong."

"You had cliques?"

"Oh sure. Every high school has those. Certain types get all bonded and form these tight-knit groups; kids with the same social status or good looks or leadership abilities. Like as not, they went to junior high school together or all belonged to the same church youth group."

"Where were you in all this?"

"On the sidelines. Way off. I wasn't even in the running, and I knew that. Didn't bother me. In fact, I enjoyed it. I felt like a spy, marveling at what went on. The thing about cliques is there aren't any hard-and-fast rules about who belongs. You're supposed to know your place. Somebody crosses the line, nobody's going to say a word. At least not in our high school. Ned Lowe was nothing, and why Shirley Ann took up with him is anybody's guess."

"Maybe he was a relief after Big Bobby dumped her."

"No question. That must have been the shock of her life. Nothing bad ever happened to her. Ned was smart enough to take advantage. He weaseled his way in and hung on for dear life."

"Did that make him acceptable?"

"No. Here's the thing, though: everybody liked her, and if she was dating him, who was going to object? All the guys wondered how the hell he rated, but there was no getting around it. For a while, at any rate."

"Then what?"

"It was like everybody switched places. Big Bobby and Shirley Ann got back together and Ned couldn't accept the fact he was out on his butt. He followed her around like a lovesick puppy dog, all sorry-eyed and pitiful. Long face like this."

She paused to make a long face that was irritating even as an imitation.

She laughed at herself and went on. "She explained and explained she and Big Bobby were back together again, but he didn't want to hear it. You know what her problem was? She tried to be nice, and her mother only made it worse. Norma encouraged her to ditch him, but she insisted she do it without hurting his feelings. He wasn't the kind of guy you could reject at all, let alone with gentleness and tact. There was no getting rid of him. The more she pushed him away, the tighter his grip."

"How did the situation get resolved?"

"It didn't. That's just it. Things got so bad, her mother pulled her out of school and sent her back east to live with her aunt. She finished high school back there."

"I assume he recovered from his broken heart," I said.

"You'd think so, wouldn't you? High school isn't the end of the world. Or maybe it is for some. The irony is when Shirley Ann came back to take care of her mom, Ned was on her like a shot—worse than in high school, and that was bad enough."

"What happened to Norma?"

"Colon cancer they didn't catch in time. Shirley Ann was here all that March and then stayed on to settle her mom's estate. By then, her father was going downhill, and she ended up putting him in a home."

"Sounds like a bad year all around."

"I'll say, and Ned didn't help. In his mind, Shirley Ann was meant for him. His one true love. So there she was, right back in the same place. Trying to get rid of him, but too polite to tell him the truth."

"Which was what, the guy's a creep?"

"Exactly. There's no way she'd ever take up with him again. She was embarrassed she'd ever dated him in the first place."

"So this was before or after Lenore died?"

"Before, but just barely. Norma passed in late March, and Lenore, well, you know, she died sometime that spring."

"Good Friday, March 31," I supplied.

"Was it? I was thinking it was later, but you might be right. Anyway, Shirley Ann went back home and had the good sense to stay put."

"How do you know all this stuff?"

"I'm friends with one of her best friends from back then, a girl named Jessica. I hardly spoke to Shirley Ann in high school. I was too intimidated. The summer she came back, I ran into Jess at church, and now it's like the three of us are best friends."

"Interesting sequence of events. Run it by me again."

"What, about her mom? Norma got sick. Shirley Ann flew out to take care of her. This was five or six years after we graduated. Ned found out she was back and he's falling all over himself, trying to fan the flames. You'd have thought not a day had passed. All moony and mopey. Every time she turned around, there he was. And he was serious about getting into her underpants. He gave her one red rose a day. I mean, for crying out loud! How corny is that? Sentimental greeting cards with all this glitter on the front. He called every day, sometimes two and three times, to see how she was doing. He just about drove her insane."

"You think Lenore was aware of it?"

She gave a half shrug. "He made no big secret of it. Lenore probably hoped she could palm him off on Shirley Ann and good riddance."

"How'd she dispatch him the second time around?"

"Well, that was the problem, wasn't it? She couldn't reject him outright without setting him off. He'd have turned into a python and squeezed the life out of her. She told him a relationship was out of the question. Never happen in a million years. She was happily married and so was he."

"*Was* he happily married?"

"No, but it wasn't her lookout. She was skirting the truth, but what else could she say?"

"I got the impression Lenore was teetering on the brink by then."

"If she was, Ned drove her to it. I know Shirley Ann felt bad when she heard, you know, what Lenore did. Like if she'd been nicer to him, he wouldn't have been so mean to his wife."

"When you found out Lenore killed herself, did you question the story?"

"I didn't know her well enough to form a strong opinion. I can see where it was the answer to Ned's prayers. He was suddenly a free man, and wasn't that convenient? Didn't cut any ice with Shirley Ann. He'd always be a creep as far as she was concerned."

"She's still living back east?"

"She is."

"Do you have a phone number for her?"

"I don't, but Jessica does. If you're interested in talking to her, I'd be happy to call first and tell her what this is about. That way you wouldn't have to go through some long-drawn-out explanation."

"I would love that. I'm hoping it won't be necessary, but I'd like the option," I said.

I went on to quiz her on a minor point or two, but essentially she'd given me the gist. I took down her phone number in case I had questions later and then gave her one of my business cards. "If Shirley Ann would prefer to have me call her, just let me know."

"Sure thing."

"Meanwhile, if you don't mind my saying so, your life turned out great."

She looked around with satisfaction. "It did, didn't it? Trick is to figure out what you want and set your mind to it."

"How'd you go about it?"

"You might not believe this, but I'm a maverick at heart. Born and raised Catholic, but when I finally decided to get married, I found me a nice Jewish boy. Everybody thought I'd turned hippie because I kept my maiden name instead of taking his. Both our mothers had conniption fits, but so what? The two of us are so stubborn, neither one of us will convert."

"Where'd you meet him?"

"Ten-year high school reunion. I'd known him since grade school. You have no idea how cute he is. I can't believe I didn't see it at the time."

"A classmate. That's perfect."

"You bet. Little Bobby Fried. He was always the better of the two."

Marsha Heddon followed me out the front door and stood on the porch fanning herself while I returned to my car. I fired up the engine and drove off, keeping an eye on her in the rearview mirror until I turned the corner and lost sight of her. Two blocks farther on, I pulled over to the curb and shut the engine down. It was time to take stock.

I'd been following much the same path Pete had taken, though he'd been operating on another plan: running a background check on Ned Lowe, or such was the claim. I assumed he was tracking Ned's family of origin in hopes of confirming or debunking rumors of his pathology. The only suggestion I'd heard on that score came from Taryn Sizemore, whose opinion was colored by her history with him. I was willing to believe he was strange, but I had no proof he'd broken into Ruthie's house or my office. In the meantime, it was my job to place Lenore's Bible and her rosary in her daughter's hands.

I left Burning Oaks at 4:00. I made good time. The back roads were more appealing as the March light waned. I passed the farm stand where I'd purchased asparagus, but neither the old fellow nor his daughter was there. I didn't look directly at the parched fields and I avoided the sight of the riverbed, which was dry as a bone. I was still rejoicing at my good fortune at having wrapped up the day's work without having to spend another night away from home. If Clara Doyle remembered to pass my phone number along to Stanley Munce, it would be well worth the time and energy.

# 27

Once in my neighborhood, I found a parking space and grabbed my overnight case, the asparagus, and my shoulder bag. I locked my car and headed for the studio. I felt great about being home until I rounded the corner of the studio. Henry's backyard had been stripped. The last of the dead grass was gone and, while the fruit trees remained, the shrubs had been pulled up by the roots. Granted, the drought had killed them, but even brown, they'd been a reminder of the yard in its glory, back in the days when water was plentiful. The two Adirondack chairs had been stacked to one side. The remaining topsoil was so dry and powdery, a passing breeze would lift it in a cloud and bear it away.

Next door, I spotted Edna on the back porch with a paint scraper in hand, chipping off flakes of white paint with great industry. This was largely for show. If she had any real intention of repainting the porch rails, she'd enlist Henry's services and then stick him with the chore.

Henry emerged from his kitchen, the picture of good cheer. The cat took advantage of the open door to slip through. Henry was saying, "There you are! I didn't expect to see you back today."

"I got the job done and couldn't think of a reason to stay over," I said. "I brought you a present." I handed him the brown paper bag of asparagus.

He opened it and peeked in. "Wonderful. Nothing better than the first young spears. I'll check my recipes and come up with something tasty."

I watched Ed pick his way across the mulch bed, shaking first one paw and then another as though he were walking in snow. When he reached the porch outside my door, he had to stop and undergo a thorough cleaning, licking himself from head to toe.

I couldn't keep my eyes off the devastation Henry had visited on his property. "This is depressing."

Henry seemed surprised. "You think?" Even when he looked around, seeing the yard as I did, his reaction was mild. "It's a work in progress, of course, but it's coming along."

"Did the book say you should rip out everything, or was this the plumber's idea?"

"It was one of his suggestions. I might have carried it a little too far, but it should solve the problem. This concept is called xeriscape—mulch, drought-tolerant plants, and efficient irrigation."

"Won't it take years?"

"I like working with a blank canvas. It stimulates the imagination."

"How can you bear it? You've always loved your garden."

"I'll have one again. For the time being, there are higher principles at work."

His tone was a teeny tiny bit self-congratulatory and I felt a whisper of irritation.

"How come nobody else is doing this?" I asked.

"Excellent question and one I've asked myself. I'm hoping others will follow suit."

"I hate pointing this out, but right now there's no water rationing in place."

It might finally have occurred to him that I was annoyed.

"You're forgetting the twenty percent cut-back," he said.

"But that's *voluntary*."

"I feel we should take steps to conserve since our usage is going up."

"How could it be going up when I was in Burning Oaks all day and you haven't watered in a week?"

"Sadly, it hasn't helped."

"Maybe you have a leak. Have you thought about that?"

He blinked. "I hadn't. I'll have Mr. McClaskey come out and take another look."

I said, "Meanwhile, your yard looks like a construction zone. Summer comes, we can sit out here in our hard hats and admire the dust."

His brows went up. "Your trip must have been a disappointment. You seem out of sorts."

I had to close my eyes and get a grip on myself. I never lose my temper with him. "Sorry. I don't mean to fuss at you. The trip was fine. I'm just tired from the drive."

"If you feel like joining me for supper, I can put together something simple."

"I'll take a rain check. I'm too grumpy to be good company. I'll unpack and shower and then get in my comfies, which is bound to help."

I could see my use of the word "shower" had set off a mental alarm. Henry was probably calculating the water I'd already used this week. "I'll keep it short, I swear."

"One would hope."

I unlocked my door and let myself in. Ed was there like a shot, sliding through the open door. As usual, he strolled around my studio and made himself at home. He hopped up on the kitchen counter and settled like a bolster pillow, with his front feet tucked under him. I wasn't sure if Henry realized where he was, so I opened the door again and stuck my head out. "Ed's in here if you're looking for him."

"Thanks. Bring him over if he turns into a pest."

"Will do."

I closed and locked the door. I set my overnight case at the bottom of the spiral stairs and turned on the living room lamps. I noticed the message light blinking on my answering machine. I crossed to the desk and pressed Play.

"Kinsey. Spencer Nash here. I'm back in town and curious what you learned about Hallie Bettancourt. When you have a minute, would you give me a call? It's Saturday, one o'clock, and I should be here until four. If you miss me, leave a message and I'll call you back first chance I get."

He recited his number and I made a note of it. I didn't want to call him or anybody else. I needed time to myself.

I trotted up the spiral stairs and set my overnight case on the bed. Behind me, Ed jumped down from the kitchen counter and followed. He had a look around, sniffed at the baseboards in hopes of mice, and finally sprawled on my bed, watching with interest while I unloaded my overnight bag, leaving the permanently packed items where they were. That done, I stripped off my clothes and shoved them in the hamper.

I had a two-minute shower and a quick shampoo. Once I pulled on my oversize sleeping T-shirt and sweats, I felt better. I holed up for the evening, tucked in bed, where I finished my book with a boy-cat stretched out along my hip. I thought he'd ask to go out, but he seemed happy where he was. Nothing wrong with being single when you can do as you please without objection or complaint. The presence of the fur ball was icing on the cake.

It wasn't until Monday morning that I caught up with Nash—or, to be more accurate, when he caught up with me. We'd played phone tag all day Sunday and I'd finally decided not to sweat it. My report wasn't pressing, and he was entitled to his weekend without business intruding. I'd try another call when I reached the office.

Meanwhile, I woke at the usual hour, pulled on my running duds, did a perfunctory stretch, and headed the two blocks to the bike path that paralleled the beach. I could jog in my sleep if it came right down to it. There was a time when I wore headphones plugged into an AM/FM radio and spent most of the run trying to find a station I liked. The music was seldom to my taste and the news programs depressed me. My fallback position was a drive-time talk show, which usually consisted of two guys blabbing about nothing in particular, their "hilarious" banter more amusing to them than it was to anyone else. Eventually, I'd abandoned the idea of listening to anything. Silence allowed me time for reflection and helped to quiet the chatter in my head.

It was now March 20 and the morning skies were clear. Despite the unrelenting sunshine, there was still a chill in the air and I was happy to be wearing my red fleece sweatpants and hoodie, which always felt good when I was starting out. By the middle of the run, I'd be stripped down to my T-shirt, my hoodie off and tied around my waist by the sleeves like someone hugging me from behind. By the time the run was over and I'd slowed to a walk, my long pants would feel like damp towels and I'd be eager to peel them off.

I was nearing the turnaround point a mile and a half down the beach when I found my attention focused on a fellow jogging toward me at a good clip. He was in loose shorts and a mismatched tank top. Like me, he had a long-sleeved shirt tied around his waist. While he was a good six feet tall, he didn't show much in the way of upper-body development. His legs were sturdy and his feet were huge. There was nothing about him that signaled danger, but I made a quick assessment of the situation. It was, after all, barely light, and there was no one else in the area except for a homeless person zipped into a sleeping bag at the base of a palm tree. I avoided eye contact as the guy ran past.

"Kinsey?"

# X

The voice was familiar, and I turned to see Spencer Nash as he was slowing to a stop.

I did the same. "What are you doing out here?"

"Same thing you are. You want company?"

"As long as I don't slow you down."

"Not a problem. I was hoping to talk to you anyway."

He turned so the two of us were headed in the same direction, jogging in tandem until we reached the recreation center. We did an about-face and retraced our steps, he taking care to match my pace with his.

I said, "I don't remember seeing you down here. Is this your regular run?"

He shook his head. "I've been off with a hamstring pull and I'm just getting back into a routine. My doc made me swear I'd take it easy, so I'm sticking to the flats."

"You live close by?"

"Other side of the freeway. A little subdivision off Olive Tree Lane. What about you?"

"I'm on Albanil. I'm out here five mornings a week unless I want to feel especially virtuous by throwing in a Saturday or Sunday."

His footsteps were a ragged, off-tempo echo of mine, and I could tell he was reining in his natural tendency to lope. I wasn't accustomed to chatting while I jogged and I was quickly winded. I raised a hand. "I gotta catch my breath." I came to a stop and bent forward, resting my hands on my knees. "Shit. I thought I was in good shape."

"You're in great shape. I pushed you without meaning to. Why don't we find a place to sit?"

We continued at a fast walk and finally perched side by side on the low wall that separated the sidewalk from a kid-size jungle gym planted in a bed of sand. Behind us, on the far side of a chain-link fence, was the kiddie pool, which was usually open from Memorial Day to Labor Day. This year, it would remain closed in the interest of conservation.

The smell of salt water was strong, the air saturated with the pungent perfume of yesterday's catch: spiny lobster, ridgeback shrimp, sea bass, halibut, and albacore.

He said, "I was going to call you this morning."

"Hey, me too. This is perfect."

He loosened his long-sleeved shirt and mopped his sweaty face before he pulled it over his head. I was cooling down rapidly, already longing for a shower despite the two-minute hosing off I'd allowed myself the night before. Henry would look askance if he knew I was taking two showers back-to-back. If the water meter spiked, would I lie to him?

Nash rested his elbows on his oversize knees, his hands loosely clasped in front of him, face turned to me. "So what was the deal with Hallie Bettancourt?"

"For starters, it turns out Christian Satterfield was waiting for a woman named Kim Bass. It threw me for a loop at first. I'd run into her earlier at Montebello Luxury Properties, but I had no idea she and Christian knew each other. It seemed an odd mix."

I gave him the short version of my round-trip to Beverly Hills, including the fact that the pair I followed had been joined by "Hallie Bettancourt" at the Rodeo-Wilshire Hotel. "Her real name is Teddy Xanakis. Theodora," I amended.

He frowned in puzzlement. "Are you sure about that?"

"Positive. I can tell you what she had for breakfast Thursday morning if you're interested."

"You know who she is," he said, as though confirming the fact.

"No clue. My landlord said the name was familiar, but he was drawing a blank."

"She was married to a guy named Ari Xanakis. The two moved to Montebello six or seven years ago. They dominated the social scene until their high-profile divorce. That was a regular knock-down-drag-out fight."

"Still doesn't ring a bell. What's he do?"

"Shipping company. Excellent Portage, only it's spelled X-L-N-T.

There's XLNT International Shipping. XLNT Courier. Maybe half a dozen other businesses."

"I see those trucks everywhere," I said. I thought about the notion of Teddy Xanakis married to a shipping magnate. "You still think she might have been involved in that art-for-ransom scheme? I take it the victim wasn't her ex."

"Nope. Someone else, though from what I've heard, she'd have enjoyed sticking it to him."

"Seems unlikely a woman of her social status would steal anything," I said.

"Let's not forget she paid you with marked bills."

"But if she came up with the ransom scheme, why would she sit on the cash for two years?"

"She might have figured it was finally safe to put the money in circulation. Or she might have been hard up for cash."

"Do you intend to talk to her?"

"Not yet. There's no point in tipping our hand. If she's a party to the scheme, let her go on thinking she's gotten away with it."

"I'm about to freeze my butt off out here."

His smile was sheepish. "I'll let you go." He stood, all six-plus sweaty feet of him.

I untied the sleeves of my hoodie and zipped myself into it, momentarily warmed. "So what now? I'm not crazy about the idea of Teddy recruiting Christian Satterfield."

"I'll bet not. Especially since you were the one who set him up."


On my way to work, I stopped off at the bank and moved money from savings to my checking account. My alarm system would go in the next morning and I'd have to write S.O.S. a check as soon as the work was done. I continued to the office and parked in the driveway between my bungalow and the one to the right of mine. As Taryn Sizemore had suggested, I unlocked and opened the door with a sense of trepidation. I didn't actually believe Ned would return to trash the place, but I paused on the doorstep and braced for it anyway. I sniffed. The air was neutral, and a quick peek at my reception area showed nothing out of place. I peered into my office proper, reassured to see all was in order there as well. Nonetheless, I did a cautious walk-about before I sat down at my desk.

I had no phone messages and the mail that had come in was quickly dispatched. One sorry consequence of being short of work was that any unresolved matter was cause for brooding—Teddy Xanakis being a case in point. Even in retrospect, her long sad tale about giving up her baby seemed just offbeat enough to be true, and while I no longer believed a word of it, I couldn't imagine why she'd wanted to make contact with Christian Satterfield unless she suffered a pathological compulsion to orchestrate personal makeovers on parolees. He'd certainly benefited from her sense of style and her willingness to spend big bucks. No harm had befallen him in that regard, but why was she doing it?

That question aside, the fact was she could have found the kid without help from me. I wasn't sure how she'd have gone about it, but she was smart and it was clear she could bullshit with the best of them. Why had she roped me in? The problem from my perspective was that I'd provided her the information and now I felt responsible. Satterfield was a big boy and he could look after himself, but I'd put him in a strange position. He was thirty-two years old, an ex-con with no job, no income, and he was living with his mom. How embarrassing was that? If I knew what Teddy had in mind for him, I could either go to his rescue or quit worrying about him.

My thoughts drifted to Vera, who probably knew all the gossip about Teddy and Ari Xanakis. I was hesitant about asking her because I'd virtually abandoned our relationship. Now I wanted to pump her for information and I had no emotional bank account to draw upon. I picked up the phone and punched in her number.

She picked up almost before the line had rung.

"Hey, Vera. This is Kinsey. I thought I'd check and see how you were doing."

"Great. I'm good. I've got three hooligans running circles around me."

"Any sign of Travis and Scott?"

"Currently, the twins are trying to kick their way to freedom, so far without success. What's up with you?"

"I was hoping to pick your brain."

"What a thrilling proposition: talking to an adult. Why don't you come on over?"

"I'd love to. What's your schedule this afternoon?"

"I'm not going anyplace. Park in the drive and let yourself in the kitchen door."

"Will do. I'll see you shortly."

On my way over, I stopped by a toy store, thinking I should come up with a "hostess" gift to atone for my neglect. In the past, I'd arrive with a bottle of pricy wine in hand, but as pregnant as she was, alcohol would be a no-no, along with spicy foods and cruciferous vegetables that in the past she claimed made her flatulent. Not that I'd give her a box of Brussels sprouts. My plan was to bring gifts for the kids and thus ingratiate myself. Their ages ranged from baby Abigail, whose date of birth was unknown, to Peter, who was close to four, with Meg's age falling somewhere between theirs. I needed something that would entertain all three. Oh, geez.

Not surprisingly, the toy store was jammed with toys and I was at a loss. A clerk followed me patiently while I drifted from aisle to aisle, pondering the merchandise. Shoppers were few and I suspected she'd offered to help for her own amusement, observing how inept I was. I rejected packages of balloons, knowing the kids would surely choke to death. I decided against guns or dolls in case the parents were dead set against gender stereotypes. I knew better than to get anything with a thousand little bitty pieces, for both the choking hazard and the certainty of plastic parts being crushed underfoot. Nothing with batteries.

I was hoping for something that cost less than ten bucks, which narrowed my choices to just about none. Well, okay, coloring books, but Abigail was probably not old enough to enjoy crayons unless she was eating them.

I spotted six racks of books, ranging from board books to picture books to books without illustrations of any kind. I turned to the clerk. "How old are kids when they learn to read?"

"Around here? I'd say ninth grade."

I finally settled on three bottles of bubble solution with those cunning wands down inside where you can barely reach them to haul them out.

# 28

I parked at the far end of Vera's driveway, where a half-moon of concrete had been provided as a turnaround. I went up the back steps and let myself in through one of the French doors that opened from the deck into the kitchen.

The furniture in the seating area had been pushed back against the walls, and the hardwood floor was layered four-deep in quilts and comforters. Vera sat with her back against the sofa, belly enormous and pillows wedged behind her for support. A voluminous tent of a dress covered her bulk and her feet were bare. A toddler I took to be Abigail stood upright beside her, a hand on her mother's head for balance. Her legs seemed a bit wobbly, but were otherwise doing what baby legs were meant to do. She wore a dress of sprigged muslin, tiny pink roses on a ground of white with puffed sleeves and pink smocking across the front. With her bare feet and plump little arms, she looked edible.

Meg and Peter were running barefoot from the foyer to the kitchen and back again. They'd invented a game that involved propelling themselves down the hall at a dead run and smacking their hands against the front door. Then they'd turn around and run toward the kitchen, bare feet thundering, and bang into the back door.

In one corner, I caught sight of Chase, their golden retriever, who appeared to have been flattened by the children's relentless energy and noise. When I'd first spotted the dog on the beach path, prancing along beside Vera and Neil, Peter was perhaps eighteen months old and Vera was massively pregnant with Meg. Now that the pooch was four, he'd mellowed considerably. He lay stretched out on the floor with his head on his paws. Now and then, he flicked an eye at the children, making sure all were present and accounted for, and then continued his nap. He didn't seem to consider me a threat.

Of course, Vera and Neil had a live-in nanny. I'm not sure how she'd have managed without assistance of some kind, though knowing Vera, she'd have done just fine. She's a big woman and she carries herself with confidence. She'd had her dark hair cut short and wore it now in a shag. With her oversize blue-tinted aviator glasses, she managed to look glamorous even with her midsection pumped up like a dirigible.

After we exchanged the requisite greetings, Vera said, "This is Bonnie." She indicated the stout middle-aged woman at the kitchen counter and I lifted a hand in greeting. Bonnie smiled in return. She'd soft-boiled half a dozen eggs, three of which now sat upright in yellow egg cups shaped like chicks. She began to slice the tops off, leaving the half shells to form vessels into which the children could dip strips of buttered toast cut into "soldiers." She'd set up three Peter Rabbit–themed plastic plates divided into compartments. In one, she'd placed diced bananas and pineapple; in another, radish flowers and spirals of raw carrot.

Vera called over her shoulder. "Hey, kids? Settle down. It's picnic time. Peter? You and Meg come sit in the clouds with me."

# X

Peter appeared from the hallway at a dead run and flung himself across the comforters with Meg right behind him, mimicking his actions. The entire house, or at least the portions I could see, had been child-proofed. Most of the surfaces were bare, and all the electric sockets were sealed with plastic devices designed to prevent children from sticking forks in the slots, thereby electrocuting themselves. There were no bookshelves with massive volumes perilously close to the edge, no knickknacks within reach of tiny hands. Lamps were wall- or ceiling-mounted, with no dangling cords. Lower cabinets were locked by means of hardware that required the swiping of a magnetic key. There were spring-loaded latches as well. Retractable gates were drawn across the doorway between the kitchen and dining room. The children had free run of the hallway. Period.

What struck me was the uncanny resemblance between Vera and her small brood. Something in her facial structure had been translated intact. They were as beautiful as small foxes, duplicates of her and variations of one another. No physical imprint from Neil at all.

Peter and Meg arranged themselves cross-legged on the floor. Bonnie set down an egg cup and a small spoon in front of each along with their plates, fruits and vegetables neatly segregated. The kids were clearly hungry and went to work with enthusiasm. Vera fed Abigail by hand, placing bites in her upturned mouth, which was open like a baby bird's.

I said, "I don't know how you do this."

She smiled. "Shall I tell you the secret? You don't do anything else. That's why most grandparents enjoy the hell out of kids. They're not always thinking ahead to something more important. Try to read or talk on the phone or undertake any task that requires focus and this bunch will be all over you. Sit with 'em like I do and they can't wait to get away from you.

"The other secret is coordinated nap and bedtimes. I see parents whose kids are up running around until eleven o'clock at night. I have a friend who claims her three-year-old doesn't 'feel' like going to bed before midnight. I'm looking at her like she has two heads. The kid doesn't *feel* like it? My kids are in bed by eight o'clock, no ifs, ands, or buts. Kids need at *least* eight hours of shut-eye. Otherwise they're whiny and out of sorts. Me too, for that matter."

"You're going to end up with five kids under the age of five?"

"Oh. I guess so," she said, as though the thought had just occurred to her. "In all honesty, I wouldn't mind adding one more just to round out the number to an even six. Neil isn't keen on the idea, but he may change his mind. Have a seat. You want a soft-boiled egg?"

"Maybe later," I said. "You look wonderful."

"Thanks. I can barely walk without wetting myself, but I'll accept the compliment in the spirit with which it was given. Is that for the kids?" she asked, indicating the bag that held my toy store finds.

"Of course."

I offered her the sack and let her peek inside.

She said, "Perfect."

Once the children had finished lunch, I gave Peter and Meg each a bottle of bubbles, first fishing out the submerged wands and giving a demonstration. Both were absorbed by the slipstream of bubbles floating above their heads. Abigail laughed one of those helpless belly laughs and then sat down on her butt. Shortly afterward, she started crying and Vera declared it was nap time. Bonnie hustled the three upstairs.

Even as well-behaved as the children were, the ensuing quiet was wonderful.

Vera said, "Ah, grown-up time. Tell me what's going on."

I filled her in on my search of the Clipper estate, my subsequent dealings with Cheney Phillips's mother at Montebello Luxury Properties, and the conversation I'd had with Detective Nash about the stolen painting that had been ransomed back to the owner in return for twenty-five thousand in marked bills.

My narrative included, but was not limited to, my round-trip to Beverly Hills where I'd spotted "Hallie Bettancourt," now known to me by her real name, which was Teddy Xanakis.

"Teddy Xanakis? You gotta be shitting me!"

"I thought you might know her."

"I can't say I 'know' her, but I sure know who she is. She and Ari Xanakis were the darlings of Montebello the minute they hit town. He donated megabucks to all the trendy charities, and she served on the boards of everything. Perfect combination. He was generous and she was smart and well-organized. She could also fund-raise with the best of them.

"They bought a big house where they entertained often and lavishly. The Montebello matrons were fawning over them. Don't tell anyone I said that. Montebello matrons think they're much too cool and sophisticated to fawn over anyone. They all claimed they genuinely liked the pair. 'So down-to-earth and unpretentious, so bighearted and sincere.'"

"I knew you'd have the lowdown."

"Oh, do I ever," she said. "When the two of them finally split, the Montebello matrons couldn't back away fast enough. If the case went to court, nobody wanted to be called as a character witness. That's a no-win situation any way you look at it. You alienate him or you alienate her and you don't know which one will end up on top. I think they finally reached a settlement after a horrific two years of trying to outdo each other. Meanwhile, the donations dropped to zero, so no more invitations for her. The only friend she has left is this redhead named Kim who used to be high society like Teddy until her husband went to prison for embezzlement."

"I've met Kim. She's now working for Montebello Luxury Properties."

"She has to work? Well, the poor thing, though she's better off than Teddy, who has no marketable skills."

"Is Kim's husband at USP Lompoc by any chance?"

"I don't know where they sent him, but that's a good guess. Meanwhile, Teddy left for Los Angeles and Ari took up with a wealthy widow. Actually, his taking up with the widow was what caused the split in the first place. His behavior was an embarrassment. The widow was half his age and a bombshell to boot. How's that for original?"

I was shaking my head. "I guess Teddy's back in town."

"Yep, which probably means they've signed off on the settlement."

"How'd she come out of the deal?"

"I haven't heard. I know she went into the marriage without a dime to her name, and here she is again, dependent on him to fund her lifestyle, only in monthly increments."

"How long were they married?"

"Eighteen years. Maybe seventeen. Somewhere in that neighborhood."

"She must have done okay, don't you think?"

"Hard to tell. She gets spousal support I'm sure, but other than that, he was determined to keep what was his and she wanted what she was owed. *Vanity Fair* ran a four-page spread, detailing their shenanigans."

"I'm sorry I missed that. What were they fighting over?"

"The big bone of contention was their art collection. He knew nothing about art and had no interest in collecting until she talked him into it. Once they split, he claimed the art on the grounds that he assumed all the risk."

"Why didn't they just add it all up and each take half? I thought that's how community property worked."

"I'm sure they're liquidating what they can, which is no fun for either one of them. She gave up her stake in the Montebello property, which she couldn't afford to maintain. There's a flat in London that ended up on her side of the ledger. She'd be better off taking up residency in the UK, where at least she can start fresh. Even with spousal support, she'll have a tough time maintaining her lifestyle."

# X

"She should have just forgiven the transgression and kept the life she loved."

"Absolutely. I forgot to mention the bombshell widow was Teddy's best friend, which made the blow more devastating."

"What happened to the widow?"

"Ari married her last month and they're about to take off on a delayed honeymoon. Can't remember where. Someplace pricy and remote. That's the new trend. Used to be you'd book a spot everybody knew about so they'd appreciate the exorbitant expense. Now you pick a resort so exclusive, no one's ever heard of it. It's even better if it's difficult to reach and requires your chartering a private jet. Does any of this help?"

"Information is always good, and the more the merrier. It still frosts my butt she put one over on me. What's her game?"

"Beats me."

"Well, whatever it is, if there's a way to trip her up, I'll be happy to pitch in."

I left Vera's house twenty minutes later, thinking she'd want to catch a few winks of sleep herself while the little ones were down. Her mention of the Xanakises' art collection renewed my interest in the art theft Nash mentioned in his initial visit. I'd dismissed the idea of a wealthy socialite stealing art unless she'd been desperate for cash. Clever as she was, she might have been perfectly willing to snitch a painting and then accept payment for its return. Possible she didn't even view it as a crime, just a minor fiddle between friends and no harm done. She probably knew who owned all the pricy pieces in Montebello and what security was in place protecting them. She might even have known which collections were properly insured and which were not.

Once back at the office, I banished thoughts of Teddy and redirected my attention to April Staehlings and the delivery of the memorabilia that had been left to her. It seemed politic to call in advance. I had no idea how much she'd been told about her mother's death. She was three at the time and I doubted she remembered Lenore at all. Ned had probably raised her on a sanitized version of the truth, if not an outright lie. With Lenore dead, he could frame the story any way he liked, and who was there to contradict him? Aside from that, I was uncomfortable with the notion of arriving on April's doorstep if she was unprepared.

I hauled out the phone book and found the Staehlings' number listed in the white pages, along with their home address. I punched in the number and listened to the ringing on the other end, rehearsing my summary of the long and convoluted story. An answering machine would have been a blessing, but not one I was accorded.

"Hello?"

"May I speak to April?"

"This is she."

Metaphorically speaking, I took a deep breath and stepped off the edge of the cliff. "My name is Kinsey Millhone. I have a mailing pouch in my possession that contains personal items your mother wanted you to have."

"You have a what?"

"A padded mailing envelope. The circumstances are complicated and I apologize for catching you off guard, but I was hoping to work out a time when I could drop off the items and explain."

Dead silence. "My *mother*? Well, that can't be true. She's been dead for years."

"I know, and I promise you the keepsakes came from her."

"*Who's* this?"

"Kinsey Millhone. I'm a local private investigator."

"I don't understand. What keepsakes are you talking about? What does that mean, 'keepsakes'?"

"I know it's confusing and I'm hoping you'll hear me out. Lenore left you her rosary and the Bible she was given when she was confirmed."

A moment of dead quiet. "I don't know what you want, but I'm not interested."

"Hang on a minute. Please. I know it's a lot to take in, but let me finish. Shortly before she died, she mailed the items to her parish priest, and he's held on to them for years."

I was omitting Pete Wolinsky's part in the matter, but I figured there was only so much she could absorb. She was already stumbling over the concept. I was talking fast, trying to convey the gist of the story before she disengaged. The speedy summation probably wasn't supporting the sincerity I'd hoped to communicate.

"Is this a *sales* call?"

"It's not. I'm not selling anything."

"Sorry. Can't help. Bye-bye." The latter was delivered in a singsong voice.

"Wait—"

"No, you wait. I don't know what your angle is—"

"I don't have an angle. I called because I didn't want to spring it on you."

"Spring what? Cash on delivery? You think I'm an idiot?"

"We don't have to talk. I'll be happy to leave the package on your porch as long as you know it's there."

"No. Absolutely not. You show up at my house, I will call the police." Then she hung up.

Shit. Now what? If I'd had my wits about me, I'd have put the old mailing pouch in a larger mailing pouch and addressed it to April Staehlings and made a trip to the post office. But somehow I had it in my head I should hand-deliver the items since Pete Wolinsky, among others, had gone to so much trouble to see that the package reached her after all these years. Lenore to Clara to Father Xavier, from him to Pete Wolinsky, and from Pete to me. I'd put in a fair number of hours, not to mention the miles I'd driven. Now I wanted to finish the job I'd started.

What was I thinking? This was one more example of the do-gooder mentality that gets me in trouble every time it surfaces.

I made a note of her street address, which I located on my city map. She lived on the north end of Colgate in a subdivision I was dimly acquainted with. I could see how it looked from her perspective. She'd assumed I was running a scam, which I knew I was not. I grabbed the mailing pouch, locked the office, got in my car, and took the 101 north to Colgate. All I had to do was drop off the mailer and I'd be done with it.

# 29

April and her husband lived in a large Spanish-style home on a lot that was probably half an acre in size. The exterior was rough stucco with a terra-cotta tile roof, arches, and ornamental ironwork. A three-car garage dominated the front of the house. Most homes on the block looked much the same, barring a balcony or two. I was guessing the Staehlings' residence had four bedrooms, four and a half bathrooms, a family room, an eat-in kitchen, and a large sheltered patio across the rear of the house. There would be a modest-size swimming pool. The neighborhood conveyed solid middle-class values. Or maybe I arrived at that conclusion because I knew William was an orthodontist and I put his 1989 annual income in the range of a hundred thousand dollars—not much in light of all the schooling he'd been required to complete. He might still be paying off his student loans.

For a moment, I sat in my car with the mailing pouch on the

passenger seat in easy reach. My call had accomplished nothing except to trigger April's hostility, and I was sorry I hadn't done a better job of explaining myself. All I wanted to do now was slip up the front walk and lay the mailer on her doorstep. I wouldn't even ring the doorbell, trusting she'd discover the package at some point during the day.

I was on the verge of exiting my car when I glanced in my rearview mirror and caught sight of a Santa Teresa County Sheriff's Department black-and-white sliding into the stretch of curb behind my Honda. For a moment, I thought the deputy's arrival was an independent occurrence. Maybe he lived next door; maybe he was doing a welfare check on the occupant. Nope.

A uniformed deputy emerged from his car and approached mine, coming up on the driver's side. I couldn't believe April had called the police and reported me, but it was clear she had. Shit. In my side-view mirror I saw the officer unsnap his holster, but the gesture was discreet; not the action of a man seriously intent on gunning me down. I glanced at the telltale mailing pouch, which I longed to tuck on the floor under the passenger seat. With the deputy so close, I didn't dare lean forward lest the movement be misconstrued as my reaching for a weapon of my own.

Traffic stops are dangerous. A noncomfrontational encounter can turn deadly in a heartbeat. I was a stranger sitting in a parked car. He knew nothing of my criminal history and nothing of my purpose. What had April complained about? Harassment? A threat to her personal safety?

I pressed the button that lowered the driver's-side window and then put both hands on the steering wheel where he could see them. I could write a primer on how to behave in the presence of law enforcement, which basically boils down to good manners and abject obedience. He leaned toward me, holding a flashlight in his left hand. He trained the light on the dashboard, not because there was anything to be seen, but because the device was equipped to pick up any hint of alcohol on my breath.

"Afternoon." He was white, in his fifties, clean-shaven, and looked like he could pack a punch.

I said, "Hi."

"May I see your vehicle registration and proof of insurance?"

"They're in the glove compartment."

He gestured. I flipped open the glove compartment and pawed through the papers until I found the documents, which I handed to him. He took his time examining both documents before handing them back. "You have identification?"

"I can show you my driver's license and a photocopy of my private investigator's license."

"I'd appreciate it."

I took out my wallet and opened it to the window where my California driver's license was displayed. "Is there a problem?"

"Can you remove the license?"

I removed my driver's license and handed it to him along with my PI license. He gave the latter a perfunctory glance and then returned it, unimpressed.

"Wait here."

In the side- and rearview mirrors, I watched him amble back to his patrol car. I knew he'd call in my plate number to see if I had outstanding wants or warrants, which I did not. April must have dialed 9-1-1 the minute she hung up. I wondered if she remembered my reference to the mailing pouch. Now I was sorry I'd mentioned it because I couldn't think how to explain why the package in my possession intended for her was addressed to a Catholic priest in Burning Oaks. If I were quizzed on the subject, my long-winded account would sound like a fairy tale and the chain of events would be irrelevant. He had arrived in response to a complaint and he wasn't responsible for verifying my claim. Briefly, I entertained the notion of having him deliver the package on my behalf, thinking surely April would be receptive if a deputy served as a go-between. Belatedly, I realized I hadn't noted his name.

I waited patiently, demonstrating what a model citizen I was. Cooperative. Unarmed. This was all part of the game. The deputy exercised control, and I showed him the obligatory respect while the mini-drama played out. Not a problem for me, officer. I could sit here all day. He'd put me through my paces, after which he'd caution me politely and I'd respond in kind.

I stared straight ahead, resigned to my fate. A car turned the corner at the far end of the block and headed in my direction. The vehicle was a late-model Ford, black, with a solo male driver, who slowed in front of April's house and pulled to the curb with his car facing mine, perhaps a hundred feet away. He got out. Caucasian, middle-aged, tall and lean, wearing a tan poplin raincoat. I knew the face. Ned Lowe looked better now than he had in high school, which I hope can be said of all of us. Given Taryn's account of him, I'd anticipated a man whose manner was intimidating. Not so. There was nothing menacing in his body language. His complexion was pale. He looked tired. Under ordinary circumstances, I wouldn't have given him a second thought.

April must have been watching for her father's arrival. She opened the front door, closed it behind her, and waited on the porch. She had shoulder-length dark hair and that was as much as I could determine, except for the short-sleeve cotton maternity top she wore. She had her bare arms crossed in front of her. I assumed she was a solid eight months pregnant. Since she and her orthodontist husband had been married a little over a year, this was probably her first.

Ned crossed the lawn to the porch, where he and April had a brief conversation, both of them staring at me. From his raincoat pocket, he pulled a small spiral-bound notebook, jotting down what I imagined was the color, make, and model of my car, as well as my license plate number in case I ever showed up again. April's next-door neighbor appeared on her porch, so I was now the object of her curiosity as well.

# X

The deputy took his time on the return. So far, he hadn't said a word about my vehicular sins. That's because I hadn't committed any. He didn't even have grounds to cite me for a faulty brake light or an expired license tag. Even so, there was something embarrassing about the whole episode, which must have suited Ned Lowe to a T. Now that I thought about it, April had probably called him and *he* was the one who'd called the sheriff's department.

The deputy leaned forward and returned my license. His name tag read M. FITZMORRIS. No hint of his first name. Surely he wasn't Morris Fitzmorris, though I've heard of parents who do that sort of thing. He looked more like a Michael; big guy, dark-haired, good posture, his back ramrod straight. "You have business in the neighborhood, Ms. Millhone?"

"Not now," I said.

Ned beckoned from the porch. "Officer? Could I have a word with you?"

Fitzmorris turned and moved up the walk in his direction while Ned approached from the porch. The two met at the midpoint and conferred. This consisted of Ned doing all the talking while the deputy nodded now and then. I had no choice but to wait. Throughout their exchange, Ned's gaze was fixed on me, and I was conscious of his scrutiny. I didn't look at him directly, but I was acutely aware of him in my peripheral vision. I knew he wanted me to make eye contact so he could establish his superior position. One glimpse was all it would have taken. In a sixth-grade staring contest, the point is to hold your opponent's gaze without faltering. The first person who breaks eye contact loses. Here, the point was just the opposite. He willed me to look at him. I kept my eyes averted, suppressing the urge.

Deputy Fitzmorris returned to my car and reported Ned's comments. "Mr. Lowe is concerned about a possible shakedown. His word, not mine."

"A *shakedown*?"

"His daughter says you wanted to deliver gifts her mother ordered before she died. It was her impression you expected cash on delivery."

"I never said anything of the sort. What gifts? I'm not delivering anything. You can search my trunk if you don't want to take my word for it." I was hoping it wouldn't occur to him to ask why I'd called her in the first place.

He kept his tone neutral. "Mr. Lowe wants your assurance you won't approach the house or initiate contact with Mrs. Staehlings."

"What is he *talking* about? I haven't stepped out of my car and I haven't exchanged a word with either one of them. Could you make a note of that in your report?"

"I will do that," he said. "I can see there was a miscommunication. I'm not sure how you two got crosswise with each other, but people sometimes jump to conclusions and the situation escalates. I think cooler heads will prevail. I'm sure Mr. Lowe and his daughter will be good with this."

"I hope so," I said. "May I go now?"

He backed up a step and gestured that I could pull away, saying, "I appreciate your patience."

"And I appreciate your courtesy," I replied.

I rolled up the car window, started the engine, and pulled into the street, my attention riveted on the road in front of me. It wasn't until I turned the corner that I let out a deep breath and then shivered as the tension drained away. I could feel a cold damp patch under each arm and I knew the flop sweat would be scented with anxiety.

I reached the office, ready for some peace and quiet so I could compose myself. As I pulled into the drive, I saw Detective Nash sitting in his parked car. He spotted me, and by the time I emerged from my car, he was getting out of his.

I paused. "Didn't I just talk to you?"

"Something's come up."

"I'm having a hard day. I don't suppose it can wait."

"Could, but I was in the neighborhood."

I unlocked the office door and left it ajar, resigned to his following. No need to invite him in when he was intent on tagging after me. I dropped my shoulder bag on the floor behind my desk and settled in my swivel chair. He took a seat in the same guest chair he'd occupied before.

"Fire away," I said.

"I had a conversation with Ari Xanakis."

"How did that come to pass? Did you call him or did he call you?"

"I confess I called him. Ordinarily, I'd keep my nose out of it. His relationship with Teddy is his to deal with, but given their rancorous history, I thought he should be aware of that business in Beverly Hills. If she's cooking up trouble for him, he should be forewarned. I gave him the broad strokes and he said he'd prefer hearing the story from you."

"I'd have to think about that. I'm not opposed to lousing up Teddy's life, but I don't want to get caught in the middle of their hostilities. From what I've heard, the two have been battling for years and this is just more of the same," I said.

"That about sums it up."

"What have you told him? Does he know about the marked bills?"

"I gave him a quick sketch of the situation. I was reluctant to brief him on an ongoing investigation, but I didn't think I had much choice. I didn't want to put you in the position of having to lie if he asked. I told him you did a job for her and that's how the two bills came to our attention."

"Speaking of which, I'm still out a hundred bucks on that score."

"Unfortunately, I can't do anything about that."

"So what does Ari want from me?"

"He understands it was your detective work that put Teddy in touch with Satterfield. He'd like to hear your assessment."

"My assessment? I met the woman once and everything she told me was a lie. I know what I saw, but I can't begin to guess what she's up to. Why doesn't he ask her?"

"Asking is usually a bad move where Teddy's concerned. If she's scamming him, she's not going to 'fess up."

"I'll talk to him. Once. And let's hope that's the end of it."

"Thanks. I owe you one. I'll get back to you."

# 30

Tuesday morning, as I was leaving the studio, I found Henry poised on my doorstep, his hand raised as though to knock. I could see his station wagon idling in the driveway. Edna was standing on the far side wearing a black winter coat and a jaunty red knit hat, her pocketbook clasped in front of her like a brown bag lunch.

Henry said, "I'm so glad you're here. I was worried you'd be gone by now."

"Late start this morning. Where are you off to?"

"Edna has a dentist's appointment. I'm tied up with my accountant this afternoon, but in the meantime, I volunteered to ferry her to and from. Someone was supposed to stay with Joseph, but the woman called just now and said she was coming down with a cold and didn't think she should expose either one of them. Could you keep an eye on him?"

I flicked a look at Edna, whose interest in our conversation was sufficient to persuade me the plan was hers. No one had agreed to "mind" Joseph. Edna was making that up. She'd left arrangements until the last minute, counting on Henry to press me into service. She knew for a fact I wouldn't have stepped in on her account. She also knew I couldn't refuse Henry's asking me to do anything. We exchanged a look. A sly smile lifted the corners of her mouth.

"My alarm system goes in today and I have to be there. How long will this take?"

"An hour and a half. Mr. McClaskey's due shortly to inspect for leaks, so I'd appreciate your leaving your studio unlocked."

"I can do that."

Next thing I knew, Henry was pulling out of the drive with Edna seated placidly beside him and I had no choice but to trot next door as agreed. I knocked twice as a courtesy, then opened the door a crack and put my head in. With Joseph in a wheelchair, it seemed inconsiderate to make him push himself through the house to let me in.

"Hello?" I stepped into the living room and closed the door behind me. "Mr. Shallenbarger?"

A massive television set dominated one end of the living room, currently tuned to a vintage Western filled with cowboys who looked like they were wearing lipstick. Sound thundered—blazing guns and horses' hooves. I could hear water running in the next room.

I raised my voice. "Mr. Shallenbarger? It's Kinsey from next door."

"In here," he called.

This was the first time I'd been in the house. The Adelsons owned the property long before I moved into Henry's studio. For years, Dale Adelson taught English literature at UCST. The previous summer, he'd taken a job at the University of Virginia in Richmond. The move had delighted the couple because her family lived in the area and they looked forward to the proximity. Meanwhile, the house had been on the market and sitting empty until the Shallenbargers bought it and moved in.

The place looked cluttered despite the fact that the furnishings were sparse. Sealed U-Haul boxes were still lined up along the walls. A big rag rug sat in the middle of the room, one of those soiled flat braided ovals you sometimes see abandoned at the curb. I'd always heard that for those in wheelchairs, carpeting and stairs were frustrating obstacles, best avoided where possible. I crossed to the kitchen and peered in.

Joseph had his back to me. It was the first time I understood how heavy he was. He'd pulled his wheelchair close to the sink, where he was washing dishes by hand. The faucet gushed noisily. Henry would have flinched to see water run at that rate, but Joseph seemed oblivious. A small plastic wash bin had been placed in the sink and it was piled high with dirty pots and pans on top of glasses and plates. The counters and sink were at an appropriate height for most adults, but at a level that created difficulties for him since his chair was uncomfortably low. He looked like a little kid seated at a dinner table. He could barely see what he was doing, and in the process of moving dishes from the rinse water to the rack, he'd trailed water on the floor and across his lap.

"Why don't you let me do that?" I said.

"I can manage."

I moved to the sink and turned the water off. "I'll just take a quick turn as long as I'm here," I said. "You go watch the movie. The good part's coming up."

"Well. You sure you don't mind?"

"Not at all. It won't take me long."

He rolled himself away from the sink and did a three-point turn. Over his shoulder, he said, "That too loud for you?"

"A bit."

He wheeled himself toward the door to the living room. The frame was narrow and the wooden threshold between the two rooms was another impediment. I crossed, took the wheelchair handles, and gave him a sufficient push to bump him over it. I waited to see what he'd do about the rag rug and noted that he rolled right over it.

He'd left the remote control on a small table near the end of the couch. He picked it up and aimed it at the set. He pushed the volume button repeatedly to no effect. He banged the remote against his palm without persuading it to work. "Batteries is wearing down," he said irritably.

"You have fresh ones?"

"Maybe in the bedroom. Edna would know. You can turn the volume down at the set if you want."

"Don't worry about it. I'll be fine," I replied.

I returned to the sink and stared at the daunting accumulation of cookware. I decided I'd start from scratch. I removed pots and pans from the hillock and set them to one side so I could get to the plates and cutlery at the bottom of the heap. Through the kitchen window, I could see the back deck, which extended along the width of the house. Edna had managed to scrape and sand chipped white paint from a short stretch of wooden handrail. I was guessing she wouldn't finish the job unless Henry and I pitched in. I would have vowed not to participate, but I knew she'd con Henry into helping and I'd end up volunteering my services on his behalf.

I tilted the plastic bin and emptied the soapy water, which by now had been reduced to a cold murky lake. I far preferred washing dishes to chitchatting with the old man. With the sound from the television set still blaring, I had no trouble following the action, right down to chairs scraping the saloon floor as the villain leaped to his feet, his six-shooter drawn.

China and glasses didn't take long, but I realized I'd have to dry them to make room for the cookware. The only dish towel in sight was damp. I tried a few drawers randomly and finally crossed to the doorway to ask Joseph where the clean linens were kept.

His wheelchair was empty and there was no sign of him. I peered to my left, where I could see the transverse hallway that led to the bedrooms and the adjoining bath. Where had the man gone? I padded across the living room and checked the hall in both directions. Joseph was in the bedroom to my right, standing in front of the chest of drawers while he struggled with the seal on a package of double-A batteries. He picked at the wrapping and finally nipped a tiny hole in the cellophane. He extracted two batteries and tossed the package back in the drawer.

I retreated in haste, and by the time he returned to the living room, I'd completed the four giant steps to the kitchen. I picked up the damp towel and swiped at a plate, trying to decide what to make of it. Neither he nor Edna had ever actually *said* he was completely disabled, but that was the impression I'd been given. I'd assumed he wasn't ambulatory, but this wasn't the case. I tucked the information away, thinking it was good he wasn't quite as helpless as I'd imagined. Also thinking I'd keep the discovery to myself.

There was a long pause. I allowed time for him to arrange himself in his wheelchair and replace the batteries in the remote. The volume diminished dramatically, and shortly afterward, he rolled into view.

I turned. "You found the batteries?"

"Drawer in the side table by the couch," he said. "How're you doing?"

"I could use a dry towel."

"Basket in the pantry," he said, waving in that direction.

I waited, expecting him to return to the living room, but he kept his attention fixed on me. This created an irresistible urge on my part to make nice.

I flicked a look at my watch. It was 8:03. "What time do you think she'll be home?"

"Depends on how long she has to sit there."

"I thought she had an appointment. Isn't she having her teeth cleaned?" I asked, thinking what the hell else would you be doing in a dentist's chair at 8:00 A.M.?

"Naw. This's an emergency. She has to have a crown replaced. She said if she called first, the lady at the desk would make her wait two, three weeks. She goes in, they'll make sure the dentist sees her right away so it won't look bad to the other patients."

"Doesn't a crown take *hours*?"

"Oh, I imagine she'll be back by noon," he remarked. "If not, she said to ask if you'd fix me lunch."

An involuntary sound escaped my lips.

He rolled himself away. "I better let you get back to work. I don't want to slow you down."

I finished the dishes, brooding darkly. I'd just wandered back into the living room when I caught a glimpse of the plumber's truck pulling into Henry's drive. "The plumber's here and I have to run next door. Henry gave strict instructions to let him in the minute he arrived. Will you be all right? It shouldn't take long."

He waved me off. "I'm fine."

I found Mr. McClaskey standing at my front door. He lifted the brown gimme cap as soon as I appeared. "Morning."

"Hey, Mr. McClaskey. Henry's off running an errand and I'm baby-sitting the guy next door, but both our doors are unlocked and you can let yourself in. You're looking for leaks?"

"Yes, ma'am. Starting with the commodes. Mr. Pitts says he has no complaints, but it never hurts to check."

"I have two toilets—one up and one down—and neither seems to be running."

"Good to hear. Comes to a leaky toilet, you got a couple ways to go. Failing flapper, plunger ball, float ball, or fill valve. You hear hissing or a trickling sound, it's a good bet that's where your problem lies."

"I hope you'll find a problem for my sake. Every time the meter goes up, he looks at me like I did it."

"If he's losing water, it's most likely the irrigation system. Also possible the leak's in your service lateral, which is the underground pipe runs between the house and the meter out there. He says his is right there along the property line. Easier to get to before he put in that two-car garage. Once I find the shut-off valve, if the meter's still running, means you got a problem somewhere between the two. Valve itself could have a leak; common with these older bronze gate valves."

"Sounds like an expensive repair."

"Can be. Most of those old galvanized iron pipes are sixty, seventy years old. You get a break, it's costly to locate and even worse to re-place. Sewer or water lines break on a homeowner's property, it's up to the homeowner to remedy the problem. It's more like I do the fixing and the homeowner pays. Any rate, possible I won't finish my inspec-tion today, but I'll be back first chance I get."

# 31

Henry didn't return with Edna until twenty minutes after one. I had to call the alarm company to push back the technician's arrival by two hours, but I was at the office in time to let him in. I left him to go about his business with his drill, his ladder, and the wiring he had to run. He said he'd mount a panel near the front door and a second one in the kitchenette, assuring me he'd give me a quick lesson in its use when it was done. I found it distracting to have someone going in and out, but he was cheerful and he seemed efficient. The locksmith arrived shortly thereafter and changed the locks on both doors.

Cullen had been on the premises less than an hour when he paused to have a word. "Your friend's here."

"My friend?"

He pointed to the window behind me. "She pulled up a few minutes ago and she's been checking the front door, so I figured she was waiting to pick you up. You want, I can tell her you're on your way."

I turned in my swivel chair and looked out. A silver-gray sedan was parked at the curb with a woman at the wheel. I didn't recognize the car. She'd parked on the near side of the street instead of the far side, so I couldn't see her well enough to determine if she was someone I knew. Cullen was correct about her interest. She leaned forward and studied the front of the bungalow. All I saw was long, dark hair. April? I sat for a moment more and finally got up. "I'll go see what she wants."

I went down the walk, and as I approached the car, she lowered the window on the passenger side. I leaned forward and rested my hands on the open window. "You're April."

"I am, and I came to apologize for yesterday. I had no idea my dad would call the sheriff's department."

Up close, I could see what a sweet face she had: large brown eyes, a hesitant smile. A swathe of freckles lay across her nose and fanned out over her cheeks. She'd had to slide her seat back to accommodate her belly.

"That was irksome, but no harm done," I said. "You want to come in?"

"Would it be all right if we talked out here? I've been watching those guys go in and out and I'd prefer privacy."

"How did you know where to find me?"

"You gave your name on the phone. You also said you were a private investigator, so I looked you up in the yellow pages. I would have called, but I was afraid you wouldn't talk to me."

"Does your father know you're here?"

She laughed. "I hope not. Is this a good time to talk? I don't want to interrupt if you're in the middle of something."

"This is fine. Why don't you give me a minute and I'll bring out the mailing pouch?"

"Thank you. I'd be grateful."

I returned to my office. The technician was somewhere in the back of the bungalow, whistling as he worked. I pulled the carpet aside, dialed the combination to the safe, and opened it. I retrieved the mailing pouch and then went through the reverse of the operation, closing the safe again and rolling the carpet into place.

By the time I reached April's car the second time, she had opened the door on the passenger side, allowing me to slide right in. Before I could give her the mailer, she held up a hand.

"Let me say this first. I should have known better than to call my dad. He's touchy where my mother's concerned. I'm really sorry."

"You had a right to be suspicious. We've all heard about scams that target the bereaved," I said. "Usually not twenty-eight years after the fact, but there you have it."

She laughed. "I couldn't believe he dialed 9-1-1. That was absurd."

I could see she was still intent on her apologies, so I headed her off. "Now that we've acknowledged the issue, let's not go on trading apologies. Peace. Truce. All is forgiven," I said. I held out the mailing pouch, which she accepted.

She studied the writing on the front and then ran a finger across the postmark. "Where's it been all this time?"

I gave her a brief account of the twenty-eight-year delay. "That's her friend Clara's return address. She mailed the package for your mom."

"Is this my mother's handwriting or hers?"

"Your mother's, I believe. I didn't think to ask."

"And Father Xavier was her parish priest?"

"He's still at St. Elizabeth's. I talked to him Saturday. Were you raised Catholic?"

"No, but Bill was and we intend to raise the baby Catholic." She put her arms around the mailer and held it against her chest. "This is warm. Does it feel warm to you?"

I put a hand on the surface. "Not particularly," I said. Since it was clear she wasn't ready to explore the contents, I tried a change of subject. "What's your due date?"

"A month. April twenty-ninth."

"You know the gender?"

She smiled and shook her head. "We want to be surprised. Bill says most of life's surprises aren't that good."

"How's his practice going?"

"Great. He's doing well."

The exchange was curious in that we looked through the windshield more often than we looked at each other. In the past I've had similar conversations; the vehicle's close quarters creates an intimacy you might not otherwise attain.

"Don't you want to open that?"

She looked down. "I'm scared. What if I find something that hurts my heart?"

"No reason to assume the worst."

"Do you know what's in here?"

"I do. The mailer wasn't sealed, so I thought it would be all right."

"Tell me. Just so I'll be prepared. Then I'll look."

"She wanted you to have the Bible she was given at her confirmation. There's also a red-bead rosary and a Mother's Day card you made for her."

"I made her a card?"

"With your handprint. You must have been three. You have an April birthday, yes?"

"The twelfth."

"She tucked in a card for your fourth."

She took another look at the postmark. "You're saying in late March, when she put this together, she knew what she was planning to do?"

I gave myself a moment to respond. This was treacherous territory. I wasn't convinced Lenore had committed suicide, but I wasn't going to sit there and suggest her father murdered her mother or drove her to kill herself. "It might have been equivalent to her making out a will. You do it for those you love. It doesn't mean you expect to die anytime soon."

She considered the idea. "You don't think she was giving things away because she knew she wouldn't be needing them?"

"I never met your mother, so I can't answer that. It's clear she loved you."

"You really think so?"

"No doubt in my mind."

"Why didn't she ask for help?"

"She did, but I'm not sure anyone realized how much trouble she was in. People were worried, but not alarmed, if you can see the difference."

"Like who?"

"Father Xavier was one. And Clara Doyle."

"You talked to them?"

"A couple of days ago, yes. Clara mailed the package and Father Xavier held on to it, thinking one day you'd be in touch and he'd give it to you then. The mailer ended up in storage, and I guess people forgot it was there."

"Why did my mom use Clara's address and not her own?"

I was walking on eggshells here and I spoke with care. "I believe she was worried the mailer might be returned to the sender. Sometimes the post office does that for no apparent reason. She didn't want it to show up at the house again."

"Why?"

April was worse than a three-year-old. What was I supposed to say? I wanted to bang my head on the dashboard, but I managed to restrain myself. I understood her curiosity. There were things about my parents I'd never know and damn few people left to ask. "Possibly because your father wasn't Catholic and she didn't want him to know she was giving you items of religious significance. This is just a guess."

"So you're saying she did it behind his back?"

"You could look at it that way."

"That doesn't sound like a loving relationship."

"Doesn't to me, either, but marriages come in all shapes and sizes. Some work and some don't."

"How did you end up with this?"

"It's a long story and really not that important."

"It is to me."

I was reluctant to go into it, but avoiding an explanation would only create more questions. "I came across it when I was going through the personal effects of a friend who died. He had this box of old files that should have gone to a shredding company years ago. I went through to see if there were documents I should pull before the contents were destroyed."

"Did your friend know my mother?"

Despairingly, I said, "Honestly, April, I wasn't prepared for all these questions. I expected to hand this over and let you make of it what you would."

"I'm sorry. I don't mean to put you on the spot."

"I don't blame you for asking. I'm just trying to tell you why I'm doing such a poor job. Your dad's the one you should talk to about this."

"I can't. He won't talk about her. It upsets him. When I was a kid, I'd sometimes ask, but I learned it was better to keep quiet. There are issues I stay away from. Things that set him off. Certain holidays— Easter in particular. The subject of his mom. Mothers in general. Sometimes women in general."

That was a topic I wanted to avoid myself lest I end up badmouthing the guy to his only child. On impulse, I said, "Did you ever meet a man named Peter Wolinsky?"

That caught her off guard. "He came to see me months ago. Is he the one who *died*?"

"He is. That was the end of August."

"Oh, well now I feel bad. I liked him. He seemed like such a kind man."

"He *was* kind."

"What happened to him?"

"He was killed in a robbery attempt."

"That is so *sad*. I used to run into him in the oddest places."

"That's because he was watching over you."

She looked at me. "I can't believe you said that. I remember thinking he was like my personal guardian angel, but I thought I was imagining it."

"Well, you weren't."

"Why would he watch over me?"

"I know bits and pieces of the story. I don't know everything. He felt protective."

"Fair enough, I guess. So now I don't understand what *he* was doing with the envelope."

"Which puts us in the same boat. I'm piecing the sequence together the same way you are. Father Xavier gave it to him to pass along to you. Fate must have intervened and he died before he could deliver it."

She was shaking her head. "Doesn't it seem odd that this is suddenly filtering back to me? This package has been out there for twenty-eight years and now I'm holding it in my hands. It's like this long-distance gift from my mother is finally reaching me, but why now? You think it's about the baby?"

"Personally, I don't believe in coincidence. Some occurrences are bound to be random. I wouldn't make too much of it."

"Do you believe in ghosts? Because I do. Well, not ghosts, but spirits."

I made a noncommittal sound.

"You don't believe in ghosts?"

"I don't know if I believe or not. There was one occasion when I was convinced there was a 'presence,' for lack of a better word, but my saying so doesn't mean it's true."

In hopes of steering her off the subject, I introduced another one. "There's something else in that package I should mention. Your mother included a photograph of your father when he was a little boy, sitting in his mother's lap."

"Frankie's another subject we don't talk about."

"Ah, that's right. You said mothers are off the list. Sounds like you and your dad are real close."

"Actually, we were once upon a time. We traveled everywhere. We ate dinners out. Really nice places, too. He took me to Disneyland for my fourth birthday."

I was temporarily distracted by the notion that he took her to an amusement park less than two weeks after her mother's death. "Do you remember your mother at all?"

She shook her head. "I have no image of her. All I remember is feeling anxious. It was fine as long as I was distracted, but at night, or when I was sick, there was just this big yawning dark hole. I can't tell you how many times I cried myself to sleep. Eventually, I got over it."

"That's not something you get over."

"You can't live in a place where there's so much pain. You have to push it down and put a lid on it; otherwise you'd be overwhelmed."

"Is that what you did?"

"What I did was grow up. We were living down here by then. I think he was hoping I'd never leave, that I'd always be Daddy's little girl. I was just the opposite. I couldn't wait to get away. The longest year of my life was between twelve and thirteen. I wanted to be a teenager. Like life would be totally different if I could only reach that age. Then it seemed like forever until I turned sixteen and got my driver's license. When I graduated from high school, he assumed I'd go to UCST, and I was thinking, 'Are you insane? I'm gone. I'm out of here.' The fact is, I didn't escape, did I? I'm here and he's a hop, skip, and a jump away in Cottonwood, which is, what, all of six miles?"

"How do you get along with your stepmother?"

She made a face. "Not so great. She's high-strung. I'm polite, but there's nothing warm and fuzzy in our relationship."

"How long have they been married?"

"Four years. He met her at an AA meeting. It was early on, when she first joined. I gather she was a bad drunk. Lost jobs, wrecked cars, binged with the best of them. She finally reached a point where she had to turn it around or die. He knew her all of three months before he proposed. The wedding was two weeks later."

"Your father's a member of Alcoholics Anonymous?"

She shook her head. "Briefly. I know it sounds cynical, but I think he was looking for a way to meet women. Celeste still goes to meetings a couple of times a week."

"He waited a long time after your mother died."

"No, no. There was Phyllis, the wife before Celeste."

"Oh, sorry. That's right. I remember hearing about her. What's the story there?"

"He married her when I was seven. I guess she didn't take to the role of mother substitute, so that only lasted a couple of years. A few years post-Phyllis, he dated a woman who worked at the same company. She was neat and he adored her. I liked her, too. He didn't marry her, but she ended up suing him anyway, so it might as well have been a divorce. By then I was off at Pomona College and missed the fireworks."

I'd have asked what the woman sued him for, but I knew we were talking about Taryn, so I let that slide as she went on.

"Essentially, if you count my mother on one end and Celeste on the other, that's only four serious relationships in twenty-eight years. That's, what, an average of one every seven years?"

"Not so bad when you put it that way."

"We'll see how long Celeste lasts. Not a lifetime, I can guarantee."

"What's their relationship like?"

"Very compatible. He's a bully and she's a mouse. They act like everything's fine, but it's not. We have them for dinner once a month, and that's as much as I can tolerate. As a matter of fact, they're coming up tomorrow night, so that's one chore I can check off the list."

"You think your relationship might change once the baby's born?"

"Like we'd see them more often? I'm sure he's hoping so, but I don't."

"I never know what to make of conversations like this," I said. "I sometimes have this fantasy that life would be wonderful if only my mother and my father were alive. Then I hear stories like yours and I want to get down on my hands and knees and rejoice."

She laughed. "I better get a move on. I need to get to the grocery store and I'm sure you have work to do."

"Could I ask a quick favor? I'd like to write to Sacramento and request a copy of your mother's death certificate, which means I'll need her date of birth."

"August 7, 1940."

"What about a social security number?"

"She never had a job, as far as I know. She wasn't even out of high school when I was born. Why do you want to see her death certificate?"

"In the interest of being thorough."

"About what? She took an overdose. End of story, isn't it?"

"I don't know if it is or not. What if her death was accidental?"

"Oh. That never occurred to me. Good point. That would be amazing, wouldn't it?"

"Seems like it's worth looking into. I'm not sure I'll learn anything, but I think I should make the effort."

"You'll let me know?"

"Of course."

She leaned forward and turned the key in the ignition.

I opened the car door and then turned and looked at her. "You won't tell your father you came to see me?"

"Oh, man. Not a word. He would blow."

# 32

By the end of the workday, my alarm system was in and fully opera-
tional. Cullen taught me the basics and told me to come up with an
arming and disarming code that didn't consist of my address, a varia-
tion on my birthdate, or any string of numbers such as 1-2-3-4 or 0-0-
0-0. He said I'd also need a one-word response code so if the alarm
went off and the S.O.S. operator called, they'd know I was the one answering and not a burglar. I settled on Henry's birthdate—February 14,
1900—which translated to 2-1-4-0 for the numerical code. My response code was "Ed." I wrote Cullen a check and he handed me an
instruction manual longer than the California Penal Code.

Once he left, I located a file that contained various forms published
by the California Department of Public Health; in this case, I was
looking for an application for a copy of a death record. I wasn't entitled to a certified copy since I wasn't related to her, wasn't a member
of law enforcement, had no court order, and had no power of attorney.

Now that I had Lenore's date of birth, I could request a Certified *Informational* Copy of her death certificate, which would be a duplicate, but printed with a legend on the face of it stating that it was "informational" and therefore could not be used as documentation to establish identity.

I hauled out my portable Smith Corona and set it up on my desk, then rolled in the blank form and filled out the section asking for my name, address, and phone. I typed in Lenore Redfern Lowe's name, sex, city and county of death, date of birth, state of birth, and date of death, including her mother's name and Ned Lowe's name where indicated. In the heading for that portion of the form to be completed was the phrase "to the best of your knowledge," which I hoped would cover any errors. When I was finished, I made a copy of the form, wrote a check to cover the fee, and put the whole of it in an envelope addressed to the California Department of Public Health Vital Records in Sacramento. I applied the proper postage stamp and set it aside to drop in a mailbox on my way home.

Then I took out Pete's list again and placed it on the desk. I'd been hoping to locate Susan Telford and Phyllis Joplin, the two women I hadn't yet spoken with. Pete had also put Shirley Ann Kastle on the list, but I was willing to believe she was alive and well and living in the east. The other two I wasn't so sure about. I started with Phyllis, Ned's second wife, who apparently now lived in Perdido. The town itself is in the same area code as Santa Teresa, though not covered by our local phone book. I dialed directory assistance and asked the operator for a phone number for Phyllis Joplin. I didn't expect to be successful and I was startled when the operator gave me the listing for a P. Joplin on Clementine. I made a note of the number and checked my crisscross to match the phone number with an address. I made a note of both as I tried the number.

A woman picked up and rattled off the name of a business, but she was too quick for me to catch what she was saying. I asked for Phyllis.

"You got her. Who's this?"

I gave her my name and occupation and told her I was looking for information about Ned Lowe. "I know you were married to him at one time."

The silence that followed was sharp and I thought she might hang up on me. Instead, she said, "What's it to you? Are you a friend of his?"

"Not at all. I'm calling because your name appeared on a list put together by a detective named Pete Wolinsky. Did he contact you?"

Another brief silence, in which I imagined her weighing her words. "Why do you ask?"

"You're aware that he was killed."

"I read that in the paper. What about it?"

"We were colleagues. When he died he left unfinished business I'm hoping to settle. I wondered if you'd spoken with him."

"He called once. I told him to leave me the hell alone. I thought he was a friend of Ned's, or how would he even know who I was? Same goes for you."

"How *did* Pete know about you?"

"He did a background check on Ned and my name came up. These days anything you do ends up in the public record."

"Why did he call?"

"That's what I asked *him*. He told me he had a theory that women who crossed paths with Ned Lowe didn't always fare so well. He asked about my marriage. I said, 'What business is that of yours?' I have to give the man credit. I unloaded a lot of guff on him and he took it all in stride. He said all he wanted was to make sure I was okay. I thought that was kind of sweet."

"Did he have reason to think you might not be okay?"

"He must have, or why would he have phrased it that way? I assured him I was fine and dandy as long as I never crossed paths with Ned again. God, I hate that man."

"Do you mind if I ask a couple of questions?"

A flicker of silence, but in the main, she was loosening up. "I divorced Ned Lowe years ago. Good riddance to bad rubbish and that's the end of it as far as I'm concerned."

I gave her a brief rundown, "brief" being a relative term. I told her about Taryn Sizemore's lawsuit, how the mailing pouch meant for April had fallen into my hands, and summed up the few facts I'd picked up in Burning Oaks. I also told her about Pete's death, which was really the starting point of my investigation.

At the end of my summary she said, "How recently did you see April?"

"This afternoon."

"How's she doing?"

"She's fine, married to an orthodontist and expecting her first child."

"Well, tell her I said hello. I can't tell you how often I've thought of her. She was nine when I left. Talk about a lost lamb."

"Actually, she was under the impression the marriage broke up because of her."

"Because of her? Where'd she get that idea?"

"She thought playing mother to a seven-year-old wasn't your cup of tea."

"Bet you that was Ned's claim, the son of a bitch. It had nothing to do with April, which he damn well knew."

"How long were you married?"

"Two years, which was two years too long. The man was impossible. Clinging and needy. Then he'd do a complete about-face and be suspicious, controlling, and paranoid. I'd say manic-depressive, but it was more like Jekyll and Hyde. The change wasn't quite that literal, but I could see it come over him and I knew enough to get out of his way. I thought of it as his seasonal affective disorder because it happened in the spring, like an allergy."

"Sounds charming. What do you think it was?"

"Who knows? Maybe he had a secret life. In the end, I didn't care if he had an entire family on the side; I just wanted out. I'd have stuck with him for April's sake, but I had to save myself while I could."

"Why did you marry him?"

"Well, that's the sixty-four-thousand-dollar question, isn't it? You think I haven't beat myself up over that dumb move? Not that this is any excuse, but I was newly divorced, unemployed, overweight, and I'd developed some sort of nervous condition that made my hair fall out in clumps. He could see how vulnerable I was and knew I'd be easy to manipulate. Which, I'm ashamed to say, I was.

"I'll tell you one more thing, and this is embarrassing. I don't even know why I'm 'fessing up except I'm sure I wasn't the first or the last woman he tried this on. We sometimes smoked a little dope back then just for the hell of it. We'd get high and hit the sack. He had this trick . . . this choking thing he did. He told me he learned it in high school. He'd take me just to the point of passing out and he'd bring me to orgasm. I'd never experienced that before and I was . . . I couldn't help it. I'm ashamed to admit sex had such a hold on me when Ned himself was so disgusting."

"I understand," I said.

"Anyway, I gotta get off the line. This is a business number. I run an accounting service out of my home and I'm expecting a call."

"I'll let you go, then. I appreciate your time."

"You need anything more, feel free to call. Nothing I'd like better than horsing up his life the way he did mine."

As soon as I hung up, I checked my scratch pad for Taryn's office number and put in a call to her. When she picked up, I identified myself and said, "We need to talk."

"Sure thing. When?"

"Soon."

"Hang on." She must have been checking her appointment book because when she came back on, she said, "My last client will be gone by six. I've got paperwork to catch up on, so I'll be here for at least an hour after that. Come when you can."

"I'll do that," I said. "Thanks."

I hung up and the phone rang almost immediately. "Millhone Investigations."

"Kinsey? Spencer Nash here with the information I promised. Let me know when you have a pen and paper and I'll give you his home address."

"Doesn't he have an office?"

"You're catching him on the fly. He's here a couple more days and then he's off on his honeymoon. He asked if there was any way possible you could meet with him today."

I looked at my watch and saw that it was just after five. "What time?"

"As soon as possible."

"Oh, why not? As long as I said I'd go, what difference does it make? Might as well get it over with."

"Love the sentiment."

"Don't worry. I'll behave myself," I said, and made a note of the address and phone number when he recited it. I took my sweet time closing up, and made a detour to the post office as I drove through town so I could drop the outgoing mail in the box.


I should have known the property would have walls like a fort. These were six feet tall and constructed of hand-hewn stone. A gatehouse had been erected at the entrance and a uniformed security guard emerged as I pulled up. I rolled down the window on the passenger side and gave him my name. I told him I had an appointment with Mr. Xanakis, then waited while he consulted his clipboard.

"I don't see your name on my list."

"What would you suggest I do?"

"You can use the call button to ring the house."

I inched forward to a point where I could push the call button on the keypad. I sat, engine idling, until a hollow-voiced stranger acknowledged me on the intercom. Before I had a chance to identify myself, the gates swung open and one of Ari's white panel trucks with the XLNT logo passed me on its way out. I eased through the open gate and continued toward the house. The cobblestone driveway was a long slow curve, landscaped so the house was shielded from view until I made the final turn. This was for the wow factor.

When I saw it, I said, "Wow."

The mansion was done in the French Country style, a term I picked up in a book about local architecture, where the house was featured prominently among others of its kind. The estate was built in 1904, so at least the aged stone facade and weathered gray shutters represented a genuine pedigree. The tall, steeply hipped roof featured overlapping slate tiles. Pairs of chimneys flanked the structure, appearing as mirror images where they peeked above the roofline. The windows were tall and narrow, and those on the first and second floors were aligned in perfect symmetry. Over the years, rambling additions had been laid end-on, like children's wooden blocks, though in perfect keeping with the original elegance. There was something Disneyesque about it. I half expected an arc of fireworks and a swelling chorus of "When You Wish Upon a Star."

I parked and made my way to the front door, which was standing open. I rang the bell, which I could hear sounding inside in the sort of soft chime that suggests the intermission is over and we should all return to our seats. While I waited, I listened to the birdies chirp. The air smelled of lavender and pine. I was wearing my usual jeans, tennis shoes, and a turtleneck that was ever so faintly stretched out of shape. No sign of my fairy godmother, so Ari would have to take me as I was.

When no one appeared after a suitable interval, I peered in. The marble-tiled hallway ran the width of the house and it was currently so crowded with furniture, they might have been preparing for a liquidation sale. Most of the pieces were antiques or very good reproductions: chairs, side tables, armoires, a chest of drawers with ornate bronze drawer pulls. A woman in a white uniform applied wax to a handsome mahogany tallboy inlaid with a lighter wood.

I took one step in, thinking someone would notice me. At the far end of the hall to my left, the elevator door stood open and two men in coveralls coaxed a rolling pallet into the hall; framed works of art were stacked against the end panel at a slant. Their progress was supervised by a gaunt woman wearing jeans, a white T-shirt, and tennis shoes with no socks. I was hoping to catch her attention, but no one seemed aware of me. There were other paintings leaning against the wall on either side of the corridor. I leaned around the door and rang the bell again. This time when the chime sounded, the gaunt woman in jeans looked in my direction. She broke away from the two workmen and moved to the front door.

I handed her a business card. "I have a meeting with Mr. Xanakis."

She gave the card a quick read and stepped back, which I took as permission to enter. She turned and walked down the hall. There was no hint of her place in the household. She might have been Ari's new bride, his daughter, his housekeeper, or the woman who watered his houseplants and walked his dogs. In the warm air that wafted from somewhere in the back of the house, I picked up the scent of roasting chicken.

Two women stood near the double doors that opened to the dining room. One was rail-thin, blond, late thirties, wearing a black velour lounging outfit that consisted of pants and a matching zippered jacket with something sparkly underneath. The other woman was also rail-thin and blond, in a snug black power suit and spike heels.

The portion of the room I could see had unadorned walls padded with a pale green silk. There were fifteen oversize squares and rectangles of darker fabric where paintings had once hung, protecting the fabric from fading. In the center of each was a recessed receptacle that contained an electrical outlet. That way picture lights could be affixed to the frame without a length of unsightly electrical wire hanging down to the baseboards. In my Aunt Gin's trailer when I was growing up, she'd sometimes have power strips hosting double and triple adapters with eight brown cords trailing from a single socket like piglets nursing at a sow. I thought all sockets looked like that.

The two women studied the room and the woman in the power suit said, "That's all going to have to come out."

"What do you suggest?"

"Quick fix? Get all that fabric out of there and paint the walls charcoal gray. That'll hide some of the flaws."

The woman in black velour looked at me sharply. "Who's this?"

The woman who'd answered the door said, "She has a meeting with Mr. Xanakis. I was going to show her to the gym."

The woman looked annoyed, but resumed her conversation without further reference to me. That one had to be the wife.

I followed my fearless leader through an enormous kitchen where a young woman in a white double-breasted chef's jacket and striped pants stood at the white granite counter chopping onions. A middle-aged man in a tuxedo vest and a dazzling white shirt sat at the kitchen table polishing silver sconces. Through a doorway I could see the laundry room. A Hispanic woman in a white uniform looked up at me as she took a damp white linen napkin from a clothes basket. She gave the seams a sharp snap, laid the napkin on the ironing board, and took up her iron.

When we arrived at the French doors along the back wall, my companion opened one and pointed. Outside, an ocean of lush grass covered the shallow hill to the swimming pool. The gym was apparently located in the pool house, a structure identical to the main house, only in miniature.

I said, "Thanks."

I took a stone path down the hill, past the koi pond, past an orchard of plum and apricot trees. Sprinklers came to life and shot out fans of water that created a rainbow against the cloudless sky. Had anybody heard about the drought in this part of town?

At the pool house below, I could see Ari Xanakis in the doorway in shorts, a tank top, tennis socks, and running shoes. I put him in his midfifties; short and barrel-chested, but otherwise trim. A lacy bib of dark chest hair spread out under his tank top. He had a pug nose, bright brown eyes, and a nice smile that showed faintly crooked teeth.

"I spend half my life down here. House is like a zoo these days. This is the only place I get any peace and quiet," he said. "Come on in."

"Are you moving?"

"We've leased out the house for a year, so we're clearing storage space. That's what the mess in the hall is about. Lot of that stuff I'm donating to a charity auction."

I followed him to the gym and watched as he returned to his treadmill, which he'd put on pause. Over his shoulder, he said, "You can forget antiques, anything with a pedigree. Stella's big on contemporary everything. Houses, furniture, modern art. Actually she doesn't much like art of any kind."

The home gym was square and had to be thirty feet on a side. The walls were mirrored and the interior was crowded with free weights and Universal machines—two treadmills, an elliptical trainer, a stationary bike, and a recumbent bike—all of it doubled and tripled in reflection. Ari mopped his face on a white terry-cloth bar towel he'd hung around his neck and set the treadmill in motion with the push of a button.

The start was slow, but picked up rapidly until he was pounding in place. He cranked up the incline and increased the speed. He was already sweating heavily, but he wasn't out of breath. His shoulders and arms had a rosy cast from exertion. I watched the belt's relentless forward motion, the seam coming around again and again. Our conversation unfolded against the mechanical grinding of the treadmill and the sole-slapping of his running shoes.

"Thanks for coming, by the way," he said. "Detective Nash says you're a busy lady, so I appreciate your taking the time to drive out. You meet the bride?"

"Not formally."

He shook his head once. "Might have made a mistake on that one. Jury's still out."

It wasn't clear whether he was referring to his wife or the interior designer, but I could have sworn it was the wife. "I understand you're about to leave on your honeymoon?"

"No worry on that score. I wouldn't file until we got back. She might turn out to be a keeper, and think of all the dough I'd save. Did Nash tell you the story?"

"He didn't."

He shook his head. "You'll hear it sooner or later, so you might as well hear it from me. I have no complaints coming because I got what I deserved. Stella's husband dropped dead on the job. He was the architect on the condominium remodel I was doing at the time. Talented guy. Forty-eight years old. Heart attack. Boom. The four of us knew each other socially. So he dies, Stella's at loose ends, and I stepped into the breach. Teddy was in LA, so I had dinner with Stella one night at the club, just being nice, and one thing led to another. Didn't mean anything to me, but right away I realized my mistake. Teddy's down at some seminar and I didn't see how she could possibly find out. She gets home and some pal of hers calls and rats me out. She filed for divorce the same week."

"She doesn't waste any time, does she?"

"Knocked me for a loop. I wasn't serious about Stella until Teddy booted me out, and then what choice did I have? When we hashed out the settlement, Teddy got the condominium where the poor guy died. How's that for irony?"

"Not good."

"Everything's gone downhill since then. Naturally, Teddy didn't want the place, so she decided to sell. Forty-six hundred square feet and the real estate agent told her it was worth a million or more, because of the location."

"Where is it?"

"Downtown Santa Teresa. The penthouse suite in a brand-new office building. Eighteen months it sat. Teddy was living in Bel Air by
then and she got the bright idea we should get the place spiffed up,
have a brochure printed, and promote the listing with real estate agents
in Beverly Hills. Sure enough, a hotshot actor came along and paid full
freight. This was a month ago. Ten-day escrow, all cash, and no contingencies. Close of sale I knew she'd whip in there and take everything
that wasn't nailed down, so I emptied the place before she could. She
ended with a million in cash. You know what I got? Only the stuff I
managed to sneak out from under her nose. Real estate goes in her
column, used furniture in mine."

He waited for my reaction, hoping for sympathy, which he clearly
felt was warranted. I made a noncommittal mouth noise. These were
not problems I could readily relate to.

# 33

I tried another subject, thinking a change in category might lighten the mood. "Do you and Teddy have children?"

"Not her. I have three with my first wife. The kids adored Teddy, but don't have much use for this new one. They can't believe I messed up. They're barely speaking to me. Anyway, enough of that."

I thought he meant he'd talked enough about Teddy and we were moving on to something else. But he said, "How did you meet her?"

"Who?"

"Teddy. I asked Nash and he said you'd tell me."

"She called my office and said she needed help with a personal matter. The address she gave was the Clipper estate, so that's where we met."

I told him about "Hallie Bettancourt" and her sob story about the baby she gave up for adoption. "I assumed it was all true. She said her father was an architect who tore down the original mansion and designed the contemporary residence that's up there now. Sounded right to me, and the setup was so elaborate, it never dawned on me the scene was arranged for my benefit."

"Teddy in a nutshell. Why'd she pick you?"

"She said she wanted to hire a woman because she thought she'd find a sympathetic ear. This was one of the few things she said that still rings true in retrospect. She also said she needed a go-between so she could keep her name out of it. I think that was true as well."

I could see the charade didn't make any more sense to him than it had to me. I went on to describe how I acquired the contact information on Christian Satterfield, which I sent her in my report; that having found out the bills she'd paid me were marked, I then went back to the property, hoping to pick up a lead to her whereabouts, but the place was clean except for a paper clip I found on the deck. "That was the end of it as far as I was concerned.

"They must have been keeping an eye on him because he was spotted in a dive called Lou's having a long, intense conversation with a woman Nash thought might be Hallie Bettancourt. He called the next day to tell me Satterfield was parked outside the Shores in a limousine. On the off chance he was waiting for the mysterious Ms. Bettancourt, he suggested I check it out. Instead of Hallie, the woman who showed up was Kim Bass. The limousine took off for Los Angeles and I followed."

"Kim is Teddy's friend from way back. I hear she and Teddy are bunkmates these days."

"Someone told me her husband's in prison for embezzlement. Do you know where he's incarcerated?"

"Lompoc. It's been rough on her. I'd say she was homeless, but that's only because she's become a serial house sitter to avoid paying rent. She's hanging in with him, but who knows why. The guy's scum. The company he worked for went belly-up after the news came out.

He's probably the one who put Teddy together with Satterfield, because how else would she hear about a bum like him? What's she want with that low-life kid anyway?"

"I thought that's why we were putting our heads together, to see if we could figure it out."

"She could be getting back at me for my little misstep with Stella. Sounds like the age difference is about the same."

"I don't think there's anything romantic going on. At the Rodeo-Wilshire, the three of them were in separate rooms. Next morning, she took him to a stylist and then bought him a new wardrobe."

"Boy toy," he said. He powered down the treadmill and stepped off the track. "Flip that if you would," he said, indicating the glowing power switch on the front of the machine.

I bent and flipped it to the Off position.

He said, "She's come back to the house a couple of times, acting like she still owns the place. I told the staff to keep a close eye on her and escort her to the door as soon as possible. So far, I don't think she's walked away with anything, but I got tired of fending her off. I finally changed the locks and alarm codes and then beefed up the rest of my security."

"Can't your attorney step in and put a stop to it?"

"Who can afford to complain? I get billed the minute he picks up the phone."

"I don't understand why you're still at each other's throats. I thought divorce was supposed to cure that."

"That's what Stella says. I tell her, hey, it's not me. It's her." He stood and toweled off the sweat. "Thing about Teddy is she's smart. There are people who're smart and people who just think they're smart. She's the real deal. She came up from nothing, same way I did. I'm not a sophisticated guy. Neither of us has a college degree, but Teddy's got a head on her and she studies up. Anything she doesn't know, she learns."

He went on with his commentary, which was largely critical, but underscored by a grudging admiration. As he detailed her many faults—grasping, insatiable, and spoiling for a fight—the unconscious smile that played across his face spoke more of veneration than distaste.

"What kicked off this latest round?" I asked.

"I've been wondering about that myself, and here's what I think it was. She calls me a couple of weeks ago and starts kissing up. Says water under the bridge, bygones be bygones, and I'm like, 'What? No hard feelings? Are you kidding me? Never in a million years.'"

I said "Uh-huh" to show I was listening.

"She says she's been thinking about the condominium because she netted a big chunk of change and she knows I got the short end of the stick. She feels bad about it, she says. So then she says if I want to work out a side deal, she'd be willing to discuss it."

"What kind of side deal? You said all you ended up with was used furniture."

"My question exactly, so I asked her outright. I said, 'What's so interesting about the shit that was in the condo?' Most of that stuff's been sitting in the basement for years."

"There must be something of real value."

"Agreed. Don't ask me what because we never did a formal inventory. Stuff's been appraised, but I don't know what's what. The previous owners came over here from England just before the turn of the century. I don't know how the guy made his money, but there was plenty of it. The house was passed down I don't know how many times. The day the last family member died, the attorney locked the doors and left it just like it was. We bought it fully equipped and decked out, right down to the Oriental rugs. Anyway, Teddy backed away from the subject, which doesn't mean she's giving up. If I know her, she'll just come at it from a different direction."

"Any chance she's sincere about making amends?"

He laughed. "Nice idea, but no. Reason I thought the two of us should talk is that whole Beverly Hills scene between her and the ex-con. Nash lays it out for me and it makes no sense. I figured he must have missed a beat, which is why I wanted to hear it from you."

I said, "Why don't you just leave well enough alone? Are you *hoping* for a fight?"

"Hey, not me. That's Teddy's MO. We finally hammered out an agreement. Everything's divided up right down to the penny. I get this. She gets that. Sign on the dotted line and we have a deal. She signs. I sign. Now she wants something else. What the hell is that about?"

"Did you ever stop to think this is a conditioned response on your part?" I said. "You're so accustomed to Teddy besting you, you can't accept peace when she offers it."

"You want a drink? Iced tea?"

"Sure."

"Wait here." He moved to the doorway, where I could see an intercom mounted on the wall. He pressed a button.

"Yes, sir?"

"Tell Maurie to bring us a couple iced teas, and not that mint shit."

"Yes, sir."

"I'll be right back," he said. He paused to pull off his running shoes and padded into the next room in his sock feet. A moment later I heard a shower running.

Three minutes later he was back wearing fresh clothes and running a pocket comb through his hair. We went out onto the patio and sat down. Maurie, who'd met me at the door, made her way down from the main house bearing a silver tray on which she'd set two tall glasses of iced tea. When she reached us, she placed the tray on the wrought-iron table between our two chairs. She'd included a silver creamer, a sugar bowl, and real linen cocktail napkins monogrammed with an X.

While we sipped our tea, we sat and looked out at the property. The gardener's leaf blower punctuated the otherwise still air.

I said, "How do you keep the lawn so green?"

"I have water trucked in."

"Ah."

I thought he had finished bad-mouthing Teddy, but he'd clearly been brooding that I hadn't been brought around to his point of view. He took up his list of grievances as though I gave a shit.

"Okay, here. I should have told you this. Typical. She gets the sterling silver flatware? Six hundred and thirty-nine pieces that price out at three hundred ninety-eight thousand five hundred. She sold it to an antique dealer in New Orleans and got top dollar. I know because the dealer called me to make sure it was on the up-and-up. Are you following?"

I was following, but I didn't think he was going anywhere. This recital constituted a peculiar form of bragging. He was elevating himself by enumerating the dollar amounts of everything he'd lost to her. "It sounds like she's stockpiling cash," I said.

"Why would she do that?"

"You still have earning power. She doesn't, unless she has a skill set you haven't mentioned yet," I said. "Who got the house?"

He seemed surprised. "This house? I did. Because she couldn't afford the property taxes or the upkeep."

"It has to be worth millions."

"Twelve, but that's down from what it was. Market's flat."

"What else did you get?"

"Well, you know. Half the stocks and bonds. I did get a Tiffany necklace she'd kill for. It was an anniversary gift, our tenth, but the judge put it in my column to offset the art she was claiming on her side. She put up a fuss like the jewelry had sentimental value, but that was strictly a negotiating tool."

"What's it worth?" I could tell I was adapting to his view of the world; every subject mentioned had a dollar sign attached.

"The necklace? A bundle. These are diamonds and emerald-cut aquamarines, a hundred and ninety carats total. Value on that beauty is four hundred and fifty thousand, and she's crying 'poor me' because I got it and she didn't."

"Where do you keep something like that?"

"I got the perfect place I'll show you in a bit. Maurie caught Teddy in my study week before last, so she probably figured I had it in the wall safe. She's ballsy. She'll try anything."

I wasn't interested in contributing to the Teddy-trashing, but I thought if I signaled agreement with him, it might put an end to it. "She's devious. I'll give you that."

"She sure succeeded in faking you out. And why is that? Because otherwise it's no fun. Teddy's not happy unless she's putting one over on you. With her, everything's a shell game. You see my problem here?"

"I do and it's a tough one."

"I'm seriously thinking about canceling the honeymoon. I can't take the chance that I'll be off somewhere. Minute my back is turned, she'll get in high gear. I come back, half the stuff'll be gone."

"When do you leave?"

"Friday, providing I don't scratch the trip. I'd lose twenty-five grand in deposits, which I'm willing to eat. Stella's pissed I'd even consider pulling the plug. I haven't done it yet, but I'm this close."

"Maybe that's Teddy's hope. To mess up your travel plans."

He looked at me. "You think that's it?"

"I'm just throwing out possibilities," I said. I felt a twinge of guilt because he'd brightened at the notion when I'd tossed it out off the top of my head.

"I got a great idea. Here's something just occurred to me. Why don't you tail the woman for two days and see what she does? It might be very educational."

"No, thanks."

"I'm serious. I don't have the savvy or the wherewithal. Nash tells me you're a whiz."

"I don't do domestic. No good ever comes of it."

"How much do you charge? I'm talking about your hourly rate."

"What difference does it make? I'm not for hire."

"Pay you a hundred bucks an hour."

"No."

"Two hundred."

"No."

"Okay, two-fifty, but that's as high as I go."

I laughed. "Listen, Ari, as much as I admire your bargaining skills, I'm really not interested."

"Here's another idea. Off point, but I could have the kid picked up. That would put a crimp in her plan, don't you think? If the police arrest the guy?"

"For doing what?"

"Parole violation. He's a convicted felon, so drugs or alcohol. Possession of firearms. Rat him out to his parole officer."

"You have him arrested and she'll just go out and find another ex-con."

"Maybe so, maybe not. He's a good-looking dude, right?"

"That is true," I said.

"Which brings us back to the boy toy idea. She's trying to get my goat. Retaliate for Stella."

"Why would she pick an ex-con? You think there aren't dozens of good-looking guys out there cruising for patronage?"

"Ex-con's easier to control. Come on. Why don't you help me out? You follow her for two days and put an end to the debate."

"No, thanks."

"Don't say no right off the bat," he said irritably. "Think about it."

Ari insisted on giving me a tour of his security system, which did seem to be state-of-the-art. In the endless stretches of basement, there was a room dedicated to closed-circuit television sets, where banks of monitors showed a succession of pictures from cameras that covered views of each room, shots of the corridors, shots of the entrances and exits, and wide-angle shots that covered the exterior. While I looked on, the views flipped like a slide show, first one room and then the next. It was hard to focus on all the screens as they rotated through.

"You have someone who actually sits and monitors these?"

"I just hired a guy. Couple of blind spots in there, but good otherwise."

"Impressive," I said.

"Glad you think so. Come take a look at this."

I followed him through the gloom to a side room about the size of a broom closet. He flipped on the overhead light and a forty-watt bulb illuminated a massive round brass-and-steel safe that resembled an oversize antique diver's helmet on a chunky base. The faceplate was jeweled and the combination lock sat in the center of the round door. A large hand crank was affixed to the front and the hinges were hefty.

"Called a Diebold Cannonball Safe. Thirty-six hundred pounds. Three time-locks you can set so the mechanism can't be opened for as much as seventy-two hours. It was the latest technology of its time."

"Which was when?"

"Late 1800s. It was in the house when we bought it."

"Is it in working order?"

"Oh sure. I had to have a guy come in and open it the first time. I had this fantasy of gold pieces. It was empty. Just my tough luck, but it's come in handy since."

"That's where you keep the necklace?"

"Better here than that dinky wall safe upstairs. Besides, Teddy knows the combination to that one. Not this."

"You didn't change the combination to the safe upstairs?"

"What good would it do? She knows how my mind works. She could probably figure this one out now that I think about it."

He flicked off the light and led the way out of the basement. I'd have thought the shadowy chambers would be spooky but the whole of it was tidy and dry, with nary a spider in sight. We took the elevator up. Walking back through the hallway, I could see that additional pieces of furniture had been brought up, some swaddled in sheets. Worker bees were still on the scene. A two-man team wrapped and packed blue-and-white glazed ceramic pieces, part of a collection of Chinese porcelains. There was no sign of Stella.

I made my exit, exhausted by the entire encounter. In spite of myself, I liked the guy. He was a bit of a blowhard, but he had a sweetness about him. I wondered if Stella had any idea what she was up against. Ari wasn't complicated. He was still in love with his wife.

While I'd continued to decline his offer of paid work, I did consider his proposal for thirty seconds on my way home. I had said no in part because sometime soon I'd need to have a talk with Christian Satterfield and I didn't want to do so with Ari's employment offer hanging over my head. One thing I've learned about money: the guy who pays has the power. Saying no kept our relationship equitable and on an even keel.

# 34

On my way to Taryn's office, I stopped off at a delicatessen, where I bought one tuna salad sandwich on rye and one egg salad on whole wheat, plus Fritos and the Pepperidge Farm Milanos on which my mental health is so often dependent. I hadn't mentioned dinner in our phone conversation, but I was hungry and I took a chance she'd be hungry as well. If she already had dinner plans, I'd take the leftovers home with me. I parked in the lot behind her building. I'd barely settled on the love seat when she came out to the waiting room.

"Your timing's great. Turns out my last client canceled, so I managed to get caught up. Come on in."

She wore tight jeans with a pair of spike heels and a dark red blazer that was open as far as the first button, her cleavage modestly veiled by a lacy white camisole. She wore the same big hoop earrings and the messy hairdo that somehow looked chic. Her lipstick was bright red and looked like it wouldn't come off on the lip of her coffee cup the first time she took a sip. I report this in detail because she's the sort of woman I want to be when I grow up. No chance of it at this late date, but all the same . . .

I held up the paper bag. "Dinner. I hope you don't mind."

"Perfect. I should have thought of it myself."

I unloaded my purchases and arranged the deli items on the coffee table. We traded sandwiches so we each had half a tuna salad and half an egg salad. She kept cans of Diet Pepsi in a mini-fridge and she popped the tops on two. She kicked off her heels and propped her feet on the coffee table. She wore panty hose, and the nylon soles were pristine.

I sat on the floor with my back against one of her two upholstered chairs. We both salted the shit out of the egg salad and then munched happily, engaged in small talk. She finally crumpled the empty paper wrappers and made an accurate overhand shot to the wastebasket before she turned back to me.

"So what's up, buttercup?"

"I need a reality check and I don't know who else to talk to. I'd like to run a few things by you and make sure I'm on the right track."

"If this is about Ned Lowe, I'm completely unbiased except for the fact that I hate the guy and hope he falls in a hole and dies."

"Fine with me."

"I can't wait to hear this."

"Saturday I drove to Burning Oaks and talked to a couple of people who knew Lenore. One was a former neighbor and one was her parish priest."

Disconcerted, she said, "You drove to Burning Oaks? What possessed you?"

"Your fault," I said. "Between you and Pete's widow, I was shamed into taking up his cause. You remember the mailer?"

"Sure. Pete hid it in the bottom of a banker's box."

"Right," I said. "The keepsakes were meant for April. I'm not sure why he didn't deliver them himself. He went to Burning Oaks a year ago and the priest gave it to him, which is how the mailer ended up in his hands. I wanted to be clear what I was getting into before I delivered it."

I filled her in on my conversation with Clara Doyle and Father Xavier and then moved on to the research I'd done with regard to Ned, Lenore, and Shirley Ann Kastle. "I talked to a high school classmate who knew all three, and she told me a convoluted story I won't go into here. Bottom line was that Ned Lowe was obsessed with Shirley Ann, who dated him for a while and then broke up with him when she and her former boyfriend got back together. Ned stalked her for weeks. Things got so bad, her mother sent her back east to finish high school. Fast-forward five years. Shirley Ann's mother was terminally ill, and Shirley Ann came back to Burning Oaks to take care of her. Ned attached himself to her as though they'd never been separated. He was married to Lenore by then. Shirley Ann was also married and she told Ned a relationship between them was impossible because of it. I'm wondering if Ned helped Lenore along, thinking he could at least rid himself of that impediment."

"Oh, man. I don't like the sound of that at all," she said. "Go on. I didn't mean to interrupt. You've got the mailer. You're back in town and now you know your mission."

"Right. I didn't think I should show up at April's unannounced, so I called her on Monday. She completely misunderstood what I was getting at and jumped to the conclusion I was hustling her. She called her dad and he turned around and called the county sheriff. I ended up in a verbal standoff with Ned and a deputy. Nothing came of it, but it was obnoxious and I was pissed."

"Shit."

"Under the circumstances, I didn't think it was smart to hand her the mailer just then. Then lo and behold, she showed up at my office yesterday and I passed it on to her."

"What was in it?"

"Lenore's Bible, her rosary, couple of keepsakes, and a photo of Ned, not quite four, sitting on his mother's lap."

"Oooh. That's bad. She abandoned him when he was four."

"Which is what I want to talk about. You think that's where all his craziness comes from? Because that's what I'm picking up on."

"You want the long answer or the short?"

"Long. By all means."

"There's a subclass of kids like him. I think of them as junior psychopaths. They're disconnected and cold and lack any semblance of humanity. Symptoms typically manifest in adolescence, which is when you start seeing aggression and antisocial acting-out. It can also show up in kids as young as three, and that's a tougher proposition. Sometimes these kids are ADHD and sometimes not—but they're always unemotional. They might have tantrums, but what looks like fury is pure manipulation. They have no empathy and they have no desire to please. They don't care about punishment. They don't care about other people's pain and suffering. It just doesn't interest them."

"You think he's one of them?"

"No question. I started following the research, or what there was of it, when I first realized what a sick puppy he is. The studies I've seen suggest low levels of cortisol, which affects our ability to feel fear. Without fear, they have no concept of consequences."

"Does this run in families?"

"The jury's still out on that one, but I'll tell you what he told me: Frankie was cold and rejecting and she punished him for every little thing he did. If he cried or wet his pants or if he spilled his milk or made noise. She burned him. She locked him out of the house. She tried to drown him in the bathtub when he was three. She'd whip him with a stick until the backs of his legs were bloody. He tried so hard to be good, but she left him anyway."

"I don't want to feel sorry for him," I said irritably.

"I'm not saying it was cause and effect. It's one small part of the whole. Growing up, he managed to acquire a thin candy shell of charm and that's served him well. It doesn't address the underlying pathology, but it allows him to 'pass' as one of us."

"Those are the kids who turn into criminals, right?"

"Some do, but it's almost a side effect. I'll give you the perfect example. When I was still in school, I worked at one of the state hospitals for six months. This was the only time I actually encountered one of these ducks. I was doing a psychiatric workup on this kid, evaluating his suitability for placement in a group home. He'd come to us by way of juvenile court because he'd pushed his little sister out a second-story window. She was two and she survived, but that didn't seem to interest him in the least. When I asked him about the incident, his attitude was clinical. She was pestering him and he was curious what would happen if he tossed her out. He had no guilt or shame about what he'd done, so it didn't occur to him to be secretive. Ned's smarter than that, but I suspect his mind-set's much the same."

"What's he do for a living? You told me once, but you'll have to tell me again."

"He's in outside sales; at least he was when I dated him. Probably still doing it in one form or another. He can be warm and thoughtful and empathetic. I was completely taken in when we first met. I thought we were soul mates. It doesn't last, but it's irresistible when he's rolling out the charm. His job is to get along with people—chin-wag and problem-solve and make nice—which might seem odd until you realize it's all learned behavior. He's human by imitation. Maybe that's why he does such a good job of it; there's no unruly emotion to get in the way of his goal, which is to dominate."

"What was the company?"

"Van Schaick Chemicals. They manufacture polymers and engineering plastics; also agricultural products. We were a small branch and most of what we handled was related to crop protection. I was in the marketing department."

"How'd you end up doing that?"

"Oh, who knows? It's not like I grew up drooling over color brochures for cutworms and fungicides."

"What about Ned?"

"He started as a crop production services advisor and ended up southwest regional manager. He was an ag major at Cal Poly with an emphasis on business, so he has solid management abilities. He's great with clients; not so great when it comes to dealing with other employees, especially women. Underneath, he's not like the rest of us."

"It's probably stupid to say this, but this guy's genuinely dangerous, isn't he?"

"More so if he starts unraveling. You can call him a psychopath or a sociopath, but what's curious in his case is that he doesn't display the irresponsibility or the chronic instability that are characteristic. To me, this makes him all the more dangerous—to use your word— because he comes so close to mimicking 'normal.' So far, his thinking's been organized. What would make him truly dangerous is losing his ability to maintain a front."

"Back up a step. If he played a part in Lenore's death, he must have felt some guilt or he wouldn't have covered up."

"That was early in the game."

"I can't believe we're doing this. We're talking about him like he's a stone-cold killer. Based on what?"

"I'd say 'intuition,' but that's not worth much. I'll tell you one thing about guys like him. And I'm just going by what I've read. They hang on to trophies. Nothing big. Just little things."

"Totem objects?"

"Something like that. He'd keep trinkets, even if he's the only one who knows what they mean."

"Because he's hoping to get caught?"

She shook her head. "Because he wants to remind himself of all the good times he had."

"This is not filling me with confidence."

"Which is a good thing," she said.

"Uh, just morbidly curious here. Did he use that choking trick on you? His ex tells me he learned it in high school and used it during sex. I gather the effects are spectacular if you don't mind being on the brink of death."

She laughed. "Maybe that's what Shirley Ann objected to. Thankfully, I was spared."

"Well, *somehow* he managed to perfect his skills. You'd think it would take practice."

"Bet you can put an ad in the personals and find like-minded playmates," she said. "What's your current feeling about April? Will you tell her what you suspect about her dad?"

"What would she do with the information? The guy may be certifiable, but I have no proof."

"It's possible she knows he's bent and she's been averting her eyes."

"I would," I said. "Who wants to admit a parent is the bogeyman? That's what adults are supposed to protect us from. What happens if your *father* turns out to be the horror you thought was hiding under your bed?"

"That's what keeps me in business," she said.


When I got to work the next morning, I turned once again to the issues Pete had dropped in my lap. Susan Telford was the only one whose story I hadn't heard. I tried directory assistance in Henderson, Nevada, asking for phone numbers for the last name Telford, and was rewarded with the sorry news that there were thirty-three. I asked for the first ten. I was already tired of the job and I hadn't even started yet. There had to be an easier way to go about this.

I considered my alternatives. Wait a minute. Let's be honest. This was me being cagey, pretending an idea had just occurred to me when it was pretty much on my mind 24/7. I never hear the word "Nevada" without thinking of Robert Dietz. This coming May, we'd celebrate our sixth anniversary of hardly ever seeing each other. Truly, in the time I'd known him, I'm not sure we'd ever been together more than two months at a stretch, and that was only once. Naturally we get along beautifully in between my being completely pissed off with him because he's left me again.

Before I could change my mind, I dialed his number in Carson City. Three rings and his machine picked up. I listened to his outgoing message, which was terse and to the point. I waited for the beep and said, "Hey, Dietz. This is Kinsey. I need a favor from you. I'm looking for a woman named Susan Telford in Henderson, Nevada, and I wondered if you'd see what you can find out. There are thirty-three Telfords listed, and it doesn't make sense for me to tackle the job from here. Pete Wolinsky put her name on a list of six women who are all connected in one way or another to a man named Ned Lowe. Pete went to some lengths to do background on Lowe, who seems like an all-around bad egg. If you have questions, call me back, and if you don't want to do the job at all, that's fine. Just let me know."

Since my typewriter was still set up on the desk, I decided it was time to convert my investigation into report form. I'd accumulated any number of facts. Granted, none were earth-shattering, but who knew what they might add up to? Working for purely personal reasons didn't absolve me of the need to be thorough. I was formulating a sense of the relationship between Ned Lowe and the six women whose names appeared on Pete's list, but so far the link existed only in my head. To be useful, there had to be an overarching narrative account that would make the information comprehensible to someone unfamiliar with the circumstances. For my purposes, I found it helpful to maintain a running résumé of what I'd done, not only with an eye to discovering gaps, but in hopes of highlighting other avenues of inquiry. I had my doubts about whether my efforts would pay off, but documentation is never a bad idea.

I kept the language neutral and, in the process, forced myself to separate my opinions from the specifics of what I'd learned. My beliefs about Ned Lowe had to be deleted even if it grieved me to do so. What I was defining, in narrative form, were the dots that I hoped to connect when all the bits and pieces were in place.

The phone rang and I picked up the handset, tucking it between my shoulder and my ear while I rolled the paper out of the carriage and placed it on my desk. "Millhone Investigations."

A gentleman with a powdery voice said, "Miss Millhone, this is Stanley Munce, formerly with the Burning Oaks Police Department. An acquaintance by the name of Clara Doyle told me you'd spoken to her about a case here some years ago. Is that correct?"

"Yes, sir. Absolutely. Thank you so much for calling. I was asking about Lenore Redfern Lowe."

"That was my understanding. I'm afraid I don't have much to offer on the subject, but I will tell you what I can. I was the coroner's investigator at the time of that young girl's death. In order to complete a death certificate, the coroner has to determine the cause, mechanism, and manner of death. If you're familiar with the distinctions, I won't go into it . . ."

"No, please do," I said. "I can always use a refresher course."

"Simply put, cause of death is the reason the individual died, as would be the case with a heart attack or a gunshot wound. The mechanism of death would be the actual changes that affect the victim's physiology, resulting in death. Death from a fatal stabbing, for instance, might be extreme blood loss.

"The manner of death is how the death came about. Five of the six possibilities there are natural, accidental, suicide, homicide, and undetermined. The sixth classification would be 'pending' if the matter's still under investigation, which is obviously not the case here. There was no question about her ingestion of Valium and alcohol. The generic, diazepam, is a central nervous system depressant, the effects of which can be intensified by alcohol. The problem arose because when the toxicology report came in, it appeared there wasn't a sufficient quantity of either to say with any certainty death resulted from the combination of the two.

"What seemed questionable, at least in my mind, was the presence of petechiae, which are tiny broken blood vessels, like pinpricks visible in the area of her eyes. Hard coughing or crying are common causes; sometimes even the strain of childbirth or lifting weights. Petechiae can also be a sign of a death by asphyxiation."

"You mean she might have been suffocated?"

"Smothered, yes. There were no fractures of the larynx, hyoid bone, thyroid or cricoid cartilages, and no areas of bruising, which ruled out manual strangulation. Mrs. Lowe had been under doctor's care. With her history of mental problems, absent any other compelling evidence, Dr. Wilkinson felt a finding of suicide was appropriate. I put up what objections I could, but I have no formal medical training, and his experience and expertise prevailed. For my part, I was never fully persuaded."

"So there was never an investigation into the circumstances of her death?"

"A cursory assessment, I'd say. Dr. Wilkinson was of the old school: high-handed and a bit of an autocrat. He was in charge, he made the judgment call, and he brooked no argument. I was putting my job at risk even to raise the few questions I did."

"It sounds like your options were limited."

"One could say that." After a moment's hesitation, he went on. "Are you familiar with the term 'burking'?"

"Burking? I don't think so."

"Nor was I until I ran across a series of murders that occurred in Edinburgh, Scotland, back in the 1800s. I'm a history buff, especially where medical matters are concerned. I was in the midst of combing through old newspapers when I chanced on the case of William Burke and William Hare, who killed some sixteen unlucky souls in order to supply cadavers to an anatomist named Dr. Robert Knox. Burke's method was what caught my attention. He and Hare would focus on intoxicated individuals and then suffocate them by covering their mouths and pinching their noses closed. The technique left little to no evidence of foul play."

"Mr. Munce, I can't believe you're telling me this. I just had a phone conversation with Ned Lowe's second wife, and she talked about a choking maneuver he used during sex."

"Ah. That would be known as 'asphyxiophilia' when it's incorporated into sex with a partner. He must have been proficient at it."

I could feel myself blink as I struggled to assimilate the information. "Why haven't I ever heard of burking?"

"You'll find references once you start looking for them. I didn't become aware of the case until many years after Lenore's death or I'd have raised the issue myself."

"What happened to the pair?"

"Hare was granted immunity from prosecution and testified against Burke, who was convicted and hanged on January 28, 1829. A short time later, Hare disappeared. To my knowledge he was never heard of again. There were the usual rumors, of course, but no sign of the man himself."

"Unbelievable," I said.

"But true nonetheless. I wish I could offer you more. It's bothered me for years, but yours is the first question ever raised about that girl."

Which was not quite the case. There had been another question raised in the matter, and that was Pete's.

I thanked him for the information, and he graciously suggested that if I had additional questions, I should feel free to call. He gave me his number in Burning Oaks.

# 35

After I hung up, I sat for a moment, trying to understand what effect his considered opinion might have. Munce's views reinforced my suspicion that Ned Lowe hastened Lenore's death without providing tangible support. I believed I was on the right track, but what good is belief without corroborating evidence?

I still hadn't met Ned's current wife, so maybe it was time I talked to Celeste. I couldn't understand how any woman would be attracted to him, but people tell me I'm way too picky, so perhaps I'm the wrong one to ask. Not that anyone had asked me.

I sorted through my notes until I found April's home number and put in a call. When she picked up the line on her end, I said, "This is Kinsey Millhone. I was wondering if you could give me a phone number for Celeste?"

"I can't believe you're calling me. I was just about to pick up the phone and call you."

"A happy coincidence. What's going on?"

"I did something dumb and I thought I better let you know. Promise you won't get mad."

"Why don't you just say what you did before you ask for a guarantee?"

"Dad and Celeste came up for dinner last night."

"Okay."

"You remember the framed photograph of my grandmother with my father sitting on her lap?"

"How could I forget? I just gave it to you."

"I know. I really love that picture and I was so happy to have a link to the past."

"That you did what?"

"I set it on the bookshelf in our bedroom. You can't even see it from the door, so I didn't think there was any way Dad would spot it. He *never* goes in that part of the house; I can't imagine what possessed him."

"He knew I wanted to deliver something, so he was probably on the alert for anything new or different."

"That's the only explanation I can think of because I swear I never said a word about our conversation. I just feel so bad about this."

"Go on."

"At one point while we were eating dinner, he excused himself and went off to the bathroom. That's the only time he left the table. Usually he uses the powder room in the hall, but for some reason, he must have chosen the bathroom off the master bedroom. When he came back, I noticed he was withdrawn. I asked what was wrong, but he waved it aside. He and Celeste left earlier than usual, but I didn't think anything of it. I didn't realize there was a problem until she called this morning. She said he was livid about the photograph. I guess the two of them got into a terrible fight on the way home. She said I should be able to display a picture of my own grandmother any-where I wanted and he was making a big fuss over nothing."

"That doesn't sound like a bright move. I thought you said she was such a mouse. Surely she's aware he's touchy on the subject of his mother."

"I know, but she'd had a couple of drinks and I guess it just came out. Now she says he's furious with both of us and in a rage at you because he blames you for everything."

"She had drinks? I thought you said she was in AA."

"She didn't have them here. She belted down a couple before they left home. I didn't see any sign of inebriation, but he says she's the master at hiding it."

"When did you talk to him?"

"He called right before she did. He says she's blown the whole thing out of proportion. He admitted he was unhappy about the photo-graph, but now he's fine with it. He says she's the one who's going off the deep end and he's seriously concerned."

"He thinks she's cracking up?"

"Well, yes. I mean, he said he didn't want me to worry, but of course I do, which is why I'm calling. I know it's an imposition, but is there any way you could stop by the house and make sure she's okay? As Dad points out, if she's drinking again, we could end up with a mess on our hands."

"I don't mean to sound cranky, but why don't you do that? She's your stepmother."

"They live in Cottonwood, which is closer to you than it is to me. I have a doctor's appointment in forty minutes, so I don't have time to get down there and back. All you have to do is reassure her he's cooled down. He said he talked to her this morning 'til he was blue in the face. He thinks she's close to a nervous breakdown."

"What if I knock and he comes to the door? He's already in a rage."

"He's not home. He called me from work. He has meetings this morning and he won't be free until noon. He's making his annual photographic retreat and he leaves town first thing in the morning. He's taking the afternoon off work to get everything done. I wouldn't press you to go down there, but he reminded me in the past she's talked about, you know, doing away with herself."

I could feel a tickle on the back of my neck, a spider of fear crawling along my collar.

"Give me the address and phone number."

The drive to Cottonwood took less than fifteen minutes. I wasn't sure what Celeste would make of my appearance on her doorstep. Her fight with Ned was obviously none of my business, but if she didn't want to talk to me, she could simply say so. I cruised the neighborhood, searching for the house number, which fell in the middle of the block. I parked on the nearest side street and walked back.

Celeste and Ned Lowe lived in what was probably a sixteen-hundred-square-foot one-story board-and-batten house painted a soft gray, with a shake roof, solar panels, and a living room with a bay window. I was guessing two bedrooms, two baths, and a kitchen in desperate need of rehabilitation. There was no sign of Ned's black sedan in the driveway. The garage doors were closed and I had no way of knowing if his car and hers were tucked away inside. I'd have to take April's word for his being tied up at work.

I rang the bell, staring out at the driveway while I waited. There was an older-model aluminum-and-galvanized-steel Argosy Motorhome parked in the side yard, white with a brown stripe that ran around its middle. The back end of the vehicle was rounded, and a unit affixed to the top suggested a working air conditioner. The license plate read FOTO BIZ, which I assumed referred to Ned's photography.

Decals from countless tourist stops had been applied in a tidy line along the brown painted stripe. This was a history of Ned's travels spelled out one town at a time in a series of slogans. FALLOWAY, TX: HAPPIEST LITTLE CITY IN THE WEST. PARADISE, AZ: GHOST TOWN OF COCHISE COUNTY. PRAIRIE, NV: HOST OF THE 1985 WILD WEST RODEO.

The door was opened and Celeste stared out at me, fair-haired and pale.

"Celeste?"

"Yes."

"I'm Kinsey. I'm a friend of April's. She asked me to stop by and make sure you're okay."

"I'm fine."

"May I come in?"

She didn't look me in the eye and she didn't reply, but she didn't close the door in my face, which I took as a good sign. She considered my request and then stepped back. I entered the house and followed her into the living room, noting that she sat in a chair that allowed her to keep an eye on the street through the picture window in the front. She was tense and thin in the manner of someone with an eating disorder. Her dark eyes were at odds with her fair coloring and seemed enormous in the delicate oval of her face.

"Are you expecting Ned? April told me he's tied up in meetings until noon."

"I wouldn't count on it. He says things like that all the time and then pops in unexpectedly, hoping to catch me unawares. He likes to keep me on my toes."

On the wall behind her, there were two enlarged black-and-white photographs that I assumed were Ned's. Over the fireplace, there were two more in stark black frames. He was apparently fascinated with rock formations: limestone worn down by chemical weathering; sedimentary layers undulating along a ridge; granite outcroppings; a massive sandstone bed that had eroded into a single towering crag. Striking, but cold.

"Are those his?"

She nodded. "He hopes to retire from his sales job and make a living from his photography. That's part of what he does on his annual treks: he goes to galleries to show his portfolio."

Her tone of voice had the flat quality of someone reading from a script. She seemed to wear her passivity like a Kevlar vest. Getting through to her would be impossible unless I could find a way to gain her trust. "Do his prints sell?"

Her smile was brief. "Lately, they have."

"April says he's leaving tomorrow."

"Unless he cancels or delays or changes his mind."

"Where's he going this time?"

"He says I don't need to know. If I press him for information, he says I'm trying to control his every move."

"When, in fact, that's what he's doing to you," I said.

She gave one of those little half shrugs.

"Are you okay? You seem to be operating in a fog."

"Ned says I'm depressed."

"Do you have an opinion of your own?"

"That's what the drinking was about. I've been depressed all my life and that's how I made myself feel better."

"But you're not drinking now."

"I've been clean and sober for four and a half years."

"That's great. I'm not sure I could do that myself," I said. "I understand the two of you got into a disagreement last night."

"My fault. I should have kept my mouth shut. When I called April this morning, I was upset. I'm better now."

"Are you aware that he called her just before you did?"

"Oh. She didn't say anything about that."

"He told her you were drinking again, which is one of the reasons she was so concerned?"

"He tells people at work the same thing. I know because one of his coworkers called me and offered to help. He told her I was flipping out."

"This doesn't sound like a wonderful way to live."

"I'm used to it, I guess," she said. "Why are you so concerned?"

"I was a friend of Pete Wolinsky's. He contacted you a year ago, didn't he?"

She nodded. "He was concerned about my safety. He believed Ned was dangerous and I needed some way to protect myself. Leverage, he called it."

"What's wrong with running for your life?"

"Where would I go?"

"There are shelters for women who need help."

"Ned knows where they are. He has friends in law enforcement. He can get any address he wants."

"That's bullshit. He'd feeding you a load of crap."

"I don't think so. The one time I left, he killed his own dog. Took him out in the backyard and shot him in the head. He said it broke his heart, but he wanted me to understand how serious he was about our relationship. No one leaves him."

"Did Pete have an idea about how to get you out of here?"

"He put me in touch with Ned's second wife."

The answer was so unexpected, I squinted. "Phyllis?"

"I met her for coffee. He said it would be good for me to talk to a woman who was sure of herself and strong. One who'd gotten away from him."

"That sounds like Phyllis," I said. "I haven't met her, but I talked to her on the phone."

"She was great. She could tell I was scared to death of Ned and she tried to set me straight. She says everyone's vulnerable somewhere and she thinks photography is Ned's Achilles' heel. She's an accountant and when they were married she was on him all the time about keeping better records. She told him if he could show a profit from his photography, he could deduct ordinary and necessary expenses. He'd have to hang on to his receipts, but how hard is that? He didn't like the idea. Most of the time, he's paid under the table and he doesn't want to declare the income. He says as long as he keeps his mouth shut, the government won't find out."

"A lot of people feel the same way until they're caught."

"She said if he's falsifying his tax returns, I can put in a call to the IRS and let the Feds take care of him."

"No offense, Celeste, but if he's willing to kill his own dog, Ned's not worried about the IRS."

"That was Pete's response as well, but he thought it was a starting place. Ned's secretive. I'm not supposed to touch anything of his. In particular, I'm not allowed in his darkroom. He keeps it locked and he's warned me a hundred times I'm not to go in there."

"Please tell me you had the gumption to disobey the man."

Her smile wasn't expansive, but it was the first time I'd seen the real Celeste peek out of her eyes. "I did. Pete pushed me to do it. Ned's job keeps him on the road part of every month. The next time he went off on a business trip, I searched the house. I found a key in an old floor register under the wall-to-wall carpet in the hall. Once I knew where he'd hidden it, I could let myself in anytime I wanted."

"Good for you," I said.

"Not really, but Pete thought I was doing great."

"And Ned didn't catch on?"

"It didn't seem to occur to him. It was the first time I realized he wasn't all-seeing and all-powerful. Next chance I had, I went into the darkroom. That was disappointing. Most of what he has in there is standard photographic supplies: cameras, film, chemicals, developing tanks. Things like that. File after file of photographs, proof sheets, negatives. One file cabinet he kept locked, but by then I understood how his mind worked. He'd hidden that key and a smaller one in a film canister on the shelf above the sink in there. In the bottom drawer, there was a locked metal box that the smaller key fit. Inside, there were receipts and some other stuff."

"Receipts for what?"

"Motels, restaurants, gasoline."

"You think he decided to play by the rules?"

"Maybe he's beginning to think of photography as a real business instead of something he does on the side. He says he may be making a big change."

"What do you think that means?"

"I don't know and I wouldn't ask."

"What else was in the box? You mentioned other stuff."

She shrugged. "I don't know; ticket stubs, a couple of parking passes for the wilderness areas he visits. He likes camping in the back country, which is where he does some of his photo shoots."

"What did you do with the box?"

"I took everything out and put it in an envelope for Pete and then locked the box in the drawer. Pete said he'd do an inventory so we'd know what we had. What happened, though, was someone offered him a job that he felt he had to take. He hadn't worked in months because of the research he was doing on Ned."

"Does Ned know what happened to the stuff in the box?"

"He does now. I told him I gave it to a friend of mine for safekeeping and if anything happens to me, it'll all be turned over to the police. That really made him crazy. At first, he thought I was lying, that maybe I'd hidden it here, so he tore the house apart. I don't know what he's doing now. I know he hasn't given up. He wants that envelope."

"Is he aware Pete was helping you?"

"Probably. He heard Pete was asking questions about him up in Burning Oaks. You can imagine how popular that notion was. Once Pete got killed, it was like Ned went underground. I think he was trying to figure out if his precious stuff was still out there somewhere. In the meantime, I can't say he's nice to me, but at least he doesn't threaten me so much."

I stared at her. "Do you know how crazy you sound?"

"I was crazy all the years I put up with his abuse. Now I've got him right there." The gesture she made would have been appropriate for pinching a bug between her thumb and index finger.

"What happens if he realizes you're as clueless as he is?"

"I hope to be gone by then. If not, I'll shoot him with the same gun he used to kill his dog and plead temporary insanity. Given what he's told everyone about my mental state, who could believe otherwise?"

"I don't understand what you're waiting for. Why not get in the car and go while you can?"

She shook her head. "For the moment, he's convinced everything's fine, which means he'll go away as planned. If he suspects anything's amiss, he'll cancel his trip. If I can just get him out of here, I'll have a three-day head start."

I was shaking my head in despair, but I didn't know what else to do. I couldn't see an alternative. She knew him better than I did. I wanted to put her in the car and hightail it out of there, but I couldn't talk her into it. "I guess you know what you're doing," I said.

"Oh, right. Something I forgot about. Along with the ticket stubs and stuff like that, he had this junky bunch of costume jewelry; mostly earrings. They were in with the rest of his souvenirs."

I felt my heart catch. "Souvenirs?"

"Well, not souvenirs exactly, but mementos; reminders of where he's been."

I pressed a business card into her hand. "I want you to call me as soon as you're somewhere safe. I mean this. If you need me to drive down and pick you up, just say the word."

"I will."

"Do you swear?"

She raised her right hand and I took that as an oath.

# 36

When I got home, I shuffled through my index cards until I'd found Christian Satterfield's home phone number. The last time I'd called, Pauline had made short work of me. I was still operating on the assumption she was Christian's grandmother. This time when I dialed, I had a better handle on the situation.

After two rings, she picked up with the same gruff "Hello."

I said, "Hi, Pauline. This is Kinsey. You remember me? Christian's friend. We met when you and Geraldine were living over on Dave Levine Street."

There was a pause while she tried to place me. "I don't believe I do, but that was some years ago."

"Never mind. It was just the one occasion. Listen, I hear Christian's back from Lompoc and I was hoping to catch up with him. Is he there?"

"He's not."

"Do you expect him anytime soon?"

"Well, honey, I have no idea. You know him. He comes and goes as he pleases."

"If I leave my number, could you have him get in touch as soon as he comes in? Nothing urgent, but I'd appreciate it."

She took down my office number as I recited it slowly.

Then I said, "Is he still hanging out at that little bar up the street from you?"

"He's there most nights. If you don't hear back, you drop in after nine o'clock, you can't miss him. I might see you there myself."

"I'll do that. Thanks so much."

Lou's Bar and Grill was right where I'd seen it last, at the corner of Dave Levine and Oliver, half a block north of Trace. The interior was small and dark, except for two pinball machines in the rear that gave off a garish glow and tinkled merrily like the slots in a Las Vegas casino. I was decked out in my usual jeans and turtleneck, but I'd swapped out my tennis shoes for my boots and I'd shrugged into my blazer, which I fancied contributed a jaunty air of confidence.

I had to park around the corner, but the walk was only a half block. I arrived at 8:45, allowing myself time to get a feel for the place, which was half full—all men, and half of them with lighted cigarettes. Like many neighborhood establishments, there was a certain proprietary air among the patrons. These were the drinkers who showed up after work and stayed until closing time. They didn't appreciate strangers in their midst. A number of them turned and stared at me pointedly before looking away. I ignored the hostility and found a seat at the bar with an empty stool on either side.

The bartender, middle-aged and male, appeared, and I ordered a Diet Pepsi just as a change of pace. Sitting at a bar alone can be a tricky proposition. On the whole, I thought it was better to be judged haughty and aloof than as a woman on the prowl. If I'd had a paperback mystery in my shoulder bag, I'd have pulled it out and buried my nose in it.

At ten after nine, the door opened and Christian ambled in. I could see him do a quick crowd assessment, searching for familiar faces. His gaze passed over me and then came back. He took his time circling the room, greeting people here and there. Eventually he came up on my right side as though entirely by accident.

"This seat taken?"

"Help yourself," I said.

He gestured at the bartender, who went about the business of making him a martini that he presented in an icy glass with two olives. He seemed comfortable with his transformation—expensive wardrobe, his hair streaked with shades of copper and pale gold. The spray-on tan had faded, but it still looked good on him.

He kept his gaze on his martini when he next spoke. "You're Kinsey, right?"

"How did you know?"

"You're the only one in here I don't know. My grandmother says you left a message for me."

"You didn't return my call."

"You left one earlier with my parole officer."

"You didn't return that one, either."

"I figured if it was important you'd get back to me, which you did. So what's this about?"

"You know what I do for a living?"

"You're a private investigator."

"Exactly. A couple of weeks ago, I was hired by a woman who claimed she wanted to locate a child she put up for adoption thirty-some-odd years ago. Yours was the name she gave me, along with newspaper clippings about your trial. I found out later she was full of shit, but by then I'd already sent off my report, in which I gave her your mother's address and phone number. I may have put you in harm's way and I thought you deserved a warning."

"Two weeks is a little late for warnings, don't you think?"

"It took me a while to figure out she'd put one over on me. I assume Teddy's been in touch."

"That's correct," he said.

He turned and looked at me with eyes that were a startling gray. Up close I could see that his teeth were good, and his aftershave suggested carnations and clean skin. These are qualities that loom large with me. For the first time, I entertained the idea that he was in Teddy's life for the amusement value. I might have found him amusing myself, though his criminal history left much to be desired. A hard-boiled private eye and a bank robber seemed like a strange mix.

"What happened to your safecracking career?" I asked.

"I wouldn't call it a career. It was an avocation."

"A hobby?"

"Let's call it a passion and leave it at that."

"What was the draw?"

"I liked the challenge. Problem solving. Getting in there and figuring it all out. I avoided vaults. Those are in a whole separate category that's way over my head. I started with home safes you could pick up and take with you to work on in your spare time. The fireproof models are lightweight, really just a shell of thin steel walls filled with insulating material to protect the contents from damage in case of a fire."

"Have you ever heard of a Diebold Cannonball Safe?"

"Oh, sure. It was a Cannonball that stumped Jesse James in Northfield, Minnesota. Burglar-resistant safes are a tough proposition. With most, you're talking about a seven-hundred-and-fifty-pound box embedded in concrete. Safe like that you have to work on in place, which is time-consuming. In those days, I didn't care about finding cash, which is good because I never netted much."

"How'd you manage to support yourself? Did you have an outside job?"

"I was *twelve*."

"So mowing lawns."

"Sometimes, sure. You know what the real problem was? Safecracking requires so much *equipment*. Drills, cold chisels, sledgehammers, electric saws with diamond-edged blades. An acetylene torch is mandatory, which means you have to have a hose and tank. Punch or drift pins you can't do without, maybe a two-twenty-volt electric cutting torch. What was I supposed to do, hide it all under my bed?"

"No blasting caps?"

"I never got into those. Practice with explosives, you can picture the complaints."

"Your mother and your grandmother didn't notice the gear you had stashed in your room?"

"I told them I was interested in how things worked. You know, tinkering. What did they care? I could fix small appliances and that was good. I spent a lot of time in my room. I was quiet and industrious. I made good grades. I wasn't truant. I didn't hang out on street corners with the bad element."

"Eventually you lost interest, is that it?"

"Essentially. Robbing banks has a bigger thrill quotient for a lot less time and effort. I got addicted to the rush. I'd walk in, calm and relaxed. Three minutes later I'd walk out the door higher than a kite with no illegal substances involved. How can you beat that?"

"You weren't concerned about getting shot to death?"

"I didn't carry a weapon. The first time a bank guard told me to drop, I'd have dropped. Meantime, I was nice about it. I didn't yell. I didn't threaten people—"

"Not ever?"

He smiled. "Okay, sometimes. In a note. I know tellers are gullible, but I tried not to take advantage. Most were beautiful young girls I'd have been happy to date. I thought of them as my ninety-second relationships. Brief, but intense. One teller wrote to me for a long time after I went to Lompoc. I can't remember her name now."

"Lucy." That got his attention, but I didn't want to stop and explain. Instead, I said, "You couldn't have enjoyed prison life."

"Uh, no. I did not. I met some very smart gentlemen and a number of thugs. I learned how to protect myself, which was not always pleasant for the other fellow."

"Why would you risk going back?"

"Look, I appreciate your concern. Especially coming in here like this. You didn't have to go out of your way."

"I feel responsible."

"You needn't. I can take care of myself."

"And you've done so well to date," I remarked.

"Don't be a wiseass. I can see you have advice to offer. You want to say your piece?"

"Sure. I think it's a mistake to get caught up in someone else's melodrama. Especially those two."

"You don't find it amusing?"

"Not even a little bit," I said. "Ari knows there's something afoot."

"Of course he does. Teddy likes it that way. Keeps him on his toes."

I pulled my shoulder bag up onto my lap and removed one of my business cards. "That's my number on the off chance you'll want to get in touch."

"I already have your number. My PO passed it on. And I'm sure Teddy knows how to reach you."

"Of course. Silly me. She's the one who set this in motion, isn't she? You expect to make money off this scheme, whatever it is?"

"If not, I got some cool threads out of the deal."

I hauled the strap of my bag over my shoulder and slid off the bar stool. I was on the verge of pulling out my wallet when Christian stayed my hand, saying, "I'll take care of it."

"No need."

"I can handle it."

"Thank you."

"You're welcome. I meant it when I said I appreciate your concern."

"Christian, those two have been knocking heads for years. End of the day, they'll still be having a good time. You're the one who'll pay."

I stepped out of the bar into night air so clean and sweet, it had the shocking quality of ice water being flung in my face. I hoped the brief walk would dispel the smell of cigarette smoke that clung to my hair and clothes. Even as I slid under the steering wheel and secured my seat belt, I knew I'd have to shower before I went to bed or my sheets would pick up the same smell.

I drove home along the beach. My exchange with Satterfield had been a letdown. I'd thought warning him would relieve me of any further responsibility, but I was not off the hook. In essence, he'd said "Thank you very much and get lost." Repeating myself would in no way produce the desired effect. I'd cautioned him and he'd made it clear he wasn't interested in walking away. He thought he was smart enough to sidestep the fallout. The problem was I had nowhere to go from here. You can't *make* someone else do anything, even if you know you're right.


The next morning as I was leaving for work, I caught sight of Henry's station wagon pulling into the drive. He parked, went around to the passenger side, and helped Edna out of the vehicle.

I went out and gave him a wave. "You're up early."

Edna said, "I needed some items at the grocery store and I didn't dare wait too long or it would be crowded."

"Mr. McClaskey arrived at seven to finish his inspection."

"He's here? Where'd he park his truck?"

"He found a spot across the street. When I told him Edna and I would be making a run, he made sure he wasn't blocking the drive."

Mr. McClaskey apparently heard our conversation and he appeared from the side of the garage. He doffed his cap at the sight of Edna, but aside from that he was all business.

"I believe I've found the source of your water loss, Mr. Pitts, if you'll just step this way."

Henry and I were both interested. Edna had certainly heard enough of Henry's complaints and I expected her to be as curious as we were, but she seemed to hang back.

Mr. McClaskey moved into the gap between Henry's garage and the board fence that separated his property from the Shallenbargers'.

He pointed at a good-size hole he'd dug. "There's your lateral," he said, indicating a pipe visible at the bottom of the hole. "And *that* is a T joint someone's cut into your line. You can see the joins right here. There's a run of PVC pipe that goes under the fence. On the other side, it comes up into a hose bib you can see if you take a look."

Edna stood at some remove, her attention drawn to Mr. McClaskey's commentary in the manner of someone passing the scene of a fatal traffic accident.

Henry and I both craned our necks to see over the fence. The hose bib had an adapter on it that allowed two hoses to be attached to the same faucet. A twenty-foot-long green hose extended from each threaded metal end. The two hoses ran in opposite directions. Both connected to portable sprinkler heads that consisted of a rounded tube with holes through which water would shoot, forming a grace- ful arc as each head moved from side to side. It was an inexpensive alternative to in-ground irrigation systems, the prime drawback being the necessity for manual intervention. At the moment, neither hose was in use but the grass was still wet from a recent watering.

We both stared without comprehension.

Henry turned to the plumber. "What *is* this?"

Mr. McClaskey lifted his chin and scratched under it, an action that gave his reply a certain droll quality. "Well. I'd have to say someone's tapped into your lateral to access your water for their own personal irrigation purposes."

"Access?" Henry blinked. "Do you mean stealing?"

"That's pretty much the long and short of it," McClaskey replied.

Henry turned to Edna with a look of dismay.

"That was there when we moved in," she said indignantly. "Of course we used it. It's in our yard, so why would we not? But we had no knowledge whatever that the hose bib and faucet were connected to your water line."

"As often as I've complained about high water usage, it never occurred to you to see what that hose bib was attached to?"

"Why would it occur to me? I don't know anything about plumbing. I don't know anything about gardening or yard maintenance. I'm doing the best I can to handle the care of a disabled husband. We had nothing to do with it."

"Of course you did. Dale Adelson didn't install that line," I said.

"I don't know your Mr. Adelson, but the hose bib has to be his handiwork because it certainly isn't ours."

Henry pointed in the direction of the hose bib. "The first time we met, you were huddled right there, burying your little doggie, or so you claimed. I said hello over the fence and that's when you told me she died. I felt sorry for you. You were probably tapping into my line right then."

"We did not put in that T. We knew nothing about it until this very minute. My husband and I are both old and he's been ill and we live on a fixed income, which provides barely enough to get by as it is. We are honorable people doing the best we can, and I can't believe you'd suggest we were in any way responsible. You surely can't suspect my poor husband of any tomfoolery when he's confined to a wheelchair and has been for the past six years."

I raised a tentative hand to refute that bit about Joseph's being confined to a wheelchair since I'd seen him amble around the house in the most casual manner imaginable. I lowered my hand again, thinking this was probably not the moment to speak up.

Henry's face was stony, but he was having the same difficulty I was in forming a response to someone making such categorical denials in that string of declarative sentences. "My water bill has doubled," he said, outraged. "You've watched me tear up my yard trying to correct the problem. And that's all you have to say?"

"What else would you have me say? Your allegations are completely false and I will not put up with it."

Henry turned to the plumber. "Thank you, Mr. McClaskey. Leave that as it is for the time being. I'll want photographs." Then he walked to his back door, banging it shut behind him as he went in.

Edna stood her ground. "I have never in my life been addressed in such a manner. We've been the best neighbors we know how, and all we get in return is spite. He has slandered us. He has tarnished our name and our good reputation. I intend to call our attorney and report this. I wouldn't be surprised if he urged us to file suit."

She looked from one of us to the other, but neither Mr. McClaskey nor I had anything to say.

"Now I suppose I'll have to tell Joseph what's happened. He'll be distraught. We both thought the world of Mr. Pitts. I can't believe the man could be so swift to judge and so unwilling to consider the facts."

She turned and walked down the driveway with as much dignity as she could muster. Mr. McClaskey and I exchanged one of those looks that confirmed we were both of the same opinion. The Shallenbargers had been pulling a fast one, never expecting to get caught and called on it.

# 37

For a merry change of pace, I bypassed the office and drove to Montebello Luxury Properties. I couldn't help but wonder what the fallout
would be from the Shallenbargers' thievery. There was no way Henry
would recoup his losses, which probably hadn't even reached the dollar amount that distinguished petit theft from grand. Henry would take
photographs, Mr. McClaskey would remove the T connection, and that
would be that. From my perspective the discovery of the illegal tap
was a boon. The sticky buns and cheery chats across the fence had
come to an end, and there would be no more shopping expeditions for
Edna. I wouldn't even have to argue with Henry about my dim view of
the pair. My only reservation stemmed from the suspicion that we
hadn't seen the last of them. Scoundrels, even elderly ones, are remarkably resilient and not so easily defeated.

When I reached the real estate office, I parked in the tiny lot and
let myself in the front door. The shopkeeper's bell jingled.

At the reception desk, Kim was smoothing one fingernail with an emery board. She looked up with an expression of anticipation, which turned only slightly sour at the sight of me. She was wary—not quite hostile, but certainly not cocky and superior as she'd been on our first encounter. Since I'd been so warmly welcomed by the company's top producer, she was probably hesitant to treat me with the same condescension.

I crossed to her desk. "Hi, Kim. Remember me?"

"Yes."

I could hear the word "unfortunately," which she'd left out. I said, "Good. I need a meeting with Teddy and I'd appreciate it if you'd give her a call to set it up."

I thought she might play dumb and pretend she didn't know who I was talking about, but she tried a different strategy. "What makes you think Teddy wants to talk to you?"

I put an index finger against my cheek, tilting my head in what I hoped was a winsome fashion. "Well, let's see. Hmmm. Possibly because I had a nice long chat with her ex-husband yesterday." I held up that same index finger. "Or. Possibly because I had a drink last night with Christian Satterfield and he was very informative. Also relevant is the fact that I'm pissed off and she'd do well to mollify me while she has the chance."

Kim broke off eye contact and her cheeks picked up a tint of pink under the recently applied tan. Really, she should have used the lighter shade. She said, "I'm not sure where she is this morning."

"Probably at your place since she's living with you. Why don't you call home?"

I could see I'd thrown her into an agony of indecision. She didn't want to make the call in front of me because she knew I'd pick up her home number simply by watching her dial. I gave her a verbal nudge. "You can use the phone in one of the empty offices. I'll be happy to wait."

She debated another few seconds and then excused herself and rose from her chair. She was wearing very high heels, no stockings, and a skirt so short, I could see her underpants.

I said, "I see London, I see France . . ."

She tugged her skirt down in back and left the reception area.

As soon as she disappeared, I reached for her steno pad and flipped through the pages until I found the notes she'd been taking about flights and departure times during my first visit. At that point, I hadn't known she was a player in the drama, so it's lucky I pay attention to these things. I ripped out the sheet, folded it, and tucked it in my bag, then flipped the pages back to the one she was using to take notes today.

She reappeared and took her seat. No eye contact, of course. "She said you should come for drinks at five." She scribbled an address across one corner of her steno pad and tore off the scrap.

"Can I bring anything?" I chirped.

She ignored the offer. I hadn't been serious, but Cheez Whiz on saltines was bound to be on the low end of canapés, even in their debased circumstances.

I left the real estate office and crossed the parking lot. It wasn't until I unlocked my car and slid under the wheel that I finally picked up on a line Edna had tossed out earlier. The remark was folded into her confrontation with Henry when she was so righteously defending herself. At the time, I'd heard what she'd said, but I'd been focused on the showdown and I hadn't picked up the significance. It suddenly occurred to me to ask myself the following: why had she said, "I don't know your Mr. Adelson, but the hose bib has to be his handiwork because it certainly isn't ours"?

How could she not know Dale Adelson when she and Joseph had bought the house from him two and a half months before? Had they completed the purchase long-distance, with papers flying back and forth and no face-to-face communication? I don't own property, so I'm not sure how these things work, but you'd think the name would have registered.

I pulled out of the lot with a quick look at my watch. It was just after nine and the county offices would be open. I returned to my office and left the car in the driveway, then hiked the five blocks to the court-house. I went up the stairs to the county clerk's office, where I sat at a small computer in the reception area and typed in the Shallenbargers' street address. I don't consider myself computer literate, but this was a simple machine with a limited number of functions, more like a type-writer with a quiet keyboard and no carriage return.

From the street address, I was able to pick up the assessor's parcel number, which in turn provided me the name of the owners of the property: Dale and Trish Adelson. Edna had given Henry the impres-sion they'd bought the property, but I don't know that she'd come right out and said so. The Shallenbargers were apparently renting the house, which clarified one point. Then I wondered if they were sticking Henry for their entire water bill or just the portion they were using for irriga-tion. I thought he'd be interested in the answer as well if he was cal-culating his losses.

The Santa Teresa Water District has offices in City Hall, some five blocks away. It was by then 9:30 and I'd caught them in a lull between customers. Both clerks were on the telephone, but one acknowledged my presence. There were four or five desks with the usual stacks of paperwork, gray metal file cabinets, upright files, fluorescent lights overhead, and a few personal items on the desktops, but in the main the atmosphere was one of industry and efficiency.

I waited only briefly before Mrs. Fremont, the administrative as-sistant, approached. She was a tall, big-boned woman in her seventies with a wiry topknot of gray curls and emphatic eyebrows that she'd penciled in herself two inches higher than one would expect. She wore heavy silver earrings and a pair of narrow glasses with black frames that rested low on her nose.

I leaned my elbows on the counter and said, "I'm hoping you can give me some help. I have an elderly couple living next door, Joseph and Edna Shallenbarger. Mrs. Shallenbarger's concerned about their water bill being so high. Her husband's disabled and neither one of them drives, so I said I'd see what I could find out. They moved here from Perdido in January and she's been shocked at how expensive it is."

"I don't know why. The rates should be the same."

"That's what I said. I wondered if they might have a leak in their service lateral. Most of those old galvanized iron pipes are seventy years old. You get a break, it's costly to locate and even worse to replace. Sewer or water lines break on a homeowner's property, it's up to the homeowner to remedy the problem." I thought I did a creditable job of rendering the plumber's point of view, and she must have thought so, too.

"Oh, don't I know it. Comes as a shock to some. Give me that name and address and I'll see what we've got."

I gave her the information and watched her write it on a slip of paper that she took with her to the row of file cabinets on the far wall. She found the proper drawer and picked her way through the documents until she found what she was looking for. The fact that there was a file in the Shallenbargers' name assured me that they'd applied for service, which would be happy news for Henry. She removed a slim file and returned to the counter. She opened the cover and leafed through several sheets of paper. The glasses worn low on her nose gave her an air of authority.

"You're not on computer yet?" I asked.

"They're threatening. I'd like to know what we'll do if the power goes out."

She pursed her lips while she read the information and then shook her head as though reluctant to contradict the elderly. "I'm not sure what she's worried about. According to our records, water consumption has stayed about the same."

"Really? Well, that's good news. You're comparing the same three months last year?"

"Yes, ma'am. They must be doing a good job of conservation."

"I can't argue with that," I said.

What interested me was the printed form on top that Edna had filled out by hand and signed. Even upside down I could see it was labeled OCCUPANT COURTESY BILLING APPLICATION. I put my finger on it. "What's that?"

She glanced down. "That would be the application they filled out when they initiated service."

"Mind if I take a look?"

She put a quick hand out to restrain me, but I'd already turned the file around. She said, "It may not be appropriate for you to read the file."

"I thought this was public information."

"Well, yes, but some of it is personal."

"I'm just looking at the top sheet."

I turned the file so we were both looking at it from the same angle. "See there. The only personal information on the application is the service address, which I already know because I live right next door to them. They asked me to come down here and so there's no breach of privacy." I pointed to the lower portion of the form. "Who's Calvin Sanchez?"

"The property owner. He's required to sign the same form, agreeing to be jointly or severally responsible for any amounts due the Santa Teresa Water District if the occupant fails to pay."

"I thought the Shallenbargers bought the place. Aren't they the owners?"

She shook her head. "Tenants."

"Really! I had no idea. You learn something new every day, don't you?" I could have told her that "Calvin Sanchez" was most likely a figment of Edna's imagination, but I thought I'd better check further before I mentioned it to anyone.

I relinquished my hold on the file, and Mrs. Fremont closed it, saying, "If your Mrs. Shallenbarger believes she's been billed incorrectly, she can always call or stop by. We'll be happy to talk to her."

"I'll let her know. Thanks so much for your time."

When I left the water department, I realized all I'd done was to burden myself with another problem. In a curious way, I knew Henry would have a hard time staying worked up about the water theft. Initially, he might have been dismayed, perhaps genuinely angry, but I knew his conscience would kick in, undermining his good sense and overruling his belief in the virtues of honesty. He'd start to feel sorry for the pair—poor sweet old folks forced to resort to such measures. It would be one of those "there but for the grace of God" moments. He'd think about how fortunate he and his siblings were: able-bodied, mentally sharp, blessed with good health, and comfortable financially because they'd figured out all those years ago that saving for the future, while not always easy, would be prudent.

I had watched Edna manipulate Henry until she only needed to sigh and he'd be ready to serve and protect. If I wasn't careful, instead of Henry feeling perturbed about the water they'd siphoned from his line, he'd be going door to door taking up a collection to help them make ends meet. In his mind, it wouldn't amount to much more than pennies a day, and why not lend a hand since he had more than they did? That was certainly Edna's attitude.

When I reached the office, I unlocked the door, disarmed the system, and then sat down at my desk. I picked up the phone and called directory assistance. When I had the operator on the line, I asked for a listing for last name Adelson in Richmond, Virginia. Apparently, there was only one: Dale and Trish. I made a note of the number, depressed the plunger, and then dialed. It was only 10:00 California time, which would make it roughly 1:00 on the East Coast.

The line rang twice and a woman picked up.

"Mrs. Adelson?"

"This is Trish, yes."

"This is Kinsey Millhone out in Santa Teresa. Henry Pitts's tenant."

"Yes, of course," she said, though I was pretty sure she wouldn't have put two and two together if I hadn't spelled it out for her. "I hope you're not calling to say something's happened to Henry."

"No, no. It's nothing like that. Sorry if I caused you alarm. Is your husband there by any chance?"

"He's off at the university. I don't expect him home until late this afternoon. Is this something I can help you with?"

"I hope so. We're concerned about your house."

"Is there a problem?"

"That's what I'm calling to find out. Do you have tenants in there?"

"No. The house is on the market, but we don't have renters. Dale asked our real estate agent about the possibility and she said being a long-distance landlord would be a nightmare. Why do you ask?"

"Because an elderly couple moved in a couple of months ago. Edna and Joseph Shallenbarger."

"Moved in? I don't understand. You mean someone's *living* there?"

"I'm afraid so. When Henry first met them, Edna said they'd moved in in January. We just assumed they bought the place. It wouldn't have occurred to me to look into it, but they actually attached an illegal T fitting to Henry's water line and they've been using his water to irrigate their grass and shrubs. We're in the middle of a drought out here and Henry's fit to be tied because his water bill's gone up. When he mentioned you, Edna had no idea who he was referring to."

She was still having trouble assimilating the introductory concept. "An elderly couple's living in the house? You mean *old* people?"

"For the past two and a half months. I didn't want to raise a question if these were friends of yours."

"Absolutely not. I can't believe this. How could someone move in like that?"

"I don't know, but that's what they seem to have done."

"Well, we'll have to evict them as soon as possible. Do you think we should fly out?"

"It might come down to that. Do you know a Calvin Sanchez?"

"Who's he?"

"He signed their application for water service, listing himself as the property owner."

"I don't understand what's going on. We own that property. We haven't authorized anyone to do anything. We've continued to pay utilities because it makes the house easier to show. Not that anyone's looked at it since we moved here."

"Well, I just talked to the water department and the Shallenbargers have put the water service in their name. I'm not sure about gas or electricity. I know they don't have their garbage picked up."

"I'll ask Dale if he's been receiving statements. If these people have put utilities in their name, the bills might be going directly to them."

"I guess we can sort this all out once we talk to them. As long as you're in agreement, we'll go next door and have a conversation. I didn't want to mention this to Henry until I talked to you."

"Well, thank you. I appreciate that, and I'm sure Dale will as well. Of course we want them out of there, so do whatever's necessary. You have our permission to take any action required."

"Perfect. We'll have a chat with them and get back to you."

After I hung up, I sat and considered the situation. I'd certainly served enough eviction notices in my capacity as a process server. A tenant can be terminated with a thirty-day, sixty-day, or ninety-day notice, depending on the circumstances. Grounds for eviction include damage to the property or illegal activity on the premises. There is also a three-day notice to pay rent or quit, but I couldn't think how that would apply to someone who wasn't paying rent to begin with.

# 38

The address Kim had given me for the condominium she shared with Teddy was part of a complex in an area called Paloma Run, located on a sheltered stretch of beach south of Montebello. Teddy was expecting me at 5:00, and I allowed sufficient time to account for rush-hour traffic. There was ample parking provided so as not to annoy the rich in their efforts to park their Mercedes, Maseratis, and Bentleys, many of which were neatly tucked into small cul-de-sacs, landscaped to disguise their purpose. We would have taken offense if we'd been confronted with an acre of unsightly asphalt.

I followed a series of flat stones that wound through the low-growing ground cover. Landscaping was limited due to a proliferation of pines that left the needle-matted ground under them impossible to plant. The building itself comprised two- and three-story sections, set at angles to maximize privacy without obstructing the views of the Pacific.

Their apartment was on the second floor, linked to adjacent units by way of open loggias.

When I rang the bell, Teddy came to the door. She was barefoot, in formfitting jeans and a loose gauzy shirt with voluminous sleeves. As was true of the caftan she'd worn the night I met her, the style of the garment was vaguely Indian—small mirrors embroidered along the bodice, the hem beaded.

She stepped back, admitting me, and then closed the door behind us. "This should be interesting," she said. "Make yourself comfortable. I'll only be a minute." She turned and padded down the hallway, disappearing from sight.

Setting my mental timer to "one minute" was a smart move on her part, as it suggested I wouldn't have time to search the premises in depth, which is how I normally occupy my time when afforded the opportunity. I circled the big open room, which served as living room, dining room, and study. The decor was nautical—no big surprise there, given the ocean beyond. Pale grays and blues, enormous glass goblets filled with sand where hermit crabs walked, leaving tracks like the stylized rake marks in a Japanese garden. Throughout, I saw bleached hardwood floors, floor-to-ceiling windows along the front and floor-to-ceiling bookshelves on two interior walls. A glass-paned door leading to the patio was open to admit an ocean breeze. A stack of coffee table books served as a doorstop, all of them lavishly illustrated with the paintings of J.M.W. Turner. There was one boxed set, two eight-by-twelve-inch volumes, one of text and the other of black-and-white and color plates of his works.

I moved out onto the balcony and looked over the rail. Below, a wooden walkway stretched from the first-floor deck across the ice plant as far as the loose sand. Waves broke in a series of thunderous reports, the surf washing up and back. I could see the appeal of living a stone's throw from the ocean. The sounds were restful and it was lovely to look out and see nothing but ocean all the way out to the horizon. On the downside, the salt air took its toll and the occasional strong storm could plant a sailboat in your front yard.

I moved back into the living room and sat down on the couch. I entertained myself by looking at the family photographs in silver frames that had been placed on the nearest end table. Children or grandchildren. There was no way to sort out which personal touches belonged to the condominium's owner and which had been brought in by Teddy and Kim to help them feel at home.

There was also a small stack of promotional brochures for what must have been the infamous condominium where Stella's husband died. I was curious to see what million-dollar real estate was looking like these days. I picked up the brochure on top; a four-fold color spread showed the living room with its high coffered ceiling, wood-burning fireplace, and abundance of light, the gleaming kitchen, the marble-lined bathrooms, the bedrooms, the gracious outdoor patio with its view to the ocean in the distance. The accompanying sales pitch was one I could have written myself. The word "stunning" loomed large.

A glossy library book about Tiffany jewelry rested open on the arm of the couch. The cover featured a necklace that looked like a baby's bib, dense with diamonds, emeralds, and gold filigree. I didn't realize Teddy had returned until she said, "I know what you're thinking, that we've hardly fallen on hard times living in a place like this." She carried a bottle of white wine and two wineglasses that she placed on the coffee table.

"Crossed my mind."

"Kim and I are housesitting for a friend. We're like gypsies. We pick up every few weeks and move to another encampment."

"But you don't pay rent."

"True enough." Her gaze drifted to the book about Tiffany jewelry. In one easy motion, she closed the book and set it on the floor by her chair.

I kept my expression disinterested. "How long have you been here?"

"A month. We have another month to go; maybe more if she extends her stay abroad."

Even in the harsh sunlight streaming through the windows, I was struck anew by her facial structure, with its angular planes, the prominent nose with the bump at the bridge. And all that excessive hair. It was a rich mahogany shade with glints of red, thick and layered, with some of the strands forming ringlets. If she was wearing makeup, it wasn't evident. I watched her use an auger-style opener to remove the cork. It was the same wine we'd enjoyed that night at the Clipper estate.

"Still drinking good wine, I see."

"Oh, please. I don't care how low you sink, there's no excuse for bad Chardonnay." She poured wine in my glass and then filled her own. She lifted hers in a gesture of goodwill and took her first sip, then eased into the adjacent chair. "Kim tells me you spoke to Ari."

"Yesterday afternoon. The place is in a state of upheaval."

"Stella's doing, I'm sure."

We were skipping from topic to topic, but it kept the tone light. I said, "I expected Kim to be here."

"It would only complicate the conversation. She's off at the gym lifting weights. We have a facility here in the complex, so it doesn't cost us anything. That's the sort of thing we have to worry about these days."

"I can only imagine the shock."

She had the good grace to laugh, but I knew I shouldn't push her too far. She was living in "reduced circumstances," and while her lifestyle was luxurious compared to mine, I felt some sympathy for her lot.

"You and Kim have been friends for a long time?"

"More so now than we were in the 'olden' days. Back then we traveled in the same social circles, but we didn't know each other well. In a curious way, we had nothing in common. Then Bret got caught embezzling from the investment firm he worked for and he went to prison. Now we're migratory birds."

"Must have been difficult for her."

"Very. They'd always lived well, and Kim assumed his outrageous salary was legitimate. Part of the fault was hers, of course, because she was strictly hands-off when it came to their personal finances. She didn't want to be bothered, and Bret was happy to let her think it was all too complicated to explain. She was lucky to find a job. She's like me in that she has no marketable skills."

"She can answer the phone graciously. That's no small accomplishment."

"She has good breeding to recommend her, which is more than I can say for myself. Also to her credit is the fact that she knows so many of the company's clients, which is both the good news and the bad. She says she feels like she's being pilloried in the public square, where her shame is on permanent display. No one says a word, but she knows they're all thinking the same thing: that she must have known he was stealing. That she'd enjoyed their ill-gotten gains and now she could take her licks the same way he did. She's a criminal by default."

"What about you? Your life's taken a distinct right-hand turn."

"No need to remind me. I went to Los Angeles one weekend, thinking life was fine. I returned Monday morning and discovered my husband and my best friend had been screwing around behind my back. I'm still not sure which makes me the more furious, his betrayal or hers. Stella was fun. She had a catty side and she skewered everyone in private. She's a great mimic and absolutely without mercy. Serves me right for laughing so hard on so many occasions. Now I'm the butt of the joke."

"Not in Ari's eyes."

"Ari," she said, and shook her head.

"How long were you married?"

"Seventeen years. He was married once before. Three kids, and I adore them. That's been hard on all of us. Well, not Ari so much as the kids and me."

"He said they were barely speaking to him."

"Good. I'm glad. Anything less and I'd feel bad about myself."

"You want to talk about our meeting at the Clipper estate?"

She smiled. "That was well done, wasn't it?"

"When you chose me, was that random or just my bad luck?"

"Oh, no. I looked into it. There aren't that many women private eyes in town. In fact, you were the only one, so that much was easy. I drove past your office and I could see from the neighborhood that it wasn't high-toned. I'm sorry for the deception, but please remember, you did get paid."

It was on the tip of my tongue to bring her up short on that score, but I kept my mouth shut. Apparently, she didn't know the bills were marked. At the very least, she didn't realize law enforcement was creeping up on her. In either case, playing my cards close to my chest put me at a slight advantage. "How did you know to mention Vera Hess? That really sunk the hook in deep."

"Kim knows her. Your name came up in the course of conversation a few months ago when she showed up at an open house."

"Was any of it true, what you told me that night?"

She shrugged. "Not Geoffrey, obviously. I invented him. Much of the rest of it I invented as well. No home in Malibu. No travels around the world. Even as I was spinning the yarn, I felt . . . I don't know . . . I guess 'wistful' is the word."

"So the Clipper estate wasn't your childhood home."

"Far from it. I grew up in Chicago. Not the nice part. Ours was one of those houses you can see from the freeway when you're coming into the city from the airport."

"Ari told me you both came up from nothing."

"That's true, and we earned every dime of the money we made along the way. Have you met Stella?"

"I passed her in the hall on my way down to the gym. She said two words and I knew she was a bitch."

Teddy laughed.

I said, "He and Stella seem ill-suited, don't you think?"

"That's because she isn't Greek."

"So Greeks should only marry Greeks?"

"If you knew any, you wouldn't have to ask."

I steered us back to the sleight of hand at the Clipper estate. "How did you do it?"

"I have a friend who's a stager."

"She must have owed you big-time."

"Oh, she did."

I picked up a brochure from the top of the stack. "Is this the condominium where Stella's husband died?"

"It is."

"The brochure was your idea, right?"

"I thought we should expand our exposure. I had no idea how effective it would be."

"Mind if I keep this?"

"If you like. It sold in two days, much to my astonishment."

"That's good news," I said. "I understand the real estate market's been depressed."

"We were fortunate to find a buyer."

"Too bad you couldn't hang on to it."

"Easy come, easy go. It's an attitude I share with Kim. It's not that either one of us enjoys being strapped for cash, but when you start at the bottom, it's not unfamiliar turf. I pulled myself up once and I can do it again. You have to have an exit strategy."

"What's yours?"

She declined to respond, so I moved on, saying, "I take it you made Christian Satterfield's acquaintance through Kim's husband?"

"Exactly, but by the time I realized I was in need of his services, he'd already been released. Bret had no idea how to get in touch with him, and I'm a complete innocent when it comes to the prison system."

"Which is where I came in."

"I must say I was surprised by the speed with which you produced his contact information."

"Workin' like a little beaver for my pay," I said. I tucked the brochure in my shoulder bag. As is sometimes the case in conversation, I was picking up a line she hadn't spoken aloud. "You haven't mentioned the story about the baby you gave up for adoption."

"I thought it had a certain ring of truth to it."

"Isn't that because it's true?"

That was another avenue she didn't care to explore.

I said, "When I met Christian, he didn't look like any parolee I've ever seen. His hair was styled and his wardrobe was elegant. Did you do that for him?" I knew full well she had, but I was curious to see if she'd own up to it.

"Being handsome counts a lot in this world. He'd never get a job looking as he did."

"Maybe Ari will hire him if he doesn't get sent back to Lompoc."

"That's not a bad idea."

"Well, whatever happens, that was nice of you."

"He tells me you went into Lou's looking for him, so you must have realized how bright he is. Why did you want to talk to him?"

"I hoped to warn him off. I got him into this and I'd like to get him out. I don't know what you have in mind, but it can't be good for anyone."

"How much did he tell you?"

"Nothing and I didn't press the point. This is between you and your ex. My only concern is to see that Christian and I don't get caught in the crossfire."

Her look was unblinking and I had no way to know if she was really hearing me or not.

"You have any idea where the baby was placed?" I asked.

She shook her head. "I did leave a letter in his file, but I've never heard from him."

"There's time yet. Does Ari know?"

She shook her head for the second time. Then she said, "So now what? So far, I don't see that we've settled anything."

"I was just getting to that. I'm going to do you a favor here. And this is purely hypothetical," I added for purposes of clarity. "Let's say two years ago you came into some money, maybe twenty-five thousand bucks in cash in exchange for missing art . . ."

I could see I had her undivided attention, so I went on.

"I'm not asking you to confirm or deny because I don't want to know. All I'm saying is that if, by some chance, the police kept a record of the serial numbers on those bills, you'd be very smart to go back, anonymously if you must, and clean up the mess. Do you know the man I'm referring to?"

"Yes."

"Does he know it was you, in this totally imaginary theft?"

She shook her head in the negative.

"Give him back the money. I know you still have it because two hundred of that is the cash you paid me for putting you in touch with Christian Satterfield. See how good I am to you? I'm not even asking what you're up to."

"I'd be prosecuted."

"Making restitution is your only chance of *avoiding* prosecution. He can look at it as an object lesson. He should have had his million-dollar painting insured in the first place."

"What makes you think this man would agree?"

"He has his painting back. If you give back the cash, what's he got to complain about? It's called making a deal. Settling out of court. It's done every day, just not quite like this."

"I understand and I'll take care of it."

"Which brings us back to Ari. Do you want to know what I think?"

"By all means."

"The way I see it, you're pissed at Ari. He's pissed at you. Neither of you have much use for Stella. You're desperate for something, but

I'm not sure what. Only that you're willing to steal it if push comes to shove. Ari's feeling ripped off and he's determined not to make one more concession to you. You're setting up some kind of showdown to make him look bad or make yourself look good, but I don't see the point. You can't battle with Ari and imagine the rest of us won't suffer the consequences. There has to be another way to work out your differences."

"So earnest."

"I am. And don't condescend."

"What do you suggest?"

"*Talk* to Ari."

"I don't want to talk to Ari. If anything, he's the one who should be talking to me."

"Good. Fine. I can set that up."

"I didn't say I'd *do* it. I'm pointing out that if either one of us is to yield ground, it should be him. He's cost me everything. My marriage, the home I love, my best friend."

"Actually, you kind of did that to yourself, slapping him with papers so fast. You could have allowed yourself a little cooling-off period."

"Too late now."

"No, it's not. That's exactly what I'm getting at."

"Have you ever been married?"

I held up two fingers.

"And how did that turn out?"

"Just because I couldn't solve my own problems doesn't mean I shouldn't have a go at yours."

"Well, I'm sorry to disappoint you, but you'll have to let us muddle through on our own."

"But you're making a hash of it," I said. "This is what I find so exasperating. I thought rich people were smart. I thought that's why you raked in all the money, because you had life all figured out."

"Wouldn't that be lovely," she said, but her expression was bleak.

# 39

When I got home, Henry's kitchen light was off. I unlocked the studio and went in just long enough to turn on living room lamps so I wouldn't have to return to a dark apartment. When I peered out the window, I could see light in the Shallenbargers' kitchen across the driveway. As Edna moved about, crossing from the sink to the stove, I realized even her shadow was sufficient to fill me with rage. I locked up and trotted the half block to Rosie's.

Henry was sitting at his usual table, working on the *Los Angeles Times* crossword puzzle and helping himself to freshly popped corn. He had a Black Jack over ice on the table next to him. "Oh good. Are you having supper here? I could use the company. Now that my water line has been repaired, I feel a burden has been lifted."

"I'm not much in the mood to eat," I said. I sat down and settled my shoulder bag on the floor by my chair. "We have a problem."

"Of what sort?"

"I did some checking today and discovered that the Adelsons are still the legal owners of the house next door. The Shallenbargers put the water service in their name and possibly other utilities as well, though I'm not sure about that. The point is, they have no agreement with the Adelsons to rent, lease, or otherwise occupy that house. They're squatters."

He blinked. "Are you sure?"

"I called the Adelsons in Richmond and discussed the situation with Trish. She proposed flying out, but I said we'd have a conversation with them first."

"How did they have the nerve?"

"It's possible they knew the Adelsons had moved out of state and thought they could slip in without anyone knowing the difference. The real estate market isn't exactly booming. Trish says their agent hasn't showed the house in months. God knows what would have happened if she *had* come by with prospective buyers. I guess the Shallenbargers would have claimed they had a bona fide rental agreement. Their agent would be furious to think they'd rented the place after she so strongly advised them against the idea, but she wouldn't be able to confirm or refute the arrangement without making a long-distance call the way I did. In the meantime, the Shallenbargers would probably just come up with another bogus claim."

"How'd they get in in the first place? I'm sure the Adelsons left the place secure."

"They probably called a locksmith and claimed they'd locked themselves out."

"What made them think they could get away with it?"

"They did get away with it, at least to date. And while we're on the subject of getting away with stuff, I can testify Joseph's no more disabled than I."

"Well, this certainly can't go on."

"My feeling precisely. You want to go over there and talk to them?"

"I don't see that we have a choice."

I waited while Henry paid for his drink and then we walked the half block to the Shallenbargers' house. As Henry rapped on the door, he murmured, "You want to talk to them or shall I?"

"Do you have a preference?"

"I should probably handle it. I'm the senior statesman," he said.

The door swung open and Edna appeared holding a paper napkin in one hand. The air was scented with meat, onion, and ever so faintly a suggestion of burning hair.

Henry cleared his throat. "I'm sorry to interrupt your supper."

She lowered her gaze, which in some people would signal humility. With Edna, it could mean anything, and none of it good. "We didn't expect to see you again so soon."

"May we come in?"

She stepped back and admitted us. She and Joseph were eating their evening meal at a card table set up in the living room. They'd arranged their chairs so both could see the television set, which was tuned to a game show that had been in syndication for a decade or more. At each place setting, there was a tin plate of the TV dinner sort, divided into compartments, which still held traces of mashed potatoes, green beans, and some sort of ground meat patty covered with gravy. Really, I don't cook at all, but I don't want to eat shit like that when I get old.

Joseph was solidly packed into his wheelchair, a paper napkin tucked into his collar. The footrest on the chair had been flipped up, so maybe he was using his feet to scoot himself around the room. He seemed uncomfortable, which is more than I could say about Edna.

She said, "I'd offer to share, but we barely have enough to feed ourselves. Would you care to have a seat?"

Henry said, "No, thank you. We're hoping this won't take long."

We remained on our feet. Edna stood near Joseph's wheelchair, one hand on his shoulder. My guess was she'd squeeze the bejesus out of him if he said a word.

Henry went on, his tone mild. "Kinsey spoke to the Adelsons this afternoon."

"Who?"

"The Adelsons. They're the legal owners of this house. They told her they don't have a rental agreement with you."

"That's because we aren't renting from the Adelsons. We signed a rental agreement with Calvin Sanchez."

"I see. I'm not familiar with the name."

"I have a copy if you don't believe me."

"We'd appreciate it."

Henry and I exchanged a quick look as she crossed to a cardboard box jammed with files. She withdrew a sheaf of papers clipped together, which she handed to Henry. The top document was five or six pages in length, with a carbon copy of a receipt clipped to the front. Henry removed the paper clip and handed me the bottom sheet, which looked like a rental application.

"This is the application you filled out for Mr. Sanchez?"

"It certainly is," she said.

While Henry leafed through the rental agreement, I ran an eye down the application, which included their prior address. I made a mental note of the house number and street: 1122 Lily Avenue. Joseph's employer was the Perdido Community Development Department, which more or less corresponded to Edna's claim that he'd worked for the city before his retirement. Under Spouse's Employer, Edna had written *N/A*, meaning "Not Applicable."

"We paid first and last months' rent and a cleaning deposit. The receipt's right there on top."

I handed the page back to Henry, who was saying, "Anyone can mock up a carbon copy of a receipt. Where is this Mr. Sanchez?"

"Well, I'm sure I don't know."

"Well, where do you send your rent checks if you don't know where he is?"

"We do it by direct deposit."

Henry was losing patience. "It might be best if we spoke to him before we go on. Do you have his phone number?"

"I suppose we have one somewhere, but we haven't had the need to get in touch."

This is where I opened my big mouth. Even in the moment, I knew it was ill-advised, but I couldn't help myself. "There isn't any Calvin Sanchez. This house is owned by Dale and Trish Adelson."

"Be that as it may," she said, "we've lived here for three months. We're good neighbors. I don't see how anyone can have a complaint."

"How about the complaint that you're in this house illegally?"

She flicked a dark look at me. "I didn't realize you were an attorney, dear. Are you licensed to practice law in this state?"

"I don't need a law degree. I have a degree in common sense. If you can show us an agreement with the Adelsons' signatures on it instead of your imaginary Mr. Sanchez, we'll concede the point."

"The point isn't yours to address one way or the other," she said primly.

"You want the Adelsons to fly out?"

"That's up to them. We're not hurting anyone. We're looking after the property. We live here in exchange for upkeep and maintenance."

"You can't just do that unilaterally. The Adelsons haven't agreed to anything."

"If your Mr. and Mrs. Adelson want us out of here, they'll have to evict us."

"I'm sure that can be arranged," I said snappishly. Henry gave me a warning look, but it was too late for that.

Edna said, "To date, no one has served us with a notice of any kind. If you do serve such a notice, we will contest it. It's clear you're retaliating because of a misunderstanding about a hose bib, of all things. You're discriminating against us because of our age and my poor husband's disability."

Henry said, "This has nothing to do with Joseph's disability. Your occupancy is unlawful."

"So now you're citing the law? Well, let me cite one for you as well. We are tenants, and as such, we are not without our rights. Even if your Mr. and Mrs. Adelson win a judgment, we'd be entitled to remain on the premises because of hardship. We qualify for low-income housing."

"You can't move into a house without permission."

"But that's what we've done. We've made no secret of the fact that we're living here. This is simply the first time you thought to question us."

"This isn't an argument between us, Edna. We'll call the Adelsons and tell them what you've admitted. They can fly out and deal with it in the next couple of days."

A smile touched her lips and dimples appeared. "You are setting yourselves up for a lawsuit for wrongful eviction. If the Adelsons take us to court and lose, they will have to pay court costs and our attorney's fees, which I can assure you will be substantial. This will be a long-drawn-out procedure—very lengthy—with countless delays— and it won't come cheap. If you think it's easy to get tenants out, you're mistaken."

"You're not tenants. You're squatting," I said.

"Also known as 'adverse possession,'" she said. "You'll find our rights in the matter aren't so easily abridged. Beyond that, we don't appreciate the name-calling. During the time we've lived here, we've improved the property, which was sadly neglected. There were so many cockroaches in the kitchen, we could have called the health department to complain. Rats, too, which are known carriers of the hantavirus. We paid for pest control and eradicated the vermin. You've seen us paint and make repairs. Whether you like it or not isn't relevant. You can't throw us out in the street. We're elderly and we won't be harassed and persecuted."

"Who's harassing you?!"

"I believe raising your voice in a threatening manner with the intent to intimidate old people would be considered a form of harassment."

"How about the fact that you're trespassing?" I said. "We should just call the police and let them deal with you."

Edna made her little dimples appear. "This is a civil matter. I can assure you the police won't want to step into the situation, especially when we can show a rental agreement in support of our occupancy."

I said, "I know a couple of detectives with the STPD, and believe me, they won't hesitate to 'step in' and run a computer check. You better hope you don't have so much as an unpaid parking ticket."

Henry gestured impatiently. "This is getting us nowhere. We'll let the Adelsons know we've had this conversation. May I keep this?"

"That's my only copy and I'll thank you to return it," she said, and held out her hand.

Henry gave her the rental agreement. Edna walked us to the door and stood there stubbornly, watching our departure with a satisfied expression. We descended the porch stairs and walked the twenty-five yards to Henry's house.

I said, "Pardon my language, Henry, but what the fuck was that?"


In the morning, I was still stewing about the tactics Joseph and Edna had employed with regard to the property next door. How could they simply move into a house and live there without paying rent? It seemed outrageous to me, but she'd defended their position with such confidence, it had to be a plan they'd executed before. The Adelsons would be forced to hire an attorney to assert their rights to a house they already owned.

In scanning the rental application the night before, I'd spotted the past address the Shallenbargers had listed, which I hoped was legitimate. Any good liar will tell you that stitching in the occasional point of fact gives a fabricated story a certain ring of truth. I pulled out my

# X

*Thomas Guide to Santa Teresa and Perdido Counties* and tracked down Lily Avenue, which was just off Seaward. I stopped long enough to fill my tank with gas and then hit the southbound on-ramp to the 101.

Once on Lily, I parked and did a quick walk-about, eyeballing the houses on either side of 1122. This was a neighborhood of middle-class houses, small but well-maintained. I approached the house at 1120 and rang the bell. There were two newspapers on the porch mat, and when I rang a second time without success, I gave it up and returned to the street.

I tried the house on the other side of 1122. My knock unleashed a noisy chorus of barks. The woman who opened the door was still shushing the assortment of rescue mutts that accompanied her. In the main, they ignored her, so excited about the company they could barely contain themselves. I counted six of them, no two alike. I knew one was a dachshund, and the small, short-haired, brown-and-white hyper leaping dog had to be a Jack Russell terrier. One of the others was a shepherd mix, and that was as far as I got in my breed identification process. Much jumping and jostling while they yapped. I'm not ordinarily fond of dogs, but this was a happy crew.

"Yes?"

I handed her a business card. "I'm Kinsey Millhone. I drove down from Santa Teresa this morning in hopes of picking up information about the couple who used to live next door. Do you remember Edna and Joseph Shallenbarger?"

She held up a finger. "Would you excuse me for a moment?" She turned to the lot of them and put a hand on her hip. "What have I told you about that?"

She had apparently told them plenty, because the barking stopped instantly and the pack arranged themselves in a line and looked at her expectantly. She made eye contact with each in turn, and their obedience was so absolute as to be comical. She reached in her apron pocket for doggie treats and gave one to each dog. "I apologize for their bad behavior."

"Don't worry about it. Looks like you have them well-trained."

"Until there's a knock at the door," she said. "I'm Betsy Mullholland, by the way."

"Nice meeting you," I said, and shook hands with her.

She stepped out onto the porch and pulled the door shut behind her. "They were calling themselves the Shallabergers then, but I know exactly who you mean. They were the worst neighbors we ever had. I wish I could tell you where they went, but they've been gone for months and they didn't leave a forwarding address."

"Oh, I know where they are," I said. "They've moved into the house next door to me, which is owned by a couple who now live out of state. Edna admits she and Joseph are squatters, but she's completely unrepentant and apparently has no intention of moving out. My guess is they've done this before, and I was hoping to find someone who had better luck persuading them to go."

"You know they're both wanted by the police."

"Are you serious? For doing what?"

"She stole a hundred and forty-two thousand dollars from the community college. She'd worked for them for years, and no one had any idea what she was up to. She'd been lying about her age, and when it finally came to light that she was seventy-five, they tried forcing her to retire. She threatened to hire an attorney to sue them for age discrimination. The school backed down, and that afforded her a few more years in which to siphon off funds."

"How'd she manage it?"

"She was senior administrative assistant to the comptroller. She set up dummy accounts and rerouted certain checks as they came in. Then she'd alter the records to reflect balances that were pure fiction. Her husband was in on it as well, forging signatures as needed. Their methods weren't original, but they were effective."

"How did they get caught?"

"An oversight. A food service contractor was owed a hundred and ninety-six dollars and he complained to the school. Her records showed the man had been paid, and he demanded to see the canceled check. She was off work that week because Joseph was ill, and by the time she got back, the state auditor had launched an investigation. Edna chose that moment to retire."

"Were they convicted?"

"Not a bit of it. They were arrested and booked, but they managed to post bail. Neither of them has a criminal history, and I guess as first-time offenders, they didn't fit the standard profile for flight risk. They didn't show up for the arraignment, and that's the last anybody's seen of them. I have all the newspaper clippings if you want to take a look. You can even have copies made if you want a set."

"I would love that," I said. "Do you remember the name of the bail bondsman?"

"He gave me his card when he came by looking for them. Hang on a minute."

She left the door ajar while she went off to fetch the business card. Six pairs of eyes were fixed on mine, and we studied one another. They seemed hopeful I might have a pocket full of treats as well, so they didn't make a peep.

She returned with a file folder bulging with articles from the local paper, which she handed me along with the bail bondsman's business card.

"Thank you. This is wonderful. This is just what I need," I said. "I don't suppose I could trouble you to use the phone?"

She held the door open for me.

# 40

I sat in my car and made a few notes before I put the keys in the ignition. It wasn't until I tucked the bundle of index cards in my shoulder bag that I caught sight of the half sheet of lined paper I'd torn out of Kim Bass's steno pad. With a little start, I realized this was March 24, Teddy's departure date. It was after 9:00 A.M. In roughly eight hours, she'd be getting on a plane to Los Angeles, where she'd pick up her flight to London. In the meantime, I hadn't heard a peep from Ari. Since I'd be driving through Montebello anyway on my way back into town, I decided it would be politic to fill him in.

When I reached the Xanakis estate, I pulled into the drive and paused dutifully while the uniformed security guard approached the car with his clipboard. I rolled down the window on the passenger side and said, "Remember me? I was here on Tuesday. I work for Mr. Xanakis."

"Right."

He returned to the gatehouse, and a moment later the gates swung open and I cruised through. I motored up the driveway and around the curve. The house was just as impressive as it had been the first time. I pulled into a parking pad big enough to accommodate five vehicles. As I approached the front door, I looked for exterior cameras. One was angled on the driveway itself, another on the front door. I gave a little wave as I rang the bell.

Maurie opened the door. Behind her, in the corridor, I could see some effort had been made to organize the assemblage of miscellaneous furniture, though I couldn't identify the underlying principle.

"Is Mr. Xanakis here?"

"Is he expecting you?"

"What difference does it make? I need to talk to him."

She glanced to her right, where I could hear voices raised. I had apparently arrived in the middle of a ruckus. I took advantage of the distraction to step into the hall.

Stella said, "I don't believe it. I do not believe you did that. How COULD you? Without so much as a by-your-leave?"

She came striding out of the dining room, dodging a glass-fronted corner piece that had been set to one side of the double doors. She wore a snug-fitting pair of teal trousers in a fabric that looked like taffeta and made a rustling sound as she walked. Over the trousers, she wore a long coat of the same material in lime green with two teal Chinese frog fasteners on the front. The coat was open from the bodice down, and she was walking so fast, the flaps lifted like two sails. She carried a folder filled with paperwork that she slapped once against her thigh. I've never quarreled with anyone while wearing an elegant outfit. You'd think it would lend an air of class to the occasion, but alas, it did not.

I could hear Ari behind her, saying, "Hey, come on now. I told you this might happen."

"No. You. Did. Not."

"Well, I told someone."

The intensity of the fight rendered the rest of us invisible. Ari appeared from the dining room in what I swear was the same workout gear I'd seen him in three days before. Shorts, a tank top, running shoes without socks.

Maurie and I were both rooted in place, neither of us daring to say a word.

There followed choice expletives on her part and his. This was like watching a foreign movie, Italian perhaps, with voices dubbed in and the lines of dialogue not quite matching the movements of their lips. I thought it safe to assume Ari had canceled the honeymoon, forfeiting the thousands of dollars' worth of deposits he'd paid to secure the reservations.

Stella's voice dropped. "You are such a SHIT!"

She turned and flung the folder at him. A passport wallet dropped at her feet and travel documents flew everywhere with a flapping sound like a flock of birds. A color brochure sailed along the marble floor and skittered under a Louis Quatorze chair. I caught a glimpse of a tropical island, bright blue waters, a palatial bedroom open to the view, sheer curtains wafting outward.

She disappeared into the kitchen, slamming the door in her wake.

Ari seemed to hesitate, probably wondering at the wisdom of following her. When he spotted me, he said, "Good. I want to talk to you. Don't go away." And to Maurie, "Put her in Teddy's office. I'll be right there."

I followed Maurie down the hall in the opposite direction, making lame small talk. She opened the door to the study and ushered me in, with the obligatory admonition to make myself at home. She returned to the hall and closed the door behind her, leaving me on my own.

The room was paneled in a dark wood and the furniture looked comfortable. There was a row of floor-to-ceiling windows on the wall opposite the door. Bookshelves, a massive fireplace, a desk with a leather top, and an oversize leather-upholstered office chair. There were two gray metal file cabinets in one corner, and those looked out of place.

Ari was taking over her office, moving in functional items she'd have frowned upon.

I saw here what I'd noticed in the dining room: sections of empty wall space where paintings had once hung, doubtless the art Teddy had fought for and won in the settlement. I could have reconstructed her collection by working backward from the lavishly illustrated art books stacked on all the surfaces. Her taste ran toward the Impressionists and seemed to trace the shift from the late nineteenth century into the twentieth.

The door opened and Ari came in. "The woman is driving me crazy. Have a seat."

There were cardboard boxes stacked on both of the guest chairs. "Here, let me move those," he said. He picked up a carton filled with what looked like XLNT bumper stickers and placed them on the floor. "You want a couple?"

"What are they, bumper stickers?"

"Magnetic signage. The company logo. I buy 'em by the case. Slap a couple on your car, I'll pay you two hundred bucks a month to drive around. It's mobile advertising."

"I don't want anyone looking at my car. I'm paid to be invisible. Slick idea, though. You can turn any vehicle you like into a company car."

As I sat down, I said, "Oh."

"What?"

"Nothing. Hang on a minute. I think I just figured out what's going on." I stood up again and moved to the door. "As soon as I take a look at something, I can tell you if I'm right."

Ari followed me out of the office and down the hall. When I reached the elevator, I pressed the Down button and waited while he caught up.

"I take it Stella's pissed because you canceled the honeymoon?"

"What'd she expect? I told her I wouldn't go until I knew what Teddy was up to. I leave and she's free to do anything she wants."

"Don't be dense, Ari. You canceled because you don't want to spend time with her. You and Stella are a bust. Get the marriage annulled."

"And then what?"

"Ask Teddy's forgiveness and beg her to take you back."

"She won't do it. You think she'd do that?"

The elevator door opened and we stepped in. I pressed "B" for the basement level and the doors eased shut. We both stood there, facing forward, while the elevator descended with scarcely a sound.

"Have you ever apologized?"

"For what?"

"For screwing around, Ari. What do you think? Why don't you just tell her you're sorry?"

"I am sorry. And I mean that. Dumbest and worst thing I ever did, and I have no excuse."

"Because what you did was inexcusable."

"Yeah, but she was a little quick off the mark with divorce papers."

"Quit trying to shift the blame. Teddy's not the type to put up with any crap. Stella doesn't seem remorseful in the least, and that only compounds the injury."

The elevator door opened onto the gloom of the basement and I gestured Ari ahead of me. "You lead. I'll get lost. I want to take a look at those CCTV monitors."

We proceeded through the basement until we reached the room where all the CCTV monitors were set up. A man in uniform sat tilted back in his chair, one foot on the edge of the counter, while he scanned the views. When he realized Ari was there he removed his foot, sat up, and assumed a posture of professional attention. Most cameras were focused on empty rooms and long, empty corridors. The system rotated through a series of static shots, revealing nothing except the well-lighted interiors.

Ari said, "This is Duke. Kinsey Millhone."

We nodded at each other. Duke was young and didn't strike me as someone with much experience. The task he'd been given is tougher than it looks. Try to pay strict attention to a set of gauges or dials, or stare out at the empty horizon from the pilothouse of a ship, and you'll find your mind wandering, making you less effective with every minute that goes by.

As we watched, the cameras continued their silent surveillance.

The chef was in the kitchen, and I could see a maid in uniform vacuuming the living room. No one in the dining room. Downstairs hall. Front door. Bedroom. Bedroom. Living room again; maid still vacuuming. Study. There was something hypnotic about the process.

I said, "I'll tell you what's been bothering me. I could see what was right there in front of me, but I didn't know what it meant. I spoke to Christian Wednesday night and he couldn't have been more relaxed."

"You should have called and told me. Why'd you talk to that bum?"

"Don't interrupt while I'm trying to help."

There were two rolling chairs available. I pulled one over to the bank of screens and took a seat. Ari pulled the second chair into place next to mine.

"I met Teddy yesterday and she behaved as though she had all the time in the world. Neither she nor Christian gave any indication they had pressing business to conduct, let alone a crime to commit. No sign of anxiety. No whiff of nerves. I expected both to be in high gear. Teddy did try some sleight of hand. She'd left a book on Tiffany jewelry on the arm of a chair. She acted like it was an oversight, but she was so casual about tucking it away, I knew it had to be bullshit. She wanted me to believe the necklace was the object of the exercise and Christian was hired for his safecracking skills. No such thing."

"So what are we doing here?" Ari asked.

I turned to Duke. "Can you run some of these tape cassettes back a few days? Not all of them."

"Sure, no problem. Which?"

"That one. And that. And these two." I was pointing to the monitor that showed a shot of the front door and the monitor showing a reverse shot of the corridor just inside. I also indicated a third camera that had a wide-angle view of the hallway, looking toward the elevator. The fourth camera was fixed on the driveway a short distance from the front door.

"How far?"

"Tuesday, the twenty-first."

He tapped instructions into his keyboard and the tapes on the four cameras I'd designated began a speedy rewind. Time ran backward. The views were populated with a motley collection of worker bees, everybody walking backward, furniture picked up and zipped to the position it was in when it first came into view. The date and hour line sped backward as well.

I watched Thursday rewind into Wednesday. Maurie. Stella. Ari. Movers, maids. Lifting, cleaning, polishing, covering and uncovering furniture. Paintings that had been stacked against the wall flipped back into the hands of those who'd set them in place. The elevator door opened and closed. Pieces were loaded and disappeared. Gradually the hall was emptied of its freight.

Late in the day on Tuesday, I caught sight of myself appearing in the corridor, backing out, then appearing at the front door, which was standing open to foot traffic. Another ten minutes disappeared, and I said, "There. Now let it play forward."

Ari said, "What is this?"

"Just watch."

All four tapes now proceeded in something close to real time. There was a slight lapse from shot to shot, so the action had a certain staccato herky-jerky feel to it. I pointed to the camera directed at the drive. At 5:25 P.M., a white panel truck pulled up. A portion of the XLNT logo was visible.

Automatically, Ari said, "That's not mine."

"I know."

A man in dark blue coveralls got out of the truck on the passenger side. Mustache, glasses, medium height. He had a clipboard in hand and he walked through the open front door. Inside, Maurie spotted him and he moved in her direction. The two chatted. He offered her the clipboard and a pen. She read the paperwork and scratched her signature on the bottom line, after which she gestured.

He crossed to the wall, where he flipped through a stack of paintings that had been left leaning there. He set five aside, picked up the painting he was looking for, and carried it to the front door.

Reverse angle. He emerged from the front door, crossed to the panel truck, and loaded the painting in the rear. He returned to the passenger side door, got in, slammed the door, and the vehicle moved out of the frame.

"What you just saw was a heist. You got robbed," I said. "You're looking at Christian Satterfield in phony glasses and a fake mustache. He didn't need the disguise because nobody here had a clue who he was or what he looked like."

"No shit. He's stealing that?"

"Pretty much," I said. "Did you see the clipboard? Maurie signed some kind of dummied-up invoice. Tuesday when I came to see you, there were half a dozen people milling around, walking in and out. As I was coming in the gate, I passed a white panel truck with the XLNT logo on the side."

"I don't use white panel trucks."

"You know that and I know that, but your gate guard didn't. He knows you own a freight and courier company called XLNT. An XLNT vehicle drives in and the same one drives out. Mission accomplished."

"Why that painting?"

"Must be something fabulous. Why else would she have gone to so much trouble and expense? She was in Bel Air when the condominium sold, and by the time she got up here at close of escrow, you'd already moved all the furniture and accessories back into the basement. She hired Christian because she knew he'd have no scruples about what she needed to have done."

"Son of a bitch."

"Here's the point, Ari. She has what she wants and she's leaving town this afternoon."

"Teddy is? Where to?"

I took out the sheet of paper I'd ripped out of Kim's steno pad. "Well, if the airport code LHR is London Heathrow, I'd say she's heading for London. Five forty-five from Santa Teresa to LAX. Her Pan Am flight's at ten o'clock. You have time to catch her if you hustle."

"I can't believe she ripped me off."

"Let's not call it ripping you off, okay? That makes it sound like she's taking something she's not entitled to. You were married for seventeen years. That's a lot of entitlement."

Glumly, he said, "I guess I'll have to give you that one. So now what?"

"Go out to the airport and intercept her."

"And say what?"

"Tell her you love her."

"That won't cut any ice. She's tough."

"Then offer her a bribe."

"Now you're getting sentimental on me. What am I supposed to hold out as bait?"

"The painting. Tell her it's a gift. That way she isn't guilty of stealing it."

"What if it's worth millions?"

"I'm sure it is. That's how she'll know you're sincere."

He sat and stared at the floor. "I don't know about this."

"Well, I do. Go upstairs and change clothes. Pick up your passport from the floor in the hall where Stella tossed it. Take a taxi to the airport and buy a ticket to London so you can get on the plane with Teddy. Her flight leaves here at five forty-five, so you have plenty of time to pack."

"What about Stella?"

"Do I have to tell you everything? Call your attorney and let him take care of it."

"She'll hose me."

"Of course. That's what money's for."

Finally, he laughed and shook his head. "I hope I don't regret this."

"You won't. Now get on with it. And when you and Teddy get married the second time? I get to be the flower girl. I've always wanted to do that."

# 41

I went home. I hadn't seen Henry since our encounter with the charmers next door and I wanted to bring him up to date. We'd just picked up a bargaining chip, and if he hadn't put in the call to the Adelsons, we could save them a trip. As I passed the Shallenbargers' house, I spotted a pint-size U-Haul truck parked out in front. Six cardboard cartons had been stacked on the front porch. Maybe my reference to my friends at the STPD had been more motivating to Edna than I'd realized at the time.

I pulled into Henry's driveway, grabbed my shoulder bag, and crossed the backyard to his kitchen door. When I knocked, there was no response. I trotted down the driveway and across the Shallenbargers' front lawn. The front door was ajar and a carton of canned goods was being used to prop open the screen. I peered in. There was no one in sight, so I tapped on the door frame. "Anybody home?"

From the kitchen, Joseph called "Yo!" apparently not realizing it was me.

I stepped into the living room. The metal folding chairs were stacked to one side and the legs on the card table had been tucked out of sight. The portions of the house that I could see were in a state of disarray. The rag rug had been rolled up, leaving an oval of dust.

Joseph shuffled into view, wearing baggy pants with suspenders, the buttons undone at his waist.

"What a miracle. You can walk," I said drily.

He'd abandoned all pretense of a disability, though he was still encumbered by his excess weight, which probably played hell on his knees. "Edna's out."

"Well, I hope she won't be long. Are you going someplace?"

"I don't know that it's any of your concern."

He turned on his heel and I followed him into the kitchen, where he resumed his packing chores. Aside from the one carton of canned goods, nothing much had been accomplished in this room. He continued to empty the kitchen cabinets, a foolish waste of time in my opinion, since they could buy the same items elsewhere. Most of what they owned was crap anyway.

I picked up a box of cornmeal muffin mix and checked the sell-by date, which was July of 1985. I opened the top. The cornmeal itself had a grainy look to it, and along the opening there were cobwebs shaped like tiny hammocks containing pupas snugly nestled in sleep. "Disgusting. You ought to dump this," I said.

I wandered into the living room and then into the hall, checking out the bedrooms. One remained untouched. In the other, the linens had been stripped from the bed and the mattress was propped against the wall. I returned to the living room and paused at the front door.

"Hey, Joseph? You know what? You're never going to fit all this stuff in the U-Haul."

No response.

"If you like, I can pitch in. I'm good at toting boxes."

Again, silence from the kitchen, which I took as assent.

I put my shoulder bag on the floor near the couch and went out on the porch, where I picked up one of the loaded cardboard boxes. I brought it into the house again and set it on the floor in the master bedroom. I went out for another box and then the third and fourth. When the porch was completely clear, I shoved aside the box holding open the screen door. I could have unpacked a few things, but I didn't want to be *that* helpful.

I perched on the arm of the couch. "Hope you don't mind if I sit and wait."

"Edna's the one who minds. She won't appreciate it if she finds you here when she gets home."

"Too bad. I was hoping to talk to her."

"To say what?"

I turned to find Edna standing in the doorway behind me. She stepped into the room and closed the screen door behind her. She wore her black coat and she had her pocketbook over one arm.

"I can't believe you're leaving us," I said. "How'd you manage to find a new place so fast? You must have checked the foreclosure filings."

"We can see when we aren't wanted."

"Oh, but you *are* wanted," I said. "Look what I found."

I reached into my bag, pulling out the handful of newspaper clippings I'd copied. I held up the first, headlines screaming, PERDIDO CC EMPLOYEE ARRESTED IN ALLEGED THEFT.

She glanced at it, unaffected. "I don't know anything about that."

I wagged a finger at her. "Yes, you do," I said. "I have copies of your mug shots, which I must say are not flattering."

In her booking photograph Edna looked haunted, eyes large, hair limp. The harsh lighting played up every wrinkle in her face. In Joseph's, his expression was startled and his skin looked wet. I'd have suggested powdering out the shine, but maybe the Perdido County Jail didn't offer hair and makeup services.

"We were never convicted of anything," she said.

"There's still time," I said. I checked my watch and pointed at the face. "Oops. Maybe not."

I was looking through the screen door behind her. She turned and caught sight of Mr. Ryvak coming up the walk. I'd spoken to him on the phone, but this was the first time I'd laid eyes on him. He was in his midforties, wearing slacks and a short-sleeved dress shirt. A halo of ginger hair and a nice freckled face.

Edna recognized him and her composure slipped. There was a note of panic in her voice. "Why is *he* here?"

"To take you into custody, sweetheart. Remember your bail bondsman? He has the right to pursue bail skips, and since he's not a government agent, he doesn't need a warrant."

I confess I chortled all the way to the office, cheered by the idea that Edna and Joseph would finally be held to account. I'd barely sat down at my desk when the phone rang. I picked up, hoping it was Henry so I could share the good news.

It was Dietz. He skipped right over the greetings and the chitchat. "What have you gotten yourself into?"

I felt like someone had thrown a bucket of water in my face. "You obviously know more than I do, so you tell me."

"I can tell you who Susan Telford is. Everybody in this part of the state knows who she is. She's a fourteen-year-old white female who disappeared two years ago in March. It must not have made the papers in California, but it was all over the news here: headlines, television coverage, radio appeals, reward offered."

I felt myself go still. "What happened to her?"

"She vanished. She might as well have gone up in smoke. She was last seen the morning of the twenty-eighth, walking on Paseo Verde Parkway in Henderson, the supposition being she was on her way to the park. Her mother reported her missing that evening when she didn't come home. The cops talked to everyone—family, her friends, teachers, the park maintenance crew, people who lived in the area surrounding the park. They rounded up registered sex offenders, vagrants."

"Nobody saw anything?"

"Eventually her best friend spoke up. At first, she was too damn scared, but she finally broke down and told her mom. Not that it made a difference. Her information was too vague to be of help."

"Told her mom what?"

"Her story was some guy approached Susan in the mall a couple of days before. He was there snapping Polaroids. He said he worked for a fashion magazine and asked if she'd be interested in some freelance modeling. According to him, this was all preliminary. He'd be coming back with a crew to do the shoot in a few days, but he was scouting the area, looking for locations, and while he was at it, had his eye out for new and fresh talent."

"Dietz."

"That was all crap, of course. The guy was obviously cruising for young girls, and she was gullible enough to—"

I cut in again. "I've heard this story, only in the version I was told, her name was Janet Macy and she lived in Tucson. She was approached by a photographer with much the same kind of line. I talked to her mother on the phone a week ago. She last saw her daughter in 1986, but she thinks Janet went off to New York to launch her modeling career. Some photographer claimed he worked in the fashion industry and thought she showed promise. He was going to help her put together a portfolio. Not even sixteen years old and she went off with him like a damn fool."

"Shit."

"Her mother did file a missing-persons report, but the officer didn't think she had anything to worry about. He took down all the information and told her to get in touch if she heard from Janet, but forget about that. All this time she's been telling herself stories about where the girl was and why she didn't write. This is Ned Lowe. I know it is. He works in outside sales, but photography has been his passion since he was in high school.

"The reason I mentioned him in the first place was because both Susan's name and Janet's were on the list Pete put together. One of the six women was his first wife, who died back in 1961. One divorced him and the other one is currently married to him. The fourth was involved in a so-called love relationship that she broke off."

"Where is he now?"

"Well, he lives in Cottonwood, but he was scheduled to leave on one of his annual photographic jaunts, which begin to sound like hunting trips. His wife said she'd call after he left, but I haven't heard from her, so maybe he's getting a late start."

"I'll have the detectives in Henderson talk to Tucson. At least they can compare notes and establish the link if there is one. Why don't you talk to Cheney and tell him what's come up. Maybe there's a way to corral the guy. You know where he's headed?"

"Not a clue, and his wife doesn't know, either."

Dietz said, "Never mind. I'll call Santa Teresa PD myself. I know more of Susan Telford's story than you do, and it'll save them some time."

I gave him Ned and Celeste's address and phone number in Cottonwood. I replaced the handset in the cradle, feeling the tension seep out of me. It was a relief to turn the whole issue of Ned Lowe over to law enforcement. I'd pursued the matter as far as I could, and now that I knew about the two missing girls, it was clear I was out of my element. Dietz had sworn he'd keep me posted, but I didn't expect news anytime soon. In the meantime, I was hoping for a way to distract myself. I pulled out two sheets of typing paper and a fresh sheet of carbon paper and rolled them into the carriage, pausing to think about how to frame the information I'd just been given.

I heard the office door open and close. I looked up, but no one appeared in the doorway. I waited briefly and then got up from my desk and crossed the room, peering out into the reception area. I looked to my right just as Ned Lowe grabbed me and locked his arm around my neck. He leaned back and lifted me almost off my feet and then flipped me so that I came down hard. I might have grunted as I hit the carpet, but that was the only sound I made. I was astonished to find myself facedown, staring at the floor from a distance of less than an inch. My cheek was pressed hard against the rug, which bit into my skin more viciously than you'd imagine. The takedown had been so quick, I could scarcely comprehend what was happening. I had that odd sensation at the bridge of my nose that denotes a hard blow. No blood gushed out, so my guess was the cartilage was intact. He had his knee in the middle of my back and he grabbed me by the hair and pulled my head up far enough to get one hand on my face. He pinched my nose shut, that same warm hand covering my mouth. I thought, *Oh shit*. I knew what this was. This was how Lenore died.

In the brief moment as I went down, I'd noted the absurdity of my situation. It was broad daylight. My office was wired, equipped with a panel where an emergency button would signal my distress and bring help in short order. The problem was while I could move my feet, I couldn't lift my hips or legs and I couldn't buck or turn my lower body. The small effort I made was futile and only burned oxygen I needed to conserve.

I converted any thought of resistance to a simple resolve to breathe. Fewer than ten seconds had passed, but his weight prevented me from drawing a breath and the panic was overwhelming. Compressive asphyxia had limited the expansion of my lungs to the point of suffocation. This crushing phenomena was precisely what I'd been avoiding by never jacking up my car and sliding under it to make homely repairs. The nose pinch and the palm pressed hard against my mouth formed a seal. My attention was most wonderfully concentrated on the need for air. Often in moments of physical jeopardy, I'm entertained by the incongruities of time and place. Once when I was bleeding on a stretch of office carpeting, thinking soon I'd be shot to death, I wondered idly what unlucky soul would be hired to clean up the mess. With blood, cold water is always preferable to hot because heat cooks the protein content, causing it to set. You don't want blood to dry, either, because you'll only compound the staining issue. Never seal your bloody evidence in a plastic bag. In short order, it will putrefy and will be worthless in court.

I wasn't concerned with any of the above just then. Oxygen deprivation is a speedy means of leaving this earth. I figured three minutes tops—unconsciousness followed by crippling brain damage followed by death. The pain in my lungs was searing, the need for air so acute that I nearly gave myself up to it. I could not make a sound. No air passed in or out of me, and the carbon dioxide in my system built so rapidly that I felt like I was being consumed from within. The hand was warm and fleshy, and if he'd been doing anything other than killing me, I might have appreciated his strength. All the times I worked late, the nights I'd stopped off at the market on my way home, times I'd found myself on empty streets in the dark. I'd always felt safe. I'd thought I was prepared.

Straining for air was pointless. I lay still, trying to signal submission. Did he know he was killing me? Of course he did! That was the point. My heart hammered and my blood pressure soared as my systems labored to feed my brain the oxygen required to continue functioning. Heat radiated through my chest and spread along my arms.

What aggravated the hell out of me, in the brief time I had for reflection, was the thought of all the time and energy I wasted learning to fight. Success at hand-to-hand combat is predicated on traction and balance, on the landing of solid kicks, on strikes with knuckles, elbows, and knees. I thought about all the orderly exercises I'd participated in, learning self-defense. In class, grabbing your opponent's arm gave you sufficient leverage to turn the tables on him, dispatching your assailant with speed. Hair grabs and forearm blocks, heel stomps to your attacker's instep, a chop to the back of his neck. Head butt, followed by elbow smash to the solar plexus. I could flip my opponent with the best of them. I couldn't remember a training scenario in which I'd been flung to the floor while my aggressor stopped my breathing by the leaden application of dead weight, mouth and nose blocked until death ensued. I pictured the books on self-defense with the stern admonitions to jab your attacker's eyes while you snapped a knee to his groin. In my current prone position, none of that was possible. I was going to die here and I wanted my money back.

I was tipping toward the swelling black. My hearing had begun to fade and a rising tone sounded in my head. The good news was that the pain was beginning to recede. It crossed my mind that you never think you're going to die until you do.

He pressed his cheek against mine, and I realized he'd eased the weight of his knee and he was no longer pinching my nose shut. This allowed me to take in a teaspoon of air, for which I was profoundly grateful. He was whispering and it took me a moment to hear what he was saying. I expected to hear threats until it occurred to me that a threat would be silly when he was already in the process of killing me. I was still immobilized, but he'd eased his weight just enough for me to suck in a bit more air; not enough for normal breathing, but enough to ease my panic. I blinked and took stock.

His breath against my ear was hot, a cloud of Listerine fumes disguising whatever he'd eaten earlier. His voice was strained. Despite the efficiency with which he'd taken me down, he'd had to exert himself, and even though my struggle was minimal, his efforts had taken a toll. He whispered hoarsely, as though short of breath himself. When I'd seen him at April's, I remember thinking he was soft. Judging from his pasty complexion and the bags under his eyes, I'd assumed he was weak. A miscalculation on my part.

He said, "I'm good at this. Really good, because I've had lots of practice. I can bring you back from the brink or take you out so far you'll never get back. Are you hearing me?"

He seemed to be waiting for a response, but I couldn't manage it. Warm breath against my ear. "Listen carefully," he went on. "You have to stop, okay? Don't insert yourself in business that's none of your concern."

I tuned him out, rejoicing at the feeling of air on my face. The pressure had lessened just enough for me to take in half breaths. I wanted to gulp. I wanted to suck huge mouthfuls down into my lungs. I didn't want to hear what he had to say, but just in case it was pertinent, I decided I better pay heed.

"Leave it alone. What's done is done and nothing will change the facts. Do you understand? No more of this."

I couldn't nod. I couldn't even move my head. He was so matter-of-fact, it was disconcerting. If I screamed, if I even managed to moan (which I wasn't capable of in any event), the mouth and nose clamp would come back. The idea filled me with horror.

"Don't make me come after you again." He spoke as though it pained him to spell it out, but anything that transpired from this time forward would be my fault.

He got up. The absence of pressure was so sudden, I thought I might be levitating. I didn't hear the office door close behind him, but I knew he was gone. I pulled myself up onto my hands and knees and then to my feet. I staggered shakily as far as the guest chair and sank into it. My chest hurt. I could feel darkness gather, my peripheral vision closing in. It would be odd to faint when I'd just stumbled back from the brink of unconsciousness.

I put my head between my knees and waited for the shimmering blackness to go away. I was clammy at the core and a line of sweat trickled down my face in a rush of heat and ice. I could still feel the weight of his knee. I could feel the warmth of his palm across my mouth, the fleshy clothespin of his fingers pressing my nostrils shut. My heart was still thumping hard, apparently not in receipt of the news that we were alive. Or perhaps not convinced.

# AND IN THE END . . .

In my final report, I must warn you there's good news and bad. In the bad news department, Ned Lowe vanished. By the time Cheney Phillips reached the Lowes' residence in Cottonwood, he was already gone. While Cheney was quizzing Celeste about Ned, he was busy burking me on my office floor.

Celeste said her husband had packed everything in the Argosy Motorhome after dinner the night before. At two in the morning, she'd been awakened by the sound of the vehicle pulling out of the drive. No note, no good-bye, no hint as to his destination. When Cheney suggested she call the bank, she discovered that Ned had emptied their checking and savings accounts, which suggested he was on his way out of one life and onto something else. Maybe this was the big change he'd mentioned to her.

Cheney put out immediate calls to the California Highway Patrol, the Arizona Highway Patrol, and the Nevada Highway Patrol. He also notified the Santa Teresa PD and the Santa Teresa County Sheriff's Department to be on the lookout. The Argosy, with its FOTO BIZ license plate, was not only highly visible, but a notorious gas-guzzler. The expectation was that the vehicle would be spotted the first time he was forced to stop and refuel. It didn't happen that way.

Two weeks after Ned Lowe left the area, the Argosy was discovered in a remote area of the Mojave, gutted by fire, its chassis warped by heat, its flammable components reduced to ash. The vehicle identification number on the front of the engine block had been obliterated, but a second VIN in the rear wheel well was still legible, having been shielded by the tire.

There was no sign of Ned. The assumption was that he'd fled the area on foot, and had perhaps hitched a ride with a passing stranger when he reached the nearest highway.

He's now been linked to a number of disappearances, all young girls between the ages of thirteen and seventeen. Twenty-three photographs were developed from negatives he left behind in his darkroom. Those pictures were published in newspapers across the country, flashed on television newscasts, along with appeals to the public for their cooperation in identifying the subjects.

Family members were quick to spot their missing loved ones. A few young women even recognized themselves and stepped forward, not appreciating until that moment how close they'd come to disaster. There was no way to determine why some had survived the encounter with Ned Lowe and some had died. I number myself among those spared for reasons I can't fathom.

In the good news department, Edna and Joseph Shallenbarger were arraigned in Perdido Superior Court on April 12, 1989. She was charged with felony grand theft, forgery, and failure to appear. He was charged with forgery as well, along with aiding and abetting the embezzlement and failure to appear. There were a few additional charges thrown in just to sweeten the pot. I'm not sure what happened to all the money Edna stole, but she claimed indigence. The pair requested and were assigned a public defender, who asked for a continuance to allow him time to prepare his case.

I wasn't present, but I heard about their brief appearance from an attorney friend who was in the courtroom for a hearing later the same morning. Joseph was once again confined to a wheelchair, claiming an injury suffered at the time of his arrest. I could have told him he was too out of shape to make a run for it. His new chair is electric, equipped with a sip-and-puff delivery system. According to my friend, Joseph sat slumped to one side, his head atilt, his right hand clawlike and immobile in his lap. It was all fake, of course, but he did a good job maintaining the fiction.

I can only imagine the conversation that took place in the judge's chambers, the assistant district attorney dreading the inevitable courtroom contretemps. Who wants to be the heartless bastard who prosecutes an eighty-one-year-old woman whose only concern is the welfare of the husband she's been married to for sixty years, who's now having to puff and sip his way through life, barely able to lift his head?

Also by way of good news, as I was closing up the office one afternoon during that same period, I received a call from Ari and Teddy Xanakis, who were happily ensconced at Claridge's in London, having the time of their lives while waiting to hear what the Turner experts had to say about their painting. They were feeling optimistic and, sure enough, by the time they returned to California on the fifteenth of April, its authenticity had been confirmed.

Months later, after Ari's marriage to Stella Morgan was dissolved, Ari and Teddy married for a second time in a civil ceremony at the Santa Teresa courthouse. Stella was not invited, but I was. I'd have insisted on my role as the oldest living flower girl on record, but it would have looked silly under the circumstances.

There's a commonly accepted assumption that the rich are greedy and uncaring and the elderly are frail and ineffectual. This isn't always the case, of course. Sometimes it's old people who lie, cheat, and steal.

Ari and Teddy are supporting all the local charities again, and their generosity is legendary.

The more I see of the world, the more I understand that justice isn't cut-and-dried. There are more compromises than you'd imagine, and rightly so. Law and order, punishment and fair play, are all on a continuum where there are far more gray stretches than there are black and white. I'm making my peace with this. In the main, I believe people are good. In the main, I believe the judicial system works.

Ned Lowe will be caught eventually. I've seen law enforcement at work, and their patience and competence tend to net the right results in the end. That's what I'm counting on, at any rate. In the meantime, both Henry and I have had our locks changed.

As for Pete Wolinsky, I acknowledge that I misjudged him and I hope he may rest in peace, wherever he may be.

Respectfully submitted,
Kinsey Millhone

# ACKNOWLEDGMENTS

The author wishes to acknowledge the invaluable assistance of the following: Steven Humphrey; Judge Brian Hill, Santa Barbara County Superior Court; Melissa Carranza, Assistant Office Manager, Executive Limousine; Santa Barbara FBI Special Agent Linda Esparza Dozer; Ventura FBI Special Agent Ingerd Sotelo; Will Blankley, U.S. Probation Department Supervisor; Dave Mazzetta, CPA, Ridgeway and Warner, Certified Public Accountants; Sarah Jayne Mack, Our Lady of Mount Carmel Church; Louise Chadwick, Office Administrator, Montecito Water District; John Pope; Joel Ladin; Jamie and Robert Clark; Susan and Gary Gulbransen; Sean Morelos; Sally Giloth; and Robert Failing, M.D., forensic pathologist (retired).